INCOGNITO

VOLUME ONE

INCOGNITO:

Volume One

by

Madison Layle
&
Anna Leigh Keaton

Cobblestone Press, LLC
www.cobblestone-press.com

This is a work of fiction. Names, characters, places, and incidents are products of the author's imagination or are used fictitiously and are not to be construed as real. Any resemblance to actual events, locales, organizations, or persons, living or dead, is entirely coincidental.

Incognito: Volume 1

Cover Artist: Sable Grey

Seducing Olivia edited by Melissa Darnell
Owning Rachel edited by Susan Greene

Published by:
Cobblestone Press, LLC
1000 Tanglewood Drive
Clinton, MS 39056

First Printing: April 2008

TABLE OF CONTENTS

DEDICATION

To our husbands for being our inspiration, but most importantly for putting up with our long nights at the computers.

AUTHOR'S NOTE

Our stories contain varying levels of bondage and other D/s activities. As with all of our stories, the characters and events are fictitious, but the BDSM community is a very real subculture of our society. As writers, we try to depict the lifestyle in a responsible way that offers the best entertainment value to our readers. Our stories are not instructional guides, however. Whether you practice BDSM in a relationship is up to you, but please remember: Safe, Sane, and Consensual.

CHAPTER ONE

"Muchas gracias," Olivia Chandler said to the doorman as she entered the deluxe hotel on the elegant *Paseo de la Castellana.* After a brief talk with the clerk, she arranged to have her suitcases stored until she called for them later, then headed for the elevator.

Keith Randall was in for a surprise, and she didn't want to waste time with a bellman carrying her luggage. The thrill of seeing her fiancé intensified as the elevator ascended, and she watched the numbers increase over the door.

By the time the doors slid open, she was almost giddy with excitement. She made a quick check of her appearance in a large gilded mirror, which hung in the hallway, before making her way to his suite. Sleeping on the plane had helped, as did the change of clothes she'd taken time to don after she landed. Her three-carat, solitaire engagement diamond winked at her as she slipped a stray strand of black hair behind her left ear.

Keith was in Madrid on a business trip and scheduled to return stateside tomorrow. She'd called him from the transatlantic flight to make sure his plans hadn't changed.

He shouldn't have any trouble postponing his flight to allow them a spontaneous pre-wedding honeymoon in Spain.

Her heart raced as she held her breath and knocked. When there was no immediate response, she frowned and knocked again.

A grumbled, "Hold on," restored her grin. Then the door swung wide, and her heart leapt into her throat.

Keith stood with a white hotel towel draped around his trim middle, his blond hair adorably mussed. He was dry, although the sound of running water told her she'd intercepted him heading for the shower.

God, I'm one lucky girl. She let her gaze climb over his muscular form to settle on his blue eyes, which went from half closed to wide open in an instant.

"Olivia..." he said on a whispered breath.

"Surprise!" She laughed, draped her arms around his neck, reveling in the feel of his solid plains against her curves, and then gave him a hard kiss.

His fingers curled around her upper arms.

"Whoever it is, darling, get rid of 'em." The woman's voice coming from the bathroom struck Olivia like a bucket of ice water. "Mmm, hurry. The water's just right."

She pushed away from Keith as shock, pain, and anger warred within her. She latched onto the cold chill that ran up her spine and let it harden her heart. Keeping her face blank, she folded her arms and raised an eyebrow. "While the cat's away, is that it...*darling*?"

Keith took her lead and met her gaze with a poker face. "What are you doing here, Olivia?"

"I should think that's obvious. I decided to start our honeymoon early, but I see you had the same idea. Only you started without me." She slipped under his arm that held the door open. "Who is she?"

"Goddammit." He released the door and grabbed her arm.

She stopped, her gaze slashing to him. "Let. Me. Go." Her voice was flat, void of all emotion, and deadly serious.

"That's your fucking problem, Olivia. You want to control everything. Everyone." But he released her arm. "Leave her alone. She didn't know about you."

"Since I didn't know about her, either, we should get along fine."

He raked his fingers through his hair, a move she'd previously found appealing. Now, it just pissed her off.

"They said you were an icy bitch," he snapped, "but I never realized how much until now." Looking like a trapped rat, he struck with a ferocious venom that left her spirit in tatters, but she'd be damned if she lost that infamous control in front of him.

As her heart bled, she laughed without an ounce of humor. "You have no idea." Hearing the shower cut off, she pinned him with a hard glare.

"Darling? Where'd you go?" The shower curtain scraped along the rod as the woman pulled it back.

Olivia spun for the bathroom, making him curse again. "Darling will be right there," she said as she slipped off her engagement ring and, with little more than a glance at the woman who yelped when she appeared in the doorway, she tossed her diamond ring in the toilet bowl and flushed.

"What the...? Fuck, Olivia, I'm still paying for that!"

Olivia dodged him as he lunged for the toilet to try

and stop the ring from vanishing. She wished the whirlpool would suck him in with it.

"Who...?" The woman held the curtain across her body like a shield. "What...?"

"You can have him. Our wedding's off." With that declaration, Olivia let the last trace of her pride carry her out of the hotel room.

She kept the tears in check until she reached the anonymity of the Madrid sidewalks.

* * * * *

Dylan Montgomery stepped from his limousine and ordered the driver to circle the block. He wanted—needed—to stretch his legs with a walk in the park after spending hours seated at conference tables, haggling with corporate executives and lawyers.

His proposed plan to expand the family business overseas, with a foothold on both coasts of the United States, was coming together. At least the first phase had been successful. It would still be months, if not a year or more, before he saw his dream become a reality.

He removed his tie and tucked it in a pants pocket, then loosened the top two buttons of his shirt. As he strolled along the paved paths, he inhaled the sweet scent of flowers and freshly mowed grass. The greenery of the city park helped him relax despite the constant hum of heavy traffic in the background.

He'd have to call his brother to let him know how things went, but... He glanced at the Rolex Cellini on his wrist and calculated the time adjustment to Eastern

Standard Time. Yes, the call could wait.

A stifled sob and sniffle made him glance around to see a petite woman seated on a park bench, her head held in her hands. Her trim, nylon-encased legs led his gaze up from elegant black heels to a hip-hugging skirt that stopped about midthigh. She wore a jewel-toned burgundy blazer to match the skirt, which broadcast her as a woman of sophisticated taste and elegance, despite her current position. Ebony strands of long, straight hair hung like a silken curtain about her bowed face.

"Perdón, señorita," he said, pulling a silk handkerchief from his jacket pocket.

She startled and swept her hair aside to peer at him with aqua eyes as alluring as the Mediterranean Sea. For a moment he could do nothing more than stare into her sorrow-filled gaze.

"May I be of some service?" he asked in Spanish.

"No, thank you," she murmured in slightly accented Spanish.

Her thick lashes lowered to fan across her damp cheeks. She blinked, and another tear trailed down her face.

He lowered himself to the bench beside her and held out the handkerchief.

She studied it for a few seconds then slowly shook her head. "No, thank you," she repeated, her hands fisted in her lap. She rubbed her thumb over her unadorned left ring finger.

He reclined against the back of the bench and silently watched her, although her hair blocked his view of her face.

"I'm not an icy bitch," she blurted out, her fists striking her lap.

Surprised by her sudden change to flawless English, he smiled and said, "Of course you aren't."

Those aqua eyes widened and turned toward him as if she'd totally forgotten his presence, or hadn't realized she'd spoken aloud.

Tilting her face with a finger under her chin, he wiped the tears from her cheeks. "You're a very beautiful woman, and whoever caused these tears is an exceedingly unfortunate and foolish man."

She caught her bottom lip between her teeth, and another tear slipped from her bottom lash.

"Allow me to introduce myself. I am Dylan Montgomery."

Her gaze dropped, her lashes again shielding her tempting eyes. "Olivia."

He let his thumb graze the lush curve of her bottom lip, released her chin, and pocketed his handkerchief. "Olivia, I know this is short notice, but would you do me a kind favor?"

Curiosity shone as she looked up.

"I have reservations at a restaurant, but I dislike eating alone. Would you do me the honor of dining with me?"

She shook her head and glanced away.

"A drink then?"

When she looked up again, her eyes were darker and...suspicious.

"Are you married?" she asked.

"No."

"Engaged?"

"No."

"Girlfriend?"

He smiled. "No."

In a move so sudden it pulled him off balance, she grabbed his lapels and roughly pressed her lips to his. By the time he recovered enough to respond, she'd already pushed away with an angry murmur.

"God, I'm sorry. I can't do anything right. Maybe I *am* too controlling, but I don't mean to be." She didn't look at him as she continued to ramble. "I don't want to be. I'm not heartless, you know. I can let go. For once in my life..."

Deciding he'd heard enough, he slipped both hands up to cradle her damp cheeks and turned her face toward him. His lips cut off her self-deprecating chatter in midsentence, his tongue diving inside to claim her honey-sweet mouth.

When her hands started to encircle his neck, he caught her wrists. Her nails scraped over his skin, sending flames of desire scorching through him, before he moved them behind her back and pinned her body against his. He swallowed her moan as he continued the kiss until they were both breathless. His cock throbbed and, surprised by the speed of his own response, he had to pause to regain composure.

His lips hovered over hers as he pulled back just enough to see her closed eyes. He held her wrists gently in one hand, while letting his other fingers lightly stroke the delicate curve of her neck, feeling excitement in her pulse's heavy, erratic beat.

"If you wish to lose control, *mi gatita*, I can show you how."

Her lashes fluttered, unveiling a confused but

intrigued haze.

One side of his mouth curved.

"Wh-what do you mean, show me?"

"Let go. Submit. Have you ever played the role of a submissive lover?"

Her look turned to one of uncertainty and skepticism. However, she didn't try to pull away. "No." He felt her tremble but couldn't tell whether it was from fear or arousal. "I don't know y—"

"Trust is a vital part of such play. The submissive relinquishes control, gaining the freedom to truly feel cherished, desired, and pleasured. The master is really the one bound, because he must adhere to strict rules to ensure his sub's experience is a memorable one."

She bit her bottom lip, making him want to suck it into his mouth again. "I don't know if I can."

"You already have." He smiled when her gaze shot to his. "I hold you in my arms, your wrists in my hand. Tell me, Olivia..." He let his fingers slide from her neck to the swell of her breasts barely visible in the V of her blouse. "...how did you feel when I captured them? How do you feel now?"

Her chest rose rapidly as her breath became unsteady. Her pulse pounded under his fingertips, reminding him that despite the blow someone had given her heart, it still beat with a need not unlike his own.

"Excited," she whispered, as if she thought sirens would sound if she made such an admission aloud. "But a little scared, too."

"More excited than afraid, I hope." He kissed the tip of her nose, and she gave him a shaky smile. "You need only to say your safe word, and I'd stop immediately."

"Safe word?"

"*Corazon*," he said, choosing the word *heart* as a reminder to her as well as himself that it, above all else, should be kept safe.

"*Corazon?*"

He released her wrists as soon as she spoke and moved back enough to break all physical contact with her.

Those beautiful eyes met his with surprise, then with understanding.

She rubbed her arms as if the sudden loss of his body heat left her chilled.

"I've never done anything like this before."

"Permit me to enlighten you? My place is—"

"No." She bit her lip. "Some place neutral."

He studied her for a moment, then nodded and said, "You choose."

She named a five-star hotel not far from where they sat. He'd had business clients stay there in the past and knew it well. The knowledge confirmed his suspicions that she was used to a life of some luxuries, if not extravagance. "You have a room there?"

"No. Not anymore..." Her gaze slid away from him, the pain of earlier shadowing her face.

He held out his hand and, after a brief minute of indecision, she took it. He led her back along the path and stopped at the street. When she turned puzzled eyes toward him, he smiled and squeezed her hand, then grinned as the limousine pulled to a stop a short time later, and her eyes rounded with surprise.

"After you, *mi gatita.*" *My kitten.* She reminded him of

one. Curious and skittish.

During the quick ride to the hotel and, as they checked in under his name, he continued to hold her hand, tenderly caressing the back with his thumb.

As the elevator rose, he sensed her nerves becoming more jumpy—a speculation confirmed when she flinched at the ding marking their arrival on the appropriate floor.

At the room, he released her hand to slide the keycard in and push open the door. "Do you wish to use your safe word, Olivia?"

She faced him, examining his face for sincerity. He held still, met her gaze, and waited without touching her, allowing her time to determine whether he was worthy of her trust.

After what seemed like an eternity, she shook her head and walked past him into the room. Her poise indicated a woman of class and confidence, yet she continued to rub her arms. He determined to help heal some of the emotional scars left by whoever had hurt her.

He tossed the keycard on the dresser and watched her turn in a circle until she faced him once more.

"It's a nice room," she said with a brief laugh at her attempt at small talk.

"Made more beautiful by your presence."

Her lips parted slightly, her tongue darting out to moisten them.

Instead of touching her, he removed his jacket and tossed it across a nearby chair. His shirt was next. Her gaze followed his hands as he worked free each button and tugged the tails from the waistband.

"Remove your blazer, Olivia." He gave the command

softly but with firm authority. He held out his hand to take it from her but was careful not to contact her skin as she obeyed. "And the blouse."

Her fingers trembled, but again she followed his order. Pale ivory lace covered her breasts, the coral nipples barely visible beneath the seductive design. His cock hardened, but he held himself in check.

As much as he'd like to sink into her hard and fast right now, tonight was not about his pleasures, but hers. She needed nurturing.

Someone had wounded her, shaken her confidence. Such a lovely woman, she'd been dealt a crushing blow by someone who should've supported her, protected her, and cherished her. Loved her. She was a strong woman, but one in need of a comforting, yet firm hand.

"Tonight, you have no worries," he said in a husky murmur. "No concerns, duties, or burdens other than to follow my command. Tonight you're mine to control, to care for...as you deserve to be. Understand?"

She swallowed then nodded. He smiled at her nervous regard.

"You have your safe word. Should you use it at any time, I'll stop instantly. But until then, I intend to master you, pamper you, and take you higher than you've ever been before."

"Master?"

Aroused adrenaline pumped harder inside him as he heard the word on her lips. He gave her an amused grin. "I like the sound of that."

She laughed, a brief but welcome sound.

"Turn around."

She did, but kept her head turned so she could see him over her shoulder.

"Unfasten your skirt."

When she complied, he took her hands and, placing his over hers, pushed the skirt down until it pooled around her feet. The top of her head barely reached his nose. His eyelids drooped as he buried his face in her hair and inhaled her fresh, floral scent.

After planting a kiss to the back of her head, he knelt behind her and slowly stroked her arms. Her breaths came out in light, quick puffs. He tucked his thumbs into her nylons and pulled them down. She wore no panties beneath the pantyhose, which pleased him, though he didn't mention it.

"Put your hand on my shoulder and lift your foot." She hung on as he removed the last remnants of her clothing, along with her shoes.

With a gentle grip on her hips, he turned her to face him as he sat back on his heels, his knees straddling her feet. Her delicate fingers clung to his bare shoulders, while he let his hands roam over the backs of her thighs and buttocks. Her skin was as soft as rose petals. He wanted to lick every inch of her creamy flesh. A small triangle of onyx curls sheltered the apex of her legs.

A growl rumbled up his throat. Soon, he thought, but not yet.

He stood, his palms resting on the swell of her hips.

"*Béseme*, Olivia," he ordered with an uncompromising stare at her full lips.

She rose up on tiptoes to comply with his demand for a kiss and pressed those lush, pink lips to his.

He let her lead during the first few seconds, but her subtle, tentative touch was too much of a siren's call for his libido. He took command and thrust his tongue inside to raid the hot depths of her mouth. She made a sound of surprise, which he drank in.

His muscles flexed as he fought the urge to press her body against his hard length. He wanted to tumble them onto the bed and power into her. His cock throbbed with the need, but he couldn't, so he tore his mouth from hers and released her hips.

After catching his breath, he said, "Lie back on the bed, puss. In the middle."

With a hint of mischief, she flashed a set of pearly whites. "Yes, Master."

He chuckled at her playful tone, and was silently relieved to see the pain that had etched tiny lines in her brow earlier had disappeared.

When she was in place, he turned off all of the lights except for the bathroom, which he left on to spill through the crack in the doorway and provide a softer, more subtle illumination. Then, returning to the bed, he sat beside her.

She lay watching him with her legs together, her hands, one over the other, across her abdomen.

"You're very lovely." He ran a finger over her collarbone, down past the curve of one breast, to circle the pebbled tip. "Control is mine, puss?"

She nodded.

As he took her hands and raised them over her head, anticipation lit up her eyes. Until he withdrew the silk necktie from his pants pocket and wound it around her wrists.

CHAPTER TWO

Olivia tensed when she saw the silky, pale blue necktie. Her breathing faltered as Dylan wound it around her wrists.

Her gaze remained glued to his chiseled Latino features. His hair was a rich brown, his skin a golden bronze as if he spent a lot of time in the sun. His eyes had an exotic tilt to them, and the color reminded her of caramel, soothing and seductive. When he'd removed his jacket and opened his shirt, she'd caught a glimpse of a hairless chest and hard abs, which made her pussy moisten.

But now her body trembled for another reason altogether. Apprehension.

As if he sensed her emotional change, he stopped after only two rotations. "Pull on your hands, puss."

She did and was free with one tug.

"That's not so bad, now is it?" He smiled, a dimple flashing seductively at her, which helped put her at ease. He took her hands again, wrapping the tie twice around and forming a single loose bow. "You can pull free any time you want, but know that if you do, or if you say your safe word,

I will stop immediately. Understand?"

She nodded and left her hands bound on the pillow over her head.

"Say it again."

"Yes, Master."

He bent down and gave her a quick kiss before he stepped away from the bed. "Don't move."

Watching her, he removed the rest of his clothes. Like his abs, his legs were trim and strong. A thin trail of dark hair led from his navel to his cock, which jutted out proud and ready.

He dug for his wallet, pulled out a couple of condom packets, and tossed them on the foot of the bed. Relieved that he'd thought of such things when she'd forgotten, she sighed and relaxed, accepting that he was in control.

Her gaze followed him when he moved to the bed and grasped her ankles. All of the air left the room when he moved her feet apart and knelt on the mattress. Despite the dim light, she could still make out the passionate desire that darkened his eyes.

He lifted her right foot and placed a chaste kiss to the inside of her ankle, making her sigh. His fingers brushed lightly over her skin to tease the underside of her knee, tickling a bit. She smiled but forced herself not to move. His lips trailed his hands up her leg, over her inner thigh, tightening her nerves until her hips lifted in a plea for his attention where she needed him most.

Instead of heeding her silent demand for more, he lowered her right leg and turned his focus to her left. The exquisite torment continued with slow deliberation until she squirmed.

"Please," she said when he kissed the sensitive pulse-point where her leg met her hip.

He licked his way to her navel, dipping his tongue inside, and her hips lifted again. He gripped her thighs and held them wide, but he refused to follow her urgings. His thumbs rubbed her skin just above her legs. So close, yet so far away.

Her head flopped back onto the pillow, while her body hummed with carnal frustration. "Please," she said again, adding, "Master," for good measure with the hope that he'd hurry.

"Patience, puss. I'm just getting started."

Oh, my...

He leaned over her, his firm body blanketing hers as he took the tip of one breast into his mouth. His hot tongue flicked her nipple. She moaned and wanted to run her fingers through his hair and hold him there. She remained still, fighting the urge to hurry him along. He sucked until she felt the pulse in her pussy match the tug of his lips. His gentle hand with long, talented fingers kneaded and teased her other breast, plucking at the peak. The torture was so exquisite she longed for *more*.

With a groan, he nipped the bud with his teeth then switched to the other nipple. She arched her back, unable to remain still.

His hands and mouth roamed her body, leaving behind a trail of sizzling skin and nerves aching for more. When he moved back down the bed, the loss of his body heat left her whimpering with need. But then all thought ceased as he spread her wide and took her pussy with his mouth.

She clamped her eyes shut and lifted for him, giving him more access. She brought both hands, still bound, to his head and sank her fingers into his thick, silky hair.

He stopped and pulled away from her grasp.

"No, don't, please...."

"Olivia, you moved."

She blinked, but then she recalled he had ordered her not to move. Surely, that didn't mean he'd stop....

He took her by the wrists and raised her arms overhead again.

"What shall I do with a disobedient pet?" He smiled, but the odd question sent a unique thrill rocketing along her nervous system.

"I'm sorry." It was her damn control problem.

"Are you really?" One dark eyebrow rose with speculation.

Yeah, she was, especially since her actions had made him stop what she'd been practically begging for from the moment he crawled onto the bed. He couldn't know how sorry she was.

He moved up beside her then, kneeling on her left side near her head, and took his cock in hand. "Show me how sorry."

Her gaze darted from his cock to his eyes and back again. After a moment's hesitation, she rolled sideways and opened her mouth.

Without her hands free, she couldn't control the speed or depth of her movements, but he did. He scooped her hair into his fist and held her head as he slipped his thick cock past her lips.

"Slow and easy. I want this to last." His cock reached

the back of her mouth.

She sucked hard and heard him draw a quick breath.

"Ah, yes, puss." His hips thrust forward on her next stroke, pushing him deeper.

After several more strokes, he pulled gently on her hair until she released him, and then held his stiff, wet cock against his stomach. "You want to lick my balls, puss? Run that tongue all over me."

His words ignited a hunger in her like never before. She buried her face between his spread thighs and licked, drawing first one, then the other into her mouth.

"Oh, *mierda,* that feels good." He released his cock to tease and twirl the tips of her breasts, which made her groan. Then he powered his cock back into her mouth, and her tongue swept the hot flesh while he set a demanding pace.

She fisted her hands in frustration. She wanted to touch him, run her hands all over him. Still, a wicked part of her delighted in knowing that she could bring him pleasure, drive him to the edge, without even laying a finger on him.

With a harsh, shaky breath, he pulled her off him and let her roll onto her back, her lungs straining for air. He quickly moved to the foot of the bed. When his fingers spread her pussy lips, her breath caught in her throat.

"You're forgiven, puss," he said with a wide grin, "but learn your lesson and don't move."

"Yes, Mast...*ah!*"

He seized her clit, sucking it hard into his mouth. At the same time, he pushed a finger inside her wet channel. He'd ordered her not to move, but her hips refused to listen to her brain. They lurched. His tongue flicked and swirled around her, driving her faster. He added another finger and shoved her unbelievably higher.

Her head tossed from side to side. The tension built until she could stand no more. The climax burst from her body, her moan of surrender harmonizing with his grunt of approval. She was still shivering with the aftereffects when he straddled her left leg and leaned forward on his arms. He dipped his head to capture her lips and steal her breath. As he possessed her mouth, she tasted her own juices, which drew another moan from deep within her.

Pushing away from her, he caught his breath, allowing her to do the same, and retrieved a tiny square packet. He held her gaze as he ripped it open and sheathed his rock-hard cock with the protective condom. Again, she was grateful to him for having enough control to remember things that her mind failed to retain.

He lifted her right leg over his shoulder, positioned his cock, and paused. His passion-filled gaze locked with hers as he slowly slid into her depths. With each inch, his jaw tightened, his eyes darkened, and her heart stuttered.

"Damn, you're so tight and hot." Her eyelids drifted closed, but he said, "No, open 'em. Look at me."

She obeyed, and he withdrew a couple of inches, then pressed home once more.

"Watch me fuck your lovely pussy." He slammed in hard, and she cried out as her muscles contracted around him. "Yes," he said without stopping the fierce pace he set. Leaning forward, he drove into her with ever-deepening strokes. His flesh slapped at hers, a rhythmic staccato amid the melody of their irregular breathing.

Her pants changed to moans, and then when he reached between them to tweak her clit, she screamed. The orgasm surged through her from her core to every extremity.

"Again, puss. Let go and come again." His breaths were short huffs, his strong arms taut. Still he powered into her with long, steady thrusts and sent her spiraling over the next precipice. One masterful stroke later, he found his own climax.

* * * * *

Two Years Later

"Thank you, Carmen," Olivia whispered as she slipped the keycard into her purse. "I owe you one."

The head of housekeeping for the exclusive Rosemont Grand hotel scowled at her. "Damn straight you do, Liv. I'm putting my job on the line for you." She glanced down the empty hallway then back at Olivia. "This guy better be worth it."

Olivia gave her best friend a quick hug. "God, I hope so. It's been two years, and no man has lived up to the expectations Dylan set. When I saw his photo in the newspaper and learned he was going to be here..." She laid her hand over her heart that beat like a timpani, and sucked in a fast breath. "I have to see if that one night was a fluke. Walking—no, slithering—out on him like I did while he slept was the biggest mistake of my life."

Carmen shook her head, pursing her lips. "If I get fired, you're hiring me for at least double what I make here, whether I know a thing about film production or not. And I want a corner office."

Olivia laughed and squeezed her hand. "Triple. And

a company car."

Her friend winked and grinned. "For that I might get myself fired anyway. Now go on. It's getting late."

As Olivia rode the elevator to the Terrace Suite on the top floor, her nerves jangled, and her palms grew damp. She could do this, she told herself. She glanced at the elevator attendant's reflection in the polished gold door and wondered if he had any idea just how turned on she was at the thought of seducing Dylan Montgomery. Or how terrified.

Dylan. The man in the spotlight of her every erotic fantasy, a one-time indulgence that, once experienced, was better left to the past.

They'd met while she'd been at her weakest. With his unfathomable compassion for a total stranger, he'd slipped past the tough, protective coating she'd long used to keep others at arm's length. She'd needed to feel nurtured, desired, if only for a moment. She'd wanted to hand over the reins of her firm control to someone, if only for a night. And Dylan had been there to give her what she'd needed and more.

So she'd taken what he'd offered and then disappeared, vowing to never again relinquish control, no matter how heavy the burden life's demands became.

Admittedly, her engagement to Keith had been a mistake, an utter failure. He'd fooled her with his charismatic personality. Ever handy with a compliment, he'd charmed her with an illusion. Always accommodating, he'd never once told her no, not even when she'd hinted at marriage. The Lothario had produced a ring within the week, while keeping his mistress hidden within the sheets of his bed.

She'd learned her lesson and become stronger. More independent. A self-reliant woman who could match wits with any businessman. She'd clawed her way up the corporate ladder using her savvy ingenuity, an attention to detail, and clear, definable guidelines. After her one night of selfish weakness, she'd shifted back into professional mode and left her private desires behind for good. Or so she'd thought.

Now her past had found her, or she'd found him. The sight of his face alone had made her long to lose control, to let go again. The desire overwhelmed her professional need for command. For three days since seeing his photo in the business section of the *Times* and learning of his arrival, she'd fought the urge to seek Dylan out. But her will had crumbled under her curiosity and need.

If she thought she regretted sneaking out on him two years ago, how much remorse would she feel if she let this chance slip by?

The soft ding of the elevator announced her arrival. The attendant gave her a courteous nod as she stepped into the short hallway. Two doors. One on the left, one on the right. She pulled from her purse the keycard that Carmen had given her and checked the number on the paper sleeve. 2301.

Her thudding heart nearly choked her. Her sex felt damp and heated. Excitement grew steadily as she stared at the door that could lead her to a night of exhilaration in Dylan's commanding embrace.

Or utter humiliation if he wasn't interested. If she'd been nothing more to him than a one-night stand, a quick lay…

No! She wouldn't believe that. He'd been too…too…

She'd been the one to run from him, from what they might have had if she'd been courageous enough to stay and find out. Before she lost her nerve and ran from another hotel, she slipped the keycard into the lock. Carmen had told her the room was empty, and that Mr. Montgomery had requested a turndown no earlier than nine tonight.

Glancing at her watch, she pushed the door open. Eight-thirty now, and Carmen had promised to cancel the turndown order.

The sitting room was spacious with rich burgundy carpet and jade green furnishings. A gas fireplace took up one corner, and a wall of windows overlooked the southern California coast beyond the quaint, garden terrace. One lamp against the far wall lit the room, so she didn't turn on any others as she made her way into the living room.

Damn, there were two bedrooms. Which one would he be sleeping in? Hard to tell since the place was spotlessly tidy. She peeked into the first one. *Jackpot.* A blue silk tie hung over the back of the easy chair positioned in front of the window. Dropping her overnight bag on the king-sized bed as she passed, she picked up the tie and ran it through her fingers. A slow smile spread over her face and a tingle, caused by her remembrance of another blue silk tie, shot through her body.

With an idea forming in her mind, she began removing her clothes. Within seconds she stood nearly nude in the middle of the room, her thigh-high black stockings the last garment remaining. She glimpsed her reflection in the full-length mirror across the room and cringed. She'd thought to lie bound and naked on the bed as she had before, but her courage fled. Just being in the room was bold enough. She went to the bed, opened her bag, and slipped into a lacy red and black teddy. Leaving her stockings on, she exchanged her professional footwear for a pair of red stilettos.

Another glance at the mirror made her chew her lip. What had she been thinking when she'd picked this outfit? Her legs looked good because of the four-inch heels, but she'd never worn anything this revealing in her life. Or this seductive. She prayed he'd find it—and her—seductive.

She stashed her bag and clothing behind the chair next to the window, tossed a few condom packets on the nightstand, and grinned. She hadn't come unprepared this time around.

Holding Dylan's tie, she climbed into the middle of the bed. The satin covering on the down comforter was slippery and cool against her skin as she adjusted her outfit, or what there was of it.

God, what if he didn't remember her? No. Of course, he would remember her. He had to.

She twisted the tie about her wrists and used her teeth to help her tie a lose knot. Lying back against the overstuffed pillows, she raised her hands over her head, just as Dylan had once positioned her. She spread her legs slightly and glanced at that mirror across the room.

She looked like a wanton. Moisture dampened the crotch of the teddy. For tonight, she vowed to be any damn thing Dylan could possibly want. As long as he did to her all the things he'd done before. As long as he commanded her body, brought her the excruciating pleasures he had before, and slaked his own insatiable lust inside her.

The sound of her own breathing brought her back to the present. Her pussy throbbed, and her nipples drew tight against the lace cups. *Please let him hurry.*

As she lay there, trying to regulate her breathing and calm her racing heart, she wondered whether tonight would go well. And if it did, could it be the start to a long-term affair?

The newspaper article had said he'd just bought a five-thousand-acre vineyard in the Napa Valley and was here on the coast to meet with investors. His main American headquarters was somewhere in Florida, where he owned a multimillion dollar mansion and two other wineries.

If he was going to be spending time here on the West Coast... She grinned and her breathing sped up all over again at the thought of Dylan calling her with that sexy Latin accent, saying, "I'm in town. Meet me at the Rosemont."

She could have the best of both worlds—daily independence and the occasional sexual guidance of a talented master. And no one but the two of them need know about her darker, deviant side. There was no point in informing the world that she wasn't always in control, that she loved it when Dylan told her to lick his balls.

She held her breath when she heard the click of the electronic lock on the front door. The room was dark now, night completely fallen outside. The only light filtered through the bedroom door from the sitting room, splashing across the bed, making her feel as if she were under a spotlight.

Straining to hear what he was doing, she thought she heard the bar fridge open and close. Ice clanked in a glass.

"Come on, come on," she whispered. What if he decided to watch television or read the newspaper first? What if she lay here for hours before he came to bed? What if he tossed her out?

Her insecurities warred with her courage. As she debated the logic of either dragging him to the bedroom or hiding until he went to sleep, a shadow fell across the bed.

His tall, lean body stopped, silhouetted in the doorway. His hand moved, and then lamplight flooded the room. He stood there in dark slacks, his cream-colored shirt open at the collar, the sleeves rolled back to reveal his darkly tanned forearms. In one hand was a glass of amber liquid. But it was the deep amber of his eyes that snared her. His intense gaze took in her body from head to toe, heating her even more, sending a thrill skyrocketing through her.

She took a deep breath for courage. "Hello, Master," she purred, her body so ready for him she could barely keep from squirming.

A slow grin spread over his chiseled features as he sauntered toward the bed. The sexy dimple that'd been her undoing two years before winked at her.

He hadn't changed much. His discerning eyes were still framed by fine lines that crinkled at the outer corners whenever he was amused. He'd kept his thick brown hair trimmed on the sides, but let it grow longer on top, which gave him a rakish look as errant strands fell across his brow.

"Well, now," he said in his deep, sexy accent, "I like the sound of that."

CHAPTER THREE

Ryan Montgomery couldn't believe what he was seeing. God bless his brother. Dylan always seemed to know when he needed a break, a little playtime when business got too hectic.

The woman sprawled on his bed was probably the sexiest creature he'd ever seen. Long sable hair flowed over her shoulders, framing her face. Flawless, porcelain skin glowed in the lamplight. He'd never seen eyes so big, so expressive, the color stunning in its unusualness. Then there was that body clad in lust-provoking satin and lace. A body designed to make even a saint sin.

Ryan had never claimed to be a saint.

"Master?" Her voice was like a caress. Sultry and filled with promise of the feast to come.

"Shh." He took a sip of his scotch as he slowly made his way around the bed to the other side, feasting on the vision of this woman. Dusky areolas were barely visible through the red and black lace, but her nipples stood out hard and proud.

He recognized his tie around her wrists and grinned.

Clever girl. He wondered where Dylan had found this beauteous treasure. No matter, he thought as he set his glass on the nightstand and saw several condom packets there. He would take his brother's gift and sate himself within her body. He definitely deserved it after the week he'd had.

She followed his movement. Her lovely blue-green eyes were wide, and he'd swear they were filled with nervous innocence, though he knew better. Innocence was one thing that had never excited him, and Dylan knew this.

As he unbuttoned his shirt, she watched his fingers. "Master," she whispered. Her tongue flicked over her ripe, rosy lips.

"Shh."

She nodded and watched his hands move down his buttons. Her intent gaze fueled his blood, and his cock grew hard. Her mouth fell open slightly, and he could hear her heavy breaths as he peeled off his shirt and dropped it on the floor, then reached for his belt. She licked her lips again, and the quick little motion was seductive in its innocence.

He made quick work of his slacks, toed off his shoes, and then sat on the bed to take off his socks. Afterward he rolled toward her, straddling her hips, letting his solid cock rest against the heated apex of her thighs.

Her breath sucked in, and her eyes widened in surprise. He grinned.

"What's your safe word?"

"*C-corazon,*" she stammered.

Heart? Unusual choice for a paid escort, but if that was her choice... "*Corazon* it is."

A slow, suggestive smile spread over her lips. He lifted his hand from beside her head and ran his thumb over the curve of her bottom lip. Her tongue snaked out and licked him, and her eyelids drooped seductively.

"You are a beautiful woman. I am honored that you have given yourself over to me this night."

Her breasts rose and fell with each quickened breath. Her pupils dilated until only a tiny ring of color remained.

"Please," she said, and her hips lifted slightly beneath him, rubbing the underside of his cock against her lace-covered crotch.

"Shh. Do not speak unless I ask you a question." He regulated his breathing, mastering his control. He would not give in to the temptation of hurrying tonight. It had been too long since he'd had a woman. And possibly never one as beautiful as this.

He lifted her bound hands from the pillow and saw the loose knot in the tie. "You wish to be bound?"

"If it pleases you, Master."

He removed the tie and refashioned it to better secure her wrists. "It pleases me. Now put those fingers to good use." He guided her bound hands to his cock, and she curled her soft, cool fingers around his heated flesh. He stifled a moan and held still while she pumped his cock. But when she raised her hips and pressed him down against her pussy, he jerked from her grasp and scowled.

"That does not please me. Hands above your head. Now."

"I'm sorry. I'm sorry. I'm just so—"

"I said no speaking. Need I gag you?"

She clamped her mouth shut with an audible click of teeth and shook her head. Her big, gorgeous eyes were pleading, and he could see how excited she was. Her hands fisted together white-knuckled above her head.

There was something about her that was different from other paid escorts he'd had. She didn't act like a trained submissive. She was too bold, had met his gaze straight on from the time he walked into the room, and obviously had no self-control. Should he take the time to train her or take what she offered and be thankful he wasn't spending another night alone in this big bed?

Perhaps a bit of both. He spread her legs with his hands so he could move between her knees. When he ran his fingers ever so lightly over the tiny snaps on the crotch of the lingerie, she sucked in her breath.

"You are wet. Aroused already, are we?"

She nodded and bit her bottom lip.

"Because you believe I will let you come?"

She nodded again.

"I thought you were here for my pleasure, not your own."

She whined and nodded some more. He bit his cheek to stifle his chuckle. No call girl he'd ever paid for had been this genuinely aroused. She wasn't pretending. No one was this good of an actress.

His blood pounded through his veins, his cock jumping at the thought of sinking into her. Feeling her hot, slick core tighten around him when she came.

He flicked the snaps open and pushed the soft fabric out of the way. He nearly groaned at the view she'd been hiding. Shaved smooth except for a perfect triangle of black hair covering her mound, her pussy lips looked delicious as they glistened with her juices in the soft light.

"Do not move," he said, his voice low and

commanding.

He thought she stopped breathing, and he glanced up at her face. She wasn't breathing. He did chuckle then. "I said don't move, not asphyxiate yourself."

Air rushed from her lungs, and she grinned at him. She was precious. There was no other word for her.

"As enticing as this clothing is, I wish to see all of you." He reached up and slipped the strapless bustier over her breasts, letting the back of his fingers skim across her flesh. She shivered and mewled like a kitten, thrusting her chest into the air, further igniting his lust.

Her breasts were generous in size and milky white. Dusky rose areolas were tipped with large, perfectly pebbled nipples. His mouth watered for a taste, but he waited, letting the tension build.

He skimmed the teddy down her belly, his fingertips trailing over her ribs, pausing to dip his little finger into her navel. Her breath sucked in, and her tummy dipped. She was shapely, but not too thin. Soft where a woman was meant to be soft.

"Lift your hips." She did, and he pulled the material free, leaving her naked except for the black stockings and heels. Ah, she was a sight.

Leaning forward on his hands, he lowered himself over her and lightly rubbed his chest against hers, letting her hard nipples scrape against his skin. She arched her back, a silent plea for more.

He nuzzled her neck just behind her ear and breathed in her freshly plucked flower scent. Her breath rasped in his ear, and he could sense the tension in her body as she fought her own need for more physical contact.

To him, the build up was the best part. Riding the foreplay as long as possible, so that when he did finally seek his own pleasure and bury himself deep inside the woman, their climax was explosive.

He licked the shell of her ear. Her breath hitched. A tiny, erotic sound slipped out of her. "No words," he whispered gruffly. "But I want to hear your pleasure."

He nipped her neck, and she groaned, pressing herself against him.

"That's it."

He nibbled his way along her jaw, nuzzled his nose and lips against her cheek, then brushed his lips over hers. Once, twice before he delved into her hot, sweet mouth. She opened to him, and he swallowed her moan.

He couldn't keep his hands off her any longer. He cupped her face, ran his hands through her hair, then wrapped his arms around her. Their tongues warred, teased, and danced.

When he pulled away, he could barely catch his breath. She was panting, but her gaze stayed on his. Her body quivered beneath him. He wondered just how close she was. He scooted down, dipped his head, and drew the rigid peak of one breast into his mouth. She cried out, and her hips pumped against him. With his legs over hers, he pinned her to the bed. Reaching up, he laced his fingers with hers then switched to her other breast. Her whole body bowed when he gently bit the tip and sucked it hard.

"Come now." He drew her in with a powerful suck before scraping his teeth over her. She screamed and nearly bucked him off the bed as she reached her first orgasm. Her perfectly manicured nails dug into the back of his hands.

Amazing, he thought as he soothed her nipple with his tongue, taking back the sting. The woman was absolutely stunning.

Before she caught her breath, he pulled his hands from hers and kissed his way down her body, letting his fingers roam over her chest, stomach, and sides.

She whimpered when he blew on her pussy lips. She moaned when he spread them with his fingers. And she cried out when he took his first taste of her creamy juices.

"That's it," he said. "Let me hear how much you enjoy my touch."

"Ahh!" Her hips rose to meet his mouth.

He couldn't get enough. She was as sweet as ambrosia.

He tweaked her clit, slipped two fingers inside her hard and fast, and curled them—just enough—to stroke the right spot. "Come *now*," he commanded. She thrust against him and screamed. He licked and suckled her through this second orgasm, and then a third. She writhed and gasped, cried and begged, and he was more than ready to oblige.

With his own body demanding release, he moved over her and reached for a condom from the nightstand. He made quick work of rolling it on before he lowered himself between her thighs.

Her skin was dewy with perspiration, her scent driving him wild. "Taste yourself," he said, pressing his lips against hers. Her tongue darted out and licked his lips, then a second time and a third. "You like that?"

She nodded.

"What do you need?"

Her nostrils flared slightly before she answered. "I

need to please you, Master."

"You do."

She grinned.

He reached up and pulled the tie from her wrists. "I want to feel your hands on me."

She wasted no time wrapping her arms around his shoulders, her hands roaming over his back.

"Ahh, yes." He teased her pussy with the tip of his cock, making her whimper. Her nails dug into his flesh. "*Mi gatita* has sharp claws. Do it again."

Her nails dug into his back, and he could wait no longer. He captured her mouth with his, delving his tongue as he plunged into her hot, tight channel.

Dios mio! She was perfection. Her inner muscles fisted him tighter than he'd ever experienced, milking a groan from him. Wanting to lose himself inside her hot core, he pushed deeper, harder on the next several strokes.

She screamed as she hit another pinnacle. He was sure her nails drew blood.

"Again," he ordered as he pounded into her, his climax imminent.

"Yes," she shouted. "Oh, God. Dylan!"

"*No!*" Too late. Unable to stop, he plunged inside her with one more powerful stroke and found his own explosive release.

Ryan collapsed on top of her, his body spent. He buried his face in the crook of her neck, inhaling the scent of her perfume, sweat and sex, and tried desperately to deny that she'd called him by his brother's name.

He slid off to one side and pulled her into his arms. When she started to speak, he interrupted. "Shh. Rest for now." He closed his eyes and bit back a silent curse. "We have all night." He pressed her head against his shoulder and kissed her forehead. One of her arms draped across his middle as she snuggled against him, her hand settling over his heart. He stared at the ceiling. He needed to think.

When her sated pants settled into the gentle breaths of slumber, he waited another few minutes, then reluctantly lifted her arm and rolled to the edge of the bed. There he sat with his face buried in his hands.

She'd thought he was Dylan. This could not be happening. But it would explain her physical response to him—so immediate, so complete.

Who is she?

He grabbed his glass of scotch and downed it like water, then went into the bathroom and cleaned up. When he came out, he searched the room for her belongings and spotted a small duffle bag behind the chair. After a quick glance to make sure she still slept, he opened the zipper and found a purse. Inside the purse was an array of receipts, some loose change, a tube of lipstick, and a compact of face powder.

He withdrew an expensive leather organizer and opened it. Behind a plastic covered window was her California driver's license.

His breath squeezed from his lungs as he read her name.

Mierda! Dylan was going to kill him. He'd just had sex with the woman for whom his twin brother had spent the last two years searching.

* * * * *

The moment he opened the hotel room door and saw Ryan on the sofa waiting for him, Dylan knew something was wrong.

Ryan had taken a red-eye flight from Florida to California and went straight to work with him after stopping off at the hotel for a quick shower and change of clothes. At the first opportunity, Dylan had sent him back to the hotel to get some sleep. So, he should've been passed out in one of the bedrooms. Instead, he was dressed in nothing but slacks unbuttoned at the waist, a glass of scotch in his hand, and the look of doom on his face.

"Did you kill someone, *mi hermano*?"

"No, but you might." He took an unhealthy gulp from his glass.

Dylan eyed Ryan warily as he moved to sit in a chair facing his twin. "Why would I do that?"

Ryan's gaze slid away from him toward one of the bedroom doors. It must be something bad if he couldn't look him in the eye.

"When I returned to the hotel, I found what I thought was a gift from you. A gift that's still here, asleep in my bed." Ryan looked at him once more then downed the contents of his glass. "I found your Olivia."

Innumerable emotions swamped him. Shock, anger, elation. Total disbelief.

Olivia is here? After all this time of trying to find her, she'd found him. He met his brother's worried gaze. *Correction. She'd found Ryan.*

He stood. So did his brother. He glanced at the same bedroom door Ryan had looked at earlier. It was closed, and he wanted to barge through it and shake her. Demand an answer for why she'd run. But he didn't. He'd waited two long, grueling years to see her again, had all but given up hope of ever succeeding, and now that she was here...

"Are you sure?" he asked, hating the hopeful pitch to his voice.

Ryan responded by lifting a leather organizer off the table, which he hadn't noticed before. "Her photo ID is in there."

Dylan opened it to see a likeness of the woman whose face was engraved in his memory forever. His legs gave out, and he collapsed back into the chair. With his arms propped on his thighs, he stared at the photo.

"I didn't know, *hermano*. I swear I didn't, not until she called out your name at the end, and even then I wasn't sure. Fuck, I'm sorry."

"*Por que?*" His voice was barely above a whisper.

"What?"

"Why are you sorry? If it is as you say, and I've no reason to doubt that it is, you did nothing wrong. Have we not shared women before?"

"*Sí*, of course, and after hearing you speak of her, helping you search for her, I'd hoped we could...but not like this. You know I'd never..."

Dylan rose to his feet again and clasped his brother on the shoulder. "What's done is done. The only thing of import now is that we do not repeat the mistake I made two years ago. We must not let her get away a second time."

CHAPTER FOUR

Olivia awoke slowly to the feel of a hot, gentle breeze on her neck and the safety of being cocooned within the warmth of someone's arms. She turned toward the soft breaths at her nape and opened her eyes, smiling when Dylan's face appeared. He lay along her right side, relaxed in peaceful slumber, similar to the way he had the morning she'd snuck away from the hotel in Madrid.

She had no intention of leaving this time.

Attempting to turn sideways and hug him closer, she lifted her left arm to discover her wrist bound firmly with a necktie to another wrist.

It wasn't Dylan's.

Adrenaline stabbed her heart as her gaze followed the male arm from that wrist to broad shoulders and...

Her scream would've registered a seven on the Richter scale had anyone been monitoring.

Like mirror images of one another, the men awoke in an instant. Despite her panicked struggles, they faced her, pinning her down. Their legs draped over hers. Each one shifted onto an elbow, her bound hands going with theirs.

Her chest heaved as she fought for air and sanity.

Trapped flat on her back, she was seeing double—feeling double—as each man placed a palm across her middle.

"Oh, God. Ohgod, *ohgodohgod*. No." She snapped her eyes shut, opened them, and looked again. "This isn't happening."

"Shh, puss. Calm down."

Her gaze shot to the one on her left who spoke. "Dylan?"

He grinned with that adorable dimple in his right cheek and bright caramel eyes. She looked from him to the other man and back. Two pair of eyes, identical in color and exotic slant, met her gaze boldly. But the one on the left... His hair was shorter, more like she remembered. Her heart continued to race, her mind reeling at seeing two Dylans in bed with her.

Lifting his unbound hand to her face, the man on her left brushed a thumb over her cheek and leaned down, his lips coming within a hair's breadth of hers.

"*Beséme*, Olivia," he murmured.

Kiss me, she translated the order, as he took her mouth in a thorough kiss. He'd said the same to her two years ago in the same seductive way. His taste, scent, and the feel of his lips on hers were like a dream revisited.

The touch of a hand on her breast made her moan into his mouth. Still, he held her face with his free hand, continuing the kiss while other fingers twirled her nipple. The other hand cupped her breast in a warm grip that declared he had every right to brand her as his own. Then a second mouth captured the tip.

Heaven help me. There are two of them.

She had no idea whether to protest or plead for more, but her body responded without conscious thought. Despite her intrinsic alarms, moisture spread between her thighs, her nipples hardened, and she couldn't suppress the encouraging sound that climbed from the pit of her stomach. "Mmm." Her back arched toward the mouth suckling her breast while her tongue dueled with the other one.

They pulled away simultaneously, as if by some silent signal only the two of them could fathom.

She blinked at them, unable to fully believe her own eyes, half expecting to wake at any second.

She watched the one with shorter hair as he studied her. Sly cognizance crept into his remarkable smile.

"Dylan," she said with certainty now.

"Are you sure?"

Dylan had a mature, uncanny perceptiveness about him. As if he could read her thoughts and found them amusing. She glanced at the other man. His gaze was identical, heated and aroused, but the depth of familiarity that could only come from having known her two years earlier was absent.

"Yes."

Both men grinned then, dimples appearing in opposite cheeks, something she hadn't noticed before.

"Very good, puss. This is my brother, Ryan. I believe you and he became intimately acquainted last night."

Mortified heat flowed up her neck like lava. She closed her eyes.

Ryan's lips brushed the sensitive skin beneath her ear, making her nerves crackle like Fourth of July sparklers. "We couldn't have gotten any closer, now could we, *mi gatita?*" He chuckled when she whimpered. "I've got the claw marks on my back to prove it."

How could she not have known? Why hadn't the damn newspaper article mentioned a twin? What the devil was she supposed to do now?

She jerked against her bindings, salving her embarrassment with a healthy dose of temper. "Do you fuck all his women?"

"Actually—"

"Do you two laugh when you switch places and they can't tell?" She glared at both of them and squirmed. "Why the hell didn't you tell me you weren't Dylan?"

He held her in place with help from Dylan. "You were in *my* bed. How was I to know you weren't an escort Dylan paid to wait here for me?"

An escort? He thought she was a *prostitute?*

She fought then, yanking and snarling with fury. "As if I'd take your damn money. I'm not some fucking street whore."

"*Mierda!* Would you stop?" Ryan twisted away to avoid her snapping teeth. "I didn't mean it like that...."

"Enough!" Dylan pinched her nipple hard enough to hurt and capture her undivided attention.

"Ouch." She frowned at him.

"Last night you both made mistakes by assumption," Dylan said. "And no doubt savored the pleasurable consequences of those errors, if you're honest enough to admit it."

Her mouth clamped shut, her cheeks heating at the memory of what Ryan had done to her, how she'd so quickly and easily succumbed to his will, his demands. A glance at Ryan showed a grin that proved he had no qualms about being honest.

Dylan continued, "You, my pet, have much to account for, however."

Her brow furrowed in confusion.

"If you didn't come here for our money..."

Her anger simmered at the accusation until he clarified.

"...And I'm quite certain you didn't, then why did you come? Why did you sneak away two years ago?" His gaze held hers with the steady regard of a talented interrogator.

She gnawed on her bottom lip. Ryan traced the edge of her areola on one breast, his eyes downcast as if he were engrossed in his activity and paying them no mind. Dylan watched her with cool patience.

She took a deep breath. "I regretted my cowardice back then. I shouldn't have just disappeared on you like I did."

"No, you shouldn't have."

She gritted her teeth.

"I've thought of you..." He paused, mouth slightly open, as if he planned to continue, but decided against it.

She couldn't face the intensity of his gaze and looked away. "After I saw your picture in the paper, I wanted to see you again, needed to know if that night was for real, or just a fluke."

He adjusted his position so that their bound hands lay next to her head. "So this was a test. Once more for old time's sake? And when the sun came up, did you intend to disappear again?"

"No, I..." She shook her head. "I wasn't sure you'd even want to see me, but I hoped...."

Ryan chuckled, drawing her attention. She raised a brow in question. He grinned and lightly pinched her nipple. "You picked a damn fine way to convince him otherwise." He leaned over her, pressed a quick kiss to her mouth, and drew away with a saucy lick of her bottom lip. "Now that I've tasted you, I think I'll keep you."

"Whoa. Hold it. I'm not some stray dog you can just take home."

Ryan opened his mouth to speak, but Dylan cut him off. "What were your intentions when you came here, Olivia? Did you want nothing more than a one-night fuck?"

"Well...uh...no." A few more than that, she thought, then realized how awful that sounded.

"Then what? You deny wanting a one-night stand, but shudder at Ryan's hint of something more."

"But I didn't come here to be with...*him*. I came for you."

Dylan's gaze bored into her as if he could touch her very soul. "I see, and yet here we both are. Are you telling me he didn't pleasure you?"

Now Ryan's gaze focused on her like a spotlight. She couldn't lie. "No, I didn't say that—"

Dylan's finger on her lips stopped her. His gaze followed his fingers as he trailed them over her chin, neck, and between her breasts. "And since waking up, you haven't once thought of what we both could do for this luscious body of yours?"

"No!" *That's a lie.* She glanced back and forth between

them, worried they could see the sinful pictures Dylan's words brought to her mind. "I mean... That's just... This is all wrong."

"Wrong? Does the thought of sharing our bed appall you? Or is it the duration of your stay in that bed that frightens you?" When she refused to answer, his voiced dropped to a challenging level. "I think you are afraid to submit to two masters."

Two? It had taken her two years to convince herself that she could submit—occasionally—to one, if that one was Dylan. How could he be so perceptive? As his fingertips circled her pebbled nipple, she knew. Her body betrayed her and gave him all the damn clues he needed.

"Frightened of commitment, Olivia?"

She cleared her throat. Tried to scoff. "Commitment? What are you talking about?"

His usually warm eyes turned hard, penetrating. "I believe you came back here to experience what we once shared in Madrid, but you've yet to convince me that your intentions extend beyond tonight."

"But they do. I mean, whenever you're in town, I'll... We could..." Her voice trailed off, and she closed her eyes, unable to look at either of them.

"We could what? Sate our lusts then go our separate ways? Is that the only reason you came back to me?"

Why did he have to make it sound so awful? "You have a life somewhere else. I understand that, but I also know you bought a vineyard in the valley. I thought we could call each other sometimes...whenever—"

"Call you?" Dylan asked. For the first time, she sensed temper in his voice. "We aren't gigolos at your beck and call. And you cheapen yourself by such an offer."

She couldn't stand it anymore, laying here with nothing on but stockings, while they still had their underwear on. He had no right to make her feel guilty. She tugged her wrists, wishing she could escape. She bit the end of one tie, trying to free herself, but Ryan jerked their bound hands away, stopping her.

"Let me go."

"If you want to leave here and never see either one of us again, you know the word," Dylan challenged. "Say it. Or make a commitment."

Her mouth opened, but the word wouldn't come. *Never see them again?* But she'd just found him.

Ryan's fingers touched her cheek tenderly. "Can you not let us show you what it is like to be cared for? Take a chance, baby."

"This is crazy. No, I can't. What kind of commitment could I possibly make with the two of you, especially with us living at opposite ends of the country?"

Dylan surprised her then by undoing the necktie wrapped about their wrists. After a brief pause, Ryan did the same with the other one. When her wrists were free, they ignored their own and rubbed hers to soothe any aches.

Dylan rolled from the bed and retrieved her bag of clothes, tossing it beside her. "Get dressed, Olivia."

What the hell?

Eyeing him warily, she dug out her outfit and put it on.

Ryan remained on the bed, watching her silently with a frown while a look of concern creased his brow. Dylan went into the other room, returning a short time later with a slip of paper in his hand.

When she stood before him fully clothed, she finger-combed her hair and tried to understand his sudden change toward her. What had she said or done that was so wrong?

Ryan got up and positioned himself beside his brother. Seeing them side-by-side, she was again stunned by the similarity.

Dylan took her arm and escorted her to the door, while Ryan carried her bag.

"I don't understand," she said, turning toward them.

Dylan grabbed her face between his hands and kissed her with a passion that scared the living daylights out of her. "An incredibly strong, courageous woman surrendered herself to me for one night. I've searched for her for two years, unable to get her out of my mind." He handed her the piece of paper. "If you find her again, if she wants something more than a single night of sex in some strange hotel room, tell her to be at that location by the time and in the manner specified. Her masters will be waiting."

* * * * *

"Did you receive the file from the courier service?" Olivia said as she glanced out the window of the taxi while she spoke into her cell phone.

"Yeah, Liv, I got it. But what the hell am I supposed to do with it?"

She swallowed and tamped down her nervous jitters. Taking this impromptu *vacation* was so out of the ordinary, and at such an inopportune moment in time, that she wanted to tell the cabbie to turn around and take her home.

"Carmen, I'm going to tell you something, but you have to swear not to totally freak out on me."

"What have you done now?"

God, she cherished her nearly life-long friendship with Carmen. That was why she was the one person she hadn't told an elaborate lie to about this unusual trip.

"I'm going to spend the next two weeks with Dylan and Ryan Montgomery."

"*What?* Wait a damn second. Now, you told me you slept with the wrong guy and everything, but what the hell are you thinking?"

Ignoring the outburst, Olivia said, "I did some checking up on them, and that's all the info I gathered." She swallowed the lump of trepidation climbing her throat. "If I'm not back by the end of the month, take that file to the police and make sure they come looking for me."

"You can't do this, Liv. You don't know anything about them."

She knew everything that was public record, including how much their company grossed each year and everywhere they had houses around the world. But she also knew them in a very strange, private way that she couldn't begin to explain in such a short amount of time.

"I'll be okay. I don't know how to explain it, but—"

"Then why the hell did you send me this file if you're so sure? You are always the levelheaded one, the one who keeps *me* from doing stupid things. What the hell has gotten into you? You'd have me locked up if I told you I was running off for a couple of weeks to have a sex-fest with *two* men."

True enough, but Carmen wasn't very good at

choosing her men. Olivia almost laughed at her own thoughts. Not that Keith had been a real winner. "Maybe it's time I did something a little wild. Besides, it's just for two weeks. Then I'll come home and be the same icy bitch I've always been."

Keith's words still hurt. Even after two years. But she'd done nothing to change that image of herself to the outside world, either. Since Madrid, she'd avoided all personal entanglements. Better to be satisfied by her trusty B.O.B. than to let her heart get bruised by anyone else. Damn good thing the Montgomery brothers were just offering some great sex and a chance to prove she wasn't a coward.

Carmen made a sound of pain. "Don't do that to yourself, Liv. You're not cold-hearted. Though, sometimes you can be a little bitchy, but that usually passes with enough wine and chocolate."

She burst out laughing. "I have to go. We're getting close to the airport."

"Where are you going with them?"

Olivia shrugged as the driver headed toward the private jet terminal. "I don't know. Dylan gave me a note that said to meet him at the Montgomery private jet at six tonight." Among other things.

"And you have no idea where they're taking you?"

"Nope." Which had made packing a bitch.

"You call me. Don't wait two weeks. I want to hear from you tomorrow, okay?"

"I'll try," Olivia said. "But..." *But they were in charge.* Though no way in hell was she going to admit that. Not even Carmen needed to know that much.

"No buts. I hear from you within twenty-four hours,

or I'm contacting the police. I don't like this one bit."

"Okay, and Car?"

"Hmm?"

"Thanks for being my friend."

"Aw, Liv, don't get all mushy on me. You're scaring me."

"I gotta go. There's the plane."

"Be careful," Carmen shouted just before Olivia shut her cell phone and slipped it into her coat pocket.

As they drove down the tarmac toward the waiting Leer jet, Olivia once again almost opened her mouth to tell the cabbie to take her home. But what might she be missing if she did that? Could she honestly throw away the chance to have the two devastatingly handsome, sexually insatiable Montgomery twins "take care of her"?

Dylan saw her submission as a strength. She disagreed. It was a weakness. Her Achilles' heel. She'd recognized that the moment her body awoke to his dominant touch. Mind over body. That kept her on the straight and narrow path to success. Body over mind would be a detour to her own destruction, if she wasn't careful.

But she'd take the little zig in the road, if only to prove she wasn't the coward Dylan thought her to be. Then it would be back to life as usual. This was like a once-in-a-lifetime trip on the Carnal Cruise Lines. She'd submit for the two weeks, taking all the hot, sweaty sex she could get, then walk away and prove to Dylan—and herself—that she was in control of her own destiny.

So here she was, getting out of the cab, dressed as ordered, and approaching the plane. She was done running. She had to be strong enough to face her fears, overcome them, and move on.

The door to the jet opened to reveal a man she didn't recognize. Her grip on her coat's lapels tightened.

The cabby removed the last of her bags from the trunk. "That'll be twenty-one dollars, ma'am."

She pulled three tens from her purse and handed them to him. "Keep the change."

He smiled, tipped the brim of his cap, and started to leave.

"Hold up, please. I need to ask you something," the man said after descending the stairway. He held up one finger toward the cabby and faced her. "I'll take care of your bags, Miss Chandler."

"Thank you. You are?"

"Enrique, your flight attendant," he said with a grin, "and copilot of the Montgomerys' private jet."

"I see."

He gestured to the stairway. "After you, ma'am."

Taking a deep breath that offered little help in calming her nerves, she ascended the stairs and stepped inside.

Ryan came to his feet and swept her into his arms, while his mouth took possession of hers. His tongue stroked hers, and she couldn't stop the shiver of desire rocking through her or the whimper of need from escaping.

When he pulled away, the rakish grin he gave her was enough to curl her toes inside her four-inch stilettos. A lock of hair fell over his forehead and gave him a playful appearance. Dressed in faded denims and a dark green shirt, his attire and physique made him look much younger than his thirty-eight years. "I was afraid you wouldn't come," he murmured as he nuzzled her neck.

She had no voice. Whatever she'd expected, it hadn't been this kind of welcome.

"If you are finished mauling the woman..."

Olivia glanced toward Dylan as Ryan slowly let his hands slip from her waist. Dylan sat in the second row of taupe leather seats, a snifter of brandy held in his right hand. The first row faced aft—two seats, separated by a narrow aisle. Dressed in black slacks and a lightweight, form-hugging sweater with short sleeves, he appeared ready for a fashion show runway instead of a flight to God-only-knew-where.

"*Bienvenido,*" he said casually, as if greeting an old high school chum, but his eyes told a different story. His gaze swept her from head to toe and back, stopping at her tightly clenched fist that held the lapels of her coat together. He took a sip then set his glass aside.

"Thank you," she said, refusing to be drawn into a Spanish conversation. She'd convinced herself that part of the attraction to him—*them*—was the evocative tones they used when speaking their native tongue. If she had any hope of surviving the time with them and returning with her sanity and heart intact, she had to keep things on a level she could tolerate. "Before we go any further, I feel some ground rules are in order."

"I agree," Dylan said with a half smile. "Come in. Be seated, and we'll discuss them." He gestured to the chair opposite him.

CHAPTER FIVE

She sat on the edge of the seat, adjusted her long coat over her legs, and looked around. Ryan took the seat next to her but thankfully didn't touch her. She didn't think she could get through a full, coherent conversation if he kissed her like that again.

Behind Dylan was a couch that faced the center aisle across from two more leather seats, a wood-grain tabletop raised between them. Further back, a matching wood-grain wall and door separated the main cabin from the aft compartment. A flat-screen TV or computer monitor was in the wall. What lay beyond the door, she didn't know, but suspected it housed the bar and lavatory.

"Care to begin?" he asked.

She nodded. "Do I use the same safe word as I did before?"

With a slight bow of his head, he said, "*Corazon.*"

Heart, she thought again. Not a bad word to remind her of the one thing she needed to protect above all else. "Okay. I also want your promise that I will retain the ability to speak it at all times."

He nodded.

"Should I be compelled to use it...?"

"Whatever is occurring at that moment stops, agreed?"

"Yes."

"Do I have your promise that you will not use your safe word at every little slight you may perceive, but only for a circumstance that you are truly unable to face?"

"Yes. Also, I want to be able to contact my office at least once a day."

Dylan's left eyebrow shot up. "Is that not excessive when you are supposed to be vacationing?"

"That's just it." She fisted her hands on her lap and glanced at Ryan. "I shouldn't be vacationing. My company is going through a merger, and this is about the worst possible time for me to leave. If I can't check in..." She swallowed hard and looked back toward Dylan. "If I can't call in at least once a day, I'm afraid I cannot leave."

Dylan pursed his lips for a moment. "Very well, that can be arranged. Anything else?"

"At the end of the two weeks I can come home and get back to work, and we'll renegotiate our...relationship...should we both—all—decide we still want to see each other."

"If that remains your wish—"

"It is."

"—then, you have my word."

She held out her hand to shake on it. He smiled but didn't move.

"Now for my ground rules."

She dropped her hand and bit her lip.

"You promise to obey Ryan and I at all times without question or complaint?"

And if they order me to jump off a bridge?

"I will, as long as your orders are within my ability to do without causing serious harm to myself or any other."

He frowned. "Of course. That goes without saying."

She hadn't meant to insult him and felt a bit remorseful for having done so.

"From this moment on, the reins are ours. We will not tolerate disobedience, but neither will we abuse you, in body or in mind. We value your trust and the strength that it takes for you to accept our offer and submit to our control." He leaned forward and looked her straight in the eyes. "We will push your limits, and you can be sure there are consequences for disobedience, but we will *never* betray that trust. Do you understand?"

"Y-yes," she said, wondering for the millionth time what she was getting herself into.

He held out his hand. "Then, you accept our offer to be your masters and agree to be our submissive for the duration of your stay with us?" That question certainly spelled it out. The sincerity she'd seen in his gaze changed to pure alpha male in the blink of an eye, and she hesitated. "The door is still open. If you wish to run, you must do so now."

Run. No. She was finished running. Wasn't that the point of all this? To prove to herself that she could face her fears and overcome them. She controlled her destiny, damn it. He wouldn't scare her off.

She took his hand and shook it with a firm grip. "I'm not going anywhere...for fourteen days."

Both men smiled. Ryan gave her hand a quick squeeze before he went to close the plane's door. Dylan pressed a button on the console. "We're ready to go."

"Yes, sir," the pilot responded. "I have clearance from the tower. We should be airborne in a matter of minutes."

"Where exactly are we going?" she asked.

Dylan reached over and buckled her in before attaching his own seatbelt.

"Some place private."

Ryan took the seat beside his brother, across the aisle from her.

Neither man spoke another word while they taxied or during takeoff. Once the plane leveled off, however, Dylan said, "Unbuckle your safety belt and remove your coat."

"Here? Now?"

He cocked a brow.

Right. Without question or complaint.

With a worried glance toward the closed cockpit door, she did as instructed. Removing the coat, she draped it over another seat and stood in front of both men like a lingerie model with a severe case of stage fright. Unable to look at either of them, she peered out the oval window at the puffy clouds and passing landscape below.

"For the past week," Ryan said, his voice low and deeply accented as his gaze roamed over her, "I have imagined you, remembered you, dreamed of you. The torture my brother must have lived through not having you..." He stopped when Dylan cleared his throat, as if realizing he'd said too much. "Thank you for honoring us with your acquiescence, if only for a short while."

Like a light switch, the thought of these two virile,

gorgeous men dreaming about her turned her on. Her nipples tightened beneath the delicate black lace of her bra. Moisture dampened the matching thong she wore.

"Come here," Dylan said.

One hesitant step, then a second, and she stood between his knees. Her pulse throbbed. Why did obeying his simple commands make her heart pound?

"Let down your hair."

Slowly, she took out the pins holding her hair in the tight French twist that was her usual hairstyle.

He didn't touch her skin as he lifted some of her hair and adjusted it over each shoulder. The feel of the ends lightly skimming her skin made her shiver. She wanted his hands on her.

"You'll leave it down for the duration of your stay."

"It gets in my eyes."

"I prefer to see it this way, wild and free, like you're meant to be."

Wild and free? She'd been wild only once in her life, with him in Madrid, but that required her giving up freedoms. She didn't see how both could apply to the submissive lifestyle she'd agreed to adhere to for the next couple of weeks.

"Kneel."

His soft order sent a thrill through her system that confused her. Why was he able to cause this reaction in her with a single word?

She kicked off her black heels and dropped to her knees.

"Put your hands together behind your back. Arms straight." When she did, he said, "Don't move." Then he pushed a button on the console. "A glass of white wine, please."

A few seconds later, the copilot who'd dubbed himself a flight attendant earlier came out of the cockpit. He didn't glance her way, but his presence alone caused a blush to heat her neck and cheeks. He went through the aft doorway to a bar on the right. When he brought the glass of wine to Dylan on a tray, his gaze fell on her. Embarrassment over her current situation battled against a wicked glee at seeing the man's approving smile.

Embarrassment won as his gaze dropped to her breasts. She lowered her head and crossed both hands over her chest.

"That'll be all, Enrique."

"Sir." The man gave a quick bow and left.

"You disobey me already."

She looked up to see Dylan frown. He passed the wine glass to Ryan, who took it without comment.

"Why did you hide yourself?" Dylan asked.

"I'm not used to baring my body to just anyone."

"Whose body?" His tone told her the question wasn't a casual inquiry and gave a clue to what answer he expected.

"Yours...for now, anyway."

"Exactly. I gave you an order to not move. My commands are to be followed regardless of who's present. For your disobedience, you shall be punished."

A shiver ran up her spine. Fear? Anticipation? She couldn't tell. What kind of punishment did he plan? A picture of being thrown from the airplane came to mind, but she quickly dismissed the paranoid thought. Dylan promised not to abuse her or betray her trust. Death by falling from an airplane without a parachute would certainly qualify as a broken promise.

"Back up," he said. When she did, he stood to retrieve something from a nearby bin. "Hands behind your back."

He unfastened her bra and pulled it off, which caused her breath to hitch and eyes to close. Her awareness of Ryan watching his brother undress her pumped adrenaline into her veins.

Around her wrists, Dylan placed fur-lined cuffs. Though soft, they held firm when she tested the bindings.

Taking his seat, he pulled her so that she again knelt between his spread thighs. The glass of wine touched her lips. "Sip."

She opened her eyes as the sweet flavor burst in her mouth. Again, he handed the glass back to Ryan.

"Everything you get comes from your masters' hands. What you drink, eat, or wear. What you feel..." His fingertip brushed lightly over one nipple. "Everything you need. That is our responsibility. Your only duty is to obey. With that obedience comes more freedom to be yourself, to see yourself for who you really are, the beauty outside and within. The limits you've put on yourself have imprisoned you. I intend to help you overcome them, beginning with the shame you display over your own body."

"I'm not ashamed...." *Well, maybe a little.* She wasn't exactly a size three by any stretch of the imagination. Her chest was too large, her hips too wide, and she never got any sun, so she was pale.

"Do not compound your error of disobedience by lying to me. Spread your knees apart."

After she did, he pulled her up so that she was no

longer sitting on her heels.

"If I wish to show you off or share you with another, then that is my choice. Remember that."

Share her with another? She glanced at Ryan and desperately hoped he was the only one who was going to be doing any sharing.

"Your body is ours," Dylan murmured, "to play with any way we choose. You gave us that right, and we cherish it." Taking the glass once more, he dribbled a bit of wine on a breast, then slowly leaned forward and licked the drops away. He sucked one tip into his mouth and pinched her other nipple hard enough to make her hiss.

When Dylan poured more wine onto her other breast, Ryan moved next to her, knelt, and took the soft weight in hand. He stared into her eyes for a long, sultry moment before sucking the liquid from her skin. Together, their hands and mouths were a distraction she couldn't withstand. Her head fell back as she took a deep breath, trying to quell the quivering in her limbs.

"You're our toy, *mi gatita*. Our pet. Do you not enjoy it when we play with you?" Dylan's fingers slipped beneath her thong panties to reveal the evidence she couldn't deny. "Mmm. Wet. See? Your body knows what it likes and is aroused by the thought of exposure after years of captivity in modest clothing."

Ryan squeezed and rubbed her butt, while Dylan pressed two fingers into her pussy. Her hips bucked to meet him. She clamped her eyes shut, unwilling to see her body surrender so easily to their mastery. Her juices soaked Dylan's fingers and, when he pulled out to circle and flick her clit, she balanced on the edge of a strong climax. Her mouth fell open as she waited for the moment when everything inside her would explode.

"Oh, no you don't," Dylan said, removing his hand from between her legs.

Ryan released her breast and moved back to his seat.

Her protest was more whimper than anything else. It usually took her a good twenty minutes to masturbate herself to completion. The brothers had damn near accomplished the same in under five minutes. If ever she needed more proof of who actually had better control over her body, this was it.

"You have to earn the right to come, puss. Be a good girl. Turn to your right and face Ryan. It's time for your punishment." She scooted around on her knees while her arousal turned into an unfathomable excitement.

What the devil was wrong with her?

Dylan tossed a small pillow on the floor at his brother's feet. "Spread your knees wider and bend forward until your forehead touches the pillow."

Together they helped her lower herself into place, her hands still cuffed and her ass in the air.

She jerked at the first swat, but then his finger slid inside her, and she moaned. Dylan's hand came down again and again, turning her ass into a firecracker of sensations, but between each hard slap, he'd finger her pussy and tease her clit.

"You're so wet, puss. I almost think you enjoy a little pain with a good finger-fucking." Two fingers entered her as another blow landed across her right butt cheek.

Her inner muscles contracted, and she tingled with desire.

"You like being punished, don't you?" *Smack.* "Answer me."

"*Yes.*" She couldn't deny it. Her body responded to his touch, whether it was for pleasure or pain...or both simultaneously.

"You want to come, don't you?" *Smack.*

"Yes."

"No." He stopped, his fingers withdrawing from her pussy, his hand no longer slapping her ass. "You don't earn the right to come through disobedience."

He pulled on her arms to help her to her feet then guided her back to her seat. Her pussy throbbed. Her butt stung, but the cool leather soothed the ache. He left her hands bound as he buckled her safety belt. Moving her hair behind her shoulders, he uncovered her breasts then separated her knees.

"Remain like that."

What choice did she have? Her hands were bound, her body buckled in. For the duration of the flight, she stayed in a position of exposure. Even while they conversed on a wide range of subjects. Even when Enrique returned to serve dinner, while the brothers ate their food, and as they handfed her portions of the meal.

"Sir, we're approaching our final destination and will be making our descent in about five minutes." The pilot's voice came out of speakers in the ceiling. "The night sky is clear, and it's a comfortable seventy-eight degrees."

Dylan looked at her. "Do you need to use the lavatory before we land?"

"Yes," she said, thinking he'd let her redress before landing.

"Okay." He unfastened her belt and removed the cuffs. "It's through there, to the left. I suggest you hurry."

She did, but when she returned, Ryan was tucking her bra into the pocket of her coat. Dylan held the cuffs up.

"Turn around," he said.

Dazed, she did as he demanded, and he rebound her hands behind her back. "But I thought..."

"I know, but we prefer to enjoy the view." Dylan helped her to her seat, redid her safety belt, and slipped her pumps onto her feet.

A short time later, the plane touched down, and her nerves rocketed into orbit. She scanned the dark scenery through the oval window, noticing lights in the distance, but little else.

"Your nipples are hard little buds. It would be a shame to cover them up now, I think." At Dylan's comment, her panicked gaze snapped to his.

The plane taxied to a stop. Ryan and Dylan unbuckled themselves but remained seated until the cockpit door opened. When the pilot and copilot/flight attendant appeared, Dylan asked, "Has our car arrived?"

"Yes, sir. Your driver stands ready."

"Excellent. Come, puss." He unbuckled her safety belt and took her by the arm.

She swallowed her fear, trying hard to not show embarrassment over being paraded in front of the two men while wearing nothing more than thong panties, wrist cuffs, and fuck-me pumps. Correction, three men. The driver gave her a smile as his gaze took in the view from head to toe. A part of her enjoyed the admiration she drew from the men, but she ignored those feelings in favor of the more volatile emotion—anger.

Once inside the limousine, she pelted Dylan with words since she couldn't brain him with fists.

"How dare you treat me like some two-bit whore to be paraded around for the whole world to see?"

He grabbed a breast and ran a rough thumb over the peak. "You see this nipple? How hard it is with arousal?" His hand ran down over her stomach to cup her pussy. "Do you feel how wet you are? I did nothing but escort you from the plane to my car. You could've ended it if you wished by using your safe word, but you didn't. Why is that, puss? Could it be that you enjoyed having an audience witness your submission? You're soaking wet." He moved aside her panties to slip a finger inside her as he'd done before. "And so close to coming, you can hardly stand it. You aren't angry over those men; you're angry at yourself for liking the thrill their presence gave you." He pulled out of her. "You can lie to yourself all you want, Olivia, but don't ever fucking lie to me."

The dam burst. A sob tore from her throat, and tears streamed down her face.

"Aw, fuck." Dylan lifted her onto his lap and held her close while the tears flowed, his hands gentle on her back. Soothing.

He was right, and she wanted so badly to hate him for it, but she couldn't. It wasn't his fault she was a sexual deviant. She'd tried so hard to ignore the urges inside her. For years she'd gone from one unsatisfying relationship to another, if one could call a single date here and there, or the occasional nightcap, a relationship. She damn sure couldn't call her failed engagement a relationship, especially since her fiancé found more satisfaction in the arms of another woman than in her bed.

The truth was sex had never appealed much to her until one day in Madrid when a stranger wiped away her tears, tied her hands together, and fucked her senseless. When he took control, she at last felt free to soar.

And how had she repaid him? By sneaking away with her guilty conscience then returning for a one-night stand.

So much for well- laid plans and good intentions.

CHAPTER SIX

"Feel better?" he murmured into her hair.

She nodded, rubbing her cheek across the damp portion of his thin sweater, somewhat embarrassed by her emotional meltdown.

"I said we would push your limits, Olivia. But we have to be honest with each other. Our relationship is a consensual one, built on trust that must go both ways."

"If we're to truly provide for you," Ryan added, "as is our desire and duty, we have to know what's in your heart. What excites you, sustains you, fulfills your needs. For us to learn that, you must first be true to yourself. Understand?"

She nodded.

"Good," Ryan said. "Now we must discuss a few more rules."

She raised a brow and looked over at him to see his wide grin. A glance at Dylan, who still held her on his lap, revealed a matching smile, which increased her nervousness tenfold. "What kind of rules?"

Dylan began by saying, "None that might prove too difficult for you. The first is how you will address me as well as my brother."

"Address you?"

"You'll refer to us both as Master. It does not matter who commands you, you respect us equally."

Ryan said, "You will not speak unless spoken to or granted permission. You may ask for that permission at any time, but we will not always grant it. You may ask us to clarify a command if confused by it."

"Otherwise," Dylan added, "the only other exception is if you should choose to use your safe word, which you may do at any time so long as it's for a valid reason, as we discussed before. Is that clear?"

"Yes...Master."

"There's more. We will decide what you wear, if anything, when you eat, sleep, bathe, and how you will do those things," Ryan said.

"We control everything for the next two weeks. It will be our pleasure to meet all your needs." With a smile, Dylan slid her off his lap and onto the floor in front of him. "Your only requirement is to obey us and enjoy your stay."

"Whenever you're in our presence, unless instructed to do otherwise, you are to kneel as you did on the plane, with knees apart and arms behind your back. Understood?" Ryan asked.

She looked over her shoulder to see him lean back and flash a sexy grin. His arms draped across the back of the seat, the privacy window behind him a dark backdrop. In answer to his question, she took up the position, which wasn't difficult since her hands remained bound behind her back, and looked at Dylan.

"Very good." Dylan pressed a button on the door,

which lowered the window between them and the driver. "How much longer before we arrive?"

"About thirty minutes, sir. Forty, if I take the scenic route."

"Do that." The window closed with a whir.

"Come here, puss." Dylan unzipped his slacks and freed his erect cock. "See what your nearness does to me?" He stroked the length, making it grow even more. "I've missed you and your sweet mouth. I've longed to have your lips surround me like they did once before. Do you remember?"

She remembered. She'd dreamed of those moments often in the private shadows of her bedroom. Only then, she thought they would forever remain memories, a figment of a past best left hidden.

Now, her mouth began to water the moment she saw him. She wanted nothing more than to taste him again, and she didn't give a damn that his brother watched.

Dylan's hand continued to slide up and down his length, tempting, tantalizing. "I tried to wait, but I can't. I need you. Do you want me?"

A slight nod of her head was all it took. His fingers dove into her hair and guided her mouth to where he wanted her. He held her head still, his cock filling her mouth, as he moved to lie down. With his right foot on the floor and his left on the seat, he rested his head on his left palm and controlled her with the other hand.

"You're so sexy with my cock in your mouth. I love watching you serve me."

"The view's not bad from where I'm sitting either," Ryan said. His voice created an unexpected spark of titillation.

She sucked harder, swirling her tongue around the soft tip, then scraping her teeth ever so gently along the thick shaft.

"Ahh, yes, puss. Your mouth is heaven." His fingers tightened in her hair, adding a little pain and spurring her faster. He grew longer, thicker, and she knew he was about to come. She hummed her pleasure at knowing she could bring him to the edge.

With an impassioned sound, he surrendered to her silent demands and pulsed into her mouth. Her lips closed around him, held him as he settled back to earth, his hand petting her head.

After a few deep breaths, he lifted her chin, withdrawing his cock from her mouth. He sat up and reached around to unfasten her cuffs. She met his gaze while he rubbed her arms and shoulders. After a brief moment of silent regard, he bent forward to give her a tender kiss on the lips.

Then she heard the telltale sound of another zipper behind her. "Go," Dylan said softly. "You have another master who needs that lovely mouth of yours."

Ryan had moved to sit in one corner, his right leg stretched out along the seat, his left foot on the floor. He held an impressive erection in his right hand. His gaze rose to meet hers and waited.

As the passing streetlights swept through the car's interior in a rhythmic fashion, she caught glimpses of what she thought was worry on his face. Uncertainty.

She understood now why Dylan had uncuffed her hands. He'd freed her to decide. Even though she'd already been with Ryan, the choice was hers to fully accept him when she now knew they were two separate people. Without saying a word, he was letting her know the ultimate choice was hers to make, and Ryan's expression proved that for him the outcome was unknown.

Almost like a dream, she crawled forward until Ryan's left hand lifted to cup her cheek, paused, and then gradually slid through her hair to the back of her head. The tip of his cock, moist with pre-cum, touched her lips, and she licked it. She watched his face as she drew him into her mouth, her tongue circling the head.

His eyes darkened to a deep, rich chocolate, but his face lit with a smile.

With half his cock past her lips, he let go of the base and held her head with both hands. "All of it. Can you take all of me?"

She didn't know, but she was damn sure going to try. Relaxing her throat, she opened her mouth and closed her eyes as he slipped farther inside. He was so thick, her mouth spread wide to accommodate him.

"Oh yeah. Stay with me, baby." He started the dance, in and out with long slow glides. His hips scooted closer to the seat's edge, each stroke diving deeper into her mouth. "Faster. Just like that."

She leaned into him a bit more, balancing her forearms against his thighs, and cupped his sac, rolling his balls between her fingers.

"Yeahhhh," he groaned.

Unable to lick around him as the rhythm increased, she tightened her lips, pushed up with her tongue to increase suction, and heard him hiss. His right foot dropped off the seat, and he used both legs to lift his hips to meet her downward strokes, slamming in to the hilt.

Her breaths were short pants, timed to his withdrawals, as he continued to fuck her mouth.

Suddenly two hands touched her ass, circling, caressing. Dylan hooked a couple of fingers into the thin waistband of her thong panties and pulled them down her thighs.

She was so glad Ryan controlled her head, so she was able to focus on the sensations occurring simultaneously at the opposite end of her body.

Dylan slipped one finger past throbbing pussy lips and into her, then two, while he skimmed his left hand around her thigh to dally with her clit. He plucked and played with the hard bud, while he synchronized his fingers' strokes with the forceful movements of Ryan's cock.

"How does that feel, puss?" Dylan asked.

Her growl of approval reverberated around Ryan's cock.

"Ah... More," Ryan said.

She couldn't agree more as the tension rose in her body like a rubber band ready to snap.

"Give and take," Dylan said without stopping his exquisite torment. "We give, and we take." He added a third finger and pushed deeper, harder into her pussy, then pinched her clit.

"Pain and pleasure come only from your masters. Yours to endure and enjoy whenever we wish."

She couldn't take any more. The orgasm seized her body. She whimpered around Ryan's cock even as he grew harder. She gripped his thighs to steady herself and wearily forced her eyes open to see Ryan throw back his head as his climax struck.

A final hard jerk of the hips, and warm, salty cum filled her mouth. She swallowed all she could while still trying to catch her breath.

Dylan released her and pulled her thong panties back into place.

She ran her tongue over the tip of Ryan's cock to clean up the last drops. He held her in place with a loose grip that was more comforting than demanding. Then he lifted her onto his lap and nuzzled her neck. His hands offered tender caresses on her shoulders. Her back. Her thighs. His teeth lightly captured her earlobe, and he whispered, "You're so fucking sweet, baby."

A thrilled shiver raced along her arms and down her thighs. She was still in that position when the limo began to slow.

Ryan kissed her softly, set her on the seat next to him, and righted his clothes. As the door opened, he gave her a gentle smile, and then he and Dylan helped her out of the car onto a cobblestone drive. Brass sconces on an elegant, Mediterranean-style mansion illuminated the way to the front door.

The chauffeur didn't say a word about her attire, or lack thereof, so she chose to ignore him entirely as she walked between her two fully clothed escorts.

Dylan stopped. "Remember the rules, Olivia. Before you enter our home, I must ask once more. Do you agree to abide by them and fully submit yourself to our control?"

She nodded, not wanting to remain outside long.

"Say it."

"Yes."

"Yes, what?

"Yes, Master."

His smile was a reward, and it thrilled her. Then he opened the door and followed her inside.

Their home reminded her of an Italian villa. Marble floors mixed with crystal chandeliers and imported furnishings to paint a tapestry of elegance and sophistication.

"I'll give you the grand tour some other time," Dylan said. "Tonight, you rest. You'll need your energy in the coming days, I assure you." His grin was pure male mischievousness.

They led her to a gorgeous staircase that split to curve up both sides of the round vestibule. On the second floor at the end of the hall, they went through a set of double doors, which opened onto a huge bedroom.

The neutral, cream color of the carpet blended with the ivory satin duvet. Obviously custom-made, the oversized bed was the focal point of the room, with intricate ironwork at every corner. The four columns were massive. Each one was made of two tall, rectangular panels combined to form right angles. In each panel, the artists had created complex metal designs of ivy and grapevines. And at the top, the corner columns braced an iron canopy with sheer lace curtains.

"Wow."

"I'm glad you approve." Dylan took her wrist, attached one of the soft cuffs he'd brought from the car, and used the other cuff to tug her toward the bed.

Ryan pulled down the covers. "Hop in."

She crawled to the middle and faced them.

"Lie down," Dylan said.

She gave him a smirk and did as ordered, settling comfortably onto the cool satin sheet and feather pillows. He propped a knee on the bed and raised both of her hands over her head, again cuffing them together.

Ryan moved to the other side, reached between the headboard and mattress, and withdrew a strap, which he fastened to the cuffs. "As you can see, the bed is as functional as it is beautiful," he said with a wink.

She chuckled. "So I see. Do you intend to leave me like this?"

They sat on either side of her and looked her over. Butterflies took flight in her tummy.

Dylan ran a fingertip from her navel down to the top of her thong underwear. "Not exactly." With that, he removed her panties and stilettos. "That's better."

Tingles erupted like goose bumps all over her body as they eyed her with heated gazes.

"Cold?" Ryan asked, skimming a hand along one side and down a thigh.

"No."

"No, what?"

"No...Master."

He smiled, gave her a light swat to the thigh, and stood. Then he lifted the fluffy comforter over her and tucked her in like a child. As Ryan walked around the bed, Dylan bid her, "Good night. Get some rest. You'll need it for tomorrow."

Surprised, she watched them leave the room, switching off the light without so much as another word.

They brought her all this way *not* to sleep with her? *What kind of crazy shit is that?*

She pulled at her bindings, but they wouldn't give. She was still grumbling an hour later when she finally drifted off to sleep.

CHAPTER SEVEN

The next morning, Olivia awoke to the sensation of warm hands skimming over her flesh.

"Wake up, sleepy head."

She stretched like a cat and realized her hands were free. "Mmm. Goodnight." She curled onto her side.

A sharp swat to the buttocks made her jackknife, her eyes popping open to see Dylan's wide grin.

She frowned.

Nobody has a right to be that chipper in the damn morning.

"You have fifteen minutes to take a shower and brush your teeth. Don't bother drying your hair. We're having breakfast by the pool, so come downstairs when you're finished. Last night you saw the French doors centered under the staircase?"

"Yes."

"Yes, what?"

She smiled at his reminder. "Yes, Master."

He tapped a finger on the tip of her nose. "Those doors will take you to the back patio. Bathroom is through there." He pointed to a white, six-paneled door, so she headed that way. "See you in fifteen minutes. And Olivia..."

She halted and turned to look at him.

His expression was impenetrable. "Don't be late."

She rushed to the bathroom, found her vanity case of makeup and other toiletries, and completed her shower in less than ten minutes. Back in the bedroom, she looked for her luggage to choose something to wear, but couldn't find them. Running out of time, she adjusted the bath towel around her body and made her way to the pool.

The scent of chlorine and salty sea breezes floating on the steamy, humid air greeted her as she stepped outside. The patio was covered in white granite tiles and sported several lounge chairs, a couple of tables with umbrellas, and numerous potted tropical plants. The pool was a large oval with a Jacuzzi at one end and a mini waterfall at the other. In between, Dylan was stroking through the water, approaching the stairs at the shallow end.

"Dylan?"

"Right here, puss." The voice coming from behind her made her jump.

"I thought..." She pointed to the pool. If he wasn't swimming, then... *Oh, Ryan.*

Dylan's brother threw back his head, sending a sparkling spray of water across the surface. The muscles in his arms bulged as his fingers combed his dark hair away from a rugged face. A thin line of fine brown hair led below the navel and six-pack abs to an impressive package of male ego, encased in a royal blue Speedo that left nothing to the imagination.

Ryan grabbed a towel as he got out of the pool, but he used it to dry his hair, not wrap around his waist, which might explain why she was still looking down when he stopped in front of her.

With a chuckle, he used a finger to lift her chin and her gaze. "*Hola, mi gatita.*" His voice was as deep and erotic as Dylan's when calling her by the same pet name.

"Hello...Master Ryan."

His white grin introduced that adorable dimple in his left cheek, like a mirror image of Dylan.

She was in serious trouble.

"What were your instructions, Olivia?" Dylan asked.

Puzzled, she answered, "Shower, brush my teeth, and get down here in fifteen minutes. I wasn't late...Master."

"No you weren't, for which I commend you. However, you are to follow instructions exactly, and I don't recall saying anything about a towel." With a quick flick of his fingers at the loose knot, he removed the only barrier she had between her and them.

Ryan immediately took both hands to prevent her attempt to cover herself. "No. No." Holding her arms wide, he gave her body a once over in the bright light of day. "I like you much better without the towel." His smile widened to a grin, and her tummy flipped.

"I'm starved," Dylan said. "Come with us, *mi gatita.*"

"Why do you insist on calling me kitten?" It wasn't as if her name was Katrina or Catherine.

He gave her a devilish grin. "Because, my sexy kitten, you enjoy lapping up my cream."

Her face burned with embarrassment, and she silently cursed herself for asking the stupid question.

"I can't think of a better way to start the day, can you, *mi hermano*?" Ryan's words made her gaze ping-pong between the two men.

"Nope," Dylan agreed. "Not when we have such a delicious pet to share."

She felt nothing like a sex kitten and a lot like a mouse caught between two tigers. Her eyes widened, and they grinned.

"This way, puss." Dylan led her to one of the patio tables where two plates of food were set out in front of two chairs. Between them on the ground was a large, square pillow.

She frowned. Where was her plate?

Dylan pulled out a chair and motioned with his index finger.

Hesitantly, she approached. He pressed down on her shoulders until she knelt on the pillow.

"Let's see how well disciplined you are."

So he planned to challenge her, did he? With an inner smile, she sat back on her heels, faced the chair, and awaited his next command.

He pulled his black bathing shorts off to release his semi-erect cock then sat. "Hold me in your mouth while we eat breakfast."

"Excuse me?" Her gaze remained on his cock, which grew before her eyes.

"You heard me. Suck my cock, but only enough to keep it hard. If you're a good girl, we'll feed you more when we're done eating."

If I'm a good girl I get to eat? Hmm, she thought. Feeling naughty, she leaned forward. Was it the challenge he offered that made her obey his outrageous order? The attraction she felt for him, knowing what he could do to her with that gorgeous body? Or was it the commanding way he gave orders? She didn't understand why she would do something others might think degrading, but she knew that he somehow made her want to please him, no matter the method. She lowered her mouth to suck him inside.

He was already hard, which gave her a private thrill, so she held as much of him as she could and tongued the flesh underneath. His hand dropped to pet her head.

All around, she heard the sounds of early morning. The clink of utensils on dishes as the men ate. The chirp of wild birds as they awoke to a new day. The trickle of the waterfall into the pool and the ripples slapping at the edges.

But all she could see, taste, or smell was the man in her mouth. His salty flavor mingled with a hint of musk to offer a powerful lure to her feminine senses.

If the other suits in her office could see her now, they'd faint dead away. Or oust her as some kind of sexual deviant.

Why were these two men, Dylan especially, capable of controlling her? What flaw made her succumb to such temptations? More importantly, would she be able to overcome that weakness and move on without them when her time was up?

Maybe she was looking at this all wrong. Maybe she should treat each command as a chance to earn what she most wanted, which was a mind-blowing orgasm. Not the kind brought on through self-masturbation, but the intense climax that could only be had at the hands of a man, or men, who knew how to really handle a woman.

"Ready to eat?" Dylan asked, his fingers combing through her hair.

Oh yeah. She answered with a strong suck on his cock, which earned her an encouraging, albeit unintelligible, sound from him. She wrapped her arms around his legs and drew him deep into her mouth. Pulling back after each stroke, she watched his face change from amused surprise to dark passion, to demanding lust. She pushed him as far in as she could stand and let her teeth graze his skin softly as she pulled back. That was the trigger that set him off.

"Aw, fuck!"

He took over. His fingers bit into her scalp. His thighs spread, his cock swelled, and his balls drew up tight. While she struggled for control, he ripped it away with each stroke. Her nails dug into his thighs, causing him to growl behind clenched teeth.

"Harder, puss. Take it all."

And she did, sucking on him until the last spurt of his cum slid down her throat.

He collapsed back in his chair, his breathing heavy and unsteady.

She tongued him gently to wipe away the last traces of his ejaculation, then licked her lips and sat up. That would teach him to challenge her. "Can I come now?" She couldn't hold back her pleased grin.

One brown eye opened to peek at her, then the other. He studied her, his expression turning from sated euphoria to one of suspicion. "No."

No? She thought steam would pour from her ears because of that one word. How dare he take his pleasure and not return the favor.

"Here, puss. Eat the rest of this." He held his plate out to her.

She crossed her arms and glared. "I'm not hungry." No way would she eat his leftovers.

Dylan knew he could handle her one of two ways. Let her go without food, which would weaken her, or he could force her to eat for her own good and risk her wrath in the process. He glanced at Ryan who shrugged.

"That wasn't a request, Olivia. Do we have to tie you up and feed you ourselves?"

Her eyes narrowed. "You wouldn't dare...."

That settled that. No Dom worth his salt would back down from a challenge cast by his sub. Ryan grabbed her wrists, and Dylan had to quickly set the plate aside to avoid her flailing limbs.

"No way!"

Dylan grabbed her legs and was damn near gelded in the process. "If you refuse to take care of your body, then we'll have to do it for you."

They hauled her bucking body over to an arbor that they'd previously modified for alternative purposes. It took a little time and effort, but they finally had their cursing, spitting pet bound upright and spread-eagle in the center of the arbor.

"Let me go, goddammit."

Dylan was still a little lightheaded from the orgasm her talented mouth had sucked from his body. As much as he'd enjoyed the oral stimulation, he suspected she'd given him fellatio for all the wrong reasons, motivated more by her own selfish desires than by any real wish to please him.

So he knew most of her pique was over his refusal to satisfy her need to come, and possibly a little over the idea of eating his leftovers. Either way, he couldn't allow her to refuse a direct order.

He left her to think and scream while he retrieved his bathing suit, then rifled through a cabinet for a flogger, which he slipped into the thin waistband behind his back.

"See if I ever suck cock again. I'll bite the damn things off first. I swear it, if you don't let me go!"

He chuckled at her threats as he returned to the arbor. At least she hadn't used her safe word, yet. That alone was telling.

"Settle down, puss," Ryan said amid further curses and vile threats against their manhood. "I've never seen someone so upset over being told to eat. You aren't on a diet, are you?" His teasing question didn't go over well, but Dylan used the distraction to step behind her so she was unable to see him or what he now held in his hand.

Ryan had combined the food on their plates—each man having left one full pancake untouched along with a couple of sausages—onto a single dish. At Dylan's signal, Ryan tried to get her to take the first bite of pancake. As expected, she clamped her mouth shut and tossed her head about until she had syrup stripes from ear to ear.

Dylan reared back and swatted her hard across the right butt cheek. She jerked with a loud, "Aww," only to have his brother stuff the bite in her mouth.

Dylan put the flogger under her chin. "Spit it out," he warned, "and you'll face a more severe punishment."

Her eyes narrowed to slits, but she chewed then swallowed. And the battle of wills began. A refusal, a swat, followed by a glare and a bite of food. With each sporadic swing of the flogger, her skin reddened. A few more sharp slaps to the buttocks led to obedience as Olivia accepted her fate and dutifully ate the last of the meal Ryan fed her.

Dylan wanted to soothe her with his hands, his lips, but knew he couldn't give in to temptation just yet. He still had a punishment to mete out.

Ryan set the empty plate aside. "Do you understand why you're being punished, Olivia?"

"For asking to come?" Her voice held a note of sarcasm.

"No," Dylan said. "You are always free to ask for whatever you want. You are not free to disobey us, however. You not only refused to accept my answer to your request, but you then rebelled by ignoring a direct order. You fought us. Challenged our authority."

When she made to speak, Ryan put a finger over her mouth and shook his head. Wisely, she held her tongue.

"What's worse is you broke your promise." He joined Ryan in front of her so he could watch her face as he spoke. "We defined a set of rules, which you accepted and agreed to follow. I will see them kept. Therefore, I cannot disregard transgressions. I must punish you for your disobedience and impertinence, if I am to keep my word to you."

Her bright aqua eyes widened like a frightened mare spooked by lightning. A glance between her legs gave evidence of arousal, but her sudden rigidity concerned him.

"You remember my promise to you on the plane? That I would never betray your trust?" He waited for her to nod. "I meant what I said, all that I've said, including that there would be consequences for disobedience. I will always keep my word."

Moisture pooled in her eyes. He touched her cheek, letting his thumb skim her full bottom lip. When he felt it quiver, the urge to soothe her mouth with his own nearly overwhelmed him. Unable to maintain the hard expression of a disciplinarian, he walked around behind her, saw her body tense, and gestured to Ryan. If she remained stiff, the punishment would be harder on her. He couldn't have that.

Ryan cradled her face between gentle hands and kissed her softly. As he deepened the kiss, his hands roamed up and down her back, lightly across an already pink ass, then up along her sides to her breasts. A whimper of surrender preceded the release of her tight muscles.

Dylan struck with a hard smack of leather across her right butt cheek. She flinched and gritted her teeth.

"Shh." Ryan's fingers returned to her face, trailing along her jaw and neck, before he kissed her again and pulled away with a whispered, "Relax. It'll soon be over."

Dylan swung again and again, covering her buttocks and thighs, making every effort to not strike the same place twice.

"Good, baby," Ryan said, cradling her cheek in his palm. "Not long now."

When her ass changed from a rosy pink to flame red, Dylan shifted from punisher to pleasure provider. With the flick of his wrist, he set a steady tempo, swinging the flogger so that the ends reached around each side to lap at more erogenous zones.

Right breast, then left, and lower.

Below her navel. Across her pussy.

Sweat beaded on his brow and trickled down his spine as he struggled to maintain the pace for maximum effect. His arm ached as he forced himself to constantly alter the strength of each swing, some light, some with bite.

Strong enough to stimulate. Never hard enough to harm her precious flesh.

Her stubborn growls and pained grunts, which had turned to pleading whines, now mellowed into aroused moans. Watching her every move, listening to her softest sound, he knew the exact moment when the pain of punishment turned to warm pulses of pleasure.

Her head fell back as his rhythm consumed her. She no longer flinched at each strike, but instead thrust out her chest or pumped her hips forward as if she wished to fuck the twenty or so leather straps of the flogger.

He hadn't intended on taking her this far this fast, but her body responded like a natural. Her innate sensuality encouraged him.

"Who feeds you, puss?" he asked softly.

Slap...slap...slap.

"Answer me." He altered again to pop her across the butt.

"Aww! You do."

"Who commands your body?"

Slap...slap...slap.

"You, Master." Her breaths were shallow pants.

"What do you need, Olivia?"

"Please, oh please, I need to come." Her head tossed back and forth.

"Not yet." Right breast, left, and lower.

Her protest was little more than an incoherent whimper.

"Will you be an obedient pussy?"

"Yes."

"Yes, what?" Left breast, right, and pussy.

"Yes, Master!"

He stopped, breathing heavily, his body rock hard and sore. He watched her sink against the bindings that still held her aloft. She was so primed. He simply nodded to Ryan who, without warning, jabbed two fingers deep into her pussy.

"Come," Ryan said, although the order wasn't necessary. The climax seized her muscles and shook her to the core. He pulled her against his chest, wrapping his left arm around her middle and holding his fingers deep inside until the orgasm lessened. "That's it. Again." He pumped them into her with a few hard thrusts, and like a wind-up toy, she took off again. When she settled against him, Ryan rubbed her clit hard and murmured, "Once more, baby."

She threw her head back, her mouth open on a silent scream. Her hips slammed hard against Ryan's hand.

"Yes, keep it going."

The sight of his brother holding her while she experienced one powerful orgasm after another was the most erotic vision Dylan had ever witnessed, a moment he'd never forget. His own cock swelled, and he wanted so much to fuck her until they both passed out. But he couldn't. Now was not the time. He must remember the goal.

Ryan looked at him over her shoulder, and he saw the same raw emotions in his brother's eyes that burned in his own heart.

Two weeks was not long enough. He needed a lifetime to fully grasp all that she was or could become. How in the hell could he ever keep his promise and let her go?

CHAPTER EIGHT

Olivia was still reeling from the most orgasms she'd ever had in under sixty-seconds when the men surprised her again. They had her under their control and could've fucked her into a stupor, but they didn't.

As soon as Dylan released her feet and hands, Ryan scooped her into his arms and carried her into the cool waters of the pool, where he sat on the steps and cradled her like a priceless Ming vase. She could feel his aroused state under her bottom, but he didn't acknowledge it.

Without a word, he massaged the aches from her arms and legs, being careful not to chafe her more tender areas. Using some of the water, he tenderly cleaned the sticky syrup off her face, as if she were a toddler in need of such assistance. His selfless caregiving made her ashamed of her earlier childishness.

When Dylan didn't join them, she looked around for him.

"He'll be back in a moment. Punishing you takes a lot out of him."

"Out of *him*?" She was the one with the stinging ass,

heightened sensitivity, and post-orgasmic languor. "He hurt me."

"And aroused you," Ryan pointed out.

She snapped her mouth shut, unwilling to discuss her illogical physical reaction to the whipping.

Ryan chuckled and tucked some of her hair behind her left ear. "Punishment isn't supposed to feel pleasant. If it was, that wouldn't be effective, now would it? However, you still reached climax afterwards."

She gave him her best scowl, which he dissolved with a grin and a kiss to the tip of her nose.

"You always had your safe word, yet you didn't use it. Why do you think that is?"

That's what bothered her the most. Why hadn't she screamed the damn word and called this whole thing off? Her gaze dropped to the water until he gently turned her face toward his.

"You're a very strong woman, a strong-willed woman. We're proud of how well you took the flogging. However, you did force our hand."

"It hurt...still does." Although the cool water had soothed some of her burning flesh, she spoke more of the pain she felt in her chest at having broken her promise to them. Dylan was right when he said she'd failed to keep her word...and she hadn't even been here a day.

"It's supposed to, so you learn from it and remember even after the sting fades. Maybe then we won't have to do it again any time soon." Ryan adjusted her on his lap so that she faced him with her legs on either side of him.

She rested her arms on his shoulders, her hands curved around his neck. The only thing separating them was the material of his tiny bathing suit, but he didn't take advantage of the situation.

"Whether you believe it or not, he dislikes disciplinary punishments. We both do."

"For something he doesn't like, he's certainly good at it," she said with a pout.

"He has to be. He's responsible for your well-being. Discipline must be wielded correctly, or he risks abusing his sub. That's something he'd never be able to live with, especially with you."

She watched him as he peered toward the waterfall. His hands rubbed up and down her arms in an absentminded manner. "What?"

"Nothing. Here comes Dylan with your next lesson."

"Lesson?"

"Obedience training," he said, giving her a kiss on the forehead then nuzzling her cheek with his nose and lips.

"I'm not a dog. I do *not* need obedience training."

"Actually you do, since you seem to forget the simplest of rules."

"Like what?" she asked, offended.

"Like addressing me with the proper title, which you've yet to do since we got in the water."

She opened her mouth to argue, but realized he was right. "Sorry, Master."

He gave her a dimpled smile and a chaste kiss on the lips. "Better."

Dylan set some towels on a table between two lounge chairs then reclined in one. Still dressed in his swimwear, he looked so sexy lying there in repose with eyes shut, his expression relaxed, as it had been the morning she left him in that hotel room. Sometimes she thought she'd give anything, do anything, just for chances like this, to see him so calm.

"Come here, puss," he said without opening his eyes.

And dominant.

She slid from one master's lap and approached another. When she neared, he held his hand out and met her gaze. Her fingers brushed across his palm before he closed her hand in his.

"Straddle me." As she moved to sit on his thighs, Ryan dried off and took the other chair.

Dylan reached for a plastic bottle and squeezed some white cream on his hands. "This will help soothe away any lingering soreness." She tensed when the cool lotion contacted her hypersensitive chest, but he eased her with a touch that was both gentle and confident.

"Are you still cross with me, puss?"

"I'd rather not talk about it...Master."

His hands moved down and around to rub cool lotion on her hips and sore buttocks. "Because you're angry over my method of correction and confused by your response to it."

She met his knowing gaze and marveled at his perceptive talents. Was she that easy to read?

"I don't understand how I could..." She shrugged, unable to fully explain her jumbled thoughts.

"Be aroused by flogging or allow me near you after such punishment?" His mouth curved into a smile.

"Both."

"Your mind tells you that you should react a certain way, while your body does what's natural. Skin is an organ like any other in the body and is just as susceptible to stimuli." His hands slid over her thighs and curved around her waist, proving his point.

"You know our rules," he said, "because we've made them clear. You accept punishment for breaking those rules because, in your heart, you trust me. You have a need to surrender, to have a strong man—or two—redirect you. Deep inside, you long to relinquish control. To feel free to explore all that we're capable of giving you."

She stared at him, his bold gaze and the firm angles of his face, and tried to hang onto her grudge. "Like a sore ass?"

His right hand dipped between her legs, a finger tracing her folds. "Like the orgasms you experienced. The tightness in your chest and desire in the pit of your stomach that happens with just one touch of my hand."

Her eyes drifted shut, closing out the sight of his face, but unable to block his seductive touch or the sound of his voice. As if they had a mind of their own, her hips rocked against his hand.

"We have so much more to show you, to teach you, if you'll submit totally to our guidance. Are you willing to learn?"

"Mmm." Her fingers curled over his hard biceps as his finger continued its tempting circles around her clitoris.

"Why do you fight yourself, Olivia? Let us take care of you, show you more pleasure than you've ever known. Let go and trust us completely."

She saw need darken his eyes. "I'll try."

His hands moved to her thighs once more as he studied her silently. "Good enough. I have something I want you to wear for the duration of your stay. It will help remind you of your place as a submissive in our home. What type of submissive you are—"

"Types, Master?"

"Subs may be slaves, sluts, or pets. They're all submissive, but the levels of bondage and dominance vary. When you think of a pet, what comes to mind?"

"Pee pads and litter boxes."

He chuckled. "Think of how pets respond to their chosen owners. Pets trust their masters to provide food, shelter, and even discipline. Because of that trust, they submit to ownership willingly. Once trained, they obey their masters. Unconditionally." His fingertip traced the lips that had wrapped around his cock earlier, his eyes meeting hers with a seriousness she'd seldom seen before. "They seek their masters' pleasure *without* any thought to their own needs. For this reason, a pet's trust is the most precious gift a master can possess."

She realized he'd seen through her deception, her attempt this morning to control him for her own selfish reasons. Unable to look him in the eye, she stared at his chest. "What about the others, Master?"

"When I say slut, what comes to mind?"

"A prostitute."

"Close. Sluts enjoy performing for their masters, including fucking whomever their masters offer them to. A pet may be a slut, or a slut may be a slave. But a pet is not a slave. They're at opposite ends of the spectrum."

Ryan proved he'd been listening all along as he took up the explanation where Dylan left off. "Slaves take submission to the extreme. They submit to total domination, which could include long periods of confinement. Slaves are forced to labor for their masters around the house as well as in their masters' beds, and they relinquish all control over who owns them, so they may be auctioned off to serve other masters."

Nothing about the last type appealed to her at all, an opinion that must've shown on her face because Dylan chuckled.

"I think we can safely say you're not a slave."

Although she'd accepted Ryan as a master easily enough, she wasn't so sure about the slut type either.

Ryan added, "Unlike slaves, pets have a say in who owns them. Like a pet bird that may fly the coop, a pet sub may end the relationship at any time. They retain ultimate control that way, while giving up all other control to their chosen masters."

"No matter the type, one thing remains constant," Dylan said. "Masters demand proof of ownership, which the sub is required to wear at all times. For slaves, that could be a host of restraints at the wrists, ankles and neck. For sluts, chastity belts are often used."

Dylan and Ryan laughed when her eyes widened at that nugget of information.

"Pets are collared." Dylan pulled a wide, black and silver collar from beneath the towels he'd set on the table. "This is a training collar. For us to continue, you must wear it willingly. The choice is yours."

They could've put it on her while she was distracted earlier by the climaxes they'd wrought on her body, or attached it while she slept last night. But they did none of that. Instead, they voluntarily relinquished control to her for the moment and allowed her to decide. She appreciated their effort to ensure she understood to what she was submitting, and that it was up to her to give that control back. So, the choice was easy.

She took the collar and put it around her neck. Dylan smiled. Ryan closed the flap on the back and set the tiny brass padlock. The soft leather lining kept the metal from chafing, while the weight of the steel band was a constant reminder of its presence.

* * * * *

"You want me to wear *what*?" Olivia stood in the middle of her temporary bedroom with nothing on but a collar and a furious glare for her so-called masters.

"Watch your tongue, puss," Ryan warned with a frown after she forgot to use their titles. It was something she'd grown accustomed to over the past few days, but always forgot whenever she got riled. He handed the roll of red tape to Dylan.

"Where's my luggage, Master? Why can't I pick something from one of them?"

Dylan said, "Your luggage didn't make it on the plane."

Enrique had said he'd take care of it. How could he have *not* put the damn luggage on the plane? Admittedly, she hadn't thought to ask until now. She hadn't needed any of her clothes since the day she arrived, but that was a moot point. She needed her clothes now.

"The bags were returned to your home at my request," Dylan said.

"What? I can't believe you'd do... No. Yes, I can. You planned this all along, didn't you?" Ryan cocked a brow, so she added a belated, "Master."

She couldn't believe she was having this argument naked as a jaybird, with them fully clothed. Actually, there were many things she couldn't believe. Her masters had given her climax after climax with their hands and mouths, but not once in four days had they actually fucked her. Except for the morning blowjobs, which had become a ritual, she seldom got close to their cocks. And last night was the third night they'd left her tied to the bed and alone with her growing sexual frustrations.

"I told you exactly where, when, and how to show up," Dylan said. "My instructions did not include bringing along half your wardrobe in three large suitcases. Besides, none of your clothing would be appropriate attire for where we're going."

Where were they going? What kind of place accepted tape as *appropriate attire*? She stared in disbelief at the roll of tape they wanted her to wear. This was ludicrous. "I can't go out in public like that. What if it unravels?"

"Enough," Ryan scolded. "Olivia, you'll wear the PVC tape or go as you are now."

Her eyes rounded, but she bit back the words, *you wouldn't dare.* She knew better than to challenge them like that again.

Dylan took a step forward with the red PVC tape. Her brain screamed for her to run, but her legs wouldn't move.

As if reading her mind and cutting off her escape, Ryan walked around behind her. She held her breath. He raised her wrists and bent her arms so that her palms were on the back of her head and held her hair out of the way.

She closed her eyes while Dylan unrolled a part of the two-inch-wide tape and began to wrap it around her breasts. He covered the middle, barely concealing both areolas, and then he ran a tight strip across the lower part of her chest.

The PVC tape didn't stick to her skin, but rather to itself, which was a relief.

After four or five revolutions, he cut the tape and started to wrap more of the red strip around her hips. His new clothing design was the shortest damn miniskirt ever. It bordered on indecent.

When she felt a tug on one foot, her hands fell to Dylan's shoulders, while he knelt in front of her. He slipped onto her foot a red stiletto with thin leather laces that crisscrossed up her calf. After he finished with the other foot, he stood to inspect his work.

"Here," Ryan said, handing him a dime-sized, ruby-colored jewel. Dylan turned it over, peeled off a paper backing, and then put the sticky side into her navel.

She looked down and saw a lot of cleavage.

"Masters. Do you have more tape? I'm gonna spill out of this top."

The men chuckled as Dylan met her gaze and tossed the tape on the bed. She eyed the roll with longing. "Not unless we want you to."

Earlier, they'd donned matching black leather pants and silk shirts of different colors. Ryan's was ivory, which really set off his bronzed skin, dark brown hair, and Latino features. Dylan chose a red one, which coordinated with the tape she wore. A thin Herringbone chain with a tiny brass key for a pendant hung around his neck. She suspected it went to the padlock on the back of her collar.

"One more thing." Ryan pulled out a braided leather cord with a loop at one end and a clip at the other. When he attached the metal clip to the front ring on her collar, she realized they had her on a leash. The word *pet* suddenly took on a whole new meaning.

"Why?" Her question came out so softly she didn't expect them to answer, but Dylan did.

"You're our pet, puss. The collar testifies to that fact. The leash lets others at the club know you're in training. They won't risk our wrath by messing with you."

Knowing the leash provided a visible layer of protection helped soothe her wounded pride. A little.

"Before we go, I want to go over some things with you." Dylan sat and patted the bed, so she joined him. "We're introducing you to a whole new world tonight. A world with its own set of rules and expectations. You'll see numerous subs tonight, along with their masters and other club-hoppers, who use these places to meet their fetish for voyeurism and exhibitionism. We feel you are ready, but if anything makes you uncomfortable, let us know."

Ryan sat on her other side. "Remember to keep your gaze lowered out of respect for the other Doms. Otherwise it could be viewed as a challenge, an invitation, or an insult. Don't speak unless told to do so or asked a direct question."

"And above all, obey us," Dylan said. "Your actions reflect upon us as your masters. Swift action will be taken for any disobedience."

CHAPTER NINE

When they arrived at the club, Olivia was surprised to see the building appeared to be an old brick mansion rather than a flashy nightclub with glaring neon, triple-X signs. Ryan pulled the Lexus SUV into the circular drive and handed the keys to the valet.

As they approached, the front door swung open.

"Dylan, Ryan...so good to have you back at Incognito. Come in."

Remembering their orders, Olivia kept her face lowered and peeked through her lashes as they walked inside. Muted music and muffled conversations spilled from beyond the closed doors on the other side of the marbled vestibule. The woman greeting them was dressed from ponytail to the tips of her toes in black latex, with kohl eyeliner darkening her eyes and blood-red lips setting off her porcelain skin.

"You're looking fine, Kat," Ryan said.

The dominatrix tapped a riding crop against his cheek. "Pity you're such a Dom. I would love to sink my claws into you."

Over my dead body. Jealous possessiveness swamped Olivia. She moved her fisted hands behind her back to hide them, even as her back teeth ground in annoyance.

Ryan laughed. "We'd rip each other to shreds, Kat. You know that." He put a hand at the small of Olivia's back. "I'd like you to meet our new pet. Katriona, this is Olivia. Puss, say hello to Mistress Kat."

"Hello."

The riding crop touched her chin, lifting her face and gaze to meet Kat's. "Hmm. You better keep this one on a tight leash."

Olivia lowered her gaze, but apparently not before Kat caught the spark of temper, which caused the dominatrix to chuckle. She waved for them to proceed inside.

"Come on, puss." Ryan held her leash, but guided her with his hand at her back. Dylan took hold of her left hand, interlacing their fingers. She knew they touched her on purpose, an attempt to lessen the shame of the leash. Their effort warmed her heart and made her smile.

As they followed Kat into the house, she passed numerous dark-wood antiques that radiated with the citric scent of furniture polish. But sex was also in the air.

"Busy night tonight?" Dylan asked.

"The usual crowd, plus a few new faces. Oh, the Masters of Sin arrived about five minutes ago. They're teamed up with Constance tonight."

Masters of Sin?

"Damn. Natalie must've not worked out for them."

Kat snorted at Dylan's comment. "It'll take a stronger woman than Natalie to take on those two. They're a lot like another pair of Doms I know, always reaching for the stars, and usually falling back to earth in flames."

"Care to name any names?" Ryan challenged.

Kat laughed. "I never name names. Not safe in my line of work."

The room proved to be a large ballroom-style space with hardwood floors and a high ceiling. Along one side was a buffet of finger foods and a bar operated by a huge, bald, African American fellow in black spandex shorts and metal wrist cuffs. Overhead, mingled with the muted glow of antique chandeliers, there was an array of pulleys and cables, which led to cranks on the outer walls. In the corners of the room stood wooden platforms with a mix of restraints. Couches, ottomans, tables and chairs were scattered throughout, many of which were occupied by people talking or making out.

Patrons mingled in various stages of undress, which made it somewhat easy to determine who was a Dom and who was a sub. Her masters had spoken the truth about her clothes. Everything she'd packed would've made her stick out. Most were dressed scantily in shades of black, red, and sometimes pink. A few wore costumes like French maids or nursing uniforms for a clinic specializing in erotic male fantasies. She hadn't seen this much flesh since she'd mistakenly visited the wrong beach on the Mediterranean coast.

She couldn't help but stare at a mustachioed man who had two redheaded women in chains licking his boots while he masturbated himself. He looked up and locked gazes with her. His lips formed a smirk.

"Stay," he said, dropping the chains onto the

women's backs, but not releasing his dick. When he headed toward her, Olivia stepped on Dylan's foot.

"Sorry, Master," she said in a panic as, realizing her error, she dropped her gaze to the floor. God, why couldn't she remember to follow directions? Why did she have to get so caught up in looking around that she forgot her masters' warnings?

"Puss, what...?" Dylan didn't have time to finish his question as the answer stopped in front of them with his cock directly in her line of sight.

She closed her eyes, her head bowed.

"I see you're still *hanging out* here, Patrick," Dylan said.

The man's laugh was a raspy sound that had the same effect on Olivia's spine as nails on a chalkboard. She peeked to see the man's cock still standing proud, his arms now folded across his chest.

"Why should I hide and deny your bitch the pleasure of ogling me? I dare not insult you and ignore her invitation."

She could feel Ryan and Dylan look at her, their silence ominous. Although there was still noise in the background—the constant flow of chatter, the sensual beat of music from hidden speakers, along with the occasional moan of pleasure—she felt as if she stood within the eye of a hurricane. Any second, the fatal winds would blow her away.

"Since we're not inclined to share her at the moment," Ryan said, "I'm sure you'll accept her apology for extending the unauthorized invitation."

She breathed a sigh of relief. An apology. She'd gladly

say *I'm sorry*, if doing so would make the man and his dick go away.

"A kiss of apology for me, and permission to watch her punishment for doing something unauthorized."

A kiss! She couldn't possibly kiss that sneering mouth without puking. Then he took hold of his cock again, and she realized where he wanted the kiss. Her hands fisted. Her right one balled behind her back. The left one's nails bit into Dylan's hand.

"On your knees, puss," Dylan said.

It took every ounce of strength in her to not look up and glare at Dylan. Then he squeezed her hand and, for some reason totally beyond her understanding, she found the gesture reassuring.

Ryan's hand slipped from her back to her shoulder and pressed down until she dropped to her knees. Her stomach churned.

"You'll obey me without deviation, puss. Understood?" Dylan's voice was hard. Cold.

Afraid she'd upchuck if she opened her mouth, she nodded with eyes closed. Maybe if she didn't look...

"Say you are sorry to Master Patrick, and then kiss the top of his right boot."

Her eyes snapped open. Her gaze locked on his boots. She saw the man release his cock and ball his hands into fists at his sides. This wasn't what he wanted, but she was elated.

Silently thanking Dylan for his creativity, she said, "I'm sorry, Master Patrick," and quickly bowed to kiss his boot. As her lips connected with the leather, she felt the leash pull taut a half second before two hands smacked her hard on the ass. Ryan's tight grip on the leash kept her from sailing forward on her face.

"Ow!" She jackknifed up, her hands rubbing her tape-clad butt.

"That's it?" Patrick asked, obviously disgusted.

"She's our pet, not our slave," Ryan said, "so brutality isn't necessary."

Dylan said, "I'm quite certain that's all the discipline she requires. Is that not so, puss?"

"Yes, Master." She nodded her head for emphasis, her gaze still on Patrick's boots. "I'm sorry I disobeyed you. It won't happen again. I promise."

With their hands under her elbows, they lifted her to her feet. She kept her eyes lowered, but still saw the man turn sharply on his heel and stalk back to his chained slaves.

"I am sorry," she whispered once more.

Dylan's finger lifted her chin, and she looked into his warm eyes. "I know. It's all new and different, a lot to take in all at once. But now you see that we give you rules to obey for a reason. So behave from now on, okay?"

"Yes, Master."

He pressed a brief kiss to her lips.

Weaving through the crowd, Ryan held her closer to his side, while Dylan walked behind her, again holding her hand. Their conscious effort to soothe her jitters helped her overcome her fears.

Peeking through lowered lashes, she could see in the center of the room where someone had put a pedestal with a square, padded cushion. Two men were attaching a buxom blonde to that pedestal, which was at the perfect height for the woman to bend over. The padded cushion was large enough to support her, but small enough that her boobs hung over one side and legs over the other. She was totally nude except for thigh-high black boots with five-inch heels. The two men were tall, at least six-foot, and wore muscle shirts and ass-hugging black jeans.

Dylan and Ryan got front row seats to whatever was going to happen. They sat in two wing-backed chairs and had Olivia kneel on the floor between them. Ryan unhooked her leash, but left it lying in plain view on his lap.

When one of the men spotted Dylan and Ryan, he swatted the blonde on her ass before motioning to his partner who was blindfolding the woman. They looked a lot alike, but obviously not twins like her masters. Both came over to shake hands.

"We were wondering when you two would put in an appearance."

"Wouldn't miss it, Jack. Let us introduce our pet, Olivia Chandler," Dylan said, lending her a hand. "Olivia, stand and greet the Sinclair brothers, Jackson..." He gestured to the one on the left, then swept to the right. "...And Jonathon. Masters Jack and Jon to you."

"Hello, Master Jack. Master Jon," she said without daring a glance up, although from what she could see of them, they were well built.

"Nice to meet you," Jon said as if he was greeting her in a public park or some other neutral location. "Permission, Dylan?"

"Granted."

Taking her chin between thumb and forefinger and lifting her face, Jon said, "I don't recall ever seeing you here before."

"I-I've never been here," she said softly, unsure

whether she was supposed to keep talking.

"Turn around, puss," Dylan said. "Let them have a look at you."

With her head bowed to hide her burning cheeks, she spun in a quick circle.

The Sinclair men chuckled.

Ryan popped her on the butt with his end of the leash. "Why don't you try it again? Slower this time."

Rubbing the stinging spot, she made another, much slower, revolution.

"Where'd you find this dove, Dylan?" Jack asked.

"At a park in Madrid. She flew the coop but couldn't stay away."

"Welcome to Incognito, Olivia," Jack said. A female moan sounded behind him. The sub they'd left on the pedestal was squirming. "We'll talk more later. Right now, duty calls."

"Back on your knees, puss," Dylan said. "You may look up and watch the scene."

As she sat back on her heels, she saw the Sinclair brothers circle their sub, each one running a fingertip over her back and sides. Her feet were separated by a bar with cuffs attached over her boots at the ankles. Her wrists were bound in leather straps, which connected to a belt that held her waist on the pedestal's padded cushion.

Olivia watched as Jack and Jon teased the woman without mercy. Jon massaged her large breasts but avoided her nipples, while Jack ran his hands over her hips, butt, and thighs without touching between her legs.

"Masters..." the woman pleaded.

Jon released her. Jack trailed a fingertip down her

spine to the crack in her ass.

"You must ask for what you want, Connie," Jon said.

"Touch me, fuck me. Oh, I can't stand it."

"He said ask," Jack said, slapping her hard on the ass before going to a nearby table that held an array of items. He selected a short chain with small, rubber-tipped clamps and a couple of silver packets, one of which he tossed to Jon as he approached the bound woman.

"We do not take orders from subs, Connie. We give them," Jon said, ripping open the packet. He opened his pants, allowing his aroused dick to spring out of its denim confines. Then he gripped her hair and hauled her head back. "Open your mouth." When the woman did, Jon added, "Ask, Connie. You must ask for what you need."

"I need your cock. I need to feel you inside me, please?" He placed the condom over the woman's lips, and pushed his cock inside. He gave a slight hiss as her lips sealed around him.

When she tried to maintain the suction and keep Jon in her mouth, Jack popped her on the ass. "Release." She did, and Jack stepped forward. "That wasn't smart, my selfish little slut. You're to follow our wishes, not seek your own pleasures." He bent down and pulled on her nipples, twisting them between thumb and finger, until she let out a cry. "Do you understand?"

"Yes," she answered breathlessly.

He took the chain and clamped an end to each nipple, causing the woman to gasp. He tugged on the chain, and the woman moaned.

"Please, Masters. Let me come."

"No. Is that all you want?" Jack stood, opened his

packet, and undid his pants.

"No, Masters."

"Maybe we should take our cocks elsewhere, my demanding little slut." He pumped his cock a few times until he hardened, all the while tugging on her chain. "I'm sure there are others willing to serve us."

"Noo. I'm yours. Please, let me pleasure your big cocks."

"Open wide." Jack positioned the condom and his cock so they just touched her lips. "Remember, Connie, our desire comes first."

Jon had moved around behind her and teased her shaved pussy with light flicks of his fingers. Now he spread her ass cheeks wide, and as Jack pushed into the woman's mouth, Jon entered her wet pussy with full force.

Olivia couldn't look away from the two men who pummeled their captive from both ends. Their muscles flexed as they synchronized their thrusts for maximum effect. The woman's cries were muffled, incoherent, but her body testified to the desire raging in her.

Despite herself, Olivia's own arousal responded. Her breathing became shallow, her pussy moist. She clenched her fists, timed to the steady strokes the Masters of Sin made. She'd never witnessed such a spectacle before, had never dreamed it might affect her so strongly. The sights. The sounds of slapping flesh. The scent of uninhibited sex.

"Fuck her harder," someone shouted from the crowd. The command echoed in Olivia's mind as she pictured herself in the other woman's place with Dylan and Ryan pounding into her. Her body reacted to each thrust and withdrawal, and she neared her own climax just from watching the ménage à trois.

"You can take more, Connie, can't you?" Jack said through gritted teeth.

Olivia could tell the men were struggling to hold back their releases. Sweat beaded on their brows, their muscles tensed as they maintained the ruthless pace.

The woman whimpered, and their rhythm increased in tandem. The force of each thrust grew stronger than the last. Jack reached around the woman and grabbed the chain. "Come...now," he said, as he jerked the clamps off her nipples and slammed deep into her mouth. The woman's scream was still audible despite the cock stretching her lips.

Olivia bit her lip and stifled her own whimper as her muscles clenched.

Jon and Jack's heads reared back as they held themselves inside the woman, their buttocks clenched, their hands holding tight to her head and hips.

CHAPTER TEN

Dylan smiled as he watched Olivia flex and fist her hands. The scene playing out before them had captured her attention, as he'd suspected it would. Her reaction proved better than expected, and he exchanged a quick glance with Ryan, who cocked a brow and grinned.

They seldom looked at the trio on the platform. His and Ryan's gazes focused on their pet, observing and recording her response. It aroused her?

Her knees squeezed together as if she was trying to hold back something, or hold onto it so it couldn't escape. Her knuckles were white. Her nails left little quarter moons in her palms. When Jon used the woman's mouth to put on his condom, Olivia licked her lips, and Dylan grinned.

He hadn't been sure how their pet would react to voyeurism, which was why he'd asked Jon and Jack earlier in the week to keep it simple tonight. Of course, he'd thought they'd have Natalie here, another sub who was fairly new to the BDSM scene, someone to whom Olivia could possibly relate. When he learned they'd teamed with Constance instead, he wasn't sure what to expect.

Connie was what the club regulars called a stray slut. She submitted temporarily to whatever Dom or Doms would take her for any given evening. Usually she required much more pain to reach orgasm, so the nipple clamps proved to be a thing of inspiration. They provided Connie with what she needed without terrifying Olivia.

She didn't look scared. She looked ready to come. When Jack yanked the clamps off, Olivia's chest rose with a sudden intake of breath. Her fingers splayed across her thighs, her hips doing a tiny bounce on her heels.

Dylan was having a hard time not fucking her and, with each passing day, that urge became more difficult to fight. But he had to stick to the plan. Ryan and he had determined to wait for her to fully submit, to completely accept them as her masters and not fight them. Another reason for the little display tonight. He hoped she caught the message. If she would release that last bit of control she insisted on having, stop arguing when she thought they weren't in the right, they'd give her anything she asked for. Everything she needed.

She'd made it clear she wanted them to fuck her and had become increasingly irritable each night they left her bound and alone in that big bed. But until she was ready and fully understood, they would withhold what she most wanted.

With any other sub to have worn their collar, he controlled and fucked them however he chose, but things were different with Olivia, the outcome more vital. She wasn't an experienced submissive. She didn't troll the clubs. Although she had natural submissive tendencies, she ran from them, denied them, or avoided them altogether. She was convinced, he suspected, that she'd be able to dabble in it for a while, enjoy a couple of weeks of good fucking, and return to her old life without any repercussions. They had a limited amount of time to convince her otherwise.

Neither he nor Ryan wanted a slave. They wanted a pet who gave herself over to them not temporarily, but for all time. Not in part, but wholeheartedly. They wanted more than her body. They wanted her heart.

Kat was right in saying they reached for the stars. They did. They wanted more than a casual fling. They wanted a lifetime commitment with someone who trusted them to care for all her needs.

The power and control weren't the lure for them so much as finding a woman who thought of them before herself and believed in them. The ultimate trust. That's what they wanted and why they kept reaching for the stars.

He'd twisted her arm to get her here by throwing out a challenge he knew she couldn't walk away from. She needed to feel strong and independent. He knew that, but what remained uncertain was whether she was strong enough to trust another—to trust them—with more than just her body. Her independence wasn't in question. The choice of a relationship with them or not, to submit or not, was the treasure they longed for, and a decision that was entirely hers. He just hoped she made the right decision, and soon.

Dylan leaned closer to her and whispered, "Spread your knees, puss."

Her wide-eyed gaze turned to him, but her knees moved apart. Since the tape barely covered her ass, he knew her movements opened her pussy to the view of anyone across the room, but he wondered whether she realized that.

He kept his gaze on hers, watching those aqua depths darken as he reached between her legs to confirm his suspicions. His fingers dipped into her moisture and pulled out. Still holding her gaze, he lifted his wet finger to his mouth and tasted her cream.

She stared at his finger as he moved it in and out of his mouth a couple of times.

"I see our pet enjoyed tonight's entertainment," Ryan said with a chuckle. "She has the heart and libido of a natural voyeur."

Dylan removed his finger and grinned, watching her blush deepen. He loved the little gifts of innocence she unknowingly offered. They made his role as her master and teacher worth every moment of sacrifice. If they could, he and Ryan would gift her with those elusive stars. She'd yet to learn that, but he'd do his damnedest to teach her.

* * * * *

After Jon and Jack released Constance, the trio joined them at one of the tables set up near the buffet. Ryan and Jack went to gather a few plates of food. Olivia was surprised when Dylan held a chair out for her and handed her the other end of the leash he'd reattached to her collar.

"Wait here," he said before he and Jon left to get drinks.

Constance sat across from her and didn't seem at all concerned about her nudity. "So, you're the Montgomery brothers' new pet."

"I guess you could say that I am. For now."

Connie grinned. "A free spirit like me, huh?"

"I like my independence, if that's what you mean."

Connie laughed and looked boldly around the room. "That's one way to put it. There really is too much variety in the bondage world to choose just one man, or two for that matter, wouldn't you agree?"

"I wouldn't know. It's all rather new for me."

"Yes, the collar and leash. Well, at least you picked a great duo to train you. They'll treat you right. Listen and learn everything you can, because when you move on to other masters, girl, you've gotta be careful. Not everyone's on the up-and-up."

"Oh, I don't think..." She let her words trail off as the men returned. Olivia lowered her gaze to the table.

The men took their seats, and the conversation turned to more casual talk of business and old times. Dylan or Ryan would occasionally hand her a piece of food or give her a sip of wine, but otherwise, they left her to her thoughts.

Was this all there was? Sex for sex's sake? When the mutual satisfaction ended, so did the relationship? Or was there more? She tried to picture herself like Connie, never settling on one relationship, going from one to another to another until she grew old and lonely.

Variety was nice for some things, but the way Connie said it, Olivia decided she didn't really want that kind of sex life. Yet Dylan had proposed only two weeks. That was what he'd written on the piece of paper he'd given her back at the Rosemont. One shot to answer any questions born from their night in Madrid. To experience submission with the safety net of knowing it was temporary.

After two weeks, it would be over, except for maybe the occasional visit whenever in town, if she could talk them into that. And that was a big *if.*

Wasn't that what she wanted? What she'd asked for?

Yes, at first she had, but now?

What was the value of independence if you had no one to share it with?

"Why the frown, puss?"

"What?" She blinked and turned to see Dylan watching her.

He smiled. "I'm afraid our reminiscing has bored our pet. You're off in your own little world." He tucked a stray lock of hair behind her ear.

She forced a smile. "I guess I'm just a little tired, Master. I'm sorry."

"Then we'll call it a night." He started to get up.

"No, please. I don't mean to ruin your evening with friends."

He took the end of her leash. "Nonsense. Our first priority is you. Besides, we'll visit with Jon and Jack again. I've invited them over for a get-together in a few weeks." He turned to the others at the table. "If you'll excuse us."

"See you later," Jon said. "Nice meeting you, Olivia."

"Thank you. You, too."

On the ride home, Olivia lay across the back seat, her head in Dylan's lap, while Ryan drove. They didn't speak. She pretended to sleep while thoughts rattled around inside her head.

What exactly did she need? Not just climaxes. They'd given her plenty of them over the past few days. That wasn't enough. She wanted to feel—no—she *needed* to know there was more between her and her masters than just a couple of weeks of enticing foreplay and frenzied orgasms. Did they care about her? Not just her body, but *her*?

Dylan's hand slowly stroked her hair.

They seemed to care. Taking her home the moment she mentioned being tired was just one example of many she could think of where they gave up something on her behalf. They weren't even sleeping with her. Why?

They were holding something back. She was certain of it. Now she wanted to know why. Was there something wrong with her?

After they pulled into the driveway, they helped her out and escorted her to the bedroom. Once inside, they removed her leash, and then Dylan gave her a mischievous grin, grabbed one end of the tape and nudged her. With a laugh, she twirled away from him until her red top fell like a ribbon to the floor. Ryan grabbed the end at her waist and spun her back across the room toward Dylan.

She stepped out of her stilettos with a grateful sigh and reached to pull out the jewel, but Dylan stopped her.

"No. Leave it for now." He knelt before her and pressed a kiss above and below her navel. Olivia's eyes drifted shut. Ryan pulled back the covers on the bed. "Hop in, sleepyhead."

She crawled to the middle of the huge mattress and lay down on her back. The men began to cuff her wrists above her head.

"Masters?"

They paused.

"Will you hold me tonight, please? Instead of the cuffs?"

The silence was deafening as they peered at her for a long moment. Then with a glance at each other, they stripped and climbed into the bed on either side of her. Lying on their sides facing her, they each draped a leg over one of hers and placed palms across her midsection, Dylan's closer to her hip, Ryan's along the bottom curve of one breast. Her arms remained above her head until the men used her shoulders for their pillows.

Hugging them close, she waited for them to go further, to try for more. Wasn't there a saying that if you gave a man an inch, he'd try to take a mile? So why weren't they pushing the envelope? They had to know by now she wouldn't turn them down.

"Good night, puss," Dylan murmured.

Both men closed their eyes. Their hands didn't move. They didn't try to kiss her, fondle her, or fuck her.

Damn it, they confused the hell out of her. And double damn it, she needed something more. Silent tears rolled from her eyes in the darkness.

CHAPTER ELEVEN

The next day, Olivia awakened in bed alone and a bit achy, but that wasn't unusual. She'd never been a morning person. Still, she did have renewed confidence. Today was a new day, and she had plans for how to make it better.

She wanted the brothers to hold nothing back, give her their all, and make love to her. So she'd decided that if the men continued to hold out on her, she'd just work harder to seduce them. Even if it meant bending to their way of thinking. She was there to look out for their pleasures, not her own. If she gave them pleasure, then it would be returned. That was what they'd told her from the beginning.

She could do this. She *would* do this. She loved it when they got all worked up when she gave them oral sex. She'd just...do it more. Without having to be told.

With a grin, she headed for the bathroom and her morning shower. She'd start by not making one of them fetch her. She would go down in nothing but her birthday suit to the pool area where they always ate breakfast. She wouldn't grumble. She'd even kneel on that damn pillow and eat their leftovers without so much as a scowl.

But she stopped dead in her tracks when she got down to the pool terrace and saw the table. Three chairs. Three plates of food. Three glasses of orange juice and three cups of coffee.

She glanced around, looking for a bush big enough to duck behind. Damn it, why'd they pick today to have a guest over?

"Ahh, good morning, puss." Dylan stepped onto the terrace fully dressed in casual kakis and a black polo shirt.

Damn, damn, damn. Where were his swim trunks? He always wore swim trunks in the morning! She glanced at the pool, but realized the clear blue water wouldn't shield her nudity from the yet unseen third person. There was a fichus on the corner of the patio, but it wouldn't cover much. She suddenly felt like Eve after eating the forbidden fruit.

Ryan came out right behind Dylan and gave her a lazy grin. "G'morning, baby." He walked up to her, cupped her cheek in his palm, and gently kissed her on the mouth.

Damn her body for reacting to his touch even when she was terrified of who else would be showing up. She gripped his biceps and returned the kiss, even as her gaze stayed firmly on the patio doors.

"Mmm," Ryan murmured as he pulled away. "A very good morning. Sleep well?" His fingers traced along her jaw, down her neck.

Her heartbeat sped, and her body tingled, but she couldn't help that. Never could help it when one or both of these beautiful men touched her. She pulled her gaze from the door and glanced at Ryan's casual jeans and T-shirt. He was dressed, too.

"Puss?" Dylan said as he moved up next to her.

"What's wrong? You look a little skittish this morning."

She shook her head and then nodded. "Who's here?" she asked in a whisper, her gaze darting back to the open doors, still expecting to see someone come out.

Dylan grinned. "Just us." Then he leaned down and captured her lips with his.

Her worry vanished under his tender assault. She moaned and leaned into him as his arms wrapped around her. Yes. This was what she wanted. This and so much more. She could feel the heat of his body, the hard ridge of his erection against her belly.

Just us, he'd said. So they were alone. And this was the perfect time to set her plan into motion. She pulled back and grinned at Dylan. "Good morning, my master."

He cocked an eyebrow at her, an amused smile playing on his sexy lips. "Yes. It definitely is."

She pulled back a bit farther and was about to go down on her knees to give him his morning blowjob, when Ryan gently caught her arm. *Okay, Ryan first.* She grinned.

"Have a seat, puss," Ryan said, then led her to the third chair at the table.

Her smile slipped. What was going on? Why didn't they want... She swallowed hard and lowered herself to the chair. Her hunger vanished, and a cold fear settled in her bones. They didn't want her anymore.

No, that couldn't be right. Hadn't Dylan's body just proven that *not* to be the case? So why was she all of a sudden allowed to sit at the table? Why wasn't she on her knees between them as she had been for the past five days? Why didn't they want their morning pleasures?

Dylan and Ryan sat in their usual chairs, picked up

their napkins, and spread them open on their thighs. That was new; they didn't usually do that. They usually had her mouth around one of their cocks while they ate.

"Um...Masters?" She spoke softly, afraid to voice her questions but unable to keep from asking. Afraid to keep guessing.

"You may speak," Dylan said then lifted his coffee mug to his lips.

"Why?" was all that came out.

Ryan took a bite of sausage, obviously deferring to Dylan to explain...whatever.

"Why what, puss? Why are you seated at the table and not on the floor? Why are you eating from your own plate and not ours?"

She nodded.

He smiled then reached over and touched her cheek, so similar to the way Ryan had. Her eyes drifted closed, and she sighed. She wondered how she'd ever live without their touch once she left.

"We told you that this relationship is based on trust. Last night you showed that you are beginning to trust us by obeying us at the club, and then even more so when you asked us to hold you."

She opened her eyes when his hand moved away. *Trust.* How could she not trust these men when they'd lain in bed with her all night and hadn't tried to take advantage? Even though she'd been more than willing. They'd simply given her what she'd requested, and that had been to be held.

Her heart pinched, and she felt close to tears.

"Your training is coming along nicely, puss," Ryan

said as he set his fork down and reached for her limp hand that lay in her lap, lacing his fingers through hers. "We know how hard this is on you, and that giving up control to us takes so much courage on your part. We cherish the fact that you are learning and trying to please us."

"Therefore," Dylan said, "since you are bending to our will, we are prepared to make concessions as well." He smiled, picked up her other hand, brought it to his lips, and tenderly kissed her palm. "As long as you behave, you will no longer be required to eat from our plates while seated on the floor." He winked. "At least, not most of the time."

She stared at them in turn, happy that she'd been given a reprieve and ecstatic that the plan she'd decided to set in motion was already rolling without her even having known. "Thank you, Masters. That means a lot to me."

Dylan kissed her fingertips, and Ryan leaned over and kissed her cheek.

"Eat, puss," Dylan said. "We've a long day ahead of us."

* * * * *

She hadn't known what to expect, but a day of shopping certainly had not been it. How many men would actually take a woman shopping? She grinned as the three of them meandered through the upscale department store.

She doubted she'd ever felt sexier than she did at that moment. The dress Dylan and Ryan had provided for her was classy, fire engine red, and had a sleeveless top and slightly flared skirt. She wore the laced stilettos from the evening before, and a naughty black thong rubbed in all the right places.

Besides the clothes, she had the two most gorgeous men with her. Dylan held her right hand, while Ryan kept a proprietary hand on her lower back, giving a light, playful tug every now and then to the dangling ends of the black silk ribbon they'd used to replace her collar.

She sighed with happiness. It just didn't get any better than this. With her demanding job, she didn't have much time to window shop. And never in her life had she gone shopping with a man, let alone two of them.

My men.

Her heart stuttered and her feet stopped moving. Her men, but for how long? Until the end of next week? Until their allotted time ended and she got on a plane to go back to California? And then she'd only see them every now and again when they were in town on business.

No!

"What is it, puss?" Dylan said as he turned to face her.

"Uh..." She glanced around, looking for some kind of escape. She had to think about this. To figure out what she was doing. How in the hell was she going to say goodbye to these two amazing men when the time came?

She'd meant to keep her heart out of this, to have a holiday of hot, sweaty sex. But that hadn't happened. No, they weren't even having sex. Well, she was having foreplay, getting orgasms on a regular basis, and so were they, but not like she'd expected.

Nothing was as she'd expected. Especially the fact that she was almost able to give up her hard-won control and let these two men take over her life. And she liked it. A lot. At least for now.

Her gaze landed on the jewelry counter a few feet away, and she headed toward it. She couldn't meet Dylan's piercing, all-too-knowing gaze. So she focused on the sparkling blue topaz jewelry in the lighted glass case.

What hurt the most, she supposed, was knowing that no other man would ever satisfy her after she'd been with the Montgomery brothers. The long sought-after dreams of a romance to last a lifetime were gone.

"Do you like those earrings?" Ryan asked as he slid his big, warm hand up her back and pointed at a particularly pretty pair of earrings in the case. "They match your beautiful eyes."

Dylan moved up close on her other side and slipped his arm around her waist. "They do," he said. He leaned in and nuzzled his nose against her ear, his warm breath sending tingles racing down her arms. "The color of your eyes haunted my dreams for two years, *mi gatita*."

She shivered at his whispered words, his sexy accent rolling through her.

Oh, yes, she was in trouble with these two. She was ready to make love to them right here and now. Their voices, their touch, their spicy scents spun through her, making her entire body vibrate with longing and need.

"May I help you with anything today?"

Olivia's eyes shot open—she hadn't even been aware they'd closed—and stared at the plump, well-groomed saleslady across the counter.

"Yes. We'd like to see that pair, there." Dylan pointed to the earrings they'd been discussing.

"Very nice choice," the lady said as she unlocked the

case. She lifted one earring from the velvet box and handed it to Dylan, who lifted it to Olivia's ear.

"What do you think, *mi hermano*?"

Three heart-shaped, aquamarine stones dangled from the fine, gold chain, gently brushing against her skin.

"*Corazon*," Ryan said softly, his dark gaze on her eyes, not the earring Dylan held up.

She glanced at Dylan in time to see him nod. "We'll take them," he said to the saleslady.

The woman's grin was huge. "Very, very nice choice."

"Wait." Olivia caught Dylan's arm as he reached into his back pocket for his wallet. "I'm sure those are way too expensive." From the saleswoman's smile, she was obviously going to land herself one heck of a commission.

"Nothing is too expensive for *nuestra gatita*." He leaned over and kissed the tip of her nose. "Besides," he said as he handed over his credit card, "we enjoy pampering you."

Pampering her. Who in her life had ever pampered her? Who had she ever *allowed* to pamper her? The answer was simple. No one.

She smiled. "Thank you, Masters," she whispered so the saleslady wouldn't hear.

Ryan squeezed her shoulder and grinned, that sexy dimple showing. "You please us," he murmured in her ear, "more than you will ever know."

Pleasure skittered through her at his words. She wanted nothing more than to please them. And starting right now, until her time ended with them, she'd prove it.

CHAPTER TWELVE

"I'm going to try these on," Ryan said, grabbing a couple of pairs of slacks off a rack and heading for the unisex dressing room. He had to get away from Olivia, if only for a few minutes. She was driving him insane.

He shut the door behind him and leaned against the wall, desperately trying to gather his wits about him. And calm the erection he'd been sporting for the last hour.

Damn his brother for making him agree to *the plan* this morning. They were to put all sex on hold for now. No blowjobs, no masturbation, no fondling. Nothing more than the occasional hug, kiss, or whispered words of endearment. They had to show Olivia that they wanted her for more than instant physical gratification. He definitely wanted her for more than sex; he wanted her for all time. And yes, he agreed with Dylan that she had to realize her stay here was more than just a two-week tryst. But, damn, she challenged his resolve. And today she was in particularly fine form.

Seeing her clothed while knowing exactly what supple beauty lay hidden beneath was making him crazy. Ever since they purchased the earrings for her, something had changed. Instead of being passive about their company, she'd begun returning the caresses and sweet kisses they'd been bestowing on her. And now... Having her soft warmth so close all day, her smile and laughter, her gentle touches— he was going to combust soon.

He pushed away from the wall, popped his jeans' buttons open, and shoved them down his legs, then almost landed on his face when he forgot to remove his shoes.

Mierda. He kicked off his shoes, stepped out of his jeans, and reached for a pair of the slacks he'd brought in with him.

Dylan's steadfast control was something he'd never understand. His brother didn't seem to be having any problems resisting her, while he on the other hand had a raging hard-on. Hell, he was barely able to walk straight.

He bent over to pull on the slacks, and the dressing room door opened. His mouth dropped open in surprise, but the words *get out* lodged in his throat. Olivia slipped in and shut the door behind her.

She was so beautiful, so sexy, yet so alluringly pure. Just looking at her made him realize why his brother had spent two years searching for her...why she engendered such heart-felt emotions.

"Hello, Master," she whispered. With a mischievous, excited sparkle to her eyes, she wrapped her arms around his shoulders and melded her mouth to his.

He dropped the pants and hugged her close. She smelled of flowers and felt like every carnal sin he'd ever imagined. He let her sweet mouth entice him for a few seconds until he couldn't stand it anymore, and then he gained control of the kiss.

Her low, sexy moan had his cock straining against his briefs. Her fingers in his hair nearly pushed him over the edge. He turned and pressed her back against the mirror as he thrust his cock against her belly.

"Yes, Master. Let me pleasure you," she whispered when his mouth left hers to trail along her jaw, her long, sleek neck, to the upper curve of her lush breasts. The time since he'd had her last seemed like years. Centuries.

His hand slipped down to her thigh, caught the hem of her dress, and lifted it. He cupped her bare ass, the lace of the miniscule thong she wore tantalizing his fingertips. She was damp. Ready.

She wound one leg around his hip and pressed her heated pussy against his straining cock. He bit back a groan, only vaguely remembering they were in a public place.

And his brother was out there, expecting him to stick to *the plan*.

"Fuck," he said in a fierce whisper as he pinned her shoulders to the mirror and stepped back, keeping her at arm's length.

"Master?" Her bright, gorgeous eyes were full of passion, need, and uncertainty.

He sucked in deep breaths, straining for control. *No more sex until she's ready to fully submit and ask for what she needs. Until she has the trust and courage to make the request.*

Ask now, damn it, he wanted to shout.

A sly smile crept over Olivia's face. "Master Ryan," she practically purred. She reached up and pulled the low-cut top of her dress down. Her full, amazing breasts popped free, her nipples as hard as diamonds. He groaned and let go of her shoulders, afraid he couldn't maintain the control he needed to resist her if he continued to touch her. He wanted her so much. Needed her. *Only her.*

He knew without a doubt that no woman would ever completely satisfy him again. And it was going to kill him to let her make up her mind about staying with them or not. He wanted to fall to his knees and beg her to never leave. But that would kind of defeat the whole Dom thing that had been such a big part of his life since college. He couldn't let Olivia see his weakness, not where she was concerned.

Her gaze lowered like a slow caress down his body, and his painful erection responded.

"Please, Master. Let me soothe your need," she murmured as she dropped to her knees and grabbed the waistband of his briefs, pulling down to free his cock.

"Olivia." His voice was hoarse. *Stop.* But the word remained buried. If he told her to stop, she had to stop. She had to obey. God help him, he didn't want her to stop. Not ever.

Her hot, silky mouth closed over the tip of his cock. With a groan, he collapsed onto the bench.

"Shh," she said then giggled. Her laughter curled around his heart, melting him, even as the suction of her mouth made his balls tighten and his erection almost unbearable.

He threaded his fingers through her long, silky hair, but let her control her own movements. Let her give him the pleasure she said she wanted to provide. He watched her breasts jiggle with her movements, relished the feel of their smooth firmness against his inner thighs.

"Ah, yes, baby," he said, keeping his voice low, even though he wanted to shout at the intense sensations.

"Harder."

She wrapped one fist around the base of his cock, while the other cupped his balls, rolling them, teasing them. She sucked him deep into her mouth, her teeth lightly scraping his flesh.

When she hummed, he felt the vibrations, and there was no holding back. He thrust his hips forward, threw his head back against the wall, and held in the fierce growl clawing at his throat as he came long and hard.

Mierda.

He tried to catch his breath.

Shit. Dylan was going to kill him.

Olivia's sweet little tongue lapped at his softening dick, cleaning him like the little kitten they called her. He ran his fingers through her hair, smoothing the mess he'd caused. Then he touched her flawless cheek.

She sat back on her heels and smiled up at him. "Anything else you'd like, Master?"

You. Forever.

"Come here, puss." He took her hand and pulled her onto his lap. She tucked her head against his shoulder and sighed softly, her warm breath against his throat.

He kissed her forehead and breathed in her sweet scent. He adjusted her dress, covering her breasts. Her hand settled lightly over his heart.

No way in hell was he letting her leave at the end of two weeks. No matter what deal Dylan had made.

* * * * *

Ryan held her snuggled on his lap for a long time, the

tender caresses of his hand a soothing presence. He hadn't turned her away, had instead enjoyed her spontaneous gift, which pleased her even though she hadn't convinced him to go any further, sexually speaking.

At least one of them was softening toward her; if only she could conquer the other one as easily. She placed a light kiss to the side of Ryan's neck and heard him sigh. Gently he lifted her from his lap, restored his clothing without a word and, taking her hand, led her back out among the racks of merchandise.

Dylan was waiting, a not-too-pleased look on his handsome face. Still, when Ryan gave her to him, he tucked her hand against his arm, his thumb making a faint sweep across the back of her knuckles.

Once outside, heading for their vehicle, he spoke in his casual way. "Did you enjoy your time in the dressing room, my mischievous puss?"

His endearment made her smile. Maybe she'd misread his expression in the store? She licked her lips. "Mmm hmm."

"You like the thrill that accompanies risk, exposure."

She'd never thought of it that way, but now that he'd mentioned it, she had to agree. "How is it that you seem to know me so well?"

He draped an arm around her shoulders as they stopped next to their vehicle. "I'm your master. To provide for you is my pleasure, my duty, my privilege. I can't very well do that without knowing you."

"But how—"

His finger over her lips stopped her. "After finding you again, I did my research. I read about you in trade magazines, your employer's Web site...the society papers."

She scoffed at that, and he laughed.

"But mostly, I watch you. For instance, you get the tiniest of lines right here..." He touched her face between the eyebrows. "...whenever you're puzzled or skeptical." He grinned. "Like now. It's really quite adorable. And your ears turn the cutest pink when you're embarrassed." With a finger he traced along the curve of one ear, and her tummy flipped. "And your eyes? They're brilliant like a cloudless, springtime sky when you're happy, and as rich in color as the Mediterranean Sea when you're aroused.... Like now."

Staring into his fathomless brown eyes, she wholeheartedly agreed. She was aroused, so much so that she wanted to yank him to the ground right there and kiss him all over, but she didn't. There were some things even she wasn't brave enough to try.

* * * * *

Dylan followed the maitre d' to the back of the restaurant where a quaint nook offered a hint of seclusion in the form of a comfortable, round booth. He paused to allow Olivia entry before slipping into the booth beside her. Ryan slid in on her other side.

"Your server will be right with you."

"Thank you," Dylan said, not bothering to look at the elaborate menu placed before him. A regular customer, he knew what entrees they offered, and so he chose to use the time to consider his options concerning Olivia.

He was still perturbed at his brother's weakness, even if he understood that refusing Olivia anything took a

Herculean effort...and a united front. Together they stood a chance; one-on-one, both were goners.

Besides, the fault wasn't entirely Ryan's to bear. He'd let her excuse herself, thinking she meant to use the ladies' room, which was located next to the dressing rooms. As much as her body language had hinted at mischief-making all day, he should've known she was up to something. He should've recognized the signs.

He watched her tongue peek out to lick her upper lip as she read the menu, and wondered whether he'd ever hear the words he longed for cross those delicate lips. The candlelight caused the gemstone hearts that dangled from her earlobes to flash with an intense brilliance—an aquamarine fire that befitted the woman wearing them.

A part of him was impressed by her creativity in turning the tables on them today. They'd pulled back further, and she'd surprised them by responding with her own unique ingenuity.

Of course, he'd also seen concern etched across her features whenever she thought he wasn't looking. Something was bothering her, and he suspected it had a lot to do with why they hadn't consummated their relationship in a manner she'd assumed would occur the moment she boarded the plane.

It would happen. Of that, he had no doubt. But it would take place on his schedule, not hers. And then only when he saw she was truly ready to take that next step for the correct reasons.

He'd bedded her in Spain because she'd needed him at the time, but the experience had been enlightening for him. Her fresh, almost innocent responses to his dominating guidance enslaved him to her almost from the first kiss.

When she'd vanished in Madrid, he'd become damn near obsessed with finding her. He'd all but given up hope of ever laying eyes on her again, only to have her reappear in his life with a cheap offer of sex-on-call. Had their first night together meant nothing more to her than a brief, albeit physically satisfying, affair?

"Ready to order?" the waiter asked without pen or notepad in hand.

Dylan did the honors and, after ordering, steered the conversation to mundane topics. They shared with Olivia humorous memories of their childhood on the Spanish coast, edited recollections of their college days as exchange students to the United States, and how they used their dual citizenship to finally settle in America.

Halfway through the meal, she began to open up about her family. She was the only child of a costume designer and a construction worker who'd freelanced by building backdrops for movie studios. Her father passed away shortly after she'd graduated from college; her mother had remarried and still lived on the West Coast.

"I used to dress up in costumes while my mother worked and pretend I was a princess in a swashbuckling film." Her laughter and blush made him smile. "Or a Hollywood starlet with all of the photographers vying for my photo and autograph."

Ryan took a sip of his chardonnay before commenting. "I'm surprised you didn't study acting."

She shook her head, making the earrings sway in a dazzling arc. "I don't need the spotlight. I've enough trouble keeping up appearances while working behind the scenes...." Her voice trailed off, and her gaze dropped to what was left of her meal. With her fork, she pushed a green bean around her plate. A second later, her smile was back as bright as ever, but a haunted sadness glistened in her eyes. "Enough about me. I'd like to hear more—"

Her hand bumped the handle of the spoon next to her plate, and it fell under the table before she could catch it. "Oops."

"Don't worry about it," Dylan said. "The waiter can bring you another."

She lifted a portion of the table cloth, glanced up, looked around, and then her gaze settled on him. That devilish gleam in her eye spelled trouble.

"Olivia..." he warned.

She flashed him a grin and slid beneath the table. Dylan met his brother's amused gaze.

"I think our little puss wants to play," Ryan said, the humor evident in his voice.

When Dylan felt her first touch, he frowned, then clenched his jaw and spread his fingers palms down on the table. One small hand slid beneath a pant leg to caress his calf. His body reacted despite his mind's commands to the contrary.

The sound of his zipper, although muffled, sounded like machinegun fire to his ears. His brother—the traitor— leaned back in his side of the booth and sipped his drink. Dylan's hands fisted, but then another fist took control of his body with a firm...*heavenly*...grip.

Fuck!

Her mouth was warm, and her tongue was doing the most amazing dance against his hard cock. "O—" He started to say her name, order her to stop, but she cut him off with mind-blowing suction and an intoxicating caress of his sac. With his hands still braced on the table, he slid his hips forward to the edge of the seat. He closed his eyes, struggling to stop the downward spiral of his blood, which plummeted straight from his brain to his cock.

Damn it. He needed to stop this, but... His cock throbbed in a rhythm that matched the tug and temptation of her talented mouth.

"Ready for dessert, gentlemen?" the waiter asked, giving the vacancy between him and his brother no more than a mild glance.

Ryan looked to Dylan as if he should answer. He scowled back, making his brother chuckle. His hands ached from the tight fists he maintained in a futile attempt to regain control.

She silently increased the pace of her hands and mouth, and he held his breath.

"No, thank you," Ryan finally said. "The check will do."

The waiter smiled, pulled out their bill, and placed it on the table. Gathering some of their plates, he said, "I'll take care of that whenever you're ready."

Dylan's wallet was in his back pocket. No way in hell was he ready to get it right now. He remained frozen in place while a hurricane of erotic torment continued beneath the table. She was so damn good; he was so fucking close....

As soon as the waiter moved away, Dylan shoved both hands beneath the tablecloth and bracketed Olivia's head.

A soft giggle, more felt than heard, made him groan.

Ryan coughed and reached for his water glass, his gaze never straying.

Dylan's fingers tightened in her hair as he slowed her movements to a steady, more manageable pattern. He'd nearly lost all rational thought as waves of pleasure pounded through him. Pulsing. Demanding. Controlling…

Control. He'd sacrificed that for this exciting, spontaneous moment of extreme pleasure. She'd stripped it from him and laid bare his need for her, or his body's need for her. But what about his heart? What about its needs?

His fingers fisted in her hair and pulled her away from him. Her whimper of protest accompanied her hands as they attempted to finish what her mouth had so effectively started.

He used one hand to thwart her progress and words to end her playtime. "Get up from there, Olivia. Now. I'm not in the mood for any more of this."

She pulled away from his hands and, after a few tense moments, resurfaced, not between him and Ryan, but rather next to his brother on the opposite side of the table. Her hair was mussed, her dress slightly rumpled, and her eyes moist. She turned those aqua pools toward him briefly, lowered her gaze, and slid from the table with a muttered, "Excuse me."

"Olivia—" Ryan began.

"Let her go."

Ryan turned on him. "What the fuck do you think you're doing?"

"I'm doing what you should've done earlier today."

"Don't give me that. I never agreed to act like an ass. It was never our plan to hurt her."

"She's fine—"

"Fine?" Ryan leaned forward, his arms crossed on the table. "You call bringing her to tears *fine*?"

"Some lessons are harder than others to learn." He found it more and more difficult to keep his voice low and calm. Harder to meet his brother's accusing glare.

"She wasn't under the table to learn a lesson, Dylan."

Olivia wasn't the only one to have learned one either, he thought bitterly, but instead said, "She's still playing a game. Give us what she thinks we want to get what she's after...sex. This isn't a damn game."

"I know that, but have you considered that maybe she doesn't? Maybe starting this relationship off with sex gave her the impression that that's what we want from her."

He'd lifted his coffee cup for a drink in an effort to calm down, but at Ryan's words, he slammed the mug on the table. "Which is why I said we needed to back off, but what do you do? You cave the moment you have her alone."

"She wasn't playing a game, Dylan. She saw my need and answered it. She enjoys pleasing us. I accept that in her, so I accepted her and what she offered, which is more than I can say for you."

"You accepted her for the sexual gratification she could provide you. I do accept her. I love her, damn it... So, I want more. I want her heart. All or nothing, and if that means holding out to get her attention... If that means bruising an ego, then so be it."

Ryan slid from the booth and stood. "Be careful, *mi hermano*. Hold out too long, and you might be left holding nothing."

CHAPTER THIRTEEN

Olivia reclined on the plush suede sofa in the library of the Montgomery mansion, reading a leather-bound classic from one of the shelves that lined the wall. She sat naked, as the rules demanded of her, save her collar. She'd become accustomed to her nudity and, knowing it pleased Dylan and Ryan, she no longer found a reason to complain. But she wasn't sure if anything else was pleasing them lately.

Over the past few days since their shopping expedition, things had been…different. Strange. There was a slight crackle of tension between the brothers, and she knew she was the cause. Knew it had something to do with the mortifying situation at the restaurant.

Dylan refused to even broach the subject when she tried to talk to him about it. He simply said that she still had a lot to learn. But he wouldn't explain what that might be, and for the life of her, no matter how hard she racked her brain, she just couldn't figure it out.

So, she hadn't volunteered any sexual favors since crawling from beneath that table, and they hadn't demanded any. Nor did they offer her any. She was beginning to wonder why, exactly, she was here. Even the morning fellatio that had been expected for the first week wasn't demanded. Other than the lack of clothing, she was treated like an equal member of the household. She ate at the table with them, watched television in the evening, sat with one or the other in the library reading, while they worked at the computer....

She laid the book aside and rested her head against the sensually soft suede.

She didn't know what to do. She didn't understand any of it. Figuring Ryan might be better to get answers from than Dylan, yesterday afternoon she'd tried getting him to talk while Dylan had to leave the house on business for a few hours.

He'd sat with her, even held her on his lap and ran his big, soothing hands down her back. Kissed her so sweetly she'd almost burst into tears. But when she tried discussing what was going on, why Dylan was giving her the cold shoulder, Ryan only shook his head. When she'd looked into his eyes, she'd seen lust there. Those rich chocolate eyes had crackled with it. And the hard bulge against her hip couldn't be mistaken for anything but a hell of a hard-on. When she'd touched his face and tried to kiss him, he'd turned his head and kissed her cheek, whispering, "What's your heart's desire, puss...for lunch? I'm starved." Then he'd set her on her feet and led her to the kitchen.

That's the last time she bothered to try talking to either of them. A small part of her feared that they thought they'd made a mistake with her. Kat's comment about them shooting for the stars kept coming back to her at odd times. Had they maybe thought she was their star only to discover she wasn't? Because she'd been so obstinate those first few days? She'd tried to change, had done what she thought they wanted….

She curled up on her side and let out a slow breath.

And then Dylan had rejected her efforts.

But even more confounding was what happened each night. They joined her in bed, one on each side, just like the first night she'd asked to be held. Even though Dylan barely touched her during the day, giving her only a cursory good morning kiss and a pat of what felt like affection here and there throughout the day, he pulled her into his arms each night, held her in a tight embrace as if… As if he never wanted to let her go.

Her eyelids slowly slid closed. The sun streaming in the floor-to-ceiling window warmed her and made her feel lazy. One thing she could get used to, she thought as she yawned, was the relaxation she felt here. The lack of responsibility to the outside world. Even if the pleasures didn't include sex, there was definite pleasure to be found in the slow ticking of the clock, the leisurely strolls through the high-walled garden.

When she first arrived, her phone calls to work had been nearly two hours long each day. Today she was only on for fifteen minutes, just enough to check her messages. Too bad she only had a few days left before returning to the world she knew and understood. Next year she'd definitely take a vacation.

They'd given her free reign of the house today, while they went on what they called a business errand. Her only instruction was that she stay nude, except for the collar, and remain indoors while they were gone, a command she found easy to follow. She should have a couple of hours to catch a snooze.

Familiar voices made her jerk upright. As their footsteps neared the room, she smiled, but that quickly vanished when she saw a fully clothed stranger walk in with her masters. She shrieked and leapt behind the sofa, ducking her body out of view of the woman wearing hospital scrubs.

"She's quick," the woman observed with an amused grin.

"You can set up on the back patio. Ryan will show you where. We'll be out in a moment."

As Ryan showed the woman out, Dylan crossed his arms. "Is that the way you are to greet us whenever we enter a room?"

"N-no, Master." She cast a wary glance at the door and moved around the chair to kneel in front of him. Though she was treated as an equal member of the household *most of the time*, she amended her earlier thoughts, there were still things they demanded. Whenever one of them had been gone from the house, when they returned she was to assume her submissive position until they released her. She still didn't get it, not really. But she kind of liked it in a weird way. For an executive who demanded respect of each and every one of her employees, she understood the guys' need for authority. And she liked giving it to them.

"That's better." His hand rested on her head in an affectionate manner, as if she really were a beloved *pet* here to greet him at the door. "Remember, puss, the rules apply no matter who is present. I'll forgive you this time, because we caught you unaware and this is your first offense, but don't let it happen again."

"Yes, Master." She hadn't been punished since that first morning, but a tingle went through her when she remembered what happened after the punishment. The incredible multiple orgasms. The way both men had treated her so tenderly after. She wanted that again. All of it.

Hmm, she thought. If she misbehaved, maybe…

"Come. We have a surprise for you."

He tucked a finger through the D-ring on her collar as she rose to her feet then led her through the house. The closer they got to the patio, the more hesitant she became.

Their backyard was several acres surrounded by a high wall and thick foliage, which ensured privacy. She hadn't felt nervous on past excursions to the pool, but knowing a visitor awaited them made her insides swirl.

Apparently sensing her turmoil, Dylan released her collar and took her hand, lifting it to his mouth for a kiss before opening the French doors.

She scanned the patio area and quickly found the woman and Ryan near a rectangular table covered in white sheets. Olivia dropped her gaze. It was just easier that way.

Ryan said, "Almost set. I'll go get the rest of your supplies, but first... Angela Patterson, this is Olivia Chandler, our pet. Olivia, greet our guest."

"Hello, Angela," she said, squeezing Dylan's hand like a lifeline.

"A pleasure to meet you. And please, call me Angie."

Olivia glanced up to see the welcoming smile on the woman's face. No censure. No curiosity. It was as if she'd expected to see her buck-naked.

"Ryan," Angela said, stopping him as he headed toward the door. "If you could heat up some towels for me, please? You can bring them out here in the silver warmer I left in the car. Thanks."

He saluted with a grin and left, making Olivia take a closer look at this Angie Patterson. She was a younger, petite woman who stood an inch or so shorter than Olivia. Impeccably groomed, she wore her frosted hair pulled back in a ponytail and had a demeanor that put her at ease. Not once did she let her gaze drop below eye level, and that helped Olivia relax.

"Angie is a certified esthetician and massage therapist," Dylan said. "Normally, she doesn't do house calls but, being friends, we were able to persuade her."

"I couldn't miss the opportunity to meet you," Angie said, holding out a hand.

Surprised, Olivia released Dylan to shake hands with Angie, wondering whether she'd fallen down a rabbit hole into another realm.

"Have you ever gone to a spa?"

"No." With her busy work schedule, she'd never had time for such frivolous pursuits.

Angie grinned. "They're paying for the full package, so you're in for a treat. I promise, once you've experienced true pampering, you'll be addicted."

Olivia didn't know what to say.

Ryan showed up with arms loaded, and Angie situated the items where she wanted them.

"Hop up on the table and lie face down, okay?" She patted the tabletop. As Olivia moved into place, laying her head on folded arms, Angie added, "I need the collar removed."

Dylan took the key from around his neck and

unfastened the padlock. When the collar's weight vanished, emptiness engulfed her. For one illogical second, she wanted to scream for them to put it back on. It had become part of her, the part that connected her to these men. Without it she… She buried her face in her arms. What kind of thought was that? *Without it she was nothing?*

What were these men doing to her head?

Angie laid a warm towel across her hips, restoring some of her modesty.

"Spoilsport," Dylan said, and there was no mistaking the teasing quality in his tone. She peeked up at him and caught him smiling, a smile she hadn't seen in days.

Her heart thudded against her ribs. What had changed? What was going on? Should she be frightened by the turn in his demeanor? It wasn't fear she was feeling, but an incredible sense of excitement.

Angie laughed. "Scoot, you two. I'll take care of her."

"I know you will, because we intend to stay and watch."

Olivia looked up to see Angela frown, then shrug. "Suit yourself, but if you're going to stay, be quiet. This is her time."

Dylan gave her a noble nod before sitting in a chair a few feet away. Ryan joined him moments later.

"Close your eyes and tune everything and everyone else out for a while. Here you go." Angie put a small headset over her ears. The soft sound of panpipes and drums flowed around her, and she couldn't help but relax and close her eyes.

Angela began on Olivia's hands and arms, clipping her nails, cutting cuticles, and massaging her forearms.

"This is called paraffin," Angie said with a lift to one earphone. After thoroughly rubbing each hand and every finger, she repositioned them so that they dipped into containers filled with the warm, citric-scented wax. After three dips, each hand went inside a plastic bag and a large, spa-style oven mitt. Next the therapist kneaded her neck, shoulder and back muscles, working in oils with concentrated pressure. Olivia slowly slipped into that pleasant dimension between sleep and awake, where everything was fuzzy and unfocused. She felt as if her body were floating.

Olivia stirred when Angie pulled her hands out and removed the paraffin, then took off the headphones.

"Time to turn over for the facial and waxing."

"Mmm hmm," she murmured before her mind registered Angie's words.

"I was going to do your legs, but you don't have enough growth on them to be of any benefit."

"What?" She raised her head.

"Turn over please."

Olivia turned over.

"Do you shave or use a depilatory?"

"I, uh...I use a cream in the shower."

"That's fine. We'll just do the Brazilian then, but first your facial."

She started to reach for a warm towel, but Olivia grabbed her wrist. "Could you repeat that?"

"Let go, puss," Dylan stood next to her table.

"I don't—"

"Lie down and behave." His hand pressed against the center of her chest and gently pinned her onto her back.

"Tell us what you don't want, puss. Tell us what you do want."

She wrinkled her brow and stared at him. His jaw set firm, he looked too serious to be discussing a damn spa treatment. "I don't want any hair ripped out of my body…Master," she added belatedly. "I am perfectly capable of shaving whatever needs to be shaved…" His jaw ticked once. "…to please you."

His eyes softened, the pressure he'd been placing against her breastbone eased, and then he nodded. "No waxing today, Angie. Shall we continue with the facial, puss?"

Olivia glanced at Angie who stood by, watching their conversation. "Yes, please."

As he withdrew his hand from her, his fingertips lightly grazed over her right nipple, which caused her to suck in a breath in surprise and instant need.

Dylan raised an eyebrow at her as if in question, but she didn't know what that question might be. Did he expect her body *not* to respond to his touch? A touch she hadn't felt in *days*?

When he grazed the back of his fingers over her nipple and then skimmed them down her belly, her entire body tensed, and she pressed her thighs together. His gaze was deep and piercing as he watched her face, as if gauging her reaction to his touch. When those fingers trailed over her and down her thigh, a tiny whimper escaped her. Pleasure coursed through her body at his feather-light touch, even as mortification swamped her because Angela, a perfect stranger and a *woman*, was standing not two feet away watching.

"All you must do, my sweet kitten, is tell us what you desire. If it is in our power to give to you, it will be yours."

Please! She bit her lip and closed her eyes. *No way. No way. No way.* She couldn't possibly say the words, even though she wanted it—*him*—more than anything. Not with this woman standing here. She wasn't that much of a deviant nympho.

Dylan's fingers tickled over her knee, then down her calf. When he reached the arch of her foot, she jerked and burst out laughing. Dylan chuckled.

"Go ahead," he told Angie.

Olivia relaxed again as a mud mask was applied. She forced her confusion into the background and enjoyed the pampering.

"While I complete the facial, would you gentlemen like to apply some lotion?" Angie asked with a chuckle. "Even though she bypassed the waxing, you're still paying for it, so you may as well reap the benefits."

With something cool and moist over her eyes, Olivia couldn't see anything, but she heard the men moving toward her. Excitement zinged through her again at just the thought of their hands on her. Warm lotion dribbled onto her skin. While gentle fingers and large hands rubbed the silky cream into her legs, another pried her fisted hands open and massaged them.

Angie completed her facial with several minutes of light, circular massage and an application of a cool toner. But Olivia's senses weren't worried about her face, they were concentrated solely on her men, her masters. Four hands traveling over her body in a tender, yet firm gliding motion.

Her breathing grew deep, labored almost, as she

battled to maintain her decency, yet take every single touch and treasure it. She wasn't sure who was where. She kept her eyes closed, not wanting to see Angie, wanting to forget the woman. Wanting to be alone with her masters.

When a finger slipped inside her pussy, Olivia's eyes shot open and a low groan slipped from her lips.

"You're so soft...and wet, puss."

At Dylan's words, her face flamed. She glanced at Angie, but the woman was busy packing away her things, her back to them.

"Thank you, Angie, for a superb job," Ryan said.

Dylan slowly withdrew his finger from her throbbing pussy, dragging ever so lightly over her clit.

She bit her lip to stifle her moan.

"Olivia, why don't you wait in the pool while we help Angie with her things?" Dylan's question, delivered with a slight tap to the thigh, wasn't a request, so she got up and headed for the pool, more than ready to escape.

She dove into the deep end and wondered how long she could hide underwater. At least until Angie left?

Her traitorous body. There was no way to keep it from responding to Dylan and Ryan. It didn't matter where they were or who was around. They controlled her in every sense of the word.

The thought was a bit frightening. But kind of exciting, too.

She surfaced and sucked air into her lungs, then swam laps for good measure, doing her best to wear her body out, use up the adrenaline, or endorphins, or whatever the hell was making her feel so incredibly horny.

And why had Dylan decided to touch her in such an

intimate way now, when he hadn't done it for days?

She was on her fourth lap when she felt the concussion of two splashes. Her feet reached for the bottom as she stood to look around. Dylan and Ryan resurfaced on either side of her, spraying her as they shook the water from their heads.

"Hey!"

Dylan cut her off. His mouth claimed hers while one of his hands combed through her wet hair, the other spanning her back.

Ryan's nude body slid up behind her, and his arms wrapped around her, his hands cupping both breasts. He kissed her shoulder, her neck, her ear.

Thank God! Whatever punishment they'd been handing her was finally over. She prayed she never again repeated whatever her transgression had been. Being pushed away by them, not being touched, fondled, petted, had been the worst torment she'd ever experienced.

When Dylan's mouth released hers so he could suckle her nipple that Ryan held between two fingers, she thrust her chest forward. "Thank you, Masters," she said on a moan. "Ahh. Thank you."

CHAPTER FOURTEEN

Her murmured words of gratitude spilled over Dylan like a warm breeze. Touching her with a cursory kiss or light pat occasionally, but otherwise keeping his distance, had been difficult enough for him; holding her close while not making love at night had been torture. Apparently, judging by her eager response to his touch today, she'd felt the absence as keenly as he had.

But had she felt it as deeply...in her heart? He hoped so, but only time would tell.

And they were running out of time.

Ryan cupped her breast for him as he dipped to taste the soft creaminess of her skin. She arched toward him and wrapped her legs around his bare waist and reclined to float in the water from the waist up. His cock responded instantly, hardening to the point of pain, throbbing with a need so fierce that he wanted nothing more than to ram himself into her welcoming core.

But he couldn't. Not until she was truly and completely theirs. Mind, body, and heart. He'd never been one to believe in love at first sight, but he'd made love to her on that night more than two years ago and had unintentionally given his heart to her the moment he chose *corazon* as her safe word. He'd slept with her once—felt the union of two like souls back then—only to awaken with her gone and an emptiness so deep inside him that he thought he'd go mad. He didn't want his brother to suffer the same fate, but he feared it was already too late.

Would she leave again when her time with them was over? Or was her heart, as he hoped, involved enough that she'd want to stay?

She groaned as Ryan licked water droplets from the slender column of her neck, stopping to lightly nip and suck her earlobe. "Mmm, so precious," he heard Ryan murmur, and he couldn't agree more.

She was precious to him, to them, which was why he wanted to give her everything he had. To provide for her every need and desire, forever, if she'd let them...accept them for who they were, their need for dominance and care-giving.

As he maneuvered them across the shallow end of the pool, he repositioned her away from the evidence of his arousal. She lay cradled in his arms, while he allowed Ryan to otherwise engage her attention. Watching his twin brother kiss her breathless ignited his passions, but her eager response affected him even more.

He'd thought about Ryan's warning. He'd been right to some extent. He couldn't hold out on her until she finally broke down and succumbed to their demands...or left them. He didn't want to break her. And he damn sure didn't want to lose her.

Her strength was one of the many things he admired

in her. No, he wanted her submission, not total subjugation. She'd need that inner strength to make such a decision for herself. A decision made willingly, not because of something they forced on her. Not because of something they said or did that guilted her into conceding. He'd used all the coercion he could just in getting her here. The rest was up to her, which was why he'd yet to share his love with her in any way other than through action. If he said the words first, would he ever know for certain that her feelings were true?

Lifting her from the water, he made his way to the Jacuzzi with Ryan trailing them. "Relax your head on my shoulder," he said, not wanting her to look around, to see the desire evident on his brother's body.

Hot bubbles lapped at his skin when he stepped into the whirlpool. A sigh escaped her throat as he sank onto a seat, carrying her into the heated water with him. He gave her a soft kiss on the forehead, tip of the nose, and lips, before swinging her upper body outward to float along the water's surface.

She yelped and tried to cling to his neck. "Relax. Lie back. We've got you."

Ryan moved into position on her other side, his hands dipping into the water to support her back while Dylan held her hips. They each took one of her wrists and extended her arms straight out. Her eyelids drifted shut, and a smile played at the corners of her delicate mouth.

He began with a kiss on her abdomen just above her navel, slowly licking an erotic path downward. He kept one hand underneath her and used the other to explore her curves. To excite her body. Touching, tempting, tantalizing.

Ryan returned to her neck, his first kiss prompting

her to tilt her head back and allow him more access, but he didn't remain there. Soon his mouth kissed a trail over her collarbone and up to suck on a perfectly round, coral nipple.

When he joined his brother by laving her other breast, her arms wound about their shoulders. He loved to suckle at her breast, the feel of her fingers in his wet hair, the heady rumbling sounds of her desire.

The roar of the jets mingled with her moans of approval, but he determined not to hurry. He'd take his time and show her the ultimate gift was in giving. Tonight was all about her. Her desires. Her needs. Her pleasure.

He lifted his head and caught his brother's glance. With one accord they moved her closer to the side, each one taking a thigh in hand.

"Whoa...what?" Her head lifted from the water's surface, and she gripped their shoulders as they positioned her feet and calves on the edge of the hot tub. Dylan moved behind her, supporting her shoulders against his chest. Ryan kept a hand on one of her breasts, a touch of comfort and familiarity, while his other caressed her inner thigh.

"Relax, puss," Dylan said when she stiffened with obvious uncertainty.

Ryan bent forward and gave her a slow, thorough kiss. Dylan took both her hands and laced his fingers with hers, then began scooting forward...forcing her hips deeper into the water...closer to the jet.

Ryan swallowed her startled sound and continued to kiss her, his hand moving up her thigh and back down into the water. She tried to close her knees, but he stopped her.

Dylan nudged her a bit more, until the jet struck her clit at just the right angle.

Her fingers flexed and fisted, her hips wiggled, and her breathing came fast and furious as she began kissing Ryan back with a renewed fervor. Dylan moved forward, sending her closer to the jet stream, and she screamed despite his brother's kisses.

"That's it, puss," he whispered close to her ear, her head resting on his shoulder. "Come for us." He moved back, pulling her away from the jet, while Ryan released her mouth to reposition her knees farther apart and held them there.

Dylan let go of her hands, and she immediately latched onto his arms. He reached around her to fondle both breasts then moved forward, forcing her closer once more. "Again...Olivia."

Her whimper stretched into a long moan as the pulsating bubbles teased her clit and pussy without mercy. Her fingers bit into his biceps, her back arched, and her thighs trembled when another orgasm rocked her body. "Yes, puss... Ride it out. Show us your pleasure."

She bucked as if she could fuck the water that tormented her, and he wanted nothing more than to feel her do the same to him. To ride him to completion until they were both sated. But this would have to do for now. He flexed his hips, rocking hers toward the jet and sending her into another spiral of orgasmic shudders.

"That's it." He kissed her cheek and moved her away from the enthralling jets, back to the center where calmer waters lay like the eye of a hurricane. "My precious puss. So beautiful." She twisted in his arms and clung to him, burying her face against his neck and shoulders as her body vibrated from the strong orgasms. He was still kneeling in the water, holding her close, when the timer on the jets finally stopped.

* * * * *

Olivia moaned as warm, strong fingers slithered down her side, over her butt, and slipped between her thighs. What a way to wake up, she thought with a slow smile.

"Wake up, sleepyhead. Breakfast is waiting."

She mumbled something incoherent and spread her legs a bit to accommodate Dylan's teasing fingers. She'd never felt more relaxed than she did in that moment. After the Jacuzzi play, Dylan and Ryan had brought her up to their room, cuffed her to the bed, and brought her to orgasmic heights time and again with hands, mouths, and sex toys until she'd fallen into a deep, exhausted sleep.

"Oo-livv-iaaa," Dylan said in a teasing singsong. "Don't you want to get up and replenish your energy?" He chuckled, and the sound was like another caress. His hot, moist mouth touched her bare shoulder, and she shivered. His fingers feathered over her pussy lips, teasing her curly hairs. "My precious *gatita*. Did we wear you out?"

She giggled at his teasing tone. He was in rare form this morning.

She loved it. She loved him. How could she not after the night they'd shown her?

But...they'd never taken her the way she truly needed. Even after hours of sexual play—their long, thick cocks engorged with their own needs—they didn't once have intercourse with her. She still didn't know why.

Olivia rolled over and realized her hands had been released from the cuffs but, so used to the position, she'd stayed with her hands stretched above her head all night.

"Where's Ryan?" she asked when she came face-to-face with Dylan sprawled on the bed next to her, his head sharing her pillow. Her voice was a bit hoarse, probably from screaming as she came repeatedly throughout the evening and night.

"He had a meeting this morning. He will return by lunchtime."

He ran a finger down her cheek, along her jaw line and neck. Then he cupped her left breast. Even as his hand moved over her flesh, his gaze stayed firmly connected with hers. And damn it all, he looked so sweet, so tender. As if he loved her in return.

She had a million questions buzzing in her mind. Instead of asking, which up until now had gotten her nowhere, she leaned into him, her hand against his silk-covered chest, and kissed him softly on the lips.

A low rumble came from him, his lips parted slightly, but he didn't deepen the caress.

She brought her hand up, forked her fingers through his soft hair, tipped her head slightly to the side, and sank her tongue into his mouth.

His arms moved around her, pulling her close, cradling her against his chest. But he broke the kiss and buried his face against her neck, his breathing labored. She could feel his cock straining his slacks, a solid presence against her belly.

"Dylan," she whispered. "I…" What could she say? He'd made it clear she wasn't to pursue his pleasure. The humiliation of the restaurant still haunted her. And she couldn't ask for what she needed. She wanted to, but how could she ask him to love her without sounding pathetically desperate? She'd tried to earn his love by pleasuring him, but that had backfired. She wanted him to love her as strongly as she loved him.

"What, puss? Tell me." He pulled back, cupping her cheek in his hand. He looked anxious to hear…something. His eyes were bright, and a small smile tipped his lips.

She wanted to make him happy, but didn't know what to say. She would not humiliate herself again. Would not beg for his affections.

"I'm hungry," she lied. "You made breakfast?"

He released her so fast she would have fallen, if she hadn't been lying down. He rolled to the side of the bed and stood up, his back to her. "Yes," he practically barked. "Breakfast is ready. Out on the verandah." He headed for the door. "Take your shower first."

He never looked back.

Worried over his sudden change in attitude, Olivia rushed through her morning cleansing routine, brushed on a bit of mascara, and was at the table within fifteen minutes.

Dylan sat at the table reading a newspaper, his breakfast already eaten. When she sat down, he laid the paper aside and served her from the warming tray. The cheesy Spanish omelet smelled wonderful, but her nerves were too jittery to enjoy it.

"Thank you," she muttered.

Dylan gave her a perfunctory nod then resumed reading his paper. His silence was unnerving.

She'd angered him. That was obvious, she thought as

she slowly chewed her eggs. But how? What had she done? Had the kiss upset him because she'd made the first move? No, he hadn't seemed upset until she spoke.

What did he want from her?

"Dylan…"

He folded down the corner of the paper and looked at her, his expression blank, unreadable.

"If I've done something—"

"Eat your breakfast, Olivia."

She bit her lip. He sounded so cold. So remote. She shook her head and reached for her orange juice.

He flipped the newspaper and continued reading.

Fighting back tears, she finished her meal. After she'd swallowed the last of her coffee, she said, "May I have my phone to call work?"

Once again he set the paper aside and met her gaze with his caramel-colored eyes. "It is in the library, in the top drawer of the desk."

She did not understand why he was sounding so… She didn't even know how to describe the way he sounded. Some combination between angry and…sad?

She had to get some answers out of one of these men. Somehow she'd get some time alone with Ryan this afternoon and make him talk. He was much easier to read. He seemed less able to deny her.

"Thank you," she finally said as she stood. "I shouldn't be long. What would you like me to do after I'm done?"

Dylan studied her for long moments, his gaze traveling over her body like a tangible caress. "Enjoy the morning, Olivia. Have a swim, or…read. Whatever you will.

Ryan and I will need to speak to you when he returns." He was calling her Olivia now. Not puss or even *gatita*. Her heart felt as if it were being torn from her body.

She nodded and moved toward the glass doors, but at the last moment turned back, walked up behind him, wrapped her arms around his shoulders, and kissed his neck. "For whatever I've done to upset you, I'm sorry," she whispered.

He didn't move for what seemed an eternity, but then he raised his hand and laid it over hers against his chest. "My mistakes are my own, Olivia. You have done nothing wrong."

She desperately wanted to know what his cryptic words meant, but she instinctively knew she'd be getting nothing more from him. She kissed his cheek before pulling away from his warmth. "Maybe," she said hesitantly, "after I'm done with my call...could we go for a walk?"

He gave a short nod, still not looking at her. "If that is your wish."

She swallowed back the hurt and pain and zeroed in on anger. It was a much safer emotion. Why was he treating her this way? If he didn't want her here, then he should tell her to leave. She only had three days left, anyway. There weren't any rules about them not breaking the deal.

She spun on her heel and stomped into the house. *Damn Dylan. Damn them both for that matter.* She'd come here for two weeks of hot, uninhibited sex and a chance to set aside her responsibilities. To be as she'd been that night years ago in the hotel room. A moment to be herself, be free to experiment. Remove the tiresome façade she always showed to the world and just let go. Explore alternatives, experience something exciting and different.

She'd followed their rules to a T. Well, most of the time, anyway. And now, after a night filled with such caring attention, she was getting the cold shoulder again.

Screw 'em. She jerked open the top drawer of the desk. She'd thought that maybe, just maybe, she wasn't the only one in this totally messed up relationship who was falling in love. But that was an illusion, a hope she should have given up on a long time ago.

She punched in the number for her voicemail back in California and plopped down on the suede sofa she liked.

She'd fucked up with Dylan somewhere along the way. He didn't even want to have sex with her, let alone love her. If he had, they would've done a hell of a lot more than masturbate for damn near two weeks. Wouldn't they?

And Ryan. She blew out a harsh breath. Ryan was sweet and funny, and she could easily see spending the next fifty or so years with him, too. But did he love her?

Ha.

Love. She could be so damned stupid sometimes! No wonder she never did anything but concentrate on work. When she tried to have a personal life, *this* was what she wound up with.

"You have forty-nine new calls. Please press one to listen to the first message."

Olivia jerked the phone from her ear and stared at it. *Forty-nine?*

She pressed number one.

"Olivia. It's Howard. All hell is breaking loose. You need to get back *now*. There's a kink in the merger negotiations. You-know-who is trying for a power play...and it's your position he's after. Thought you'd want to know, so get here...."

Olivia's heart skipped a beat. Howard Kendall was VP of Finance and a longtime friend and confidant. *You-know-who* was another executive who'd been pissed when the board selected her over him as CEO five years ago. She'd managed to keep him in line until now. *Damn it! I should've known something like this would happen.*

The next message started. "It's Howard again. Damn it, Liv. Call me!"

Each message she ran through was from Howard, sounding more and more panicked.

She skipped to the end. The last message had been left ten minutes ago. "Liv. This is it. There's a dinner meeting this evening at eight with the Big Three. If you're not there, you're out of a job. Bob says no matter what happens with the merger, if you don't show, you're outta here. I hope your vacation is worth it."

Holy shit. The Big Three was the company they were merging with; their representatives weren't due to arrive in California until next week...originally. And what the hell was Bob, the Chairman of the Board, doing there?

She glanced at the antique grandfather clock in the corner of the room. Almost ten o'clock. If she got on a plane by three, subtract three hours, add five for the flight...she'd make it. She had to. The entire career she'd spent years building was on the line.

She dialed Howard's office even as she ran up the stairs to her room. Clothes. Clothes. She threw back the door to the closet where Dylan and Ryan kept the dress she'd worn for their shopping day.

She flipped through the rack, settling on the least daringly sexy outfit. A beige A-line skirt and matching blouse. The blouse would be a bit form-fitting, but—

"Kendall here." There was no mistaking his harried tone.

"Howard! It's Liv. I'm coming back. I'll make the meeting even if I have to hijack a plane."

"Oh, thank God. Where the hell are you?"

"Florida. I'll call and let you know when to send the car to the airport."

"Okay. Hurry. Jeez, Liv, this is cutting it too damn close."

"I know. I'm sorry. Gotta go, but my phone will be on the rest of the day. Call me with updates." She disconnected the call and found the number for her favorite airline programmed in her phone.

CHAPTER FIFTEEN

With just her little personal grooming bag and her phone in hand, wearing a pair of three inch heels she'd found at the back of the closet that matched the outfit she'd chosen, Olivia descended the sweeping staircase to the main floor.

Her heart thudded too hard against her ribs. She set her bag down on the table by the main entrance, but kept her phone clutched in her hand as she went in search of Dylan.

Oh, how was she going to tell him she had to leave early? How was she supposed to say goodbye to him? And Ryan… He wasn't here. How could she leave without saying goodbye?

Dylan still sat at the table on the terrace. He was leaning forward, his chin propped on his hand while he stared out at their acres of lush garden. When he heard the door open, he turned. The smile on his lips faded.

"What is this about?" he asked, pushing to his feet. Confusion with a hint of anger replaced his contented look of seconds before. "Why are you dressed? You know the rules."

She nodded, a jerky movement. "I have…" She cleared her throat. "I have to go back. Today."

His face went blank. "You agreed to two full weeks, Olivia. Do you break your word?" Even his voice lost every bit of emotion.

She shook her head. "You don't understand. That big merger I told you about… There are complications. If I don't get back by tonight, I'm out of a job. I have to go." She walked up to him, needing to touch him, but he turned away.

After he rounded the table, he faced her once again, his arms folded over his wide chest. "And your career is your life, is it not? Isn't that what you intimated before?"

Her heart was cracking open, and he looked as cool and detached as ever. The *bastard*. Didn't he care one little bit?

"Yes," she said, hardening her own heart against the pain. "I've spent my entire adult life building my career. Without it, I have nothing."

With a shake of his head, he dropped his arms to his sides and slipped both hands into his pants pockets. "Do you...have nothing?"

"Look," she said. "I know I didn't fulfill the agreement. Maybe...maybe when you come out to the West Coast next, I could make it up to you. We could get together for a few days." She'd do anything for this to not be the end.

To never see him again? Both of them? God, this just might kill her.

"A few days...? Then what? Renegotiate a new deal for a few more days...when you have time?" Dylan shook his head. "It ends here. If you leave, our agreement is void. It's over."

Her breath whooshed out of her. He might as well have driven a knife into her chest. Tears burned her eyes. "No..."

"You know the rules, Olivia. You knew it going into this arrangement. If you back out...walk away—"

"I *want* to see you again. You and Ryan." How could he be so hard? So cold? Did this time together mean *nothing* to him? Didn't he feel *something* for her? "Are you saying you don't want to see me again? Ever?"

He shrugged. "It is your decision. Not mine to make. If you wish to leave now, you know what must be done."

She opened her mouth, but only a squeak came out. What was her decision? She had to go back to California. There was no choice in the matter. She couldn't lose her job over...over...over obviously nothing, she realized as she stared into Dylan's unfathomable eyes.

They stared at each other for a small eternity while she tried to be strong, to draw out her icy bitch persona. Why couldn't she find it? Where had that cold, unfeeling woman gone?

She wanted nothing more than to rush into Dylan's arms and cling to him. To beg him to feel for her just a tiny bit of what she felt for him. She wanted to cry her heart out and plead with him to hold her forever, take care of her always.

No.

No, she was stronger than that. She needed no one but herself. Hadn't she overcome a failed engagement and numerous other tribulations in her chosen, back-stabbing career field? She firmed her resolve and her shoulders.

"I guess this is it, then. I'm sorry you feel that way." She turned away, praying he wouldn't see the pain in her eyes, the black hole her soul had become.

"Your decision is made then?"

She nodded, afraid to speak.

"Very well." She heard his footsteps as he came toward her. She prayed he'd touch her, hug her. He walked past. "I will call for the jet and a car."

She followed him inside. "I already have a plane ticket waiting for me at the airport."

He stopped mid stride and turned. "And I suppose a taxi is waiting outside?" Anger seemed to have replaced the nothingness. His tone had turned harsh, nearly a shout.

She cringed, shook her head. She'd wanted to wait until Ryan returned. She had to say goodbye to him. Maybe he'd be willing... She couldn't lose them *both*. She just couldn't!

"Then I will arrange for your ride. No need for you to waste one more minute here if you wish to leave." He strode into the office and lifted the phone.

Olivia leaned against the wall, her knees weak and shaking. She didn't want to leave, but he apparently didn't care. Judging by his reaction, he wanted her gone. Maybe it was for the best that she go. Immediately. Tears burned her eyes, but she fiercely blinked them back. She didn't need Dylan. She didn't need Ryan. She would make it on her own.

"The car will be here in ten minutes."

Olivia shut her eyes, couldn't bear to see Dylan's beautiful face.

"We must finish this now."

Her eyelids popped open. "What?" She couldn't breathe. What was he talking about? Finish what? Hadn't he just finished *everything* by telling her it was over?

He unbuttoned the top two buttons of his shirt and withdrew the gold chain that held the key to her collar.

Her collar. She'd forgotten about it. She reached up and ran her hand over the metal and leather. It'd become such a part of her. She didn't want to lose it. But she couldn't exactly show up for a meeting with the Big Three still wearing it.

"Say the word, Olivia."

She shook her head. She couldn't. She didn't want it to end. She didn't want to go. She didn't want to give up what she'd found in Dylan and Ryan.

"You may not pass the front door alone without saying the word."

She grasped the tiny padlock on her collar—the urge to run and hide from him and the key so strong, she nearly bolted.

"Do you wish to stay, then?"

If he would just show some kind of emotion. Something for her to cling to. But he didn't. His eyes were unreadable, his face a blank mask of...nothingness.

Yes, she wished to stay! But she couldn't. Her job...her life...her...future. Her empty future alone with nothing but her files to keep her warm at night. Her paperwork didn't tease, didn't tantalize. Didn't sit and talk with her. Didn't make her feel, for the first time in her life, like a real, loveable woman.

But then again, Dylan wasn't making her feel that way right now either. She'd obviously been less to him than he and Ryan had been to her.

She was Olivia Chandler, an icy bitch. Destined to be alone. Destined to never again lay eyes, or hands, or mouth on the Montgomery brothers.

She pushed away from the wall and stepped in front of Dylan. Then she lifted the lock for him. *"Corazon,"* she said, proud that her tone had gone as dead as Dylan's.

Did he flinch? She couldn't be sure. Maybe.

"Very well." He lifted the key and with a tiny *snick*, the lock opened. He removed the lock then lifted the collar from her. Not so much as a fingertip of his grazed her flesh.

She gritted her teeth against the pain. The loss. The missing weight from around her neck was too tangible. Too real.

Without another word, Dylan turned away and moved toward the foyer. He opened the door and moved to the side, inviting her to leave.

Pain twisted in her gut, but she swore she wouldn't show it. She walked past the small table and picked up her toiletry case. "I'll send the dress back."

He said nothing. She wanted to say so much more.

A long, black limousine pulled up outside. Her heart twisted. Her breath lodged in her throat. She looked into Dylan's eyes one last time. Did she see pain there, or was it only a reflection of her own?

She reached out and touched his cheek with her palm. His gaze never wavered. Nor did he try to return the caress. "Goodbye, Dylan," she whispered. "Tell Ryan..." She swallowed. "Tell him I'll..." Her chin started quivering.

Why won't you touch me? Hug me? I need you, Dylan!

She turned and ran for the car. The driver held the

back door open, and she practically dove in.

Tears streamed from her eyes. The driver closed the door. She leaned forward and buried her face in her hands as harsh, empty sobs tore from her throat.

The car started.

The door next to her flew open. Dylan leaned in, clasped her face between his palms, and kissed her deep and hard, sucking all the breath from her lungs.

"I will miss you, *mi gatita.*"

And then he was gone.

Before she could react, the door shut, and the car began to move. She scrambled around in the seat to see out the back window. Dylan paused on the top step before the big double doors, his hand resting on his chest, right over his heart.

Her heart, she thought as the vision of him became blurred by her tears. She'd given him the word, but she'd left her heart, all her love, within the walls of their home.

* * * * *

Ryan pulled his red Mitsubishi 3000 into the garage and parked next to his brother's Lexus SUV. He picked up the box from the passenger seat and ran his hands over the plush black velvet.

This had to work, he thought. It had to. They were running out of time, and nothing they did seemed to be working. Olivia wasn't any closer to admitting her feelings for them, and Dylan's mandate that she be the one to speak first was killing him. A slow, torturous death.

He flipped up the lid on the box and ran his fingers

over the cool platinum choker, the little lock, the two keys. Would she accept their gift? Would she accept what it meant? Would she stay?

He snapped the lid shut and closed his eyes, let out a slow breath, ran his hand over the slight ache in his chest. This was the big test, and he prayed his brother was wrong. Dylan had said it was too soon. Ryan worried it was already too late.

How Dylan could remain so aloof to Olivia was beyond him. Never had a woman made him feel so…needed. Yet, so terrified.

He pushed open the door and stepped out of the car. From the moment he'd walked into the hotel room on that fated night and found the beautiful Olivia in his bed, his life had turned upside down. She never left his thoughts. She invaded his mind every waking moment. And at night, lying next to her, it took all his willpower not to take her and make her his, to tell her exactly what was in his heart.

Walking into the utility room from the garage, Ryan set his features and tried to calm his racing heartbeat. This was it. Dylan said they'd have lunch before presenting Olivia with the choker and explaining what it meant if she accepted their gift.

As he headed through the house for the terrace, he slowed his steps. Never had he and Dylan taken such a huge step with a woman. Not in the nearly two decades since Jack and Jon Sinclair had introduced them to the alternative lifestyle of dominance during college, had they been willing to ask for a lifetime commitment.

What if she said no? What if she felt she couldn't handle it? This was still all so new to her. Would she understand that she was committing to both of them the type of commitment that a woman normally makes with only one man?

He had no doubt that she knew they were sexually compatible. He'd never seen a woman respond as fast and fiercely to sexual stimuli as she. And that was the crux of Dylan's worries. That she still thought of this as an affair, a quick dalliance, something that she'd one day look back on fondly. Something left in her past.

Ryan walked out onto the terrace to find Dylan seated in a lounger by the pool. He didn't see Olivia. "I have returned, *mi hermano*. Is our pet on her phone?" He held out the velvet box to Dylan.

Dylan eyed the box then raised his gaze. Ryan had never seen such a shattered, pained expression in his brother's face.

"She is gone, *hermano*. She has returned to California."

Fury shot through Ryan. He dropped the box to the tile deck and grabbed Dylan by the front of his shirt, dragging him to his feet. "What the fuck do you mean, she's gone? We have three days left! What did you do to her?"

Dylan didn't fight. He simply stood there, his shoulders slightly rounded, his eyes as dark as midnight. "I did nothing to her. She called her office this morning...." He shook his head. "She made her choice. She chose her job."

Ryan shook Dylan. "You let her go? You fucking *let her go*. I could kill you right now, *hermano*."

Dylan's expression never changed, nor did he try to get away from Ryan's rage. He nodded instead. "Death would be a relief."

Ryan shoved him away. "Where is she? When does

the plane leave?"

"I don't know. When I offered to have the jet readied, she said she already had a flight booked. I assume she's leaving out of Miami."

Ryan grabbed up the jewelry box and turned for the door.

"Where do you think you're going?"

"If you won't do anything about this, I will. I'm going after her."

"You cannot go after her, Ryan. She made her choice. We must abide by her choice."

"Screw her choice."

"You don't mean that—"

"This is our life, too. She made the decision she did because she doesn't understand. Why can't you see that?"

"She understands more than you think she does. She left once before."

"That's different."

"The only thing different is that she didn't sneak out in the middle of the night this time. But I'm telling you, she knew exactly what she was doing, what it meant when she gave me her safe word."

"Her safe... She said *corazon*?"

Dylan nodded.

Ryan frowned. "I don't care. I'm still going after her." He headed for the garage. He'd find her. He'd find her, and he would never let her go. He heard his brother's footsteps behind him. "What do you think you're doing?"

"I do care. I'm coming with you," Dylan said.

Ryan snorted and jerked open the door of his car. "You're wrong about her."

"Perhaps..."

CHAPTER SIXTEEN

Nothing would make Dylan happier than for him to be wrong about her. But he'd been the one who woke up alone in that hotel bed all those years ago. And he'd been the only one looking into those beautiful, aqua eyes when she tossed his heart back to him as if it was worthless.

Neither he nor his brother spoke a word to each other as Ryan raced to the airport, although Dylan phoned the limo driver to confirm his suspicions about where she was flying out.

And he prayed. He prayed that he was wrong, that he'd misread the stubborn anger in her eyes, that Ryan wouldn't be devastated by her departure. Although he knew his hope in the latter was useless. His brother, albeit more prone to emotional eruptions, couldn't be any more heartbroken than Dylan was.

So he also prayed that the damn flight was delayed.

By the time they reached the terminal, his pulse raced with an eager expectancy that equaled the urgency in Ryan's strides through the crowd of travelers. They both searched the departure monitors like pirates in search of buried treasure.

"There!" Ryan pointed to the screen.

"I see it," he said, already heading in the direction of the ticket counter.

"We still have time... Hey, where are you going?"

He pointed to the line at the security gate. "We can't get through there without tickets."

Ryan cursed and followed him to the shortest line at the counter.

"Your tickets?" the agent asked with a smile.

"We need to buy two...roundtrip."

"Destination?"

While Dylan responded to the litany of questions, Ryan fidgeted, making him wonder whether they'd be arrested as possible hijackers before he could even pay for the tickets. The suspicious activity didn't help matters when the agent asked about luggage.

"We like to travel light. Besides, we're going there to shop." He grinned. "Clothing is first on the list."

The agent giggled, but the look on her face told a different story. Maybe she thought them nuts, but once he had the tickets in hand and was through security, he didn't give a damn.

Unfortunately, they'd just cleared the checkpoint when they heard the final boarding call for her flight, and the fucking gate wasn't right around the corner. After a shared glance, he and Ryan took off running.

The empty seats in the waiting area were his first clue, and he knew even before the window came into view. They were too late.

"*Goddammit!*" Ryan said, slapping a hand on the thick

glass as the plane backed away from the gate.

Dylan collapsed into an uncomfortable chair and rested his face in his hands, propping an elbow on each knee. His emotions had never ridden such a roller coaster ride before. The pain of loss, yet again, was almost too much for him to bear.

"What now?" Ryan asked.

He rubbed his temples and muttered, "What do you mean what now?"

"Don't give me that. Those tickets you bought... Are they for the same destination?"

"Hell if I know where I told that woman we were going. I was just trying to buy our way through security."

"Call for the jet. We have to go after her."

He sat up and watched his brother pace, his face turned toward the window. The plane had taxied out of sight.

"She came back to us once before," he said, trying to sound encouraging. "If she loves us enough, she'll return again in her own time."

Ryan spun toward him with an angry stride, his voice rising with equally volatile emotion. "Don't try to pretend you're okay with this. I can't believe you're just going to let her go. Does she mean nothing to you?"

Dylan shot to his feet. "Of course she does. What? You think you're the only one here who's hurting? Is that it? Well, think again. I love her, too. Just as much as you do." He jabbed a finger toward the vacant spot where the airliner had been. "My heart's ripped out and on that damn plane!"

"Why didn't you tell me?"

The familiar feminine voice made both men spin on

their heels. While Dylan fought to get his lungs working again, Ryan stepped toward her, but her raised hand brought him up short.

Her aqua gaze never left Dylan.

Finally, when he was able to give sound to his thoughts, he asked, "Tell you what?"

"That you love me. You never said I had your heart."

"Olivia... How could you not know? You've had my heart from the moment I gave you the safe word, *corazon*."

Tiny stars of moisture glistened on her lashes and fell to her cheeks.

He wanted to take her in his arms, hug her so close they never parted again, but instead, he swallowed hard and said, "You missed your plane."

She blinked, another teardrop fell, and her lips trembled with the hint of a smile. "I couldn't leave my hearts behind. I love you both too much."

She took one step forward and collided with them as they sandwiched her in an urgent embrace. Then with a joyous whoop, Ryan lifted her off her feet in a tight hug and spun around, which had her laughing aloud. He silenced her with an impassioned kiss before setting her back on solid ground.

When she turned to look over her shoulder at him, Dylan held out a hand. With a timid smile, she lowered her gaze and placed her palm against his. He let her move to within inches of him then lifted her chin with a finger.

"Say it again," he said.

"I love you, Dylan."

He closed his eyes and savored the sound, the emotions engendered by the combination of her voice and those words. Tenderly, he pressed his lips to hers, savoring the softness and warmth.

He pulled back only far enough to see her face. "Never again, puss. Or you have my word; I'll tie you to our bed and spank your ass for even considering the idea of leaving us."

Her reaction somewhat surprised and completely pleased him. With a cheeky grin and a wink, she murmured, "Mmm...Master, you promise?"

* * * * *

She never would've thought they could get her home so fast, but the Montgomery brothers were nothing if not exceedingly resourceful. While one drove, the other distracted her so well that the return trip seemed but a fraction of the original ride to the airport.

Of course, another reason might be the change in her mood, which was drastically altered by the reversal in direction. On the way to the airport, she'd been plagued by the look on Dylan's face as the car pulled away. She'd struggled with the guilt of having left without a word of any kind to Ryan and questioned why....

Why was she in such a rush to head back to a career that offered little more than financial stability? Yes, she'd busted her ass to climb the corporate ladder, but what had she really gained? Nothing other than a reputation as an icy bitch, and a pool of underlings waiting for the slightest fuck-up so they could stab her in the back and climb over her corpse to reach the top rung of that ladder.

Did she really want to exchange what she'd

experienced with Dylan and Ryan for a stressful job and a lonely apartment? No. A resounding *no* had echoed in her mind and increased in volume as each mile stretched the distance between her and the place she'd come to call home.

By the time she made it to her gate, she was a distraught mess and knew she couldn't go through with it. She couldn't leave. So, rather than board the plane, she'd slipped into the ladies' room to freshen up and fix the damage her crying had done to her makeup. A good thing, it turned out, since she'd heard familiar voices the moment she stepped out of the restroom.

Once home, the men spared her a few minutes to make some phone calls. She placed one to Carmen and one to Howard. Exhausted from the stress of dealing with Howard's dismay over the phone, and grateful all of that was behind her now, she climbed the stairs to the second floor. She'd fax her official resignation to the Personnel department in the morning as a matter of protocol.

She stopped short in the doorway to the master bedroom.

Dylan and Ryan had prepared the bed with what appeared to be ropes of some kind, but she didn't pay the cords much attention. No, her focus was on her men who stood bathed in soft candlelight and completely nude next to the bed.

She blinked, and her heart skipped a beat. To think, she'd nearly exchanged this heady vision before her for a tedious cross-country flight and a stressful business dinner.

"Come here, puss," Dylan said.

She approached with sure steps, stopped in front of them, and dropped to her knees. "Masters..."

"Up with you, now." Ryan gave her a hand and led her to the foot of the bed. "You're a bit overdressed for what we have in mind. Remove your clothes and lie down."

She quickly undressed, leaving her garments and shoes wherever they landed. Then she climbed onto the bed as ordered and discovered the purpose for the ropes, which had soft cuffs attached to the ends.

A few moments later, her hands and feet were stretched toward the four corners of the bed, but her body wasn't on the bed. It was hanging face-up a couple of feet above the mattress, courtesy of the soft leather straps attached to her limbs and waist and the ropes tied to the bed's iron canopy.

"I told you our bed is multifunctional," Dylan said, his fingers gliding from one ankle to her hip. "How do you feel?"

"High, Master." She felt as if she were floating in midair.

He chuckled. "We're going to make you ours, Olivia. Completely ours. From now on. Do you understand what that means?"

She had a damn good idea and nodded.

The flicker of candlelight, which they'd used to light the room, multiplied her sensation of floating. Unable to hold her head up forever, she let it fall back, her neck exposed, her hair brushing the sheets below her. Her world flipped upside down.

Dylan drew one fingertip over her neck. "You're missing something, puss."

My collar. She hadn't retrieved it after returning to the house. She didn't even know where it was.

"We have something for you." Ryan moved into her range of view. In his hand was a velvet box. "Do you submit to our ownership, Olivia?"

"Do you entrust us with your care," Dylan added, "and accept our vow that we will love and cherish you above all others from this day forward...forever? Will you accept our offer to be your masters and agree to wear our collar?"

Tears welled in her eyes and, in her current position, when she blinked, the droplets ran over her temples to drop onto the bed below. "Yes...my masters."

With a broad grin, Ryan opened the box, and she saw that it did not contain her old leather collar. Instead, on a bed of black silk lay a shimmering silver choker. At its center was a tiny, heart-shaped lock encrusted with diamonds.

Dylan pulled the piece of jewelry from the box and put it around her neck. She wanted to touch it, rush to a mirror, and view it. But that would have to wait since she remained hanging spread-eagle several inches above the bed.

Ryan slipped a hand under her head and lifted her so that he could plant a brief kiss to her lips. "You're a treasure, Olivia. Our priceless treasure."

Her heart swelled, and she fought to keep from bawling like a sappy, sentimental fool. Her love for these two men overwhelmed her so much that she thought her chest might burst.

Dylan crawled onto one side of the bed with something else in his hand. "Today, we want you to feel like you've never felt before. So we're going to blindfold you."

Okay, she could admit it. That scared her. Tied up *and*

blind? Her pulse sped up. Her breathing grew shallow. As he wrapped black PVC tape around her head, covering her eyes, she tumbled into total darkness. *Helpless.* She was utterly helpless.

Panic spurred her heart and lungs and clawed at her mind. Fear of the unfamiliar, the unknown. Yet, she didn't feel as if she were in danger—no, her trust in the men nearby prevented that from happening. They wouldn't harm her, although they would no doubt push her boundaries.

Then soft, sultry music wove its way through the blackness like a mythical siren's call. Her fear subsided as anticipation gained new ground. She waited, wondering what they planned next.

They didn't begin where she expected them to start. They didn't do what she thought they would do. Instead, they rubbed jasmine-scented lotion over her arms, massaging as they went, then her feet, calves, thighs. They dribbled some of the cool lotion on her abdomen and slowly worked it into her skin. By the time they finished, every inch of her body was cocooned in a warm, mellow sensation.

"You're doing well, baby," Ryan said. "I'm so proud of you. I know you're nervous about the blindfold, but we need you to trust us even when you can't see and don't know our plans. Can you continue to do that for me?"

"Yes, Master."

"Do you trust us, puss?" Dylan asked.

"Yes, Master." The answer came quick and sure. She did trust them. Neither had ever betrayed her confidence.

"Good. I'm going to put a ball gag in your mouth." Something touched her lips, but he didn't force it in. "I remember my promise, and I'm keeping it. There are no straps, so you can spit it out if you wish to use your safe word. But otherwise, you must hold it. Understand?"

"Yes, Master."

"Open wide then." The ball was large enough to fill her mouth, but not so big that it was uncomfortable. It was soft and tasted of latex.

Someone circled her nipples, flicking them, tugging on them, twirling them between fingers and thumbs. Then she felt the sharp pinch of rubber clamps on each bud. She groaned around the ball gag and bit down on it. The weight of a cold chain lay between her breasts and slid over her right side.

Her thoughts scattered when fingers walked past her navel to slide between her legs and tease her. They vanished for a second only to lightly slap her pussy, which made her jerk. One finger circled her clit, pushing around and around, then another series of quick slaps. She couldn't help but moan as moisture flooded her sex.

The chain moved, lifted, and settled down the center of her body. Fingers pinched and separated her pussy lips. Then the bite of two more rubber clamps on those lips had her grunting and chewing on the ball gag.

The initial pain soon mellowed to a dull ache that radiated throughout her body and throbbed from the tips of her breasts to the apex of her thighs. When she inhaled, her chest rose, lifting the nipple clamps, which tugged on the chain they'd aligned directly over her clit. Every breath created an unbelievable friction that propelled her closer to a climax.

"Your skin is so soft," Dylan said, running his fingertips lightly over one side of her tummy. "Your breasts, so full." A warm hand cupped one.

Ryan said, "We love seeing you stretched out before us, bound, helpless."

"Unable to move unless we allow it. Unable to do anything but feel as we explore what belongs to us." Dylan gave a gentle tug on the chain.

She growled around the ball gag.

"Your thighs, your hips, your breasts..." Ryan's hand glided over each place he named then slipped between her breasts to gently curl around her neck. His fingertips stopped over the point where her pulse thumped, and he murmured in her ear, "Your heartbeat."

Despite her bondage, she shivered. Their words penetrated her brain, seduced her mind, while their talented hands and fingers titillated her flesh.

The men moved around her, one settling at the head of the bed between her outstretched arms, the other between her legs. It wasn't until Dylan spoke again that she knew who was where.

Dylan's voice was whisper soft against her ear. "You're ours, aren't you, Olivia? Ours to play with any way we choose. We can nibble on you." He nipped her earlobe, which shot a bolt of electricity down her back.

"We can lick you all over," Ryan said. Tugging the clamps on her pussy lips apart, he suckled her clit.

"Mmm." That was all she could manage around the gag.

Dylan said, "We can bring you pleasure...or pain that's pleasurable." A drop of something hot fell on her right breast, which made her lurch and grunt in protest, but it cooled quickly. Then another drop struck her left breast, and she realized it must be a candle's wax. A few more drops fell in a line below her navel, on her thighs.

She whimpered around her gag, the slight sting of the heat spurring her even higher in her sensory overload.

"Shh," Dylan said as he continued to dribble tiny droplets of warmth at key erogenous points on her suspended body. After a few more, though, he stopped and pulled the ball gag out of her mouth.

While Ryan caressed her thighs, hips and butt, Dylan slid his hand over her breasts, squeezing them gently, then down and around her neck. With that hand, he supported the back of her neck. With the other, he pressed on her chin to open her mouth. "Your mouth, Olivia, is mine, isn't it?"

"Y-yes, Master."

"Then serve me well." His cock demanded entry, and she gave it gladly. Her upside down position wreaked havoc on her senses as he powered into her. "Hungry for cock, puss?"

"Mmm hmm," was all she could manage since he didn't withdraw to allow a response. He pushed in several more times, easily reaching the back of her throat. His groan of approval was music to her ears. Then he pulled out. "Your tongue is mine too, isn't it?"

"Yes...Master." She panted between words.

"Use it, puss. Lick my balls."

"Nnn."

"All over. That's it. You want to suck 'em, don't you, puss?" He scooted closer. "Suck 'em hard." His palm pressed the back of her head, supporting her, pushing her between his legs. She concentrated more on her task. "Aw, fuck yeah. Just like that. Don't stop."

Ryan remained busy as well. She could still feel the occasional pull on the chain, a flick of a finger on her clit, the stab of two others into her moist pussy. Then he moved again, his voice now coming from beside her. "Do you need to come, puss?"

"Nnn hnn."

"Not yet."

She whined but didn't stop what she was doing to Dylan. At least not until he backed up, pressed his cock into her mouth a couple more times, then moved out of the way so Ryan could take his place. As they repositioned themselves, their hands roamed over her body unchallenged, and she reveled in the feelings their touches generated.

Their efforts had brought her to the edge and kept her poised there with astonishing efficiency.

"My turn, puss." Ryan's dick touched her lips. "You want to taste my cock?"

"Yes, Master." She tried to lick the tip, but he pulled out of reach.

"How bad do you want it?"

"Very badly. I want it very much." She opened her mouth.

"Ask me nicely."

"Please, Master. Please, let me have your cock."

He slipped in as far as he could go, stretched her mouth, and gave her all he had. "Such an obedient little pussy...cat. Lick my cock, baby. That's so good.... Serve me well, and I'll let you come." Ryan's hands fondled her breasts, lifting and tugging on the chain between the nipple clamps, as he repeatedly drove his dick into her mouth.

"Go, Dylan. Suck her tits."

Dylan leaned over her from between her outstretched legs and removed the clamps. Blood rushed to the peaks, making them more sensitive. He laved her right breast while he tweaked the other stinging nipple. His body pressed on the clamps pinching her pussy lips and rubbed the chain against her clitoris. Though suspended by her bondage, she writhed under the onslaught of such staggering sensations.

Ryan continued pumping into her mouth and then, without warning, Dylan slammed his cock home. The climax shattered her world.

So long. It had been so long since she'd felt Dylan's powerful touch deep in her womb. She wanted to scream for joy.

"Again, baby. Come for me." Ryan shoved his cock deeper into her mouth, cutting off any cry she made as orgasmic waves rocketed through her body.

The ropes tied to the bed allowed for a little give, turning her into a pendulum for their pleasure...and hers. When Dylan pounded into her, he swung her onto his brother's cock, and Ryan's thrusts sent her back.

Time ceased to exist for her as the men took her body to new heights. She lived for the men ravishing her, knew nothing outside of the cadence of their strokes. They'd wanted her to feel things like never before, and she did. It was almost more than she could handle.

When the orgasm settled down, Dylan pulled back just enough to remove the clamps from her pussy lips and toy with her clit, which sent her splashing into another whirlpool of sensations.

The swinging slowed to a stop. Ryan withdrew from

her mouth and lifted his wet cock so his balls touched her lips. Without being told, she licked his sac. "Yes. Slow and easy," he said, the words little more than a breathy whisper.

"I want all of you, Olivia," Dylan said. His cock slipped out of her pussy and moved lower to rub against her anus.

When she paused, Ryan gave a slight nudge of his hips and murmured, "Keep going." She resumed her licking.

"Today," Dylan announced, "we accept your gift and take all that you are...everything that is ours." He held her butt cheeks apart and pushed against her. The tight ring of muscles gave way, and the head of his cock slipped inside and stopped.

"Keep going," Ryan said softly, still supporting her head with one hand. Unsure whom he spoke to, she continued to tongue his balls, but her mind and body focused on what happened between her legs.

Dylan grabbed her hips with both hands and, with a deep male groan, took her ass in one long, slow stroke. There was pain, but there was pleasure, and the two were so twisted together, she became a mass of raw nerves.

"Fuck, Olivia," Dylan said on a huff of air, holding himself motionless inside her while every muscle she possessed contracted. Locked up, quaked. "Do you feel that?"

She could, but was unable to answer. Ryan had backed away and was now kissing her on the mouth as if there were no tomorrow.

"Is she okay?" Dylan wanted to know.

Ryan stopped, removed the blindfold of tape from around her head, and gazed into her eyes. With a smile, he said, "Yes. She's perfect," and stole her breath with another kiss.

His words were like a green light. Dylan began to pump into her with deep, steady strokes that created a sizzling burn with each penetration, which seemed to go on and on. Hands cupped, tugged, and kneaded her breasts. Fingers stroked her abdomen and bit into her hips, her thighs...thumbed her clitoris. At each thrust of Dylan's cock, her nerves rippled with orgasmic fury. Then with a loud shout, he poured himself into her.

Ryan's tongue dueled with hers, and he drank in the sounds of her pleasure.

When Dylan pulled out, Ryan moved between her legs to take his place. He rubbed his cock along her pussy and slipped inside her soaked channel several times. "*Dios mio, mi gatita.* You are...you feel so wonderful," Ryan said as he pressed deeper inside her body.

She couldn't agree more. Wonderful didn't begin to describe how these men made her feel. She groaned with approval and delight at each stroke of Ryan's thick cock.

After a while, Dylan returned to her side, climbed onto the bed, and sat between her outstretched arms. He lifted her head. "Watch, puss. See how much pleasure you give him?"

She was having a hard time concentrating on anything because of the pleasure Ryan bestowed upon her. She was nearing another climax when he withdrew to aim for her ass, his initial entry made easier by Dylan's slick cum. As he slowly pressed deeper, however, she winced. He stopped. Ryan's head reared back, his teeth clenched, eyes closed. His bronze skin pulled taut over bulging muscles as he fought for control.

"Fuck. She's too tight, Dylan. I'll hurt her." His chest heaved with every breath. His fingers curved into a bruising grip at her waist. He started to pull back.

"No, please," she said. Tears brimmed on her lashes.

Ryan opened his eyes, his gaze locking with hers.

"Don't stop, Master."

They stared into each other's eyes as he acknowledged her plea and pushed forward once more. He took her slowly, giving her time to get used to him, until finally, every inch of his thick cock was inside her ass. By then she was breathing heavily, but so was he. She smiled.

With a deep breath, he slid back and thrust forward again, stretching her flesh, claiming it as his own. What pain she felt drifted into the background as she saw his face take on a look of passionate bliss.

Dylan gave her a kiss on the cheek and continued to support her head as they watched his brother.

With a half smile, Ryan quickened his strokes in her ass and dipped two fingers into her pussy. When his thumb rubbed her clit, her eyes glazed over, and she lost herself in another sea of nirvana. Two more harsh thrusts and Ryan joined her with a shout of completion.

*****

A short time later, the men had cleaned her and themselves, using the opportunity to tantalize her already over-sensitized skin. They'd released her from her bondage as well, and now she lay on the bed sprawled out in post-coital lethargy.

The bed dipped as the men took up positions on either side of her. Each man faced her, propping himself up with an arm and laying a hand across her midsection.

She smiled and lifted sluggish eyelids to glance at them. Their hands, like their facial expressions, were gentle and warm.

Love. They loved her. Not because she held a coveted position of power in the corporate world. Not because she projected herself as a person of means, a talented professional with a reputation for an aggressive, no-nonsense business façade. Not even because of what her body could provide them. No, they'd proven they could withhold their own pleasure to cater to her needs. She understood that now. How had she been so blind?

As she stared into their eyes, studied their faces, she knew. They loved her because of who she was. Heart and soul.

She'd once thought Dylan—her Spanish stranger— seduced her into desiring this decadent lifestyle with promises that were impossible for him to keep. And that maybe, if she slept with him once more, she'd see that she was a fool to succumb to such overbearing dominance.

She'd thought she could dabble in uninhibited sex and have her heart come out untouched. Impossible, she realized now. Their mastery of her body went far beyond the flesh; it penetrated to the bone, even to her very soul.

She'd chosen her masters well. Those words sank into her mind, and she grinned. She had selected them, sought them out, traveled across a nation to surrender to their dominance...and indulge in their care.

If her obedience was all they requested of her in

payment for their care giving, that was a small price to pay. Silently, she vowed to give them more. Her love. Her heart.

"Why such a sly smile, puss?" Dylan asked, again proving how in tune he was with her every thought.

"I was thinking of something you said to me when we first met in Madrid."

Ryan's hand slid over her breast and up to her neck to thumb the tiny lock on her choker. He smiled at her when she glanced at him.

"What's that?" Dylan asked, drawing her attention back to him.

"You told me that you'd master me, pamper me, and take me higher than ever before. Do you remember?"

His lips curved. "I do."

She gave a light chuckle. "You do know how to keep your word, don't you?"

"With you...always, *nuestra amor*."

Our love.

"Mmm," she said on a sigh. "I like the sound of that."

The End

OWNING RACHEL

by

Madison Layle

CHAPTER ONE

"I've tried everything to get them to stop, Doc, but nothing succeeds. Isn't there a sleeping pill or knock-out drops that can prevent dreams? I must find something that works. I refuse to let them win."

Dr. Jonathon Sinclair scribbled on his notepad as he listened to his patient bemoan recurring fantasies his other female clients would give their eyeteeth to have just once in their lives. Hell, even he'd like to have them. "They're dreams, Rachel, not defense attorneys. Don't look at it like a competition. No one's on trial here."

Her right hand fisted in obvious frustration, the perfectly manicured nails biting into her palm. Her lips pouted in disapproval as he knew they would. They shimmered a pale brown today. The ladies probably called the color *Man-Trap Mocha* or some other such nonsense.

"I know that, Doc. I'm not crazy."

"I didn't say you were," he responded calmly.

She sighed, her trim body sagging into the plush couch. "What I meant was that I refuse to fail. My career is important to me. I can't take much more of this. I'm not sleeping well. I can't concentrate. These dreams are invading my consciousness now."

"How so?"

"The other day in the middle of my closing arguments, a memory of one orgasm in particular came to mind. I broke out in a sweat, lost my train of thought, and couldn't catch my breath. I nearly died of embarrassment, but honest to God, I couldn't help it at the time. It just struck so fast. I had to ask the judge for a five-minute recess." She turned pleading amber eyes toward him. "If the evidence hadn't been so strong and clear-cut, I could've lost the jury's trust entirely. I might have ruined my chances of winning a conviction with that stunt."

He'd bet his life savings that Rachel Morrissey never failed at anything in her life, which explained why she was so rattled over her recent episode. She'd first come to him about six months earlier, dressed in a ruby-red power suit with a hip-hugging skirt that stopped just shy of her nylon-encased knees. Her coffee-colored hair was always impeccably styled and her makeup subtle. In conservative pumps that showcased some impressive legs, she had a walk that broadcast confidence, a handshake that testified to experience in a man's world, and a smile that could make a guy forget his own name. He'd wondered then what the woman could possibly need with him.

Most of his female patients were disillusioned housewives who needed help putting a spark back into their marriage beds, or feared their husbands had already discovered that spark with a younger woman. Few, if any, were successful, independent career women with fantasies that could make an adult film star blush.

"Was this orgasmic fantasy one we spoke of before?"

Her cheeks pinkened. The pulse in her throat doubled

as the explicit daydream no doubt replayed in her mind.

"No," she whispered. Her hips raised a fraction.

He removed his reading glasses. Leaning forward to better watch her, he kept his tone smooth and encouraging. "What makes this one any different?"

"There were two." Her voice was soft, her eyes closed.

"Two orgasms?"

She shook her head.

"Two what?"

"Two men."

He sat back, silently drew in a deep breath, and tried to prevent the images her words gave his imagination. He'd concluded months ago that Rachel was a sexual submissive who lived publicly as a dominant prosecuting attorney. Her fantasies of being forced to submit control of her body over to an imaginary male Dominant was a clue even a Psych freshman at the junior college could interpret, but he hadn't seen this twist coming. He adjusted his position in the leather recliner.

"Doctor?"

He blinked, grateful for the notebook placed strategically in his lap. "Yes?"

"This isn't normal, is it?" She glanced at him briefly before turning her gaze toward the cream-colored ceiling. She quickly wiped away the single tear that spilled from the corner of one eye.

For some patients he would've offered a tissue. He didn't believe she'd appreciate the gesture, so he pretended not to notice.

"I've always been so in control. Driven. You know? I

knew what I wanted, went after it, and I got it. These thoughts aren't like me at all."

"Maybe that's the reason."

Curious amber eyes turned toward him.

"You're a beautiful woman with an insatiable sex drive, which you've kept suppressed in favor of other desires. Your career, for instance. What you've done isn't wrong, just unbalanced. Subconsciously, your body and mind are telling you they need relief from the demanding lifestyle you've chosen. It can't be easy to always be in charge, to take on pressure after pressure without caving. At some point, you have to give yourself a break. Learn to relax and let others take some of the burden off your shoulders."

She snorted and stared at the ceiling.

"Do you want to stop these fantasies from controlling your life?"

She blinked at him. "Of course."

"And if I suggested that the only way to do that was to give in to them?"

A tiny line appeared between her delicately arched brows. "Give up, you mean. I can't do that." She shook her head forcefully. "I'm not a weakling. Women have struggled for centuries to be independent."

"And they've gained all the headaches and stresses that come with bearing the burden of that independence without ever considering, for one second, that two can carry the load farther and longer than one can alone."

She sat up and gave him a look he was certain made many defendants quake in their boots. He smiled.

"If you're telling me I should turn in my attorney's license for an apron and spatula, you can think again."

He'd bet she'd look sexy as hell in nothing but an apron, but he forced that thought away and chastised himself. She was his patient, something he had to remind himself of repeatedly with her on his couch. His code of ethics prevented anything beyond professional dialogue and platonic observation. He'd never touched a patient, never crossed that line. Still, Rachel Morrissey tempted him.

"You expect me to throw away all I've worked for to grovel at some domineering man's feet. Not a chance, Doc."

"I didn't suggest—"

"I thought you were saying I needed a man."

She did, but he wasn't fool enough to announce it to her face when she was in what he called her cross-examination mood. "Not exactly."

"Exactly...what did you say then?"

"When was the last time you took a vacation?" At her blank look, he continued. "I thought so. When was the last time you had sex...with a living, breathing man, not a battery-powered toy?"

Her eyes widened before she hid her surprise behind a cool façade of indifference. "I don't see how that has anything to do with this."

He grinned. "You're having sexual fantasies to rival the steamiest erotic novels, and you think sex has nothing to do with it?"

She leaned back and crossed her arms. "I'm no virgin, Doctor. I've had sex plenty of times before."

"When was the last time, Rachel?" He put enough authority in his tone to make her answer.

She shrugged. "A year. No. Two...three? I don't know. I've been too busy to think much about it."

"That's your problem. Maybe it's time you did think about it."

"'All work and no play...' Is that what you're preaching now?" A teasing smile played at the corners of her mouth.

He maintained a serious expression, but the inside of one cheek would pay the price for the effort. "Rachel, you are a successful career woman. I'll grant you that. But you're still a woman with needs. When's the last time you allowed yourself or someone else to meet those needs?" He didn't bother explaining that those needs were as much emotional as they were physical. She'd just deny it. Still, no sexual relations for several years could only mean she'd also avoided any chance of an emotional commitment.

"I've been out with plenty of men. They didn't give me anything that my vibrator couldn't provide for a lot less trouble. Couple batteries, a few minutes of my time..."

"I don't hear you fantasizing about vibrators." That got her attention. She had a lot to learn about what men could provide a woman. Unfortunately, as her psychiatrist, he couldn't be the one to show her, but maybe another man... "Submissives like you have often fought against their natures, substituting—"

Her laugh cut him off. "I don't have a submissive bone in my body."

"Then explain the fantasies of bondage, forced orgasms, dominant lovers—"

"I can't explain them! That's what I came to you for." Exasperation turned up the volume on her words.

"What you are in your professional life is not all that you are."

"I'm no weakling."

"You're stereotyping." Her gaze snapped to his. "Weakness is a typical misconception. Submissives are not the weaker of true D/s couples. It takes great courage and strength to submit one's mind and body to another. More so if one commits one's heart. The relationship is a matter of trust—a consensual exchange—more than forcing one person to bend to another's will."

"I'll take your word for it."

He studied her face, read the skepticism in her eyes. "The issue here is that while you may be a domineering woman in the courtroom, you are having fantasies of submission, and that troubles you because you refuse to accept that part of your nature. We've concluded through our past sessions that your longings aren't the result of some past trauma."

"We have?"

"I have," he corrected. "You were never molested as a child, never sexually assaulted or raped. Even if you had been, that usually has the opposite effect on the victim. Your previous love affairs were consensual but lacked passion and frequency—"

"Hey, my sex life is just fine, thank you very much."

"You consider being too busy to think about it, or even remember when you last had sex, 'just fine'?"

"My sex life, or lack thereof, isn't the issue, Doc. Insomnia is. You tell me I need to think about sex, but that's the problem. I can't stop thinking about it. These damn dreams won't go away."

"Your dreams both arouse and appall you because you fail to understand them and refuse to even try. Until you face them with an open mind, they'll continue to torment you."

"There's a promising diagnosis. Thanks, Doc."

He ignored her sarcasm. "By your own admission, they have you shaken up. I might even venture to say they frighten you."

"I'm not—"

"Whether you admit it or not is incidental. When you're ready to deal with them, you will. Until then, there's nothing more I can do as your psychiatrist to help you overcome something that you can clearly handle without assistance." He closed his notebook and walked to his desk.

"Now wait just a minute. You can't turn me away." Honest anger infused her command. She was a woman used to getting her way, which was only part of her problem— although he was sure she wouldn't agree.

He turned to see her standing opposite him, his wide, mahogany desk between them. "What I cannot do, Rachel, is continue to waste my time and take your money when you're obviously not ready to deal with your problem. In that, I've failed you, and I'm sorry, but I have other patients who also need my help. If you won't take my advice or even consider my professional opinion, then there's nothing more I can do for you."

She tried to appear contrite, but succeeded in looking panicked. "What if I take your advice, go out on a few dates and have a one-night stand or two? Do you really think that will get rid of the fantasies?"

"If a person is frightened of something, the best way to overcome that fear is to face it head on. However, your fantasies are specific. I doubt a vanilla romp between the sheets will exorcize them. How many men do you know who are experienced Doms?"

"Doms?" One thin brow arced. "None that I know of. Any suggestions?"

He removed his reading glasses to stare at her for a long moment. His private life had never intersected with his professional life before. He'd prided himself on keeping them separate. His patients didn't need to know his sexual preferences as long as he was capable of using his knowledge and training to assist them with their sexual troubles in a professional, clinical manner. But if he said more, she would know...or at the very least, suspect. What she did with that knowledge could destroy his career and reputation.

He wasn't naïve enough to think that his preference for bondage and sexual domination wouldn't adversely affect his patients' opinions of him as a professional psychiatrist. All of the degrees and licenses in the world wouldn't help him with some of his straitlaced clients.

As much as Rachel fought against her own submissive instincts, he was unsure whether she'd be open enough to consider an alternative lifestyle. If he came right out and admitted his own experience, she might clam up—use his admission to disregard his opinion entirely. But there was a slight chance she might respond if he handled this correctly.

Taking the risk, praying he wasn't wrong about her, he pulled out a small piece of paper and wrote a number on it. "Entering the world of BDSM is potentially dangerous for the inexperienced," he warned, "but there are honorable people, experienced trainers, willing to introduce subs to an alternative existence."

Her lips parted.

After a slight pause, he held out the slip of paper. "This is a cell phone number."

She stared at the number for several seconds before taking it from him. Suspicion wrinkled her brow. "Whose? Yours?"

He shook his head. "I meant what I said. As your psychiatrist, I doubt I can do more for you in this office, but if you're serious about dealing with your fantasies, then call that number. You need only say that you're ready. The rest will be taken care of."

He escorted her to the door, his hand placed on the small of her back. A warm tingle zinged up his arm.

"How do you know this will work?"

"I don't. That lifestyle is not for everyone. Many have found they were more comfortable with the fantasy than the reality, but you'll never know until you try." He pointed to the paper still in her hand. "Call it *only* if, and when, you're ready."

* * * * *

A month later, Rachel sat in her office, staring at the number on the wrinkled slip of paper. She knew the number by heart, yet had not made the call. Neither had she returned to see her former psychiatrist.

With a brief rap on the door, Pamela poked her curly, red-haired head around the door. "So tell us, is the rumor true?"

Rachel set the paper upside-down on her desk. "Is

what true?"

"That the ice queen is really, finally, taking a vacation."

"Yes."

"Ha! Pay up," she said with a glance over her shoulder at someone behind the door. A few seconds later, Pamela came in with a wide grin. "Whoo-hoo!"

Her enthusiasm made Rachel smile. "That glad to be rid of me for a few weeks?"

"Nope, but I did just win fifty bucks."

"Against whom?"

"Carmichael."

"That figures."

"You have to admit, history was on his side. I mean, you haven't taken a real vacation in... Who knows? At least since I met you as a legal intern." She leaned over the desk to peek at the calendar. "So, where are you going for three long weeks? Got any hot plans? A sexy stud waiting in a closet somewhere?"

Rachel shook her head. "I just had a break between cases and thought I'd relax a little."

Pamela snorted. "You, relax? You'll go crazy within forty-eight hours."

"Such a vote of confidence." She laughed.

Pamela stood.

"Where are you headed to now?"

"I'm going to go catch up with Carmichael. Maybe I can convince him to go for double or nothing."

"Going to bet against me, huh?"

Pamela paused at the door, gave her a considering look, and then said, "You make it three weeks, and I'll split my winnings with you."

"Rigging a bet's illegal."

"Yeah, well, I figure it's worth jail time. It's about time you took a break, don't you think? Now, go get laid." With a wink and a laugh, she dodged a flying wad of paper and retreated.

She could still hear her best friend's chuckles after the door closed.

Picking up the scrap with the phone number on it, Rachel pictured Dr. Sinclair. Seeing a psychiatrist hadn't been her first choice. She'd always plowed over any obstacles in the past and considered herself fully capable of handling anything life threw her way. But when the minor wet dreams turned into full-blown erotic nightmares, she knew she had to do something. What sane woman got turned on by being bound hand and foot and then fucked into submission?

So what if her love life had never really measured up to her expectations? The men she'd slept with hadn't all been that bad. They just seemed to rush toward completion, which often left her seeking climax later with her trusty vibrator.

She laid her head against the back of the high leather chair and closed her eyes.

She liked being in control, whether on the job or at home. Her life was well organized, even if a tad stressful. Okay, very stressful. Dr. Sinclair had been right about that. Sometimes she wished she could toss everything into the air and run. Let someone else pick up the pieces and struggle under the burden for a while. But as soon as the thought crossed her mind, she discarded it as a sign of weakness.

If there was one thing she refused to be, it was weak.

Unfortunately, the dreams no longer hid in the darkness of the night. As the months passed, kinky ideas and risqué images plagued her mind day and night until she wanted to scream her frustration to the world. They left her body on edge and her mind exhausted. So she'd spilled her feelings of guilt, embarrassment, and need to a psychiatrist.

Pamela suggested the good doctor after going to him herself for what she called a temporary anxiety disorder. Rachel had thought of it as on-the-rebound depression. But after seeing the melancholy Pamela transform into the vivacious friend she remembered from their college days, Rachel decided to give the man a chance.

Now he was suggesting she submit her body to some sexual deviant to exorcise unwanted fantasies. Only she didn't understand how replacing the fantasies with a potentially worse reality could possibly help.

What if someone in the legal community got wind of what she did on her one and only vacation?

What if the memories of real sexual encounters disrupted her life more than the imagined ones?

What if she took the risk and discovered a sensual utopia?

She laughed at her own wishful thinking.

You'll never know until you try. His words challenged her as the memory of his chiseled features haunted her.

The doctor might know her fantasies, but there was one aspect she'd kept from him. Before she first met him, the dominant man in her dreams was faceless. A masked man of mystery. But as she shared her thoughts with him, hearing his deep voice encourage her to open up her mind and soul at each consultation, the mysterious Dom morphed into the face of Dr. Sinclair, with his black-as-sin hair and mesmerizing blue eyes.

Could she do what he suggested and go to another man? Let a stranger lead her into an exploration of submission and bondage? Then again, he was the psychiatrist, trained and licensed to give unprejudiced clinical diagnoses. What could a little adventure hurt if that was what the doctor ordered? Maybe the solution was as simple as Pamela's earlier command. It had been a long time since she'd gotten laid.

She picked up her phone and, before she could talk herself out of it, dialed the number.

A commanding baritone answered on the second ring. "Hello?"

"Hi. This is Rachel. I'm ready."

"We'll be in touch. Soon." The line went dead.

She stared at the phone, dumbfounded.

What the hell did he mean by that? And who were *we*? Trepidation and exhilaration raced along her nervous system. How soon was *soon*?

That night she left work later than usual since she had a lot of loose ends to tie up before taking her vacation. Besides, until they—whoever *they* were—got in touch with her, she didn't really have any plans to speak of, so she needn't hurry. She'd pick up a DVD from the video rental store and scarf down a bowl of popcorn if they stood her up.

When she stepped off the elevator into the parking garage, a prickly sensation erupted across the nape of her neck. She glanced at the security camera in the corner and waved, reciting a silent prayer that George was watching from the guard booth.

Cautiously walking to her car, she noticed brake lights come on; they belonged to a midnight blue Suburban parked several spaces away. With no one else in sight she relaxed, knowing there was at least one witness should a mugger leap at her from the darkness.

The Suburban's engine turned over, and the driver backed the vehicle out of the slot. Rachel hurried to her car before the only other human in sight could vanish around the corner. She reached her Jag just as the Suburban halted behind her car.

Thinking the driver meant to ask for directions, she paused and looked up. The last thing she remembered was thinking that the large truck blocked her view of the security camera near the elevator doors.

CHAPTER TWO

Rachel awoke to a pungent smell that made her jerk her head back. Thankfully, the odor of smelling salts soon vanished. Other sensations, however, didn't. Scared beyond any fantasy she'd yet to dream up, she realized she lay on her left side in a loose fetal position, her hands bound tight, although not painfully, behind her back. And everything was pitch-black dark.

Something soft—probably a pillow—propped up her head, but she couldn't be sure since she was blinded by what felt like a snug hood. She pursed her lips, moved her jaw, and blinked her eyes. All to no avail. She couldn't see, and the hood wouldn't give way. The mask covered her face and head completely, although there must be holes for her nose, since she had no trouble breathing. However, her fright did make the normally simple task more difficult.

She tried to move a leg and found her ankles also secured to each other. A wail boiled up her throat as fear clawed her spine. Squirming, she tried to loosen anything.

"Calm down, Rachel. You aren't hurt. That's not our intention."

She froze. She recognized the husky baritone voice,

but that did little to soothe her nerves. He was the same man she'd called, but who was he? Where was she? What did he intend to do with her?

Would she survive the ordeal so that she could kill one prominent psychiatrist she'd been naïve enough to fantasize about and stupid enough to trust?

The man's deep rumble of humor filled the room. What the hell did he find so funny?

"I can almost envision the questions churning in that pretty little head of yours."

Fully awake now, the realization that she was at the mercy of some stranger, who could take her life as easily as stopping up whatever air holes existed in her mask, sent a renewed panic through her system.

"Don't worry, Rachel. All your questions will be answered in time. With time comes understanding, acceptance, and we hope, mutual satisfaction and trust."

A warm hand on her shoulder made her jerk. The man's fingers curled over her shoulder, giving a brief squeeze of...reassurance?

"Feeling a bit jumpy is understandable." The baritone voice came from behind her, making her question the direction of the earlier caress. Were there two men in the room or only the one? The man's tone said her reaction pleased him. Did he enjoy her fear?

The platform she lay on dipped behind her as he moved on what she now recognized as a bed. When a hand settled on her knee, she forced herself to remain perfectly still, even when it slowly moved down her calf.

"Remember, Rachel, you called and claimed to be ready. The method of extraction is one way of confirming a new submissive's readiness."

He considered abduction a test of readiness?

"Panic, helplessness, that's expected, but what about arousal? Lust?" The hand moved back to her knee and slipped beneath her skirt.

She bucked, trying unsuccessfully to dislodge it.

"Our pet still has some defiance left in her." Amusement tinged the observation.

She'd show him defiance. She'd show him the inside of a jail cell if she made it out of here alive. Sure, she called, but she expected to meet face-to-face first, openly discuss a plan, and take it slowly. Not get kidnapped, hogtied, and fondled on the first night. Or second... Exactly how long had she been out? Hours? Days? No, hours, she decided. She didn't feel rested enough to have been out for days.

"Mmm, thigh-high stockings. I'm impressed. The hard-nosed, straight-shooting attorney has a softer, sexier side." His fingers started to force one of the nylons down. When she pressed her knees together, his chuckle was a warm bass rumble. "And a stubborn side, too, I see." He used two hands to accomplish his mission. The nylons bunched around her ankles.

The bed shook a bit as he moved around behind her. His fingers traveled up the outside of her right thigh, pushing her skirt higher. She squirmed so much that he grabbed her around the waist and pulled her back to his front. The position pinned her bound fists against his denim-clad crotch. She could feel his heat and hardness. Maybe she could...?

"Don't even think about it," he warned as if he'd read her mind, or more likely guessed her intention when her fingers flexed. His left arm wrapped around her neck and made his point very clear.

She swallowed. Would he kill her if she pushed him too far?

He didn't choke her or even attempt to. He just held her in place while his right hand splayed across her abdomen, spreading warmth and a tingle she didn't dare acknowledge. His lips brushed her ear as he whispered, "You want this, don't you? That's why you called. Yet, your mind struggles against the one thing your body craves. Do you feel it, Rachel?"

She felt something all right, something she didn't want to feel, and hated herself for it.

Without sight, her hearing grew more acute, more attuned to the stranger's voice, tone and breathing. Every touch had more impact on her skin even through the barrier of clothing she still wore. Adrenaline pumped through her veins as fear waged war against arousal.

"Do you see how your body responds when touched in all the right places?" He pressed a kiss to the sensitive spot on the side of her neck, and she wondered how he knew.

A finger circled her nipple and, despite the thin silk of her blouse and bra, it pebbled in response to the attention. Then a hand cupped and kneaded her breast until, against her better judgment, she arched her back, forcing her breast farther into his firm grasp.

"That desire deep within longs for you to surrender, to feel the pleasure that's only possible under the capable hands of a master...or two."

There *were* two men! Her mind caught up to what her

body already knew. The one spooned behind her couldn't possibly be the one fondling her breast, not unless he had more than two hands. That thought sent shocking tremors reverberating through her body.

She should not be reacting this way, her mind screamed.

Fight! was her first thought. *Both of them, while trussed up like a Thanksgiving turkey?* was her second.

The arm remained around her neck. The hand on her breast pinched her nipple while another lifted her skirt and discovered her long-kept secret.

"No panties, Miss Prosecuting Attorney? You surprise me."

She moaned, unsure whether it was from mortification or arousal. She chose the latter when his finger found her clit.

"What would the judge say about such naughty behavior in his courtroom?" He pressed a finger inside her. "Does your pussy throb every time he slams the gavel down?"

Two hands caressed her breasts, unbuttoned her blouse, and unfastened her bra.

His voice dropped to a sensual purr. "Does the thought of getting caught make you all moist and horny?" Another flick. A second finger. In and out, around and around, pushing her higher, closer to the edge.

The alluring baritone whispers continued. "Are you brave enough to experience the adventure, Rachel? Are you strong enough to submit?"

She didn't know if she'd survive the ordeal, but the two men were certainly starting to sway her opinion.

"You're so wet. Such a responsive little pussy. I wonder...do you want to climax now?"

Yes! She shoved her hips toward his hand. *Please*, she thought as the pressure built. It had been so long since she'd peaked without having to do it herself, and she was so close. This was so much better. But then he pulled away. The other's hands vanished as well, which left her wanting and confused.

"Not yet, my pet, but soon." He rolled off the bed.

She realized how quickly he'd played her. Like the master he professed to be, he'd coaxed her with words and, together, the two men had teased her body while remaining in complete control. Anger simmered until she noticed they were releasing her ankles.

They removed her stockings. She had no clue where her shoes were.

"Your response has earned you a boon."

One of them disconnected the cuff on a wrist and gently repositioned her arms above her head. She groaned as a dull ache tore through muscles that had grown stiff from confinement in one position for so long. A pair of hands spread her legs then massaged her calves and feet. Another pair proceeded to massage away the aches in her arms and shoulders.

Now on her back, she experimented with a tug on her arms only to find them re-secured to something, most likely a headboard. Her blouse hung open, her skirt remained hiked up above her hips, but none of that mattered as long as they continued to knead away the soreness from her tired body.

Her second captor had yet to say a word, which made

him even more mysterious than Mr. Baritone. What did he look like? Could he talk? Did they use alternative methods of communication? she wondered, since their movements often complimented each other's.

Her body was a limp noodle when Mr. Baritone stopped with a chuckle. "Feeling better?"

"Mmm," was her only response.

"You've just had your first lesson, my pet. Please us, and reap the benefits."

That was fine by her.

His voice dropped. "Disobey, and face the consequences."

Uh oh.

"With obedience comes pleasure. With trust comes added liberty."

The bed dipped as the men repositioned themselves on either side of her.

"You professed to be ready to experience the submissive lifestyle. You've now had a brief taste of it, but there's more to learn. More my brother and I can teach you if you are bold enough to submit both body and mind into our care."

She squirmed a bit, having trouble keeping her head aloft, and turned in the direction of his voice. The silent one placed another pillow beneath her head and back.

"Thank you," she mumbled, though the mask distorted and muffled her voice. His hand squeezed her hip in reply then settled on her abdomen, a warm reminder of his presence.

"Our rules are simple. We expect complete and immediate obedience, but we also understand that it takes time to develop trust between a sub and her masters." A finger drew a hypnotizing pattern of loops on her thigh as he spoke. "As Doms, we are here to command and train you, protect you, and provide for you. We can introduce you to your limits and help you reach beyond them, if you wish. We do not seek an unwilling slave, but a consensual relationship, which you have the power to end at any time. I will give you a safe word should either of us push you beyond what you are capable of enduring. Your safe word will be...*fantasy*."

She could hear the smile in his voice, and wondered how much Dr. Sinclair had told them.

"If you use it, whatever is happening ends right then." The hypnotic circling finger froze. "The adventure stops. We will release you immediately, return your clothing, and take you home. You'll never hear from us again. Nod if you understand everything I've explained."

After a brief pause, she did. They rolled away and got up.

"My brother will remove the restraints around your wrists, but the mask remains for now." After she was free, they helped her up. "As you stand before us unbound, we must know. Do you wish to continue?"

The silence in the room was deafening as she pondered the answer to that loaded question. If she said yes, what would they do to her? If she said no, what would she miss out on? Did she trust them to keep their word and let her go if things got to be too much for her to bear?

"Your choice, Rachel."

His words, and willingness to let her make the choice, helped her decide. Hoping she wouldn't regret her decision, she nodded. A sense of relief flooded the room.

"Very well, my pet." A new pride or joy infiltrated the man's voice, and she knew he was smiling. "From this moment forward, you'll call me Master and my brother Sire. You must use these titles whenever addressing us once the mask is removed and you are able to speak unimpeded."

Okay, that was a little high-handed, but what had she expected them to do? Announce their real names as if meeting for the first time on a blind date?

"Kneel."

Why did that have to be his first command? She gripped one man's hand as she obeyed.

"Spread your knees apart. Wider."

She had to slide up her skirt to comply.

"A little more. Yes, like that. Now place each hand palm-up on a thigh and bow your head... Good. When ordered to kneel, or whenever you are in a room we occupy, you'll take up this position at our feet. Understood?"

She nodded, wondering why the thought of such an act sent a thrill through her system. Her mind argued that she should be appalled, but the rest of her body refused to listen.

"The position with bowed head is one of respect," he explained. "The spread thighs are to show your acceptance of your body, a display without shame. The open hands represent your willingness to accept change, to comply with our wishes instead of your own."

A lot of symbolism for something she'd always viewed as groveling.

"Now, rise and remove your clothing."

Her head snapped toward his voice despite her

blindness. Had she heard him correctly?

"Get up, pet. Take off your clothes. Do not make me repeat myself a third time."

She rose to her feet on shaky legs, took a step back, and collided with the bed. A hand gripped her upper arm until she was again steady. A lump lodged in her throat, which she forced down, her swallow audible and revealing.

"Do you wish to use your safe word already?"

Did she? They'd seen and touched most of her body anyway, and brought her so close to a climax in the process. Didn't he mention something about accepting her body?

They'd have to call it quits. Not her. If viewing her in her birthday suit sent them packing, then so be it. She could return home to plan her revenge on one Dr. Sinclair.

She shook her head and pulled her blouse free of her skirt, which had fallen back into place when she stood. The blouse dropped to the floor. Next came the bra. She wished she could see their faces. Then again, maybe being blind was better. The skirt's zipper had the effect of nails on a chalkboard. Her nerves ripped apart her intentions.

When she stopped, the silent brother...Sire...moved behind her, while Master murmured a soft, "Keep going." Sire's hands touched her waist and slid south, pushing the skirt until it fell at her feet. His palms, hot on her cool skin, stayed on her hips, holding her in place. Even blinded, she could feel their gazes explore her body.

"Beautiful." Master's whispered praise did a lot to settle her nerves until another natural urge made its presence known.

For once, she was grateful of the mask that hid her blush as she muttered, "Bathroom," and rocked onto her toes. She hoped they'd get the message soon, and they did. Sire's reaction was swift. He lifted her off her feet and carried her into another room. When she felt cool tile instead of plush carpet beneath her feet, she knew she was close. Her hands swept out to seek the toilet, but she needn't have bothered. Sire put both hands on her shoulders and pressed down, forcing her to sit and give off a muffled yelp.

Unfortunately, at that moment, her body decided that performing for an audience wasn't part of the program. She fisted her hands on her thighs. The urge to urinate evaporated.

Then Sire turned on the faucet. The sound of trickling water was more than her body could stand. The pressure inside popped. Her face flamed with embarrassment as she peed. Couldn't the man give her some privacy?

Maybe he did. She couldn't see whether he faced her or turned his back. Uncertain, she chose to believe the latter to save a small portion of her pride, but then even that was snatched from her grasp. Her hands searched for the toilet paper only to collide with an arm. She heard him tug several sheets free of the roll, and before she knew of his plan, he'd already reached between her legs and completed the necessary task.

She didn't bother to hide her mortified groan. Her pride sank with the sound of the flushing toilet.

She wasn't an invalid. If they'd remove the mask, they'd see that. Determined to show them herself, she reached for the mask and discovered laces and a buckle on the back. Before she could loosen either, Sire's hands grabbed her wrists and forced them away from her body.

Still sitting on the toilet, she stamped her foot in

protest and tried to kick her captor.

"Ever the self-reliant one, aren't you, my pet?" Master's voice came from her right. He seemed amused by her show of defiance, but there was an underlying edge of authority in the question. "Do you think we are remotely attracted to urine? I can assure you we're not. There's nothing appealing about it."

Which was why I prefer to do it without an audience, she wanted to shout.

"However, peeing is a very natural bodily function. There's no need to act prudish about it."

How dare he! A prude? She was not the one who was wrong here. What was so asinine about demanding a little privacy? She tried to yank her hands free, but Sire's grip held firm.

"My brother provided everything you needed just now, as is a master's duty to his sub. How do you respond? Instead of feeling grateful for his care-giving, you repay him with a deliberate act of disobedience."

She shot to her feet to give them a piece of her mind, but all thought was suspended when Sire again scooped her up and carried her back to the bed. Surprised by the move, she didn't even squirm until she found herself facedown across his lap.

With a quick grasp of the situation, she struggled in earnest, but was no match for their combined strength. Master sat beside his brother, pulled her halfway onto his lap, and held her hands over her head. Sire pinned her hips in place with an arm across her back and left her legs to kick uselessly.

"We told you there'd be consequences for

disobedience," Master said.

Swat. Sire's hand came down on one butt cheek.

That hurt! She grunted in fury, bucked, twisted or at least tried to, but escape proved impossible.

Swat. The sting of punishment spread heat across her ass as the hand came down again and again. By the fifth blow, she was flailing like a trout out of water. By the sixth, she was kicking like a rodeo bull, and by the seventh time, she was whimpering in wanton frustration.

The spanking stopped.

"Will you attempt to remove the mask again?"

She'd die in the damn thing if that's what they wanted. She shook her head viciously.

"That-a-girl."

They rolled her over and turned their laps from a platform of punishment into a cradle for her body. Uncertainty made her spine tense.

"Relax, pet. It's over," Master whispered as he hugged her closer to him, his arms banding her in warm comfort.

Large hands that once restrained and punished now caressed and cajoled. They massaged her limbs into a subdued state of relaxation. The tension of her prior struggle slowly seeped away.

While one strong arm supported her back, Master's other hand cupped her breast and thumbed the peak to pebbled hardness. Soon, his mouth joined his hand, causing her to throw back her head. Sire ran his palm up her thigh, slipping his hand between her legs to tease her clit and very damp pussy. Soon, a slow burn joined the sting as her body awoke in their arms.

With steady, reassuring strokes, they picked away at the iceberg that other men seldom scaled. She marveled at the response they drew from her. The pair worked with a synchronicity that enthralled her. Sire flicking and plumbing her pussy with his fingers. Master sucking and teasing her nipples with his mouth.

"Pain and pleasure." Teeth nipped her breast as thumb and finger plucked and pinched her clit. "Both come from your masters. Both are yours to experience and enjoy." The acute pain added to the carnal sensations.

Seeking more, her back arched, her hips lifted, and a moan rumbled from her throat.

"That's it, pet. Almost there."

Their cocks were hard beneath her, but they ignored the desire of their own bodies while they pleasured hers.

"Come for us, pet." At Master's command, Sire's fingers pierced her pussy in a hard thrust that sent tremors throughout her body.

The mask muffled but couldn't silence her cry of fulfillment as the powerful orgasm ricocheted like a whiplash through her system. Her chest heaved with effort to take in more oxygen.

Fingers moved inside her, drawing out the climax until she thought she'd pass out. Lips continued to suckle with less and less intensity until they finally stopped.

"Good girl."

Her body collapsed across the men in sated relief as post-climax lethargy swept her into the first peaceful sleep she'd had in months.

* * * * *

Owning Rachel

Rachel awoke to find herself lying on her back in the center of a human pretzel. The weight of arms and legs crisscrossed over her body, making it impossible to rise. After much work, however, she was able to extract one of her own arms. Her hand went to her face where it contacted the leather mask. Feeling her way, she discovered two holes rimmed by metal located just below the tip of her nose. No other openings existed. It covered her head completely and followed the curve beneath her chin, as if it had been custom designed to fit her face.

Temporarily blinded, she had no sense of day or night but assumed it was early morning.

"Still trying to remove the mask, my curious pet?" Master's voice was husky with sleep.

She snatched her hand away and shook her head. He chuckled and adjusted his body along her left side into a more comfortable position. His movements brought a sleepy protest adorably muttered from the man on her right, the first sound she'd heard Sire make.

Beneath the mask, she smiled.

A gentle touch traced her lips through the supple leather. "In a few moments, I'll replace your current mask with one more to my liking. I want to see your lips, allow you to answer my questions with more than a nod or shake of the head."

She met the news with mixed emotions. She was excited with the idea of being able to speak freely again, something that the current mask made difficult if not impossible to do. But she'd hoped they would remove her mask and reveal their identities today. After all they were demanding of her trust, they weren't returning the favor. She longed to balance the scales, but then a part of her enjoyed the challenge and thrills the mystery offered.

"Come on. It's time to get up and shower." Master rose and lifted her to her feet. Taking her hand, he guided her from the carpet back to the tile. Unable to see where she was and unsure of what he expected her to do about it, she stood still and listened as he moved around her in the bathroom. A moment later, she heard water running in the shower.

He grasped her shoulders and turned her to face away from him. "Close your eyes. Do not open them, or you'll face consequences much harsher than yesterday's."

Party-pooper. She squeezed her eyes shut and nodded her understanding.

He unbuckled the strap and loosened the laces. The mask pulled away, and temptation to peek flooded her mind.

She sighed, but heeded his warning and kept her eyes closed. Next, she felt him place what seemed like a pair of goggles over her eyes, with loops that hooked over her ears. Curious, she reached to confirm her suspicions and opened her eyes. She saw nothing. The lenses were black as pitch.

"These are only temporary while you're in the shower. Afterwards, we'll exchange them for something else."

She frowned but kept silent. He turned her again then placed a thin stick in one hand. She heard him turn on the tap in front of her, and awaited instruction.

"Go ahead. There's toothpaste already on the bristles. I hope you like mint-flavored gel." The vigorous swishing of a second toothbrush told her he, too, wanted to remove all traces of morning breath.

Finding the situation somehow amusing, she brushed her teeth, and tongue for good measure, then leaned forward and spit, hoping she hit her target. He placed a paper cup in her hand for her to rinse out her mouth, which she did.

A click signaled the opening of a shower door. He moved her toward the origin of the sound. "In you go. Watch your step."

Easier said than done with goggles for blinders. At least the water was warm. She leaned her head back under the water and smiled. She held out her hand, expecting him to give her shampoo and soap as he'd done with the toothbrush, but he stepped in behind her.

"Hold still."

She heard him squirt something before he began working the substance into her hair. She loved a good head massage. Her eyes closed, and her lips parted on a sigh.

The door opened again and shut with a telltale click.

"You're late," Master said.

Sire snorted as he moved in front of her. She couldn't help her giggle.

"Our pet's in good spirits this morning."

"Why do you call me that?" she asked, mildly shocked by the sound of her own voice.

Master chuckled from behind her. "And still as curious as ever."

Sire's hands distracted her as he soaped up the front of her body and paid close attention to her breasts. For several minutes she luxuriated in their care, which took on an erotic allure as she blindly concentrated on the feel of four large, male hands sliding over damp skin. They scrubbed her body until she imagined her skin rosy-pink. Fingers cleansed and teased her from head to toe, inside her pussy, and all around her ass cheeks. She was so close to a climax she could almost taste it, and her condition didn't go unnoticed.

"Ready to climax, pet?"

"Yes," was all she could manage.

Abruptly the hands vanished. *So not fair!*

"Lean back. Let me rinse out your hair."

She did as instructed and felt the suds wash away along with some of her excitement.

Belatedly, she noticed he hadn't answered her earlier question. "Why do you call me 'pet'?"

"That's what you are to me. I prefer to own a pet instead of a slave."

In her book, pets were animals and slaves were human. But in his book, some other distinction must apply. "What's the difference?"

"Do not forget your place, pet. You must refer to us by title."

"Sorry," she said, then repeated, "What's the difference, Master?"

Master chuckled. Sire tweaked her nipple playfully.

"For some, not much. Both are submissive by nature. There are Doms and subs that enjoy role-playing as masters and slaves on a part-time basis. That's fine, but it's like fantasies. Unreal. For my brother and me, unsatisfying. A true slave is someone who gives herself over to enforced captivity 24/7. We know of several sold from one owner to another and another."

"That's illegal!"

"Not in the way you think. Slaves voluntarily enter the BDSM world when, like you, they respond to their curiosity and seek out instruction. Their trainers identify those who prefer the ultimate dominance of uncontrolled ownership."

"So they aren't really forced?"

"Not in the manner you envision. Consent and trust is vital in BDSM. If either is missing, then it's not true BDSM. Still, force is part of the allure. Slaves need it, and it's their masters' responsibility to provide it. Obedience isn't offered. It's enforced. A slave may have a safe word. Most do, but few ever use them as they're auctioned off to the highest bidder. Lengthy confinement is not uncommon, and a slave is required to not only meet her master's sexual needs but also labor in his house."

"Oh." A shiver coursed through her body.

"On the other hand, pets are like the domesticated animals often associated with the term. They submit to their masters' ownership willingly. Completely trust in their masters' ability to care for them. They aren't auctioned off like slaves can be, and they aren't forced to labor for their owners. Instead, they provide comfort and companionship in their own way."

His fingers combed through her wet hair as he spoke.

"Discipline is required, of course. Pets must be trained so they know and can adhere to their masters' wishes. The responsibility of ownership is stronger, more demanding for that of a pet than a slave, and the rewards far greater. Pets offer loyalty and obedience without regard to their own needs, yet they retain control."

"How so?" she asked, uncertain whether she believed the owned could have any control over the owner. "I mean, how so, Master?"

"Because they make the initial choice of who owns them. Just like a dog can run away from its owner. A pet can end the relationship at any time. Control is theirs to give, which makes it the ultimate gift for a master to honor."

Put that way, she was glad he considered her a pet rather than a slave. She liked knowing she wouldn't wind up the victim of some twisted form of slave trade, and he said she could end the relationship or his ownership anytime she wanted.

"Thank you, Master."

He squeezed her hand and started to turn off the water.

"Wait...please."

Surprisingly, they obeyed her request. She pictured single eyebrows raised in curiosity as they awaited her next move. The water continued to beat down upon them.

She turned about, seeking the soap until one of the men guessed her intentions and handed it to her. She worked it between her hands until a good lather formed, then held it out so he could take it from her again. Tentatively, she reached out again until her hands collided with firm flesh. Curiosity swamped her, and she reveled in being able to see them with her hands.

"Master?"

"Yes." The word hissed out from the man she touched and made her smile.

Her fingers slid over his firm chest, following the

curves of broad shoulders and muscular arms. Down and up, they returned to circle tiny, hard male nipples. She took her time, rubbing and wandering over his plains. Moving lower, she traced the shallow hills and valleys of six-pack abs.

A plop sounded as the soap hit the shower floor.

CHAPTER THREE

Her fingertips brushed lightly across the hair above his cock. She heard him suck in a harsh breath and wondered if she'd find his cock as hard as his abs. Leaning forward, she pressed her wet body to his and reached around to rub down as much of his back and buttocks as she could reach.

Yep. His cock was rock-hard and ready. It rose proud and hot between them. His butt cheeks tightened under her hands.

"Rachel," he growled. A warning or a plea, she didn't know.

Savoring the thought of revenge, she left him hard and wanting as she turned toward Sire and reached out to repeat the torture. She could feel the rise and fall of his chest, the rapid pulse of his pounding heartbeat.

The men moved to stand side by side so, when she again stopped just above Sire's cock, instead of hugging him, she felt two hands—one from each man—grip her shoulders. They pushed down, their message clear.

Kneeling, she found the soap on the shower floor, so she lathered up again then placed one palm on each man's thigh. Feeling a bit mischievous, and loving the idea of having two men under her control, she avoided their cocks. She rubbed up and down each leg, hoping to draw out the anticipation. A couple times, the back of her hands brushed their sacs as she scrubbed the insides of their legs. Fingers dug into her shoulders.

Finally, she cupped their balls then wrapped her fingers around each man's cock.

Master grabbed her head with both hands and guided her toward his cock. "Suck it."

Sire's fingers banded her wrist, holding her hand in place around him.

That quick, they'd regained command.

The soft tip of Master's cock touched her lips, and she opened to let him in. Her tongue barely circled the head when he pressed deep to fill her mouth. He reached the back of her throat, triggering her gag reflex. She tried to push away with one hand—Sire refused to release her other one— but Master pulled back himself. Then he bucked forward again in a shallow thrust she could handle.

Sire wrapped his fingers over hers and slid her hand from root to tip. After two pumps, he released her to continue the rhythm as instructed. Finding it hard to concentrate, she matched the movement of her hand to Master's cock as he slowly fucked her mouth.

"That's it, pet. Ah, yes. Suck harder."

Thin streams of water struck her back, butt, and legs like tiny whips as she knelt before the men. Master's fingers wound through her wet hair, holding her head in place for his thrusts. Sire's hips jerked forward in direct opposition to her movements, his body forcefully colliding with the side of her hand. She tightened her grip and heard him hiss.

She'd intended to tease them and leave them wanting as they'd left her, but moisture unrelated to the shower's spray collected between her legs. She wanted to please them, to know that she could bring two powerful men to an orgasmic precipice. She increased her suction on Master's pumping cock.

He jerked once, the tip lodged in the back of her throat, his fingers biting into her scalp. He groaned as salty cum pulsed into her mouth. She was so focused on swallowing every drop, her hand stopped moving and flexed around Sire's hard length. He yanked her hand away.

Master pulled out of her mouth and turned her head, just as Sire pushed passed her open lips. She latched onto him without thought and sucked hard. His hands replaced Master's as he climaxed after just two hard strokes. Salty seed shot down her throat, and she swallowed it greedily. He moved in and out a few more times before he slid free, releasing her to sit back on her heels.

For a moment, she sat exhausted and panting. Her mind reeled at what she'd just done. Heavy male breathing registered on her senses, and she grinned. She'd done it! Excitement renewed her energy.

Without a word, they helped her stand, led her out of the shower and toweled her dry. They rubbed lotion over her skin. The scent reminded her of honey and cocoa butter. Then they combed and dried her hair.

All this pampering could spoil her, she thought giddily.

"Close your eyes."

Crap. Here we go again.

The exchange didn't take as long the second time, and her replacement was more blindfold than facemask.

Master lifted her chin, murmured, "Very good, pet," and then kissed her soundly on her exposed mouth.

She enjoyed the feel of flexing muscle beneath smooth skin, and since he didn't complain, she let her hands roam. His hair was soft and his body firm. She had no idea what his face looked like, except that he was clean-shaven. He tasted of mint. Fresh and clean.

And oh, what a talented tongue he had. Her hands curled around his neck to prevent escape but he tore his mouth from hers. She gulped in much needed air as her equilibrium twirled out of control. Master spun her around and lips again devoured her mouth, only this time they belonged to his brother.

Sire pulled her against his chest, and she couldn't help letting her fingers explore the soft curls of hair that lightly covered the hard plains. Like his brother, he stood a head taller than she did, had broad shoulders, and sported no facial hair.

His hands were possessive, his tongue demanding, but the hardness of his cock against her body held her attention.

If these two kept this up, she'd be a horny, groveling mess.

Moisture gathered between her thighs in preparation for what she hoped would be the climactic sequel to Sire's rapacious kiss.

Instead he released her mouth and held her at arms length. His abrupt stop bothered her. Only his heavy breathing and the memory of his hard cock testified to his approval of her kiss.

Denied the warmth of their bodies, she rubbed her arms as goose bumps erupted across her skin. Her legs were unsteady. Her lungs strained to fulfill the need for air.

"Come with me, pet," Master said, having obviously composed himself. His hand curled around the back of her neck. He walked her back to the room with plush carpet and a bed. Despite his guidance, she faltered, her hands stretched out in front of her.

"We must work on your trust skills."

Could she help it if she didn't like walking around in the dark?

"Kneel and wait here."

As she obeyed, she wondered what he planned to do next. She didn't have to wait long for the answer. Judging from the sounds, they were getting dressed without her.

"Excuse me, but when can I get dressed?"

"When you learn your place. How were you told to address us?"

Recalling all too well her previous punishment for disobedience, she decided now was not the time to take a stand. "Sorry, Master."

Didn't a girl deserve a little leniency after what she'd just done for them? Instead they got her all aroused again with suggestive kisses then left her kneeling unsatisfied on the floor while they got dressed. This hot and cold rollercoaster ride was driving her crazy. They definitely wanted her—their rock-solid erections told her that—and hadn't she already given them the green light by "submitting" to this wild adventure? What were they waiting for? *Here I am, one hot and horny woman in need!*

"Now that you're capable of unhampered speech, your training begins in earnest."

What? Like roll over, speak, and play dead? No, better not think along that line.

"What do you mean?"

"What do you mean...what?"

She pursed her lips. "What do you mean, Master?"

"I believe you just answered your own question. Obedience training, if you'd like a name for it."

Since that made her feel too much like a dog, she decided to make up her own name for it, like Submissive Instructions, Compliance Course, Appease-the-Master Apprenticeship. That thought caused a giggle.

"I'm glad you find it amusing. I doubt you'll find it easy."

Was that a threat?

The silent one knelt in front of her. His fingers brushed her cheek in a soft caress. How did he look when he touched her like that? She feared she'd never find out.

"When do I get to remove this blindfold, Sire?"

Silence...

"Master?"

"When you've earned it."

"How?"

"Trust us, and you'll see."

Could the man be anymore cryptic?

Sire took her hand and placed something in it. Leather. A buckle and a metal ring. It felt a lot like a dog collar.

"Oh, no. No, and double no." This was too much. She'd never fantasized about being treated like a dog.

As if he hadn't heard a word she said, Master said, "Unlike many slaves who are forced to wear leg, wrist, and neck shackles, a pet requires only one proof of ownership. Of course, they must don the collar willingly. That is a training collar. Do you agree to wear our collar, Rachel, while within the walls of this home or in any place we deem appropriate until such time as our ownership ends?"

Her mouth opened but no words came out, so she shook her head instead.

"Do you give up?" He dropped the question like a challenge. "To quit, you must speak your safe word."

Give up? Quit? She'd never backed down from anything in her life. But a dog collar? How humiliating was that?

"The collar or the safe word, Rachel. It's your choice. We will abide by whatever decision you make."

Sire's fingers cradled her face, his thumb lightly moving across her cheek. Did he understand how hard this was for her? She hoped so.

Whatever the case, she wouldn't quit. *Couldn't* quit. Although their method of introduction left a lot to be desired, they seemed to sincerely care and hadn't harmed her. The spanking was only a mild, albeit humbling, annoyance better left in the past. And better still, she'd slept soundly for the first time in ages after spending one evening with these two. She'd see this thing through to its conclusion.

Taking a fortifying breath, she put the collar around her neck and murmured, "Thanks," when Sire helped fasten it in place. Afterwards, he surprised her with a chaste kiss on the lips. It affected her more than the voracious one he'd bestowed on her after their shower.

"I'm hungry," Master said in typical male fashion. "Let's eat."

A suspicious click sounded before each man grabbed a hand and pulled her to her feet. When they released her, she reached for her neck and found confirmation of what she feared. They'd attached a leash to the collar.

Sire's kiss had made her feel special. The leash irritated her. This was not the stuff of her fantasies. Well, the kiss was, but the leash was not. Hadn't Dr. Sinclair told them what she expected? Bound? Yes. Fucked senseless? *Absolutely*. But treated like an animal? Degraded, as if she were less than human?

Tears burned her eyes, but she squeezed her lids tight and bowed her head. A tug got her feet moving. She shuffled from the room, her hands hanging limp at her sides. If she fell or ran into something, it would be their own damn fault. In silence, she followed the pull of the leash until a hand at her navel stopped her.

"You're on the first step to a staircase that curves around to the left. There's a railing, but you won't need it." The men stood one on either side. Each took one of her hands and tucked it in his arm, then escorted her down the stairs as if formally presenting her to a royal court. At the bottom, they let her go, and the illusion disintegrated with another tug on the leash. She trailed behind the sway and pull of the leash until prompted to stop again.

"Kneel, my pet. I'll return shortly."

As she knelt on a pillow apparently placed there for her convenience, she heard his footsteps move away, then silence. He was gone so long she was tempted to take a peek, but she hadn't heard Sire leave and feared a trap. She would not disobey a direct order, but no one had said anything about keeping silent.

"Sire?" she whispered, then added, "Why won't you talk to me?"

No response.

Was he there?

The leash remained attached to her collar and hung away from her body. She gave in to curiosity and followed the braided cord to discover the other end looped over the back post of an unoccupied ladder-back chair.

"Sire, are you there?"

Silence, except for faint noises of food preparation in another room.

With a sigh, she scooted off her knees, sat on the floor closer to the chair, and propped her head up with an elbow on the seat.

"Tsk, tsk, tsk." The sound of Sire's disappointment came from directly behind her and made her snap straight.

At least she hadn't peeked, she thought sourly.

"Sorry that took so long," Master said, coming back into the room. The aroma of eggs and hot, buttery biscuits accompanied his return and mingled with other enticing fragrances she was unable to distinguish.

"Are you allergic to any foods we should know about?"

Impressed that he would think to ask such a question, she answered, "No, but thanks for asking...Master."

Remembering her earlier question, this time she posed it to the more vocal brother. "Why won't Sire speak to me, Master?" She didn't consider a tisking sound verbal conversation.

"He's a man of few words."

"Tell me about it," she mumbled.

"Watch your tone, pet." Master's warning came out more amused than angered. "I imagine he'll speak to you when the time is right."

He sat in the chair to her left, the wood scraping the floor as he scooted it toward the table. The sound echoed to her right as the silent Sire took the seat attached to her leash, and left her on her knees between them.

Something's definitely wrong with this picture.

"As our pet in this house, you'll eat only what you obtain from our hands. Understood?"

Let her recline on a chaise lounge while he fed her one grape at a time, and he had a deal. But kneeling like a dog begging for scraps from its master's table?

"Understood?"

No, but she nodded just the same then waited, her lips parted slightly.

"Good. Don't move."

Their knives and forks clinked as the men ate breakfast and ignored her.

She huffed out a frustrated breath but otherwise kept quiet. She recited the alphabet in her head, then the Preamble to the U.S. Constitution. She counted to one hundred then reversed back to zero, and allowed her anger to boil. The smell of a fresh, home-cooked meal made her stomach feel hollow. Could they not see she was starving? Her feet had fallen asleep, her knees hurt despite the pillow, and her nose itched. She flexed her hands, wrinkled her nose, and squirmed.

Finally, Master's chair moved. After several intolerable minutes that seemed like hours, one of her *owners* decided he knew of her existence after all. His hand brushed her neck when he tucked a finger into her collar's D ring and pulled her between his knees. She scooted forward on the pillow, still sitting on her heels. The arc of the leash hung higher against her arm.

"Are you thirsty, pet?"

"Yes...Master." She remembered to include his title and failed miserably in hiding her pique.

"I see."

A zipper sounded, his hand pressed on the back of her head, and his cock forced open her lips. Shocked, she hung suspended, her gaping mouth filled with thick male flesh. Her hands sought purchase on the floor, chair, and finally his legs. She prepared herself to claw her way free if necessary, but he just sat there.

"Tell me, Rachel, what is the first rule every submissive must learn?"

He wanted to test her now?

"We've given you plenty of time this morning to think about it...." He pulled her back an inch or two and pushed home again. "Unless you were too busy worrying over your own needs."

Her needs had changed drastically in the past few seconds. Against her will, her body responded. Her parched mouth watered. Her tongue twirled around his erect length as if it were a treasured lollipop.

His cock withdrew, the soft tip still a temptation on her bottom lip. "Answer me."

"Uh...obey?"

"Not exactly." He pushed inside again. Two, three, four times then out for another pause. She got the picture.

"Okay...second guess... Suck cock whenever ordered?"

"Minx," he said with a chuckle. "Try again."

"I think I need a hint, Master." She licked a dollop of pre-cum from her lips and smiled until he pressed her mouth into service once more.

"You have all the hints you deserve, pet," he said, a bit breathlessly.

She sucked hard to keep him in, but he pulled free with a pop.

"Tell me," he ordered.

"Seek to fulfill her master's pleasure without regard to her own needs."

"Good answer. Now drink your fill."

He pushed on her head, but she needed no encouragement. Her hunger, sore knees, and itchy nose forgotten, she focused on her "drink". She licked and nipped and sucked with the hope of driving him wild.

Suddenly hands seized her hips and forced them higher. Sire shoved her knees apart and knelt behind her. His fingers roamed at will across her flesh.

She tried to stop, slow down, and take in what was happening around her, but Master retained dominion. With a firm grip, he controlled the tempo as he pushed her down on him repeatedly. She opened her mouth wider to take as much of him as she could.

The loose collar spun around her neck as Sire pulled the leash taut. The abrupt tug on her neck was a titillating trigger, an unexpected aphrodisiac that offered a new, unique stimulation.

The forceful urgency of their movements propelled her excitement. She'd dreamed of this, fantasized of having two men want her so badly that they lost control and weren't afraid to show it. They had to have her as much as she needed the rush of desire.

Sire ran another hand up her spine. He reached around her side and pinched a nipple, which forced a moan from her throat that vibrated around his brother's cock.

"Yes, pet. Yes," Master hissed and the pace increased. "Fuck her."

A zipper ripped open. Fingers flicked her clit, stroked her pussy lips, and jabbed inside.

Anticipating the pressure of a large cock, she sucked harder on the one in her mouth. Her short nails dug into Master's clothed thighs.

He groaned. "Ah, fuck, yes. Fuck her now!"

Sire's long, hard cock slammed into her, pushing Master's dick farther into her mouth. Their hands clamped her head and hips as Sire pelted her pussy repeatedly.

Her head spun, her gut clenched, and orgasmic pleasure rocketed through her body until every muscle trembled uncontrollably. Still, they pounded in and out of her mouth and pussy like storm-tossed waves on a battered beach. The tension built inside her womb, a rising tide that burst forth like a blow hole onshore. With one last, fierce thrust, Sire reached new depths in her body. He filled her with seed as the moist, salty flavor of Master's cum shot into her mouth.

When they let go, she collapsed to the floor, her ass in the air as if she bowed before an ancient ruler. Sticky liquid trickled down her thighs. A drop of cum remained on her chin. She didn't care. She'd just had the best orgasm of her life and wanted to enjoy the moment a bit longer. So there she remained, panting in a sated lump, as the men cleaned themselves and righted their clothing, their ragged breaths pleasing to her ears.

The chairs grated when they resumed their seats. A tug on the leash forced her head up, although she still couldn't see a damn thing.

"Sit up, pet, while we finish our breakfast."

Still tingling from a superb climax, she found the pillow, knelt, and placed her hands on her thighs, palms up. *What the hell.* She'd sit for hours while they ate as long as they promised to fuck her into submission like that again.

She heard one pour something. A second later, the rim of a glass touched her lips, and she smelled the citric fragrance of orange juice.

"Drink."

"I thought I already did," she teased, but drank the cool liquid as he tilted the glass and chuckled.

The men proceeded to take turns feeding her bites of eggs, a strip of bacon, and a biscuit with grape jam...A pill?

"It's your birth control medication," Master said, placing the tiny pill on her tongue. "The refilled prescription was in your car. Very helpful of you, by the way, or at least convenient timing. It saved us a trip to your place."

After the meal, they used a moist napkin to wipe away any crumbs from her lips and the dried cum off her chin. Then they cleaned her thighs and pussy.

"Stay here," Master said. The clink of china and silverware told her he was collecting the dishes before the sound of footsteps announced his departure from the room. She heard him in what she guessed was the kitchen, which made her wonder what their house looked like. She knew it was two stories at least, and the staircase seemed rather grand. Did they live together in this house or spend time here only when they had a sub to train?

She frowned. How many subs had they trained? Did they own another pet? The bitter taste of jealousy surprised her. Why should she care how many they had, before or now? She was only here to learn what she could while on vacation and then return to the real world.

The leash swung as Sire lifted the end off his chair. Did he lead another woman around by a leash? Did she offer him more pleasure?

He took her chin and turned her to face him. When his thumb caressed her bottom lip, she realized he'd noticed her frown. She could hear the unspoken question in his touch, but refused to offer any explanation. If he wanted to know, he'd have to ask aloud. She pasted on a tentative smile, though she doubted he was convinced. That doubt grew when he gave her another chaste kiss, as if he apologized for some wrong.

Master's footsteps approached. "Come, pet. Time for your next lesson."

Sire stood and led the way with the leash through the house. She held her hands out a bit, but found it unnecessary as they touched and turned her to avoid any obstacles. She went from the smooth floor of the dining room to carpet to what felt like polished marble tiles before the leash drooped and a hand signaled that she should stop.

A door opened to the melodic chirp of songbirds.

Owning Rachel

"Let's go, pet. We're taking you for a walk."

CHAPTER FOUR

The leash pulled taut, and still, she froze. A tug made her shake her head. She was naked except for a damn dog collar, and they wanted to take her for a walk on a leash like a pet Pomeranian. Outside? She had *not* signed up for this.

"Do you want to say your safe word?"

She nodded, but her mouth didn't move.

"You either trust us to care for you or end this now by saying your safe word."

Trust. There was that word again. Did she trust them? She thought she did until she heard the song of nature through the opened door. She listened for the whir and click of cameras catching one of the city's prominent prosecutors in a most humiliating condition. But she heard only the cheerful sounds of chirping. She didn't even hear any traffic in the distance. No car horns or sirens. Nothing that indicated she was even in the city at all.

"Rachel? What's it going to be?" Master stood a few feet to her right.

She took a small step forward. Her heart leapt three miles ahead.

A thumb brushed across her cheek as she took

another tiny step toward the door.

Master's hand grabbed one of her fists. She latched onto him like a lifeline.

"Watch your step. Across the threshold, there's a deck, then some stairs that lead down to a stone patio."

He continued to hold her hand as she made her way over the physical and mental obstacles on her first ever jaunt outside in the buff. After reaching the cool stone of the patio, she took several more steps before her toes met cool blades of grass.

"It promises to be a beautiful day. Only a few white clouds in the sky." He spoke in a casual manner, as if they strolled in a public park. Of course, *he* was fully clothed.

The blackness she saw behind the blindfold was brighter outside, but still scary. They continued to walk across the lawn, Master's hand offering more comfort than he could possibly imagine. The leash swayed in front of her, a constant indicator of Sire's location.

"Feel the heat of the morning sun on your skin, pet. Let it seep inside and warm your body."

The summer sun did feel good. His hand swung with hers as they kept up with the slow, steady pace set by Sire. A balmy wind kicked up and played with her hair.

Master breathed deeply.

"Feel that cool breeze, pet? Yes, I see you do."

She turned her face toward him.

"Your nipples are hard, sexy little pebbles." His words made her chest rise involuntarily, her lungs filling with fresh air.

Her heart beat triple time. She squeezed his hand and concentrated on each step, the grass soft and plush under her feet.

"You like those cool gusts in the city, don't you? I bet they feel good lapping at your pussy as you walk around without underwear."

She stumbled, but he caught her.

He leaned closer to her and murmured, "Do you ever go to the park and lift your skirt as you sit on a bench?"

She shook her head in quick denial.

"We'll have to try it some time." Her jaw dropped in surprise, which caused him to laugh.

As for her lack of underwear, what would he think of her if she told him the truth? She only did that because she didn't like the visible lines they created when she wore her form-fitted skirts. Too unprofessional.

The idea of public exposure was new. Although, he might not believe her if she told him so. She'd never dreamed of committing such a risqué action in the city park. None of her fantasies had taken place outside. As raunchy as they were, they'd always been in a safe, private bedroom. Maybe Dr. Sinclair hadn't realized that during their sessions, or maybe he just hadn't relayed that little piece of the puzzle to these guys.

Besides, she seldom went to the park; it a waste of time better spent in preparation of her latest case. Her only walks were twenty-minutes on the treadmill in her bedroom or the frequent treks from office to courthouse.

"Here we are."

Here? Where was here?

"Hold still, pet." She tried, although the trembles were unavoidable as she felt him remove the leash. "Now take one step forward."

They didn't touch her anywhere, so her step was tentative.

"A little farther. That's it. Now stand with your feet apart. A little more. Good. Raise your arms over your head and don't move."

Curious, she raised her hands as if surrendering to a cop. One of the men locked her wrists together using soft cuffs of some kind. Then she felt an upward tug that turned into a constant pull until her arms extended straight up, and she rose onto her tiptoes. When she moved her feet closer together to regain her footing, something swatted her butt.

"Ouch!"

"Quiet," Master said softly. "Spread your feet apart and don't disobey again."

Her feet inched apart until one of the men grabbed her ankles, forced them wider, and attached a bar between them. She stood on tiptoes, exposed, unnerved, and much to her amazement...aroused.

A fingertip dove through her pubic curls to slip between her labia. One stroke and a flick of her clit made her twist and jerk on her bindings.

"You're already wet, my pet." Master sounded pleased by the discovery, yet his finger didn't remain, at least not between her legs. "Taste," he said, then slipped the moist digit into her mouth. He held it there until she'd licked every inch.

"Feel how wet our pet is, brother?"

Sire used two fingers to stroke her pussy, collecting more of her juices and teasing her until she bucked against her bindings.

"I think our pet enjoys being naked outside," Master

said to his brother.

"Mmm hmm," Sire murmured, surprising Rachel. "Again," came the softly whispered command as Sire finger-fucked her mouth.

Master said, "Suck 'em clean, my naughty little pet."

She did feel naughty, even shocked by her own actions, and so damn hot she thought she'd self-combust.

"Shall we see what else she enjoys?"

Uh oh. She strained to hear Sire's response.

Nothing.

"Don't go anywhere," Master said before moving away.

For a second, she almost laughed. Where could she go, tied up without clothing? She waited, anticipating his next words or touch. Several minutes passed, and she began to worry that they'd left her hanging out alone. Literally.

Then something soft stroked across her back. The light, almost ticklish touch moved down her spine and swiped over each butt cheek. Gently, it traveled down and back up each leg. It felt like a feather, and when it flicked her underarm, she was certain. More downy soft strokes fanned across her sensitive skin. She giggled helplessly and twisted, trying to get away from the delicate torture.

"Brother, she's so hot," Master said. "I don't think a feather will do."

The feather vanished, and something cold and wet replaced it. The chilly object touched the tip of one breast, causing the breath to freeze in her lungs. She struggled to remain motionless. The cold touch circled her nipples, which became stiff, damp nubs.

"You like this, don't you my naughty little pet?"

She couldn't answer. Her breaths changed to pants.

Drops of cold water trickled down her body as Master continued to rub each tip with the melting ice cube. Her only moment of reprieve came when he stopped to grab a new, seemingly larger cube. He drew a figure eight around her breasts then ran it down to dip in her navel. The sun's hot rays rained down on her skin in direct contrast to the chilly trail made by the ice.

She grinned. He blew a cool breath of air across the damp trail adding more sensation. She sucked in her tummy, but couldn't escape.

He continued down to the edge of her curls. On reflex, she tried to close her thighs, but the bar kept her legs apart. She hung before him, unable to stop him. Unsure whether she even wanted to.

Chilled fingers spread her open, exposed her to the cube, which drew closer. Unchallenged.

She shook her head, her bottom lip trembling. She begged, "Please, no."

"Tsk, tsk. You're forgetting the rules already, pet." He slipped the cold ice cube between her pussy lips.

"Master!"

Her thighs shook. Her inner walls clamped on his finger as he pushed it in. Shivers spread throughout her limbs. She gasped for air as her entire body focused on the cube melting from her heated core.

He slipped in a second finger, shoved the cube deeper, and pulled out. Her head tossed back, and her arms yanked against the ties that held her in place. The cube continued to melt inside, trickling small, cold trails down her hot inner channel to drip from her pussy. She bucked her hips as if fucking an invisible cock in a vain attempt to dislodge the object that held her enthralled.

Then fingers returned, thumbs holding her open again. She moaned, fearing another cube. Instead, hot breath bathed her cunt, and a warm tongue lapped at the moisture.

"Do not come." Master's voice whispered the stern warning into her ear, and she realized Sire knelt between her legs.

She held her breath, trying to fight the growing tension. The battle was lost as Sire's tongue toyed with her clit and sank deeper inside. Each lick pushed her closer to the peak. She bit the inside of her cheek, her nostrils flaring like a racing steed. Still, the pleasure built as more cold water tickled her inner muscles.

His mouth sucked hard, almost painfully, on her clit. She teetered on the edge of a climax. His finger rubbed her pussy, spreading the moisture between her legs. When he reached the puckered skin of her anus, he circled it, and fear lanced through the erotic haze.

She shook her head violently. She fought against her restraints to no avail.

She screamed, "No," but he pushed in. The jolt of pain shattered her resolve as the orgasm took her by storm. *Yes!* Her anus clenched, yet he continued to move in and out with steady, gentle strokes. Her pussy gripped the cube until it disappeared completely, and Sire drank up the juices of her uncontrolled pleasure. *Oh, yes!*

Slowly, she returned to reality and hung listless as Sire stood up. A carnal haze engulfed her as little aftershocks sparked along her nerves.

"You disobeyed us." Master's voice was deep, hard,

and brooked no argument, but she gave him one anyway.

"What? That's crazy."

"I did not give you permission to climax."

"I can't help it if he's so damned good at that." Over her shout, she heard one of them—probably Sire—chuckle at her off-handed compliment, which only made her bolder. "No flesh-and-blood woman could've avoided a climax after what you two just did to me."

"Maybe, but other women are not you, pet. Their pleasure and obedience are of no concern to us. Yours are."

"You pleasured me just fine. Thank you."

"And you're lippy. Your punishment continues to grow."

She gulped. Maybe she shouldn't have picked a fight when she was hanging here like a slab of beef. "What punishment?"

"Care to rephrase that?"

She took a breath. "What punishment, Master?"

"Better, but not enough to reduce the penalty you've earned. You disobeyed a direct order to not come. If we want to suck you for hours, that's for us to enjoy and you to endure."

He tweaked a nipple. When she tried to twist away, he pinched harder and hung on. She snarled. He released her nipple, moved behind her, then reached around and squeezed both breasts. An obvious show of possession.

"Your body belongs to us, to do with as we choose. Yet, you climax whenever you want without any consideration for our pleasure. When told of your transgression, you forget your place. You don't accept my word, but challenge it."

"Sorry, Master," she said, hoping to appease him.

"Sorry? Maybe sorry that you face an unknown discipline. Somehow I doubt you truly regret your actions, but we'll see." He let her go.

The ties that held up her arms lowered. Sire unhooked her cuffs, leaving her hands bound in front of her. He rubbed away any soreness from her arms without comment while Master unfastened the bar from between her ankles. Standing back up, Master reattached her leash and, with a murmured, "Follow me," he led her a few feet away.

He took her hands and guided them until she felt a padded beam in front of her. It was about six inches wide and positioned at about waist level.

"Lean forward until it runs down the center of your body from the hips up."

She did as instructed and discovered that the beam's padding stopped at her shoulders, while the beam itself extended farther than she could reach. Hands quickly separated the cuffs at her wrists and refastened them to wooden legs that extended away from the beam in an upside down V. She was on a modified sawhorse of some kind. Her ankles were also bound to a pair of support legs at the end.

Trepidation set in. Why hadn't she yanked off the blindfold and ran when she had the chance? *What if the punishment is too much?* Was she strong enough to take it?

What was her safe word? *Oh, fantasy. That's it.* They'd stop if she used it, wouldn't they?

She trembled as she settled her right cheek on the beam and awaited her punishment.

"Raise your head." When she did, trying to look over her shoulder, he corrected, "No, turn your face so that your chin, not your cheek, almost rests on the beam."

She did, and he rolled something forward on the beam above her head.

"Sire will sit in this seat while you receive your punishment."

Sire took his position, scooted forward, and draped a leg over each of her arms on either side of the beam. His crotch touched her nose.

Well, isn't this cozy, she thought, tongue-in-cheek.

Her humor fled when something slapped her thigh.

"This is a flogger."

He slapped her other thigh, no more than a mild tap that offered little pain, if any. She could handle this.

"Have you ever experienced a flogging before?"

She muttered, "No," since Sire had her head pinned between his rock-wall thighs.

"No, what?" Another slap, this one a little harder and with a bit more bite.

"No, Master," she said with gritted teeth.

"You are to receive a whipping for your disobedience and for the disrespect you showed me with your tone. While I punish you, pet, you will hold Sire's dick in your mouth." On cue, Sire unzipped his fly and slipped his semi-erect cock past her stunned lips.

"Do not suck on him unless he is soft, in which case you'll lick and suck him until he's again hard and then stop. At no time are you to bring him to completion, unless specifically told to do so. If at any time you disregard my orders, he'll signal me, and I'll adjust the punishment accordingly." He trailed the flogger's ends lightly down her spine. "You let your mouth run away with you. We're going to put it to better use."

Sire nudged her mouth. She started sucking.

The flogger's touch vanished, but the icy fingers of uncertainty remained. She heard a squirting sound behind her that puzzled her. When Master put a hand on her back, she flinched, expecting the snap of the flogger instead of his warm palm. Just as she started to relax with relief, he slipped something cold between her butt cheeks. She jolted and tried to turn her head, but Sire's thighs and now-fully-erect cock held her head in place. So she wiggled her butt instead.

"Hold still. It's just anal lube."

Anal what?

"Relax, pet. This will go in easier if you do." Master rubbed his finger over her asshole.

She stiffened.

"I said, *relax*." He swatted her butt. Then while she concentrated on the sting, he slipped in a slick finger to coat the inside of her rectum.

"Gah!" She managed good volume, but couldn't say much more with Sire's dick stuck in her mouth.

Master pushed deeper, and her body jerked against its restraints.

"Settle down, pet. A lack of control is what got you into this situation in the first place."

No. What got her into this was trusting her former, no-account, good-for-nothing psychiatrist who refused to just take her money and let her chat away her hour while stretched out comfortably on his couch.

Master removed his finger, and she sighed in relief until she felt him squirt more lubrication inside her, straight from the tube. Then something else pressed forward to gain her undivided attention. It was wider than his finger and stretched her more as he pushed it in a bit then pulled back and tried again.

"Gaaahhh." The pain was not intolerable so much as it was unfamiliar, so she squirmed in retaliation, and earned a sharp five-fingered smack to the ass for her trouble.

"Aaaaw."

Sire's cock lay hard and full in her mouth. His hand petted her head. He made no move to stop the torture that continued at the other end of her body.

In, out, a slight twist and then a final push.

"This isn't the largest butt plug we have, but it'll do for starters," Master said.

Behind the blindfold her eyes were as big as saucers.

"Besides, it has a feature I need for your punishment." He must have flicked a switch or something, because a slow vibration suddenly radiated from her ass.

In reflex, her lips and tongue closed in a tight suction around the cock in her mouth, and Sire fisted his hands in her hair.

With a swish, the flogger slapped her right thigh hard enough to smart...and make her release Sire. Master swung the flogger again, this time landing across her upper back.

"The vibrations are set to bring you to peak and then stop, leaving you unfulfilled. You are under a standing order to not come unless instructed to do so. If you disregard this order, you will remain tied up and left to the mercy of the vibrator for the rest of the day."

Another swat and another, seldom in the same spot. Rarely with the same force.

When Sire's cock softened a bit, he pushed against her as a reminder. She began to suck him and lost herself in the bliss of feeling him come alive. When she failed to stop soon enough though, the flogger fell with full force across her butt. She jerked and stopped sucking.

The plug's vibrations did exactly what Master warned. They built in intensity until she thought she'd explode. Then the plug quit, leaving behind nothing but the full pressure in her ass and a few residual tingles.

More lashes rained down across her flesh, never breaking the skin, but leaving behind a warm pain that spread through her body. The combination of pain and pleasure mingled into a euphoric fog that disintegrated when Master stuck something solid, long, and thick in her damp pussy.

Startled by the unexpected intrusion, she sucked Sire's hard cock deeper into her mouth and received another sharp whack across her backside.

The object returned to press inside her pussy. Master pulled it nearly out and pushed home again. His thrusts joined the vibrations in her ass, which started up again.

"You like being fucked by the handle of my flogger, don't you pet?"

All she could do was moan and struggle against the building tension.

Again she reached the precipice. Again the vibrations ceased, but this time the thrusts into her pussy remained.

"Your skin is gorgeous when it bears my marks, but don't worry." Master's fingertips trailed tenderly over the tiny stripes that crisscrossed her back. "They'll fade quickly."

The multitude of sensation nearly overwhelmed her. Hard cock, soft touch, rhythmic thrusts and erotic vibrations. Her hands fisted. Her legs pulled against their bindings. Her mind blanked.

Master shoved the penis-shaped handle in farther, withdrew and repeated the stroke. His thrust pushed her face into Sire's crotch, so she licked him and felt pre-cum spill onto her tongue.

"Your pussy is soaked, my pleasure pet. I must say you enjoy a little pain when you're fucked." He pulled the flogger free and rubbed her clit in a circular fashion.

The vibrations started again. She thought she'd faint. She couldn't explain it, would probably never understand it, but he was right. She did enjoy the mix of a little pain with a lot of pleasure.

Master ran the thin leather strips lightly all over her heated skin, keeping her body fully awake for the titillation that emanated from her ass.

The fine hairs around the base of Sire's cock tickled her nose as he pushed the tip to the back of her throat. She sucked huge amounts of air through her nostrils in a futile attempt to calm down. The scent of sex and man surrounded her.

The sound of a zipper showered across her senses like Fourth of July sparklers. Anticipation and dread swamped her. She desperately wanted to come, and didn't know whether she could hold it off if Master entered her, or if the damn vibrator didn't stop soon.

And she couldn't ask for permission with Sire's cock lodged in her mouth.

Her back, butt, and thighs were on fire. Her asshole

tingled. The vibrator notched up to another level at the same moment Master rammed into her with a fierce thrust. She screamed around Sire's cock, causing him to groan, but she didn't come. Yet.

"Very good, pet," Master said huskily. "Hold off a little longer, and I'll give you what you most desire."

She didn't know if she could, but she'd try. *God knows, I'll try.*

Master moved back and, with a tight grip on her hips, powered into her.

"Suck him, pet. Suck him hard."

She obeyed, hoping she could concentrate on giving Sire pleasure and avoid her own as long as possible. He held onto her head and slid the seat closer. She almost gagged but forced herself to relax and take more of him. Deeper. Harder.

Master pumped his cock into her pussy with strong strokes that had his thighs slapping against hers. Each time he collided with her, his body nudged the plug in her ass. It was like being double-fucked. His thick dick combined with the vibrating butt plug to fill her more than she'd ever been before.

"That's it, pet. Damn, you're so tight."

He leaned forward and held her shoulders, enabling him to hammer harder into her willing body. Simultaneously, Sire increased his pace and the vibrator kicked up another notch.

No. I'm not going to make it!

"Ah, fuck, yes." Another thrust deep inside sent Master over the edge. His cum gushed warm inside her, and a second later Sire reached his peak.

"Now. Come, pet." Master didn't have to say it twice. She was already obeying. Rachel swallowed all of Sire's cum that she could, but some escaped to trickle down her chin. Her ass held the vibrator in a death grip, while her pussy clamped onto Master's cock, and her whole body shook with orgasmic fury.

Master switched off the vibrator but left it in place while she trembled uncontrollably. Another wave hit her, and the contractions continued. With a sated moan, Master rocked gently into her, then pulled back and slammed forward to the hilt once more. She passed out.

CHAPTER FIVE

Rachel awoke to blackness, but instead of disturbing her like before, she felt soothed by its familiarity.

She had no idea how much time had passed, but she suspected a lot since she felt clean, refreshed, and lay on the plush softness of a bed. She stretched and was surprised she didn't feel restraints. Neither did she experience any of the stiffness she usually associated with first waking up.

She relaxed into the pillows with a satisfied sigh and listened to her environment.

Male voices sounded from the other room, but they were too faint for her to successfully eavesdrop on the conversation. A short time later, she heard the door open.

She smiled as she heard the men pad across the room.

The mattress dipped. "How do you feel, pet?"

"Renewed, Master."

He chuckled and, leaning over her, gave her a quick kiss on the lips. Simultaneously, she felt what could only be Sire's hand caress her calf.

"You were out quite a while. We were starting to worry."

"I'm sorry, Master."

"Don't be. I'm glad you got some rest. I understand you haven't been sleeping well over the past few months."

She frowned at the reminder. What would happen when her time here ended? Would her return to reality mean a return to insomnia?

"I'm fine," she said.

"I know. I trust you'll tell us otherwise should the situation change." He and Sire took her hands. "Come. It's getting late. We've a dinner date."

She slid off the bed. "What do you mean, dinner date?"

She heard the smile in his voice. "We're going to wine and dine you in one of the finest Italian restaurants the city has to offer...in a cozy little corner booth."

"Like this?" she squeaked.

He gave a loud bark of laughter. "No, my pet. Not exactly."

Not exactly? She was beginning to hate that phrase.

Her nerves settled down, however, when they presented her with a dress and shoes. She couldn't tell what color they were, but the dress's material was soft and fluid. Before she could put it on, they gave her fifteen minutes in the bathroom without the blindfold to put on some makeup and fix her hair. She checked her back and found Master to be true to his word. He hadn't left a single mark. Any welts were gone and most of the redness as well. Before her time was up, she took a quick moment to relieve herself. Then she opened the door, holding the black silk cloth over her eyes.

"Got 'em closed?" Master asked.

She nodded.

"Okay. Hold still." She dropped her hands when he

took the scarf and placed a pair of glasses on her. They wrapped around her face like a sleek pair of sunglasses.

"Open up."

When she did, she saw black in front of her and to the sides, but if she looked down her nose, she could see herself and a little of the floor. The carpet was a deep, rich burgundy.

She scowled. "Master, when am I going to get to see you two?"

He laughed and leaned forward. "When you've earned it," he whispered teasingly in her ear. He took her hand and led her to the bed. There, he slipped the dress over her head and removed her collar.

She touched her neck. Funny how she felt naked without it.

The dress fit her perfectly, and a peek down told her it was fire engine red, one of her favorite colors. Thin spaghetti straps over each shoulder held it in place. The bodice dipped low enough in the front to display some cleavage and farther in the back to eliminate any doubt of whether she wore a bra.

She sat to let Master put on her shoes. Peeking, she noticed he wore a gold watch on his right wrist and no rings. His hands and forearms were tanned and sported a mild dusting of black hair. *So, Master's a left-handed, dark-haired man who enjoys outdoor activities.* She could attest to what type of outdoor activities he liked. She giggled.

"Are you peeking?"

Her giggles stopped. She shook her head.

"What's so funny?"

She wasn't about to admit to the lie, so she gave an

alternative truth. "I just realized I've never had a man dress me before."

A long pause followed her statement and, for a second, she thought she'd been had, but then he stood and pulled her to her feet. The stilettos added quite a bit of height to her modest five-foot-five-inch frame, and they promised to kill her feet in record time. She hoped they parked close to the restaurant.

"To any observer, the glasses will appear to be those worn by the blind." Something silky wrapped around her neck. "This ribbon will temporarily replace your collar without drawing undue notice." He tied it in back and let the long ends hang free. "The loose ends will give you the illusion of the leash and remind you of your submission. Now, let's go. We don't want to be late."

As he escorted her down the stairs, she saw the risers were painted white with the treads a deep, rich cherry wood. Applause greeted her as she stepped off the last one.

"Sire approves, and I must agree. You look absolutely breathtaking, pet."

Their praise made her tummy flip and brought a wide grin to her face. "I'd say the same about you, but I'm not allowed to see for myself," she teased.

"Cheeky pet," Master murmured before popping her playfully on the behind.

Sire placed something in her hand, which turned out to be an evening bag that matched her dress. Something was inside, and she started to open it....

"You're peeking."

Her gaze lifted, and her hands dropped to her sides. "Sorry."

"You're forgiven, this once," he said with unhidden amusement.

They escorted her through the front door and down a sweeping set of stone steps to a cobblestone driveway where another surprise awaited her.

"Good evening, gentlemen...and ma'am." She didn't recognize the stranger's voice at all and couldn't see a damn thing, so she had no clue how to respond. Hold hand out for a shake or just stand there and smile?

"Hello, Fulstrom. Pleasant evening, is it not?" Master asked.

"Indeed it is, sir. Your car's ready."

The vehicle turned out to be a stretch limousine and Fulstrom, the chauffeur. Sire got in first and held her hand as she followed.

"Watch your head, my pet," Master said, keeping a protective hand over her head before joining them inside. The door closed and, a few seconds later, the engine purred to life.

Rachel settled in between her two lovers and tried to ready herself mentally for the very public dinner ahead. The limo was a nice touch even if she couldn't see the surrounding luxury.

"So, Master... Do you two rent limos for every dinner date?"

"It's not rented, my curious pet."

"Oh."

"It belongs to my company. We serve some very wealthy clients who expect the star treatment whenever they're in town. I find it more affordable and convenient to have a chauffeur on staff."

She paused, unsure whether he'd willingly share more information about himself, but how else was she to find out unless she asked? "What kind of business are you in?"

"I buy and sell real estate."

"You're a realtor?" She was so surprised, she forgot his title.

He laughed. "More like a high-dollar real estate financier."

"Oh!" She pointed from him toward Sire and back. "So the house is...yours?"

"Ours, yes."

Taking a chance, she asked, "Sire, what do you do?"

He took her face between his hands and leaned forward until their noses touched. With a quick laugh, he gave her one heart-stopping kiss. When he let go, she heard Master laughing.

"Nice try, my pet, but enough questions for now," Master said. "We have a few rules to discuss with you before we arrive."

Rules? A huge lump settled in her stomach.

"From the moment you leave the limo until you return, you are free to speak as you normally would. However, you will refer to us as 'sir' instead of the usual titles." Two hands tugged her knees apart. "At no time are you to cross your legs or sit with your knees together. Maintain a distance similar to the way they are now. When seated, you must lift your skirt so that your pussy is on the seat and not the material of your dress. This will remind you of your nudity."

As if a girl could forget with these two men around.

"Adjust your dress now."

With a hint of naughty excitement and a healthy dose of worry, she lifted her skirt out of the way and sat. The leather was soft against her skin. *This isn't so bad.*

"Good. Like that, the front of your skirt rides up to barely cover your pussy."

The large lump shot to her throat. What if the restaurant didn't use tablecloths?

"I want you to sit up straight at all times, chest out. They're lovely breasts, so don't be afraid to show them off."

He pulled her hands away from the hem of her skirt.

"Don't fidget. Also, for the purposes of this dinner date, you'll know our names as John and Jack Smith."

How original, she thought and almost asked if she could be Jane Doe, but wisely held her tongue.

"Don't forget, pet. You are to refer to us as 'sir'. Obey us without question or challenge. Understood?"

"Yes, Master."

"What is your safe word? Say it now."

"F-fantasy."

"Good. Use it only if you must. If you do, we'll call you a cab, pay for your fare home, and send your things to you in the mail. You retain control over when our journey together ends, but we control the path we take on that journey."

As the restaurant drew nearer, her trepidation increased. What if they asked her to do something she couldn't possibly do? Would she have to use her safe word? What if she ran into someone she knew? What if that someone saw her skirt hiked up to her waist?

"Relax," he said. "Trust us." He ran a finger up her

inner thigh. She opened for him without hesitation.

Sire grazed her neck and shoulder with the back of a finger, pushing the spaghetti strap off. As Master dipped a finger past her pussy lips, Sire dipped his finger lower to reveal one breast. Rachel's head fell back against the seat.

Sire used teeth and tongue to nip and suck the tip into his mouth. Master slipped a second finger into her channel to explore as deep as he wished, much to her contented delight. After a few heart-pounding minutes, the men switched places as Master took her other breast into his mouth, and Sire pinched and teased her clit.

Her hips lifted. Her hands pulled the skirt higher out of the way.

The climax neared, and the limo rolled to a stop.

Immediately, the men righted her dress and gave her quick pecks on each cheek.

"All set," Master said as the door opened.

Rachel wanted to jerk him back so he could finish what he started.

He tugged on her shaky hand, and Sire's palms cupped her ass as they guided her out of the car. She listened for paparazzi cameras or the dreaded greeting from an acquaintance, but heard none.

Once standing, she smoothed her skirt and tried to settle her nerves. Her body made that difficult since it still hummed with unrelieved arousal and pent-up frustration. She could smell her arousal and feared others could, too.

"This way, my pet." Master took her arm in his and started forward. Sire's hand settled on her lower back, touching skin and the dangling ends of her "leash".

The maitre d' apparently recognized them because as

soon as they walked up, he said, *"Signori...* Welcome. The booth you requested is ready. Right this way."

Master released her arm, giving her over to Sire's care, as they made their way through the restaurant. The lighting was dim. Maybe they relied on candles to provide a softer, elegant illumination for patrons. Fine for those sitting down but, for her, it made navigation damn difficult. Rachel kept her gaze aimed at the floor as she faced the gauntlet of tables, chairs and bustling servants. She prayed one didn't decapitate her with a serving tray.

Sire remained behind her, his hands at her hips or back, safely guiding her through the maze. "Almost there."

The shock of hearing his whispered words would've landed her flat on her face if he hadn't held onto her.

"You pick a fine time to talk, sir."

His chest shook silently against her back.

"Ah...Jack, good to see you." The unfamiliar male voice stopped Rachel in her tracks.

"Sorry we're late," Master said. "Have you been waiting long?"

"No, not at all." The answer came from a woman who was either very short or already seated in the booth.

"Olivia, you're as lovely as ever."

"And you're still the charmer," she said with a laugh.

"John..." The man's hand came into her limited view. Sire reached around her right side, his arm pumping as they shook hands. His left one remained on her back.

"And this must be Rachel."

Her eyebrows shot into her hairline, her lips parting. They used her real name?

The woman in the booth laughed. "Apparently we're

a bit of a surprise." While the man had a European accent, hers was All-American.

"Shame on you, *amigos*," said the stranger, although his tone was anything but disciplinary.

Master took his seat while she toyed with the idea of running for the door. "Sit, pet. I'll make the introductions."

Sire's hand held her in check. A slight nudge made her move forward, and she reached out blindly until Master took her hand. She scooted in beside him and found her only chance at escape gone when Sire sat on her other side.

With head bowed, she laced her fingers together on her lap. Bracketed by her lovers, the space seemed tiny. In reality, the circular booth provided plenty of room.

"Adjust your skirt, pet." Master kept his voice low, but that didn't prevent her face from flaming. She finished the task quickly, hoping the other couple was too far away or too busy to hear his command.

Her cheeks burned as two hands, one belonging to each man on either side of her, wedged between her knees and pried them apart.

"This is Dylan and Olivia Montgomery," Master said. "They're close, personal friends of ours. Rachel is our new pet."

The new pet wanted to kill her master. Instead, she said softly, "Hello."

"I can see Jack didn't tell you we'd be here," Dylan said. "He does like to test a person's limits. But if it'll set your mind at ease, Olivia belongs to me."

Rachel raised her head.

"You couldn't ask for better owners," Olivia added. "They'll treat you well. Trust me."

She appreciated their words and tried to resolve her feelings of helplessness when ambushed by their presence. Master must have decided she'd faced enough for now since he changed the subject and steered conversation to more mundane topics.

The server stopped to take their orders. Master and Dylan spoke for everyone. Sire held her right hand beneath the table, his thumb rubbing her skin in a calm, hypnotic manner. Master's arm draped over her shoulders.

"Are you thirsty, pet?"

Her head snapped around, her eyes wide, as his question brought back memories of another time he'd used those same words.

CHAPTER SIX

He read her reaction accurately and chuckled. "I mean for some water." He took her left hand. "The glass is here."

Her fingers curled around the slick, icy goblet, and a breath rushed from her lungs. "Thank you, Ma—I mean, sir."

She took a sip, which turned into a lengthy swallow. Trying to anticipate her owners' next moves wore on her nerves. Even the most innocent of questions sent her mind into erotic orbit. She was jumpy, not to mention still aroused from their play in the limo. Her palms were embarrassingly moist, and she'd no doubt leave a damp spot on the seat.

Thank God for the tablecloth.

The server arrived with the food. The pasta topped with Italian herbs and spices gave off a delicious aroma and made her mouth water. She found her place setting to the right of her plate and unwrapped it from the cloth napkin. Then, putting the napkin across her lap, she picked up her fork only to feel Sire's hand on her wrist.

She held her breath. Were they going to feed her here, too?

"That's no place for a napkin," Master said. The covering slid off her thighs. He folded it and placed it under her hand, next to her plate. "Enjoy the meal, pet, but never deny us the pleasure of such a lovely view." He and Sire scooted the hem of her skirt a little higher.

Her heart skipped, her breathing tripped, and the fork in her hand rattled against the dish.

All around her, she heard people gathered to savor friendly conversation and gourmet meals, those at her table included. However, she sat frozen for several minutes, praying the moist signs of her arousal wouldn't leave a mark on the bench's cushion between her open thighs. Her pussy throbbed with unfulfilled need, for which she put full blame on the shoulders of the two men beside her. Knowing they could look at her...down there...only made the need worse.

"Do you wish us to feed you here, too, pet?" Master's words yanked her out of her trance.

She shook her head and leaned forward to take the first bite, using what little field of vision she had to guide the fork to her mouth. The sauce was heaven on her tongue.

"Mmm."

Sire chuckled, and Master said, "Glad you approve. Eat up. You'll need the nourishment for later."

Refusing to let his prediction bother her, she dug in and was halfway through her meal before anyone spoke again.

"What do you do for a living, Rachel?" Dylan asked.

Thankful that she'd just taken a bite, she used the time chewing gave her to formulate a response. Should she lie? Tell the truth? If she did lie, would the men beside her call her on it? *Probably.*

"I practice law."

"Interesting. Would I recognize the firm?"

She hesitated again, unwilling to announce outright that she worked for the state as a prosecutor. "I...I doubt it's one you'd know." She held her breath, waiting for her escorts to reveal her fib, but they kept her secret.

"Hmm, well, no matter. Olivia here was a CEO."

"Was?"

"I retired after meeting Dylan," Olivia said in a cheerful, adoring tone. "He made me an offer I couldn't refuse."

"I had to have you, puss."

Uncomfortable and not understanding why, Rachel tried a change in subject. "How did you meet my...uh..." Although she realized she had begun thinking of them as her owners, she wasn't brazen enough to admit that publicly. "...the Smiths?"

"We went to college with Dylan and his brother," Master said. "They were exchange students."

"And you taught us how wild you Americans can be."

"I thought I did that," Olivia said. The men laughed, including Sire. Even Rachel grinned.

"Ah, *mi amor*," Dylan said, "you showed me how it feels to possess the stars."

The soft sound of a kiss, combined with his words, poked a hole in Rachel's heart. Dylan owned Olivia. He'd said so, yet they spoke like life-long sweethearts. She'd never felt such love before and didn't know how to react to witnessing it now.

She bowed her head and concentrated on turning her

fork to gather more noodles.

No one had warned her that a life like this could lead to such a strong relationship. She'd expected them to be temporary flings whereby each party received mutual physical satisfaction before parting ways. The lifestyle offered great sex—a lot of great sex—but did training lead to love? Surely not. Dr. Sinclair said these two were experienced trainers. They must've trained plenty of subs only to release them out into the world of BDSM. Hadn't Master called her his *new* pet? Wouldn't that imply he'd had an old one?

She frowned.

Maybe she was getting in too deep. She shouldn't even be thinking of love. This was just her chance to live out a few fantasies before returning to the real world. She had a life beyond the collar and leash. Sooner or later, she'd have to return there. And unlike Olivia, she wasn't willing to give up a thriving career for life-long subservience to one man, let alone two.

Master's hand on her thigh made her jump. "Sorry, Master...sir."

"You're not eating."

"I'm full," she lied.

Sire interlaced his fingers with hers. She almost cried.

Why was she suddenly so damn emotional?

"I think you have a lot on your mind," Master said. "Let's see if we can help you focus a bit."

Her spine stiffened. "What... What do you mean, sir?"

"Just relax."

In the background, muted conversations hummed amid the tinkling of utensils and the sounds of footsteps. All noise from across the table had stopped.

Oh, damn. How could she relax with an audience?

Sire released her hand and began stroking her right thigh. Master rubbed her left leg. She breathed easier. That wasn't so bad. It felt kind of nice, actually.

Master continued a casual conversation with Dylan, who responded in a voice laced with good humor. Rachel was too busy concentrating on where their hands went to listen to the exact words. Their fingers repeatedly moved closer to the apex of her thighs. Her head fell back against the seat.

The server stopped to ask if their glasses needed refilling. Only the fact that his voice came from Dylan's side of the table kept Rachel from sliding beneath it with mortification. Her tormentors' hands paused, but their fingers continued to move while Master answered.

"Yes, more water please. Lots of ice. Thank you."

Ice. Rachel bit her lip to keep from moaning, but a whimper still escaped.

"Is she okay?" the server asked, deepening her blush. She must be as red as her dress by now.

"She's fine," Master said. "Just a bit flushed. The ice water will help."

Knowing what he could do with an ice cube, she doubted that, but held her tongue.

When the servant left, she sat up straighter and tried to compose herself. "I'm all better now, really. Thank you, sir. Both of you."

For a second their hands remained, and she thought they'd try to push her further, but then they released her. Taking a relieved breath, she retrieved her fork and took another bite of pasta.

"Have you never come in public before, pet?"

She damn near choked to death. Her eyes watered; her throat burned. Master gave her a napkin. Sire handed her the water glass.

Amused, Dylan said, "You've rather impeccable timing there, *mi amigo*."

"Kiss my ass, Dylan," Master said.

"*Gracias*, but I already own a lovelier one that's more to my taste."

The server stopped by with the refilled water pitcher and asked with some concern, "Does she need a doctor?"

Taking the advice of a doctor—a psychiatric doctor—had gotten her into this situation. Suddenly Rachel found the whole thing hysterical. Her coughs turned to peels of laugher, and tears ran down her cheeks. Her humor was contagious as the others at the table joined in.

Obviously stumped, the server filled the water glasses and excused himself. She wished she could've seen the look on his face.

Her gut hurt by the time her laughter subsided.

A thumb and finger lifted her chin and turned her face toward Master. "Feel better now?"

She grinned and nodded.

Sire's hand sat like a soothing heating pad across her thigh. She laced their fingers together and turned to give him a smile. He leaned forward and kissed her, a tender, all-too-brief touch of his lips on hers.

"Before you risk another bite or sip of water, pet...You haven't answered my earlier question."

Slowly she turned back toward Master and gave a

quick shake of her head.

"After your tears, I think you may want to freshen up in the Ladies Room. Take your purse." That comment was unexpected. "With Dylan's permission, Olivia will accompany you."

"Granted," Dylan said.

"Once you pass the door, you may remove your glasses. Put them on before returning. Also, when you get inside, you're to open your bag. You'll find a few items that I want you to put on...or insert under your dress. You'll know which orifice when you see it, but if not, Olivia can guide you. Don't return without all of them in place. Understood?"

"Yes, sir," she said softly. Her mind raced with curiosity.

Sire helped her scoot out, the skirt falling back into place the moment she stood. Her feet didn't move, however, until Olivia took her arm.

"This way, hon'."

"I can't see a damn thing," she whispered to her guide, who gave her a sympathetic pat on the arm.

"I know. Don't worry. They didn't give us a deadline, so we can take our time."

Grateful for small favors, she let Olivia lead the way until finally they passed through the door into the bright fluorescent lights of the restroom. Rachel yanked off the glasses and had to blink several times.

"The light's harsh after being in the dark for so long, isn't it?"

"You had to do this, too?"

"Oh, yes. Dylan blindfolded me for a solid week once when I chose to disbelieve something he told me." They headed for the mirrors on the wall.

Olivia didn't talk or look like a CEO. No monotone suit or conservative pumps. She was dressed in a sleek, black strapless dress that barely reached mid-thigh. Her high heels had long straps that crisscrossed part-way up her calves. Her ebony hair swept away from an oval face, and around her neck hung a silver choker with a padlock pendant in the shape of a heart, encrusted with a few diamonds. She had a pretty, white grin.

Rachel looked around to see they were alone. "What for? I mean, being blinded for a week seems rather cruel punishment for a minor infraction."

"On the contrary. Trust is the most important thing in this kind of life. There's a lot at stake when a sub puts her trust in a Dom. The masters know that, which is why they treasure a sub's trust so highly. It's a confidence each Dom must earn and constantly reinforce. Look at it this way. How would you feel if your masters betrayed you?"

"I'd take them to court and sue the pants off 'em until they were nothing but homeless, lice-infested beggars, crushed under my feet."

"Attorneys." Olivia laughed and rolled her eyes. "I think you get my point. When a sub doesn't believe her master, it's viewed as a major insult."

"I see." Still, she wondered. Would she be kept in the dark for a week or more?

A woman in a pastel dress came in.

"Here," Olivia said. "I should have some powder you can use to touch up your makeup. Tears of joy are nice, but they can leave you looking a bit streaky."

They spent the next few minutes primping and

waiting for the other patron to leave. When she did, Rachel stepped into the handicap stall, leaving the door ajar, and opened the purse.

The contents were small, but she did know what to do with at least one of them. She left the bullet-shaped vibrator in the bag as she dug around for the rest.

"Here, allow me." Olivia cupped her hands together so Rachel poured out the contents. Two tiny rings joined the bullet. She looked at Olivia, who grinned. "Nipple rings. They're like clamps, but these conceal easily under clothing. They just make you look like your tits are constantly cold."

Rachel grinned. "Okay, how do they work?"

Olivia demonstrated how to expand them then stepped out of the stall to wait.

Rachel pinched and twirled a nipple to make it pucker, then positioned the ring and released the spring. Feeling its bite, she quickly did the other one before she lost her nerve. The sting lasted a while before numbness set in. When she replaced her dress, she keenly felt the rub of material against each tip.

"You got it, or do you need some help?"

"No, I'm coming." Realizing what she said, she laughed. "Well, not yet, but soon."

She pushed the bullet-shaped device into her pussy, which was already damp. Concerned that it might fall out as she walked back to the table, she shoved it up a little higher and clamped her butt cheeks together. Why hadn't they let her wear panties or jeans? At least then she wouldn't have to walk through a busy restaurant as if she had a corncob up her butt.

"Ready?" Olivia asked when the stall door opened.

"No. What if this thing falls out?"

"It won't. Hold in your tummy and squeeze your muscles together. You'll be fine."

The return trip was slower because Rachel refused to walk with a normal stride, but they did make it with the device still in place.

"I was beginning to think I'd need the Jaws of Life to pry you two out of that room," Dylan said as he and Sire moved out of their way to let them in.

"Cute, dear," Olivia said, "but as you know, perfection takes time."

Rachel was too worried to say or do anything but perspire. How had she allowed these two men to talk her into this predicament?

"What did you two chat about?" Master asked with an amused cheerfulness to his tone.

"About how marketable a cock-sized tampon would be," Olivia answered, causing Rachel to laugh in spite of herself.

"Would you mind putting your pet on a leash, Dylan? She's running a bit wild, don't you think?"

"With pleasure, *mi amigo*."

Rachel couldn't see what Dylan did, but Olivia gave a sharp yelp, a giggle, and said no more.

"Your hard nipples attract the eye, my pet," Master said. "Wouldn't you agree, Dylan?"

"Indeed."

The tips tingled under their regard.

"Tell me, pet. Did you feel the gaze of every man on you as you returned?"

She hadn't thought about it then, but she did now.

"You forgot something, my pet."

Her hands went to her face. The glasses were in place. The device was inside her. What had she forgotten?

"Your skirt, Rachel. Lift it for us."

"Oh. Sorry, sir." She made quick work of moving the material out of the way and noticed that while seated, the device felt almost nonexistent.

"We took the liberty of ordering another round of drinks...and dessert," Dylan said.

A glass touched her lips.

"Take a sip, pet." White wine spilled over her taste buds.

"Going to get me drunk, sir?" she asked as a joke.

"No, we're going to make you come...while we enjoy dessert."

Master almost accomplished his goal with the boldness of his statement alone. Her dress rubbed her nipples with each shaky breath she took. Her pussy was already saturated.

Sire leaned closer, his lips at her ear, and whispered, "Not a sound."

The bullet awoke inside her. She didn't know who held the remote. Not that it mattered one way or the other. Like a rifle scope, her focus targeted that bullet as its pleasing vibrations ricocheted through her body.

"Do you like dipped strawberries, pet?" Master asked.

"Hmm?"

"Dipped strawberries, do you like them?"

"Yes, sir." Her lips parted, expecting to taste a chocolate covered strawberry.

Instead, he took one of the fruits and ran it along her pussy, back and forth over her clit, until the berry was thoroughly soaked and she had lost her mind. Then, leaning close to her ear, he took a bite of the *dipped* fruit. "Mmm, so do I."

She lifted her hips, seeking more of his decadent touch. Her thighs fell open as someone turned up the vibrations.

Sire took her right leg and draped it over his left thigh. Master did the same with her other leg so that she sat with knees wide apart, her hemline bunched around her waist, and her pussy fully exposed to their view.

She pressed her hands into the seat on either side of her hips and closed her eyes. The soft brush of the tablecloth offered a vague sensation across her bare thighs. Otherwise, she forgot where she was, who was around, everything except for the two men beside her and the buzzing inside her body.

Someone flicked her clit. Sire? Master? She didn't know and didn't care as her body responded with more wetness. Another flick, and she peeked down. They were again working in tandem, taking turns teasing her throbbing flesh with strawberries.

"You really must try the fruit, pet," Master said, lifting the tip of one to her mouth. "It's very good."

She bit into the berry. Its sweet flavor burst into her mouth, along with the taste of her own juices.

Master's finger entered her, followed by a second from Sire's hand, and the tension grew. They didn't go deep. They didn't have to. She was so close to the edge already. Her chest heaved.

She wasn't going to last. She felt a scream rising as the orgasm drew near.

Sire's finger withdrew, and he grabbed her chin, turning her face toward his. Master pushed deeper.

"No sound," Sire whispered again before taking her mouth to ensure she obeyed.

Master pulled out, rapidly plucked and rubbed her clit, and then said, "Come, pet."

She did, and the rush of arousal was like white water rapids. Whatever sound she would've made drowned in Sire's kiss, which didn't stop until after the last of the waves subsided.

"Amazing." Dylan's voice—part awe, part unfathomable moan—was a wakeup alarm. Every muscle she had tensed. Her face flared hot as the sun's surface.

Master used her shock to his advantage. He reached inside her and took out the bullet before she could recover her senses. "If you're concerned about an audience, my pet, don't be. We chose this booth because it offers the right amount of seclusion."

"But Dylan and—"

"Dylan could only watch the look of pleasure on your face, which was quite remarkable, by the way. And Olivia...? He's had her too busy to see much of anything."

"That's enough, puss. You can get up now." At Dylan's breathy command, Rachel tilted her head, listened, and heard Olivia climb from under the table as she returned to her seat.

"I'll be damned," Rachel whispered.

The men laughed.

"I can't believe she did that."

"Any more than you can believe what just happened to you, my naughty pet?"

Master has a point there. Her wet thighs and soaked seat was enough evidence to convict her.

"Here." He gave her a cloth. "Wipe off your legs."

After she did, Sire pulled her onto his lap while Master took care of the seat. In her new position, she noticed that "John Smith" had a healthy hard-on. He might be soft-spoken, but his body spoke volumes. She fought to contain her pleased grin.

Later they said their goodbyes to Dylan and Olivia, promising to meet for dinner again sometime. As Sire paid their bill, the maitre d' asked if they enjoyed their meal. Master replied, "The strawberries were delicious."

Rachel laughed all the way to limo.

* * * * *

The next morning, Rachel awoke to the clink of chains.

"What the hell?"

"Good morning, pet." Another rattle accompanied Master's greeting.

She was again naked, since they'd made her remove her dress and shoes as soon as she entered the house the night before. Her original dog collar replaced the soft ribbon, and the blindfold was back in place.

"Good morning, Master."

"Last night, you exceeded our expectations and ventured into public obedience sooner than we anticipated. We're very pleased with your training so far."

She couldn't prevent the proud thrill his words sent zinging through her body. "I'm glad."

"We think you're ready for the next stage."

Next stage?

In the first stage, she'd already learned a lot about her own sexuality, thanks to them. Even though she enjoyed the aggressive nature of the justice system, she liked being the recipient of an aggressive nature in the bedroom even more. There was something to be said for letting go once in a while, allowing someone else to take the lead. She better understood why her previous relationships with men seldom went beyond the first date. Few were able to identify her insatiable need to submit behind the ice queen façade of her professional persona.

What more could she learn?

Another clink made her ask, "Is that a chain I hear, Master?"

"Yes, my curious pet."

"What's it for, Master?"

"You'll learn that after you shower."

Giving him a grin, she climbed off the bed.

He led her to the bathroom, but stopped at the door. "You'll find everything you need inside. Your pills are on the counter. Don't forget to take one. Replace the blindfold before coming out."

"You and Sire aren't joining me?"

"Not this morning. Go on with you."

Puzzled by their absence, she hurried through her morning routine eager to see what they had planned for the next stage. When she stepped out of the bathroom, a pair of hands she recognized as Sire's silently led her downstairs then down another flight and into a room she'd never been to before.

"Put her on the table," Master said.

Rachel tried to back up only to collide with Sire. He forced her forward with gentle but firm hands. When he lifted her off her feet, she clung to his neck. He had to pry her fingers apart.

"Lie on your back."

"Master?"

"Trust me, pet. Lie down."

As soon as she did, they secured her arms above her head. Next, they put her feet in stirrups and attached cuffs to her ankles. She felt as if she was on a padded examining table about to have a pap smear. She hated physical exams.

"I see you didn't shave this morning," Master said.

She planned to and would have, but hadn't found a razor in the bathroom. "I was going to, but—"

"We're going to remove the unwanted hair."

She tried to get up. The restraints and two pairs of hands held her down. "Master—"

"Quiet, pet."

"But Master, I—" A ball in her mouth stopped her words. She tried to spit it out, but couldn't. The gag had a pair of leather straps that stretched from either side of her mouth and another pair that crossed between her blindfolded eyes and extended over her head.

Sire paused before fastening all four straps around the back, as Master drew near and asked, "Is this more than you can handle, pet? Do you want to use your safe word?"

For a silent moment, she waited then shook her head. She felt the straps tugged into place, the buckles fastened.

"We want your pussy smooth and hairless." The snap of latex sounded as Master apparently put on gloves.

She whimpered as someone fastened a belt under her breasts to keep her body in place.

Master's voice whispered soothing words of encouragement as male hands stroked her belly, the insides of her thighs, and fondled her breasts. They couldn't distract her from the heat of the wax. He began with her underarms then proceeded to do each leg. She fought her bindings every time he ripped the cloth strips away. They added other ties to secure her legs and hips when her movements became too troublesome.

"If you'd relax, this wouldn't be so difficult for you."

Then you should try it on your own body some time!

Drool spilled from around the ball gag.

He trimmed her pubic hair, and then used the wax on her bikini area. Tears streamed from her eyes to soak the blindfold. Still, when he asked again if she wanted to use her safe word, she shook her head. Other women survived a wax job. Some even paid to have it done, so why did she have to be such a baby about it?

Ouch, damn it!

"Almost over, pet. Just a little longer now."

Fingers spread her open. "Hold still now. I don't want to cut you with the razor."

Every muscle in her body locked up. Her teeth bit hard onto the gag.

"Good girl," he said with a chuckle. He rubbed something on her mound, then gently and slowly shaved her folds until all the hair was gone.

Fingers played with her nipples. A dry cloth wiped

the drool from her chin, and a cool cloth soothed away any pain from the waxing.

"See? That wasn't so bad, was it?"

She grunted around the ball. Some of the restraints were removed from across her body, except for the belt just under her breasts. They also left her ankles attached to the stirrups and her hands secured over her head.

"You have a sexy pussy," Master said as his hand slid over her hairless mound. "So soft and smooth. Feel, brother."

Sire's fingers replaced Master's. "Mmm, wet," he whispered with a quick nip of her earlobe. If he kept touching her like that, she'd be flooded with moisture soon.

Master said, "Many women who keep their pussies bare feel more sensitive during intercourse. They say it heightens the experience."

Two hands stroked the inside of her thighs, brushing against bare flesh that was proving to be very sensitive indeed.

"I love a shaved pussy. Sire loves a shaved pussy." Master kept talking while Sire moved between her legs to bend down and lick her delicate folds. "You don't mind providing us this one pleasure, do you, pet?"

She shook her head, fast and hard. She was bare as a newborn babe, and if that's all it took to make them do what they were doing now, she'd stay bald down there.

Sire's finger rubbed her clit as his tongue darted between her pussy lips.

Master's mouth sucked hard on her left nipple, making her moan around the gag. He stopped, but Sire didn't. Master's hand lifted her head. Fingers unfastened the straps and pulled the gag out. He wiped away the saliva.

Sire sucked her clit, forcing her to draw in a harsh breath.

"Rachel, whose breasts are these?" Master asked, his thumb rubbing one hard nipple.

"Mine," she said, barely able to concentrate on the conversation.

"Wrong, pet. That's the lesson you've yet to learn." He pinched and rolled the nipple. "A submissive, whether pet or slave...bitch or slut... She belongs to her owners."

Sire fingered her pussy as he continued to lave her clit. She couldn't think when he did that. Master unfastened her wrists, and she sank her fingers into Sire's hair until he pulled away from her, leaving her breathless, hot, and needy.

"Touch yourself, pet," Master ordered.

"What?"

"You heard me."

Tentatively, she obeyed. Knowing they watched made her feel very wicked. Her skin was smooth. Moisture coated her fingertips.

"Fuck yourself, pet."

She stopped.

"Push one—no, two fingers into that bare pussy. In and out, pet. You know how."

She did know how, had masturbated countless times, but never with an audience. Neither man touched her, although she could sense their presence on either side of her. Reluctantly she obeyed, and noticed the sensations didn't appeal to her as much as Sire's touch had. She went from decadent to insecure in a split second. Her hand froze.

"I said, fuck yourself." A swat on a thigh had her fingers moving again as ordered.

"That's it." He took her wrist and guided wet fingers to her mouth. "Taste yourself." After she did, he put her hand back between her legs. "Keep going."

She heard a chain rattle, felt a tug at her neck, then heard a lock click closed.

"The short chain locked to your collar will prevent you from sitting up or leaving the table." He unfastened the belt beneath her breasts. "Keep masturbating until you climax, pet. Use only the one hand." He ensured her obedience by restraining her left hand in a cuff at the side of the table.

"But, Master—"

"You have your instructions, pet. You have only your body to please, so take care of its needs. Pleasure yourself."

The tears began before their footsteps made it out the door. She didn't want to bring herself to climax, wasn't even sure she could anymore. What had happened to her?

CHAPTER SEVEN

"You're taking a big risk, Jack. What if she's able to bring herself to climax?" Jonathon Sinclair sat in a plush leather chair in their office and watched the naked woman on the security monitor.

His brother glanced at the screen, finished pouring himself a drink, and then sat in the opposite chair. "It's a risk I'm willing to take."

Jon frowned. "That's obvious, but it's not my point."

"If she comes, then we have more work to do."

"It'll set her back."

"Maybe, but if this works..." He grinned. "I want her. All of her, and I know you do, too, or you wouldn't have even considered this plan."

Jon stared at the amber liquid in his own glass that reminded him of her eyes. He did want Rachel, had wanted her since she first stepped into his office—full of fire and ice. When he'd learned of her dilemma and the cause, his own fantasies had begun, which he'd shared with his brother. He'd never dreamed he'd fall for a patient, had always prided himself on keeping that cardinal rule. But the more erotic her fantasies became, the more he wanted to be the man—or one of the men—to bring them to reality.

He'd only held off as long as he did because he hadn't been certain she would be interested in having two Doms. Then, she'd admitted to that last daydream in the courtroom, and he'd been unable to avoid his baser instincts any longer. So, he did the only ethical thing he could. He released her as a client to seek alternative treatment.

He hadn't forced her to call Jackson's cell phone, a fact that soothed some of his guilt, but neither had he admitted her second trainer would be her former psychiatrist.

"Three weeks isn't much time," he said, "and we aren't even sure she'll give us all of that."

His biggest fear now was her reaction once she learned of his duplicity. Would it prevent him from achieving his primary objective? Could they still win her heart?

"The real problem is your secrecy," Jack said as if reading his mind. "I understood the reason for it at first. She needed to face her fears and desires without any interruption from a familiar face. But if we are to have any chance of succeeding in making her our pet forever, she must turn to us. That takes trust, and she's not going to give us that if we hold out on her much longer."

Jon took a large swallow of bourbon, let the liquor burn his throat. "We're not even sure she's in this for the long haul. You know as well as I that she only took a few weeks off of work. What happens when she returns to that career she's loved more than herself?"

His brother shrugged, but he could see his own insecurity mirrored in Jack's eyes. "If you love something, set it free...."

Jon sighed. "...If it comes back, it's yours."

"Exactly. If she's unwilling to stay, we can't keep her chained up. You don't want a slave any more than I do."

"Of course not." But that didn't help appease his doubts. He watched Rachel's head toss from side to side. Her fingers moved inside her pussy in agitated thrusts. "She has to accept both sides of her nature. She's already tried forcing herself to give up one for another. I can't do the same. It would destroy her. I just worry about whether my part in all this will ruin any chance we have with her."

Jackson laid a hand on his shoulder. "Better to know sooner than later. You knew of the risk when this began. We have to be willing to face her anger to win her love."

* * * * *

Rachel was getting nowhere. She pushed three fingers in deep, but still the peak eluded her. Her arm ached. Her fingers were tired. Anytime she neared the edge, thoughts of Master and Sire made her efforts fruitless. She couldn't picture their faces, but she wanted their hands on her body. She wanted to hear their words and sounds of encouragement. She wanted to please them, feel them reach climax with her.

She didn't want to be alone, couldn't do this alone.

She no longer controlled her own body. It craved something more than she could provide.

"Master, Sire... Please!"

"What is it you need, pet?" The question came from somewhere near her feet, as if he stood between her spread legs.

She nearly cried at the sound of Master's voice, at the touch of Sire's hand on her shoulder. She vaguely wondered how long they'd stood by and watched her, but the reality of their presence made the thought irrelevant.

"I need you. I need Sire. Please." She started to reach for him.

Master gripped her wrist to keep her hand between her legs. "I told you to fuck yourself to climax, pet. Do you wish to disobey me?"

"No, Master." She shook her head to emphasize the answer.

They each took a breast in hand. She arched her back for more.

"Whose breasts are these?"

"Yours!"

A finger traced her lips. "Who owns this mouth?"

"You do. You and Sire."

"And this lovely pussy you're finger-fucking? Who controls it?"

"Both of you."

They released her from the table with lightning speed. The cold links of the chain remained attached to her collar and dangled freely between her breasts. After she slipped off the table, she dropped to her knees. She left her head bowed as she listened to them unzip their pants. The sound sent ripples of excitement expanding through her body. From now on, she'd always equate that sound with indescribable pleasure.

"On your feet, my little pet bitch." Master made the word sound like a sweet endearment.

She scrambled to her feet. Her pussy throbbed with need. Her mouth watered. They'd turned her into an insatiable animal, but she couldn't fight the desire any longer. A hand grabbed the chain and pulled her forward until she leaned across the padded table.

"Lift your head," Master ordered with another tug on the chain. His cock touched her lips. She opened immediately, but he didn't move.

"Who do you belong to, Rachel? Who owns you?"

"You do, Master. You and Sire." His cock brushed her lips as she spoke.

"Can you speak without our permission?"

"No, Master."

"Eat without our permission?"

"No, Master."

"Wear anything without our permission?"

"No, Master. You provide everything." She licked the tip of his cock, but he refused to enter her mouth.

"Can you climax without us?"

"No, Master."

"Ask for what you need."

"I need you and Sire."

"What do you need? Be specific."

"I need you to fuck my mouth. I need Sire's cock. I need you both inside me. Please."

"Only from us, Rachel."

"Yes."

"Take what you need."

As she sucked him in, fingers dug into her hips, and Sire's thick cock impaled her. Master twisted the chain around his hand and pulled her closer to his pumping hips.

She slurped and licked his hard length. She stretched up on tiptoes, which gave Sire an even better angle for his deep thrusts.

They took her hard and fast. The sounds and scents of unbridled sex filled the room.

"Take all of me," Master ordered, pushing as far as he could go. "Just like that. Yeah. That's it. Now, finger your clit."

She obeyed without hesitation. Reaching between her trembling legs, she twirled the tiny bud. Her cunt contracted.

"Ah, yes," Master hissed. When Sire slapped her butt, his brother encouraged him. "Yeah, take our hot little bitch. Fuck her hard."

Sire pounded faster into her body, stretching her inner walls. His finger slipped between them, tangled with hers, collecting moisture. Then between two strong strokes, he pushed his damp finger into her ass.

"Aaaaahhh," she screamed. The trembles exploded as they filled her everywhere. Her legs gave way. Her body sagged on the table, and still they pressed her climax on.

"Here it comes. Fuck, yeah." Master jerked forward, his cock throbbing as he ejaculated into her mouth. "Drink...all of my cum...pet."

Seconds later, Sire wiggled his finger in her ass and buried his cock as he emptied his seed into her womb.

For long moments, the three of them stayed there, sweat-slick skin connected. Sated.

She wasn't sure which one lifted her into his strong arms until he pressed a chaste kiss to her forehead. *Sire.* He always seemed to plant such kisses on her when her heart was at its weakest. The tenderness behind his actions warmed her heart as much as the dominating tone of Master's voice aroused her.

Still, their hidden identities disturbed her. She had a glimpse of their bodies and liked what she felt. But how could she feel the way she did with men whose faces she'd yet to see, whose real names she still didn't know? Would the attraction end when her blinders vanished? Was she that shallow?

She told herself it wouldn't matter what they looked like. She'd enjoy the short time they had together and would keep the memories close to her heart. That would be enough to get her through the rest of her life. It had to be.

The men pampered her in a big Jacuzzi bathtub before presenting her with some clothing. Sort of.

"These aren't meant to cover up," Master explained, "but to enhance the view for our enjoyment."

They wrapped a garter belt around her waist then attached it to thigh-high stockings. Her pussy and ass remained bare.

"Hold your arms out."

She did while one of them took the bra from her hand, slipped it into place, and hooked it around back. The straps were thin, fine lace with tiny hooks that connected to her collar. The cups curved under her breasts to push them up and out while leaving her nipples and cleavage completely exposed. They reattached a pair of nipple rings like those she'd worn at the restaurant, only these had the added weight of what felt like tiny chains with little beads on the end. Like mini-floggers, they brushed against her areolas when she walked in her stilettos to the dining room.

There, the men fed her from their plates while she knelt in her usual position. Knees apart, chest out, palms up, and mouth open. Amazingly, she relaxed, unconcerned about what would happen next. Something inside told her they would take care of whatever need she had. It was a sense of comfort she didn't often experience. Most of her time revolved around the worries of her job, the stress of having to do everything for herself at home. She liked not having to bother with the finer details for once.

Every now and then, one of her owners would tug gently on her nipple rings, delicately stroke her neck, or tuck a stray lock of hair behind her ear.

After the meal, she followed the leash into another room, which she learned was their study.

"Although this is Sunday, we do have some work to do, since we both intend to be out of the office for the next several days." Master removed the leash.

"Because of me?" She'd knelt when they stopped and now turned her face toward Master's voice.

They both chuckled, but Master answered. "Yes, my curious pet, because of you. I told you taking care of a pet could be very demanding. We intend to take very good care of you."

"Oh." She ducked her head, but secretly grinned. Having them take time off to be with her, even for only a few days, meant more than she would've guessed.

"We intend to take advantage of the time available and see that you're properly trained. For now, your lesson is patience. Get up." She did, and he backed her against a wall. "Turn around and spread 'em."

As she did, she heard Sire open a drawer nearby and

then approach.

"Scoot your legs back some so you're leaning forward more. There. That's good." Master's fingers pulled her butt cheeks apart while Sire spread lubrication over her asshole. She couldn't avoid the jolt of mild pain when his finger pushed through the puckered opening. A couple pushes later, he withdrew. Then a larger object sought entry. She winced as Sire worked it into place.

"You okay?" Master asked. "How do you feel?"

Stuffed was the only word she could think of to describe the sensation. That, and pain. She bit her bottom lip in reaction to the hurt, which soon turned into a dull throb.

"I'm okay."

"That butt plug is a bit larger than the one I used on you before, but you'll adapt to its size soon. Come here, pet." Master tugged on her nipple rings to move her where he wanted. "Feel this ottoman?"

Her hands touched a thick, padded cushion. The wide, leather-upholstered ottoman was hard to miss. It had to be at least four feet square.

"I want you to kneel across it, knees apart, face on the cushion." He helped her into position, which left her ass in the air for all to see. "Excellent. Stay there just like that. Keep quiet now, while we work. If you must speak about something urgent, ask for permission first. Otherwise, remain silent and let us enjoy the view."

Why his words made her cheeks heat, she'd never understand, but they did. No doubt he could also see the fresh moisture his comment brought to her pussy.

Sire felt her ass, squeezing each cheek, before moving off to do some work—whatever that involved.

After a few moments, she heard computers power up and then a lot of typing. Master made a few phone calls, most of which involved him rearranging his schedule next week to provide him with a few days off.

She crossed her forearms, laid her face on them, and relaxed into her bowed position. Her eyes closed behind the blindfold, and she waited. She'd nearly fallen asleep when a finger stroked once across her pussy lips.

"How are we doing, pet?"

"Fine, Master."

He twisted the plug in her ass, making her groan. "Good. We won't be much longer."

"Thank you, Master."

"For the remainder of your time, I want a different view. Sit on the very edge of the ottoman. Lean back on your elbows, and let your head fall backward."

She followed his instructions. "Like this?"

"Beautiful. Spread your knees a little wider, arch your back. That's perfect." He ran another finger over her pussy.

She caught her breath.

"Stay."

She wasn't going anywhere. Knowing she was on display like a centerpiece for their pleasure excited her. She could almost imagine herself posing for an artist in the nude, something she never would've considered before meeting her owners. She pictured their frequent glances, and hoped their smiles were as big as hers.

Soft music, slow and sultry, played in the background. The typing continued. Pages of a book turned. Another phone call made. And she stayed poised on a peak.

A hand spanned her tummy below the navel. She

raised her head and took a deep breath.

"Tell me, Rachel. Are you pleased with our ownership so far?"

She smiled. "Yes, Master."

"Are you willing to see how far this can lead?"

"What do you mean?"

Sire leaned on the opposite side of the ottoman. His finger drew invisible circles around her nipple ring.

"I think you are a natural submissive," Master responded. "We both do, but only you can decide whether this life if something you want to pursue fulltime."

She frowned.

"You have a career, I know. We're aware that you only took a little time off from work and intend to return to it in a few weeks. We aren't asking you to give that up."

"Oh. Okay."

"One of the reasons we've kept our identities secret is because of the temporary nature of our current relationship."

So they were just as uncertain about her intentions as she was of theirs. She'd assumed they'd train her then bid her farewell as they explored the challenges of training other pets, but the longer she considered that possibility, the more she wanted to tie them up until they agreed to remain her owners forever.

Something he said struck her. "You said 'one of the reasons'. What's the other reason?"

A long paused descended on them.

"Me," Sire whispered so softly she almost missed it.

"I don't understand," she said, but as the words came out, realization dawned. "Oh, God. I know you, don't I?"

He didn't answer. He didn't have to. That was the reason he never spoke above a whisper. He wasn't trying to be mysterious. He knew she'd recognize his voice.

She reached for the blindfold. His fingers banded her wrist.

If he was Carmichael from her law office, she'd die. Or one of the many defense attorneys she went up against in the courtroom. Or a judge? God forbid!

Wait…she knew what his body felt like, had a good idea of how tall he was, and if he was like his brother, she knew he had dark hair. Who in her life fit the description?

Carmichael was out. He had a nice body in a suit, but he wasn't as tall as Sire. Attorneys…neighbors…

"It's time I trust you, Rachel," he said aloud. "I hope you'll continue to do the same toward us."

She knew that voice. "Dr. Sinclair?"

He released her wrist. She removed the blindfold, blinked several times, and then covered herself as much as was possible without the benefit of clothing. The butt plug reminded her of its presence when she drew her knees up to her chest.

She buried her face and groaned in mortification. As much as she'd fantasized about the man, she hadn't expected to be this embarrassed.

"Stop that, pet." The words were sharp, authoritative, but they didn't come from Master.

Slowly, she raised wide eyes to Dr. Jonathon Sinclair…Sire.

"You hide your body from me as if you're ashamed of it." He took her arms and pulled them apart. "You deny me my pleasure because of a fear to face reality? I won't allow it."

"You won't allow it? You lied to me!" She couldn't hide her body, but she tried to hide her fear behind anger.

"I didn't lie to you, and you will address me with respect, pet, or pay the consequences."

She stared into his familiar blue eyes, sat up straight, and crossed her legs. Her arms folded over her breasts. The butt plug felt as if it were permanently stuck in her ass.

He knelt beside the ottoman to her left. She glanced to the right and saw matching sapphires peering at her from under a jet black head of hair. Twins? No, but definitely brothers. Different, yet very much alike. She looked away.

"You did lie to me," she said, too angry to heed his warning. Her gaze bored into the opposite wall. "You denied that phone number was yours. You said you couldn't help me, but once I was blindfolded, here you are."

Sire—no, Jonathon—took her chin, made her meet his penetrating gaze. "The number isn't mine. It's Jackson's, and if you'll recall my words correctly, I said I could no longer help you *in the office*. Both statements are true. I can't help you as a psychiatrist. I *can* help you as a Dom."

Without reading glasses perched on his nose or the notebook in his lap, he certainly didn't look like the all-business psychiatrist she'd come to expect of Dr. Sinclair. The top three buttons of his short-sleeve shirt were undone. His hair slightly ruffled, he looked adorably rumpled, virile, and very real.

Being blind had enabled her to deal with her sexual escapades as if she remained in a constant fantasy world. With those blinders removed, reality stared her in the face.

"The question," he said, "is whether you are still bold

enough to complete your training."

She studied the many facets of his sapphire eyes. Determination. Uncertainty. Hope. All were there for her to see. Challenge also showed in the chiseled face. She heard it in his voice.

He may have spoken the truth, but he still lied by omission. Now what? Could she overcome her doubts about him and continue what they'd started?

"Pet." Master—Jackson took her hand. "You may say your safe word, and this will end. I hope you don't. I know Jon hopes you don't, but the decision is yours."

The word was on her tongue, but the emotion in Jon's eyes stopped her.

"Three weeks, Rachel. What's that in the grand scheme of things? Give us three weeks to show you that you were made for this life. Made for us."

"One week." The bargaining words that slipped out of her mouth were as much a surprise to her as the men.

"Two," Jon countered with narrowed eyes.

"Ten days. No more." She held her breath.

He frowned, glanced at his brother. Jack nodded.

She stuck her hand out. Jon cocked a sinful brow, closed her hand in his, and gave a single shake. His gaze dropped to her chest, reminding her that she sat nearly nude while negotiating terms with two fully dressed men who could imprison her in their home if they wanted.

She tried to release his hand. He pulled her onto her knees and against his chest. The hug caught her by surprise. Her hands hung limply at her sides.

"Ten days. Such a short time to fit in a lifetime of memories." He cradled her upturned face in his palms. Her hands traveled up his shirtfront. As his lips approached, her eyes closed. "No. Keep them open. I want you to know who you're kissing, Rachel."

His kiss was not the possessive, demanding invasion of her mouth or the chaste peck he'd often bestowed on her before. Instead, his lips caressed hers, his tongue teasing her mouth like a seductive lure. Slow. Thorough. Infused with emotions she wasn't ready to contemplate.

His hands trailed down her body before falling away. He stood up, stepped back.

Her heart thundered under the palm she placed between her breasts. Her lungs labored for air. She turned at a tap on her shoulder.

Jon's brother knelt with his hand extended and a mischievous smile. "The name's Jack...Jackson Sinclair. I must say that it has been an absolute pleasure to officially meet you, Rachel Morrissey."

She blinked then burst out laughing. Rather than shake his hand, she gave him a big hug. He quickly took advantage, cupped her ass, and kissed her senseless.

Afterward, she sat back on her heels and grinned. "So, what do we do now?"

CHAPTER EIGHT

"First, a tour of our home and a recap of the rules," Jon said with a tone that screamed Dominant. He reattached her leash and flashed a grin when she scowled at it.

"I don't think that's necessary anymore. I mean, I was hoping we could move on now. You know...maybe reenact a few of my dreams." She smiled at the thought.

Jon didn't. "Let's go, pet."

She knew he used 'pet' to reestablish boundaries, which was fine, except those boundaries had been a lot easier when she couldn't see. Having her sight back meant her nudity glared at her like a neon sign. The difference in their dress unnerved her more now, since she could pretend they were all naked before.

Trying to ignore the fullness in her ass caused by the butt plug, she got up. Her hands positioned to hide her pussy, she followed Jon's lead.

He had a firm ass. His slacks fit like custom-made gloves. Jack's faded jeans and polo shirt offered a more casual vision. Slightly different haircuts and a tiny mole on Jack's left jaw line provided additional clues to their individuality.

"The house has three floors. Our office, the formal dining room, kitchen and the great room are on the second, or main level. The bedrooms, five in all, are upstairs. There's a bathroom on every floor, with a few more expansive ones upstairs. We have a weight room on the lower level, among other rooms."

They made their way past the grand staircase, her heels clicking on the marble floor. The décor was simple, tasteful and elegant. Nothing like the bachelor pads she'd visited in college. The brothers had done well for themselves, and it showed.

"You have a lovely home, as grand as I suspected."

"You were peeking," Jack teased with a tug on one of her nipple rings.

"I plead the Fifth." She grinned.

The leash dangled loosely between her and Jon since she could easily keep up with him now. He opened a door onto a downward staircase.

"What other rooms are down there?"

Jon tossed a lopsided smile over his shoulder. "You'll see." He descended with an uncompromising pull on the leash.

Dread raced through her veins until she saw that the space wasn't anything like a medieval torture dungeon. The stairs ended in a large room. Finished and well illuminated, it was a game room. A pool table held center stage. Nearby sat a card table. A mini-bar occupied one corner to the left of a hallway.

Jack and Jon stood side-by-side facing her.

"What are you supposed to do upon entering a room we're in?" Jack asked.

She answered by kneeling.

"To review the rules, pet," Jon began, "you will address us by our proper titles. That hasn't changed, even though you can see."

"If you have a question, first ask permission to speak," Jack said. "Otherwise, remain silent unless spoken to."

"The only exception is your safe word, which you may say at anytime. You'll wear only what we provide, if anything. You'll eat only what we hand you. You're not to pleasure yourself unless told to do so, and you must obey our commands without pause or complaint. Are the rules clear so far?"

"Yes, Sire," she said without looking up.

"If you should break the rules, we will discipline you as is our right as your owners. The form we use is also for us to decide. You have no say-so." He lifted her chin with a finger. "There is no appellate process, Miss Prosecutor."

Her lips twitched at Jon's use of judicial jargon.

His pull on her leash made her stand. "This way." Down the hall, he opened the door to a dark room. His hand on her back, she entered hesitantly. "Kneel."

She did, and Jack flicked the light switch. Across the room, she recognized the examining table she'd lain on earlier as he'd shaved her pussy. Around the room was a collection of other binding platforms, among them a large X-shaped object, a padded sawhorse, eyebolts and chains. A cage.

Shivers ran the length of her spine. They spread to her legs when Jon opened the cage.

"Get in, pet." His face showed no emotion. No smile

of encouragement.

Without comment, Jack unhooked her leash. The collar moved slightly. Rachel's body ached for his touch, but he was too careful. She glanced from him to Jon, put one foot on the floor, and started to rise.

"Crawl."

Jon's order tested her limits. His eyes were a hard challenge. His stance whetted her appetite.

She took his command as a dare, which helped her overcome the humiliation that settled in her stomach. She crawled across the floor, the pressure from the plug in her ass swaying as she moved. Entering the cage, she winced when the door clanked shut behind her.

Bars enclosed her on all four sides and overhead. The cage, which was bolted to the floor, was tall enough for her to sit up, but not stand, and wide enough for her to turn around on her knees.

Jon locked the door and pocketed the key. His hand reached through the top and stroked her head. "How do you feel?"

"Strange." She couldn't explain the assortment of emotions that flashed through her. A part of her was terrified, but chasing the fear was excitement. Adrenaline pumped in her veins. Arousal pulsed in her pussy. Her lungs, however, inflated in a calm, steady manner.

She trusted Jon and Jack, didn't she? They'd take care of her, not bring her harm. At least not any harm she couldn't handle. She hoped her trust wasn't misdirected.

Humiliation argued with her need to obey. Sanity screamed for her to break free and flee. She gripped the bars with tight, damp fists, realizing any chance of escape was now gone.

"Good enough," he said. "I want you to understand your place, pet. Accept it. A moment ago you spoke to us as equals, and we allowed it. Despite your negotiations of a time limit, however, our ownership of your body will be complete. As long as you remain with us, you are ours to do with as we choose. Day and night, in this house or not, you belong to us. We can play with you when we want...or not, if that is our wish."

He walked out of the room.

"Wait!" She turned a pleading gaze to Jack. "Let me out. Don't leave me in here."

"Jon's right," he said. "We'll honor your desires and keep our promises, because as owners, that's our responsibility to our pet. But you must understand that this is no game. It's a chosen lifestyle, not a vacation from reality." He thumbed her cheek, wiping away a tear that had escaped her efforts to hold it back.

When he left, she screamed and rattled the cage. She yanked on the door handle, but the lock held.

"No! Let me go. Don't leave me here alone. Master! Sire! Please..."

Her shouts ceased when, her throat raw, she realized they wouldn't return because she demanded it of them. They were in charge.

The cage trapped her body, but her mind was free to wander.

At first, she let anger boil. How dare they treat her like this? She was a powerful attorney. She could land their asses in a jail cell if she wanted. If they ever let her out of here.

But hadn't she, of her own free will, crawled inside? They hadn't pulled her in by the leash, hadn't shoved her in physically. No, the decision had been hers even though the order had come from Jon.

Time stretched into the silence. Her confines became more acceptable, easier to endure. She sat without removing the butt plug, subconsciously knowing they wanted it to remain in place.

She pictured the faces of her captors...her owners. She'd begun to think of them as Jack and Jon, treat them as equals. She'd even started to view them as sexual servants to help fulfill her needs. But they had other plans and made them perfectly clear.

She was their property, theirs to do with as they wanted. They'd scared her a bit, but not frightened her to death. Tested her limits, but never pushed her beyond what she could endure.

Lying on her side, she made herself comfortable. More time passed. It must have been hours, although she couldn't track the passage of time.

They'd effectively taken command, allowing her to let go of the reins and enjoy the spontaneity of life. Her only requirement was to submit to their wishes. While with them, she had no other obligation, no other responsibilities to stress over. That helped her to relax.

She accepted that they'd return when they wanted to. Or when they perceived she needed something. They'd imprisoned her, but deep down she knew her release was only one word away.

With trust came understanding. She didn't want to say the word, fantasy. She realized why they'd chosen it.

They picked the perfect safe word for her and taught a valuable lesson in the process. She didn't want to use the word because deep down she didn't want the fantasy.

She wanted the reality.

A small metallic sound prompted her to action. She opened her eyes, got to her knees, and watched. The key turned in the lock, the mechanism opening the cage door. Physically she was free now, but she willingly remained bound in mind and spirit with the man who held the key, and to the one who knelt down and slipped a finger between her collar and skin.

"Come out of there, pet," Master said with a tug on the leather.

She crawled out, stopped, and knelt by his feet, her head bowed. Her hands lay palms up on her thighs. His hand settled on her head.

Her new position awoke a pressure in her bladder. She squeezed her knees together.

Apparently noticing her discomfort, Sire said, "Follow me to the bathroom, pet."

She paused, uncertain whether he expected her to crawl or walk. His hand at her elbow decided for her. She stood and wanted to run to the toilet.

He didn't need to make her sit. She did that as soon as she saw her porcelain throne. Relief escaped on a sigh as she emptied her bladder. When she was done, she looked up to find him watching her. Her cheeks warmed, but she met his gaze boldly and waited for him, which brought a pleased smile to his face. Instead of wiping her off, he nodded his permission for her to finish the task. She did and found that it wasn't such a bad thing after all. It was part of life.

Nothing to be ashamed of, especially with people who accepted her as she was.

She stood. He moved aside to let her wash her hands.

"Turn around," he said when she finished.

She did and noticed Jack standing in the doorway. He moved into the room.

Jon turned on the faucet behind her again.

Jack gestured toward the toilet. "Bend over. Spread your legs."

Her body responded to his command like a spark that ignited a wildfire. She put her hands on the back of the toilet and widened her stance.

"Hold still." With one hand curved around her right hip, his other gripped the butt plug and pulled it out.

The men changed positions behind her. Then a warm washcloth touched her. Jon wiped between her legs and butt, and she didn't feel the least bit uneasy.

"Go stand with Jack."

He was beside the door, so she went there. His hands turned her around, pulled her back against his clothed chest, and settled in a loose grip over her bare pussy. He didn't play with her, and she didn't think to care. She was too busy watching Jon set up an odd looking bench in the space between the toilet and the sink.

When he was finished, he looked up. "We plan to claim your body, pet. All of it."

In the bathroom?

"Does it belong to us?"

With a hard swallow, she nodded.

He put a hand on the bench. "Before we do, we want you as clean as physically possible. As we've said before, using the bathroom is a natural requirement of life, but we do not find it the least bit attractive. An enema will clean out any waste and leave you refreshed and ready for our use. Come here. Lie down."

She paused until Jack propelled her with his hands on each hip. They removed her garter belt, stockings and shoes in a methodical manner. Jack positioned her so that her butt hung over the open toilet, her legs bent with her feet on the back of the toilet.

"Keep your knees together and your feet apart," he said softly. His smile helped her relax some, but the nervousness remained. He ran a soothing hand over her stomach, cupped a breast, and thumbed her nipple.

She could hear Jon moving around, but couldn't see what he was doing until he knelt beside her. He held a full hot water bottle with an attached hose. He hung the bottle on a nearby towel hook and kept the hose pinched off as he positioned it under her legs. She caught a glimpse of a plastic, douche-like tip at the end of the hose.

"The solution is warm. As it goes in, you'll start to feel full. Don't fight it. Relax. When your rectum is full, you'll expunge the solution naturally." He slipped the bulbous tip past her sphincter and released pressure on the hose.

She closed her eyes and took deep breaths, until Jack kissed her. Together, the men effectively used caresses and gentle kisses to distract her, while ensuring her comfort during the procedure. Afterwards, they wiped her off and helped her up. As Jon cleaned up, Jack took her back into the other room.

"How do you feel?"

She thought about the question and smiled. "Refreshed, Master."

He grinned. She started to kneel, but he stopped her.

"Not yet." Handing her the black stockings, he said, "Put these back on."

With a mischievous chuckle, she turned her back on him, knelt on first one knee, then the other, to work the stockings up to her ankles. Then standing with her feet apart, she bent at the waist to slowly pull each one up her legs.

Master's hands settled over her butt, kneading the bare flesh.

"Our pet is playful," Sire said, walking into the room.

"Undoubtedly," Master agreed with a grin. He attached her garter belt, after which she put on her shoes and dropped to her knees. The position felt so natural to her now.

Sire made a complete circle around her and stopped in front of her.

Her heart sped up. Her arousal rose like mercury during a heat wave.

"I think we'll give her something to play with," he said.

She fought the urge to look up.

"What do you have in mind?" Master asked with obvious amusement.

"Bring her here."

Master held her hand as she rose to her feet. Curious, she stood watching Sire run a rope from an eyebolt in one wall to another. The rope stretched across one corner of the room at about waist level. As he tied off the ends, she saw more eyebolts secured at regular intervals in a line up each wall from floor to ceiling.

Sire draped a folded strip of velvety cloth over the rope so several inches hung on either side.

"Come here, pet." He held out a hand, which she took as she stepped forward. "Bend over that."

She did. Her face was in the corner, her hands on the walls.

"No. Keep going until you can grab your ankles the way you did a moment ago."

Oh. She bent her back and reached for her ankles. The rope was low enough that she kept her stilettos on the floor and knees slightly bent.

"Move your feet apart so you can see me between your legs."

When she did as told, she saw both men kneel. Each one cuffed her wrists to her ankles then pulled her feet farther apart to secure them to eyebolts in the wall. The spread forced her to put all her weight on the padded rope.

Sire rested a hand on her exposed ass. "Are you okay?"

"Yes, Sire."

"Excellent." His hands moved to his pants.

Zip. The sound made her mouth water.

One finger flicked her clitoris. "Don't go anywhere." With a wide smile, he stood to remove his pants.

Another zip told her Master undressed, too. Like some upside-down striptease, the two men shed their clothes with slow, steady ease. Gorgeous tanned skin and impressive hard-ons filled her view. She pulled against her restraints, gulped in inadequate breaths, and felt her own moisture build.

Kneeling out of reach, but not out of sight, Sire laughed. He held his cock, his thumb stroking along one blue vein. "Do you see something you want to play with, pet?"

"Yes, Sire." She stretched her neck like a starving baby bird.

"Beg for it."

"Please, Sire. I want to suck your hard cock. Lick it, taste it."

"My cock is not your toy, pet." He inched forward. "You're mine."

Her eyes focused on his aroused dick so near, but not close enough. Pre-cum moistened the head, and she experienced a hunger like none she'd ever had before.

"Sire, please, take what's yours. Fuck my mouth. Let me pleasure you. I beg y—"

His cock cut off her words. She tried to lick him, but he pressed deep to fill her mouth. She gagged, making him pull back. Only a little bit.

"Yes, pet. Swallow my cock." He pushed forward again and this time, she fought the reflex to choke.

With a tight grip on her hair, he moved her mouth up and down his hard length. She opened wide and let him control her head. After several thrusts, she caught onto the rhythm and began to suck.

"Just like that...ah, damn. That feels so fucking good."

His fists pushed her onto his cock, causing a little pain at her scalp, but she loved it. She reveled in making him lose control. She sucked harder, longing for that moment when his control would collapse and flood her mouth with his salty flavor.

Another pair of hands trailed up and down her thighs, over her ass.

"Open her for me," Sire said.

Master's fingers pulled her pussy lips apart so Sire's mouth could latch onto her. As his tongue darted in to torment her own control, she groaned around his cock. The position in which they'd bound her provided the perfect exposure for their splendid torture. She gasped for air and fought the impending climax.

"Come for me, pet."

No problem. She went off like a rocket.

"Ah, that's it. This once, you can come anytime you wish. As often as you like. I want to see it, taste it, and feel it take over your body."

Abruptly, Sire pulled his cock out of her mouth, stood, plunged it into her pussy, and sent her spiraling over another precipice. She couldn't speak, couldn't move. He pumped into her with shallow movements, drawing out more aftershocks.

"I'm going to fuck you in every way possible, pet," Sire said between heavy pants and more forceful thrusts. His fingers bit into her butt cheeks. His thighs slapped against her sweat-soaked skin. "You're going to take it, aren't you?"

"Y-yes, Sire," she hissed. Her muscles pulled taut in anticipation.

As his cock slipped in and out of her pussy, he gathered her juices with his fingertips and rubbed moisture across her asshole.

"Then...it'll be Master's turn...to play."

She moaned, unable to form words.

"I need more lube," he said but didn't leave, his cock still tunneling deep inside her channel.

She heard Master move away. A few seconds later he returned, and she felt something slick rubbed around her asshole.

"Who owns your ass?" Master asked, having knelt to peer at her from between his brother's legs.

Panting, she had to force her mind to concentrate on his words, to form a coherent reply. "You do. You both do."

"Damn right," Sire said and pushed his cock into her virgin ass.

She gritted her teeth, threw back her head, her eyes clamped shut.

The butt plug had done its job, prepared her for his invasion, but it wasn't as long as he was. Her muscles stretched to accommodate him. The pain radiated throughout her body, causing her legs to quiver and her arms to jerk against the cuffs. It wasn't unbearable, but instead turned into a sizzling, seductive lure.

His fingers held her butt in a bruising grip as he worked his cock in to the hilt. When he paused, she opened her eyes to see Master watching her closely.

He smiled, and she did, too. "She's fine," he said.

His words prodded Sire to action. He fucked her ass with long, steady strokes, his testicles slapping her engorged pussy.

Master scooted closer to reach forward and pinch one of her nipples. She heard a scream, vaguely realizing it was her own voice.

Deep in the throes of an intense orgasm, she gave up her body to their control. Sire pushed in several more times and with a shout, found his own release in her ass. When he pulled free, Master moved into place, easily entering her soaked pussy. In and out, his harder thrusts brought another orgasm. Her inner walls contracted around his length in a vain attempt to keep him inside.

"You're so wet." He slapped her ass.

She whimpered as another aftershock ripped through her body.

Master pummeled her pussy until she'd lost all track of time except for the steady cadence of his thrusts. When he slid out, he knelt before her face, his hand cupping the back of her head.

"Lick me."

Her tongue came out and circled the circumcised head, tasting her own juices.

"You taste that?"

"Nnn."

"Lick all of me." He held the tip and moved his hips closer so she could lick him like an ice cream treat. "You're such a hot little pet bitch. So wet and eager for our dicks, aren't you?" He prevented any possible answer when he stabbed his cock past her lips. "Suck my dick."

Unlike Sire, he didn't guide her head, so she stayed still and sucked as much of him as she could into her mouth. He pumped his hips, shoving his cock deeper. His hands kneaded her thighs just above her stockings. The touch sent a new thrill straight to her core.

More cream trickled from her pussy. Her ass felt soaked, but she couldn't dwell on that with his cock diving into her mouth. He fingered her ass as his lips sucked her clit with hard nips that torpedoed her senses. She knew nothing that happened beyond the man who used her body for his own pleasure and gave her unbridled pleasure in return.

After several deep strokes down her throat, he pulled away and stood. His hands on her ass spread her cheeks. His stiff cock pushed against the puckered flesh. Well lubricated, the tight opening was no match for his physical demand. He entered in a single thrust that buried him to the hilt.

Again she screamed as the pleasure-pain shot up her spine. Her flesh clamped around him like a fist. He halted briefly, his harsh breaths audible over her unintelligible sounds.

"So fucking tight. That's it. Grip me hard."

Her pulse thundered in her head. Her legs and arms hung limp. Her mind and energy centered on the cock that moved in her once more.

"Take it, my little bitch. Take all of me."

He drove her higher, stretching her flesh as he fucked her ass without mercy and annihilated her temperance.

Her self-imposed constraint shattered. She went wild, thrashing against her bonds.

Sire's voice penetrated the haze. "Very good, Rachel. Feel it rise. Let it out." His hand reached between his brother's flexing legs to touch her stomach, her navel, and her breasts. His tender caresses were a direct contrast to the vehement strokes that pierced her ass. Pain and pleasure. They gave her everything she needed and more. Tears rolled from her eyes unchecked.

"Who do you belong to?" Sire asked calmly.

"You," she shouted.

"What are you?" Master gritted out the words without stopping his powerful pace.

"Yours."

Hot cum shot into her ass as orgasmic tremors wracked her entire body.

"My what?"

"Your bitch!"

CHAPTER NINE

When she finally came back to earth, gentle fingers were unfastening her hands and feet. She hung motionless over the rope, her legs unable to hold her weight. A warm, damp cloth comforted her skin, wiping away cum and lubrication. Then the rope loosened.

"Careful," Sire said, guiding her body to the floor. As weak as a newborn babe, she collapsed into a fetal position on her side. Hands kneaded her arms. Another pair rubbed her legs and removed her shoes. They undressed her completely while she lay like a rag doll. Subdued and sated.

Strong arms lifted her against a damp chest. Her head settled on his shoulder.

"Just rest, pet," Master murmured in her ear. He moved through the house with Sire clearing the way.

Upstairs, he waited for Sire to fill a spa tub then sank into the water with her on his lap, her back to his chest. Sire removed her leather collar before climbing in. While Master cleaned her torso, Sire lifted each foot and rubbed away the aches caused from walking in stiletto heels. Both men touched her with a tenderness that made her want to cry.

Her sore weakness turned into contented inertia.

After they finished, they dried her off and carried her to bed, settling her exhausted body between them. She closed her eyes and drifted off to sleep with feelings of peace, protection...and love.

* * * * *

Over the next week, she refused to think about the love she'd felt that night. They'd never used the word, and she wasn't about to bring it up. She'd made her deal in good faith and wouldn't balk when it ended.

So she focused on making the most of her limited time and enjoyed the way her owners made her body come alive. She gave little thought to her life beyond their arms. Each day they challenged her to go further than she ever thought possible. Every limit she'd set in her mind gave way to their persistent influence. With each lesson her trust in their care grew.

They started feeding her in bed rather than forcing her to kneel at the table. While the collar remained, the leash had been retired, as her obedience earned her greater liberties, and she accepted their guidance by word alone.

Many times they cuddled with her and shared fun-loving stories of their childhood spent on a dairy farm of all places. The youngest two of six children, they'd kept their parents on their toes until college beckoned and they sought out the lights and joys of the big city.

She had also grown up away from the hectic pace of city life, although her childhood hadn't been as idyllic. The only child of a weak woman too afraid to leave an abusive husband for a better, if not richer, existence. Although he'd never raised a hand to her, Rachel witnessed his attacks, both verbal and physical, against her mother. She determined that she wouldn't become like her mother. She'd never be that weak, never give up her hard-earned independence for any man. Yet, here she was kneeling at the feet of not one, but two.

She learned that irrational physical abuse was not the same as consensual discipline wielded by one who cares. They proved that not all men were like her father, on an angry power trip. There was a difference between attacks that demeaned a woman, and dominance motivated by an urge to provide and pleasure.

They showed her the contrast of a lonely, self-imposed freedom and the strength behind submission. They hadn't forced her to labor in their home once, although they'd done chores together. Most often they seemed to revel in caring for her.

She'd asked them once what attracted them to this lifestyle. What did they get out of it?

Jon's response was, "A woman is a man's treasure. Sure, we like the power evident in controlling her, but the real attraction comes from knowing she's completely ours. Her needs, wants, and desires are ours to provide. With that responsibility, we're blessed with her faith in us and the pleasures of her body, mind, and..." He never finished his thought, but she'd never forget the tender longing in his eyes.

They showed her through both words and deeds that the real gift lay in providing for others. She discovered the rush of pleasing them without any concern for her own needs. With them, giving up her independence proved worth it as they fulfilled her sexual desires and comforted her lonely soul.

"Before our time is up, pet, we want to present you to a few of our friends." Sire sat on the couch, his booted foot across his right knee. "You've already shown great promise in public displays of obedience. This is the final step in the process of complete submission."

Her face heated as she remembered the orgasm in the restaurant. She kept her head bowed.

They'd since taken her shopping, fucked her in a dressing room, made her pleasure them in a movie theatre, and had her masturbate in the backseat of Jack's Suburban as they drove through rush-hour traffic. They long ago convinced her that it wasn't a game. It wasn't a dream, but it could be her reality.

She wanted this kind of life and all the daring thrills that went along with it. Her job and its daily pressures hadn't even crossed her mind as they kept her busy with more than great sex. Her career remained an exciting challenge, but she knew now that she needed a way to let go of her daily worries, surrender herself to someone she could trust to share the burden. Someone to share her thoughts, feelings, and private desires. They'd given her that. Shown her what was missing most in a life she'd believed was full but now found utterly lacking.

How would she ever live without them?

Her head down, she closed her eyes to hold back the tear that threatened to spill over her lashes. It escaped anyway to drop on her thigh.

"What's wrong, pet?"

Damn. "Nothing, Sire."

Master's voice was sudden and stern. "We know better, and you know not to disobey us."

She looked up. He leaned down and fingered the tiny drop on her thigh.

Her gaze lowered. "I'm sorry, Master."

"You wronged Sire with your lie and will face your punishment from him."

"Get up and lie across Master's lap."

She did as told, making herself comfortable facedown across Master's thighs. He held her in place with a light hand on the small of her back and a firm grip on the collar's D ring at her neck.

"Do you know the reason for your punishment, pet?" Sire asked.

She nodded.

"Tell me."

She heard him cross the room, open a drawer and return.

"I lied to you when you asked me what was wrong."

The first blow was sharp, quick, and made her gasp.

"Have we lost your trust?"

"No..." The paddle fell again. "...Sire!"

"Yet, you lied to me?"

Another swat. "Sorry, Sire." After each slap, his hand gently touched the spot, making her keenly aware of his concern. And her arousal.

"Lying destroys trust." *Slap!*

"Yes, Sire."

After one final smack of the paddle, he knelt before her.

"Will you do it again?" His pained expression

brought more tears to her eyes than the punishing blows.

"No, Sire."

He kissed away the teardrops.

"Does the thought of meeting our friends frighten you?"

"I...I don't know if I can do it. I'm afraid I'll disappoint you."

Sire cradled her face in his palms. "You could never disappoint us as long as you remain true to your heart...and honest with us."

Another tear fell onto her cheek. His thumb wiped it away.

"You're ours, pet—if only for a little while longer—and we'd like to show you off. We believe you're ready. Do you doubt us?"

She shook her head. Her ass still stung like the devil from the paddling, but his words struck the more painful blow to her heart. *If only for a little while longer.*

Her self-imposed time limit was fast approaching, and once that time was up, she would have to return to the real world. A real world where polygamy was illegal and prosecutors remained on the right side of the law.

She could've had three weeks to build more memories with the two men who'd somehow wormed their way into her heart, but wouldn't that just make leaving them later more difficult? When the time came, she'd leave. After all, she'd negotiated the damned deal. Now, she'd have to live with the regrets.

* * * * *

Her last night as the Sinclair pet came all too soon. With each passing second, her trepidation increased, as did the tension in the house. Her owners kept themselves busy and refused to share any details about the night's events. So she paced and worried and thought up all manner of possible things that could go wrong, her worst fear being somehow to let them down or embarrass all of them in front of their friends.

She took a long time to prepare, spent extra time on her nails, makeup and hair.

She turned at the sound of a knock on the bathroom door.

"It's almost time, pet," Master said. "We've something different for you to wear tonight."

Surprised and curious, she walked naked into the bedroom to see an unmarked box on the bedspread. Since she'd spent much of the past week with only the dog collar on, the idea of wearing clothes in the house was a bit of a shock. She wasn't sure whether she felt relief or disappointment.

"Close your eyes."

"Again, Master?" Disappointment won out. She really did not want to spend her last night with them blind as a bat.

"Only for a little while, so behave," Sire said with a grin as he stepped forward and removed her collar.

She frowned at the loss of its touch encircling her neck.

Both men were already dressed for the evening, Sire in dark slacks and a cobalt blue silk shirt with no tie. Master wore black pants and a burgundy shirt unbuttoned at the collar like his brother's. The rich colors brought out the brilliance of their sapphire eyes, complimented their bronzed skin, and made her want to rip the material off to uncover what was beneath. Alone, each man was attractive enough to turn any woman's head. Together they devastated her senses.

"Finished looking, pet?"

At Sire's amused question, her gaze shot from his crotch to his eyes. The temperature rose up her neck just as fast.

He touched her eyelids, forcing them closed. "No peeking."

She waited.

His fingers skimmed against her skin as he pulled something around her neck. A soft material draped like a whisper over her shoulders and fanned out down her back to flutter across her butt and the backs of her arms and legs. Then he lifted some of the material to let it settle over her head and brush against her face. With a soft click, he attached something else around her neck.

Fingers pinched and twirled her nipples until both were erect. Tiny loops slipped around each bud and pulled tight. A chain dangled between her breasts. Next, she felt an unexpected pinch to her clitoris that made her hiss. Although the fingers released her, the pressure on her clit remained, and when she shifted her feet, she heard tiny bells.

Lifting her feet one at a time, he put a pair of very high heels on her.

"Turn toward my voice, pet." When she did, Master said, "Open your eyes."

She couldn't believe the reflection in the full length mirror. "I..."

A sheer black cape hung across her back. It gave the illusion of cover while concealing nothing. The gossamer cape cascaded down her arms and framed her exposed front. Attached at the neck, it had an equally transparent hood that hung over her head and draped across her entire face like a see-through veil. Over the material around her neck was a beautiful silver choker with a clasp sealed by a tiny padlock.

Threaded through the loop of the padlock was a delicate silver chain that led downward to nipple rings, from which dangled round diamonds. Between her legs were little silver bells attached to a silver clamp on her clit.

"You're breathtaking," Master whispered.

"I'm speechless," she said, making them laugh.

"We intend to push your limits tonight," Sire said, "as far as you're willing to go."

Attending a party dressed in little more than an invisible veil was already so far beyond any limit she'd ever considered before, it might as well be on Pluto.

"Um...exactly how many people are going to be here tonight?"

"A few couples and hired help. No more than that." Master tilted her chin up. "You aren't considering backing out on us now, are you?"

She'd thought about it, but this was her last night with them. She didn't want to spoil it by going timid now. If they thought she was bold enough—ready enough—to do this, then she would trust them.

"I didn't get all dressed up for nothing," she said, hoping her bravado would convince them, even if she didn't buy it for a second.

Sire grinned. "That's my girl. Remember, there are a few additional rules you must obey tonight. Unlike at the restaurant, you are not free to speak unless we tell you to, or one of the other Doms asks you a question directly. You will also keep your eyes downcast unless given permission to look a Dom in the eye."

"Yes, Sire."

"Obey us immediately, and all will go well. We know you can do this. Make us proud, pet." He lifted the veil and gave her the type of chaste kiss that always punched her heart.

She did not want to—No. She *would not* let them down.

"One final thing." She turned to see Master lift a piece of black, cone-shaped leather with silver buckles.

"What's that?"

His smile was wicked. "Something guaranteed to heighten the suspense. Hands behind your back, pet. Arms straight, palms together."

He moved the cape aside briefly to slip on the unusual device. The leather was a sleeve that stretched from her wrists to a few inches above her elbows. It held her arms locked in a V-shape behind her back, forced her chest out, and definitely boosted her anticipation.

Apparently satisfied with her appearance and bondage, they took her downstairs and made her wait, kneeling on the ottoman, as guests started to arrive.

Rachel had no trouble keeping her gaze lowered. She was too nervous to look anyone in the eye. Fortunately for her nerves, the first to appear were Dylan and Olivia.

"What a beautiful centerpiece, Jack," Dylan said.

Her whole body tingled under their regard.

"We think so," Master agreed. "Pet, say hello to Master Dylan."

"Hello, Master Dylan." She didn't look up.

"You are even lovelier than the last time we saw you, Rachel."

A lot more naked, too, she thought. Her face warmed. A shiver vibrated up her back. "Thank you."

"Dylan, I believe you know Mistress Katriona," Sire said escorting the next arrivals into the room.

"Indeed. A pleasure as always, Kat."

Out of the corner of her eye, Rachel watched Dylan greet Kat with a kiss to the cheek. While Dylan wore a custom-tailored, blue-black suit that broadcast classic style, Kat appeared to have fallen into a vat of pitch latex. *Wall Street meets the S&M Dungeon Mistress.* The contrast was almost comical, but Rachel kept her lips sealed and head bowed.

Beside Kat was a man clothed in a pair of skin-tight, black spandex shorts and no shirt. He wore metal cuffs on his wrists, ankles, and around his neck with chains connecting each one to a belt around his waist. Olivia was in a form-fitting dress similar to the one she wore at the restaurant, only this one was cherry red, and she'd removed her shoes. She and the chained man knelt next to their owners. Seeing the subs clothed in more than she was increased Rachel's unease tenfold.

"You gentlemen remember Carl, my slave?" Kat popped him across the bare back with a small riding crop. He didn't even flinch, but he caught Rachel peeking through her lashes and grinned. What on earth would make a man want to submit himself as a slave?

"Greet our hosts properly, slave," Kat said.

Carl murmured a greeting to the men, which she didn't quite catch, and bowed until his forehead touched the floor. Kat petted his ass in approval. When the dominatrix stopped and suddenly approached her, Rachel forgot how to breathe.

"So, this is the reason the Masters of Sin have been absent from our little club?"

Masters of Sin?

"Mistress Katriona, this is our pet, Rachel," Sire said.

"Greet our guest, my pet," Master said.

"Hello, M-mistress." Unlike Carl, she didn't budge from her position on the ottoman. If her owners had wanted her to bow, she felt certain they would've instructed her to do so.

"Hello, bitch," Kat said, turning Rachel's downcast gaze into a glare. The dominatrix raised a brow as she circled the ottoman like a critic finding fault with a sculpture.

Master had called her that, too, but his tone compared to Kat's was like the difference between sugar and sand. One was palatable and sweet; the other wasn't. "My name is Rachel."

"Lower your gaze, pet. Now!" Sire snapped.

She damn near hissed, but obeyed, catching a satisfied smirk on the latex witch's face before her gaze drilled a hole through the floor.

"Disrespectful bitch, isn't she?" Kat asked. "I can see why you've been away so long. Must have taken days to break her."

"She will accept her punishment for any disobedience," Master said.

Like hell! Not for something she didn't do.

"She knows who her masters are, Katriona. You should remember it as well when you use that tone of voice to address our property."

Yeah! Take that, asshole!

"I suggest you use her name," Sire added, "so that you don't risk offending us."

After a silent pause, Katriona said, "As you wish. No offense intended."

Master gestured toward the door as a servant in bondage attire entered with a tray held aloft. "Please, make yourselves comfortable while drinks are served, and we dispense with the necessary punishment. Afterwards, we'll adjourn to the dining room for dinner."

Punishment, my ass.

Her Doms took up book-end positions at her side as the others moved away. The uniformed servant went around the room in a manner so normal that she wondered how many other dinner parties he'd worked for clients with bondage fetishes. Was there a caterer who specialized in this type of thing?

Sire helped her off the ottoman.

Taking her place on the ottoman, Master sat with legs apart. He forced her to face him on her knees and then lifted her veil out of the way. "Do you understand the reason for your punishment, pet?"

She gave him a bold stare. "No, Master."

Sire stood off to her right. "Did you forget that you

were given strict rules for this evening?"

She turned her face to him, her eyes wide.

"I see you recall my orders. Did you not directly disobey me?" His hand held the flogger Master used on her previously. He slapped it once against his thigh. When she continued to stare, he asked, "Do you not still disobey me?"

Damn it. Rather than trusting them to handle Kat's caustic offense, she'd reacted by speaking out of turn and looking up. She broke both rules in one fell swoop and played right into the hands of that latex witch.

She lowered her gaze. "Forgive me, Sire. I'm sorry."

Master fingered her chin to regain her attention. "You know what we do when your mouth gets the better of you?"

She nodded and watched him unzip his pants. She did love their form of punishment, usually, but the audience made this time daunting.

Since her arms remained bound behind her, they had to help her into the position they wanted. Her chin rested on the edge of the ottoman, her back parallel to the floor. The silver chain dangled from her nipples and choker. The tiny bells between her legs tinkled.

Master's semi-erect cock pressed for entry to her mouth. "Put your mouth to better use. Remember, pet. Hold, but don't suck to completion." As her tongue worked to arouse him to full hardness, she was grateful for his thighs which blocked out any view of the others in the room.

Sire parted her knees slightly so her pussy was exposed to the air, and no doubt the view of everyone else in the room. When he moved the sheer cape out of the way, she'd never felt so vulnerable in her life. Her heart leapt into action as moisture dewed on her labia.

Just then, the last guest arrived.

"Sorry, I'm late," the man said with a rich accent similar to Dylan's.

While she remained in a tenuous position, her owners greeted the new arrival as if nothing was amiss.

"Ryan! Glad you could make it. How was the flight?" Master asked.

"Delayed in Detroit. Just got in and came straight from the airport. Dylan told me about your new pet." He laughed. "I see you have her well in hand."

"*Hola*, brother," Dylan said, much to Rachel's surprise. "Welcome home."

Ryan's footsteps moved toward his brother's voice. "It's good to be home, but it'll be better soon. Olivia, puss, where's my welcome?"

Rachel heard Olivia jump up with a gleeful squeal and kiss him soundly on the mouth.

"Welcome home, Master."

Olivia had two masters?

Several long seconds later, Ryan said, "Now that's what I call a homecoming."

The Doms laughed.

"Come, puss. Sit on my lap for a while. I've missed you too much to leave you on the floor." The leather couch sighed as they took their seats beside Dylan. "So have I missed much?"

"No," Sire said. "We were just getting started."

Rachel's back tensed in anticipation of the flogger's blow, but instead she felt the suede ends lightly brush across her butt, between her legs. The bells rang.

"Our pet forgot some of the rules tonight. We're

reminding her of our preferred use for her mouth and tongue."

Ryan chuckled.

Master nudged her lips into action.

The flogger trailed up and down the back of each thigh, and then the handle rubbed her cunt. She expected a sharp blow across her ass, but instead she got a light flick of the flogger, the thin strips perfectly aimed at her pussy. With one mild strike, Sire shoved her to the edge where she teetered in shocked alarm.

If he strikes there once more...

She moaned a warning around Master's stiff cock and tried to look up. If she climaxed without permission, she knew the punishment would be more severe. But worse, she'd disappoint her owners in front of their friends. She didn't want to do that.

But the flogger's ends didn't return. Instead, the penis-shaped handle did. Sire pressed it slowly into her wet sheath, moving in shallow strokes that she could better handle. When he'd lodged the entire length inside her, he left it there. The suede strips hung out of her like a tail and tickled her thighs.

She started to close her legs and felt a sharp, five-fingered stop sign collide with her right butt cheek. "Aaaw," she said, although the sound was muffled by the dick in her mouth.

"Suck harder, pet," Master said. His hands forced her head to his preferred pace and intensity. "A little longer."

Yep, he was getting longer. She would've smiled if her lips weren't spread wide by his thick cock.

The flogger remained embedded in her pussy. The

cape draped across her ass once more, but did nothing for her modesty.

Master pulled her mouth off him. Tiny lines of strain appeared etched in his chiseled features. "Are you thirsty, pet?"

Sitting back on her heels, she licked her lips and smiled. "Yes, Master."

He raised a brow. With a frown, he tucked his ramrod dick back into his pants and leaned close. His words were a husky whisper in her ear. "Then earn it."

She couldn't believe he was stopping. Not now. She'd brought him within seconds of climax. What did it matter who watched her? "Master..."

His hard look chilled the longing in her voice.

Her punishment was not the flogging she'd expected, but rather a denial of what she wanted. She eyed the tell-tale bulge in his slacks as he stood. Unfortunately, the knowledge that Master was forced to forego his own pleasure made the punishment that much harder for her to bear.

"If you need some relief, Master Jack," Kat said, "my slave is at your service."

Rachel seethed, but she'd bite her tongue off before she'd fail them again. She kept her head bowed and waited for her master's response.

"I appreciate the offer and will keep it in mind. Right now, however, I'm hungry for that delectable lobster I smelled cooking in the kitchen earlier. Shall we?"

Sire helped her up with a whispered, "The flogger stays put...for now."

CHAPTER TEN

She held her breath as they walked her into the dining room. At least they hadn't made her crawl like a dog with a tail. A literal tail, since the flogger still hung out of her pussy.

In the dining room, she saw pillows on the floor and realized she wouldn't be sitting at the table. With a resigned sigh, she waited for orders, which came from Master this time.

"Kneel, pet."

The flogger was less noticeable as she took up her position between her owners' chairs. The table was glass, held up by two marble sculptures, so she had an easy view of the others as they took their seats. Except for Olivia and Carl, who remained on the floor like her.

As the meal progressed, Rachel was able to forget the flogger and noticed a difference between the Doms. Like her own owners, Ryan and Dylan fed Olivia from their hands. However, Carl didn't eat. He prepared Kat's plate, positioned her napkin, and essentially served her throughout the meal. Once, he dribbled a bit as he lifted a bite to her mouth. She made him lick off the spot then bow at her feet licking the top of her boot while she enjoyed the rest of her meal. Finally, after eating only about half her portions, she set the plate on the floor and allowed him to eat her leftovers.

Rachel found the whole thing appalling. As much as her owners had put her through, they'd never treated her poorly. A part of her questioned whether she was overreacting. Wasn't she doing the same by eating portions of her owners' meals from their hands? Maybe so, but at least the way they chose to feed her was more palatable. Then Carl glanced up from his plate and grinned at her. Apparently he enjoyed servitude to his mistress, so who was she to complain?

Conversation continued throughout the meal as Ryan caught everyone up on his business trip and the others reminisced about various moments shared over the years.

"How are things at the club?" Master asked Katriona.

"The renovations are complete since the last time you two were there. The Plexiglas panels are a big hit for our voyeuristic crowd. There are a few subs, however, who are lamenting your absence...Constance, for one."

Would they go back to the club after tomorrow?

If Rachel wasn't mistaken, Sire's response held a trace of warning. "I'm sure you're quite capable of finding others willing to meet her needs."

"When do you plan to bring your latest pet to the club for a...demonstration?"

Sire's hand caressed the back of her head. Master gave her a bite of lobster. "Not before she's ready."

Master's answer didn't show any doubt in her ability to someday face such an ordeal, but it was vague enough not to give away the fact that their relationship ended after tonight, which prevented any chance of a demonstration at the club.

"Permission to speak, Master?"

His gaze fell to hers. "Granted."

"What's the name of this club?"

"Incognito."

Katriona wouldn't give up. "Are we to be entertained with a demonstration tonight, then?"

Master studied her eyes as if trying to determine whether she was ready for what he had in mind. She met that gaze boldly. Challenges had always been her Achilles heel. She felt compelled to rise to the occasion, even if by doing so she allowed others to take pot shots at her.

"Certainly," he said at last, lifting her veil back into place.

They all went downstairs.

"Feel free to use anything in the room for your own property," Sire said as the other Doms browsed the room and its many contraptions of bondage.

Rachel knelt in the center of the room. Tension rose with each passing minute. Her owners stood nearby watching as the other Doms secured their subs.

"I believe you're overdressed, puss," Ryan said with a toothy grin.

"Apologies, my Master." Olivia stripped nude and wound up bound to the padded sawhorse, her head facing the center of the room.

Carl lost possession of his spandex shorts after Kat ordered him to a tall wooden post in one corner where she locked his wrists over his head. His attention remained on his mistress as she roughly dragged the shorts down his legs. Although not as well endowed as the Sinclair brothers, the slave still had an impressive erection.

Realizing what she was staring at and that she'd raised her head to watch, she quickly lowered her gaze. Neither Master nor Sire gave any indication that they'd witnessed her disobedience.

All five Doms gathered around her. She couldn't breathe. What did they have in store for her?

Master stood in front of her. "Stand, pet. Look at me."

As she did, the flogger slipped out of her pussy that had grown increasingly wet as the night progressed. Her tiny bells jangled.

"Leave it," Sire said from behind her. "Assist us, Doms?"

She tried to ignore the others' movements and stared at Master. His intense gaze didn't sway from hers.

Sire removed the collar, which released the chain attached at her nipples to slap against her tummy. Ryan lifted her veil over her head. Kat released the hook-n-eye fastening of the cloak. The material fell in a puddle at her feet.

Her breathing became difficult.

Dylan, Sire, and Kat worked to unbuckle the straps of her leather arm restraints. Ryan removed her nipple rings.

Her hands fisted behind her.

When Kat reached toward her crotch, the panic in her eyes must have shown.

"Wait," Master said. His hand reached out to stop the mistress. "Do you wish to say something, pet?"

She had no desire to have Katriona touch her between

her legs. No woman, for that matter. The idea shattered every ounce of arousal and replaced it with anxiety. She'd tried to remain calm while the others stripped her body, because Sire had requested their help. Though their touches were impersonal and business-like, she'd grown increasingly terrified. Even Ryan's fingers on her breast unnerved her. She couldn't explain it, but she didn't want—couldn't stomach—anyone else's hands on her body. No one but Sire's and Master's.

She hated to disappoint them, had vowed to make this night memorable for them all, but they'd reached a limit she hadn't realized existed until this moment. She didn't want her time with them to end this way. Her nose burned as tears gathered in her eyes. One teardrop escaped to plow a wet path over her left cheek.

Master watched and waited, as did all of the rest circled around her.

"To feel another's touch is to me a...fantasy."

Master showed no emotion, no change in expression whatsoever, but the other Doms must have realized something had changed because they moved away. All except Sire, who walked around her to stand beside his brother.

She turned her face away in shame. She'd let them down. Ruined their last night together.

"We've reached your limit, Rachel?"

Her hands, now free, hung by her side. She closed her eyes, nodded, and let the tears fall.

"Before, we told you what we would do should your 'fantasy' overwhelm you."

"I just...I can't...I'm sorry to let you down." Not

knowing what else to say or do, she dropped to her knees. The tinkling bells brought more sadness than cheer.

Neither man touched her as she knelt before them, bare in body and spirit. So much time passed as they stood over her, she feared what would happen next.

"Get up, pet," Jack said.

She wiped her damp cheeks as she obeyed. Unable to look them in the eye, she kept her gaze lowered.

"Gentlemen...ladies," Jon began, "This room is at your disposal. You may continue to use anything here as you wish. Please, forgive us as duty to our pet requires we leave."

They left the room with her between them. She expected them to call a cab and toss her out the front door along with her clothes, but instead, they took her to their bedroom suite, watched her dress, and escorted her to the Suburban.

Jack drove through the dark streets while Jon sat in the back beside her. She fidgeted with her skirt's hem and stared out the window in silence.

As they neared her house Jon asked softly, "What's in your heart, Rachel?" He sounded again like the professional psychiatrist, so calm and interested. She nearly smiled, but her heart hurt too much.

"I don't want the night to end. I'll do anything for you, but...just you. Your touch, Sire...Master. My body longs for that, but..." Again the words wouldn't come.

"You need our touch?"

She looked at him. "No one else's."

"So that's the boundary..." He exchanged a glance with Jack's reflection in the rearview mirror. "...Your limit has more to do with not wanting others to touch you?"

She nodded and turned back to the black night out the window. "I failed you tonight, and I'm sorry for that."

"You didn't fail us, pet," Jack said from the driver's seat.

If she hadn't failed them, then why did she feel so pitiful?

He pulled into her driveway and set the brake. Her home, a quaint bungalow, sat at the end of a cul-de-sac. Her Jag was in the driveway, which made her cast a questioning look at Jon.

"We took it from the parking garage that night so it wouldn't draw attention. Fulstrom drove it over here the next day for me."

She got out. Jon did too.

Jack opened the driver's door and handed her purse to her. "Your keys are inside."

Unable to speak, she nodded and stared at the bag. She wanted to ask them to come in but knew they'd refuse. How pathetic would she be if they declined?

Jon took one of her hands. "Thank you, Rachel, for giving us the pleasure of your company...the gift of your trust...if only for ten days."

"You didn't disappoint us, pet," Jack said. "We understand that the use of your safe word tonight was only to avoid the touch of the other Doms and not a direct response to us. We accept that and respect your wishes."

Then why were they ending the night so soon?

"At the same time, we must keep our word and fulfill the promise we made to you should you feel it necessary to use that word."

Owning Rachel

But she wouldn't hold them to that! Not if it meant she could have a few more hours with them.

Jon said, "As much as I'd like to imprison you forever in my home, sometimes one must let go." He thumbed her cheek and smiled. "Know that for us, you became our pet the moment you called Jack. But we also know that you have another life that requires your attention. Go back to that life. Get away from all of this. Only then can you hope to find balance."

"Only then will you be free to decide," Jack added before he gave her a tender kiss on the lips and got in his vehicle.

"Go on," Jon said, giving her a brief kiss as well, his fingertips brushing her jaw line. "We'll wait to make sure you're safe inside."

Tears clung to her lashes. By the time she made it through the front door, they were streaming down her face.

She knew Jon was right, and she hated that. They'd introduced her to another world, peeled away a layer of her own nature, and forced her to face the consequences. Like forbidden fruit, that lifestyle was so different, tempting and totally incompatible with her other life.

Crawling between the cool sheets of her bed, she curled up fully clothed and cried. How could she ever hope to find balance when they'd ripped the scales from her grasp?

* * * * *

Several days later

"Damn it. You said three weeks, not two. I lost the bet. You're not supposed to be here!" Pamela stormed into her office and froze. "What's that?"

Rachel stared at the words on the card. "Flowers."

"Right. What are they doing on your desk?"

"Carmichael brought them in a few minutes ago."

Pamela's mouth gaped. "Carmichael?"

Rachel laughed. "No! They aren't from him."

"Oh. So who are they from?"

She held out the card. "What do you make of that?"

"If you love something, set it free..." Richard Bach

Pamela's brow furrowed as she read the bold handwriting. "I've heard the saying before, but who's Richard Bach? You meet him on vacation?" She grinned. "Did you take my advice and get laid?"

Rachel smiled. "Bach is an American author who was born during the Depression."

"Uh...Okay...bit old for you isn't he?"

"He didn't send the flowers. He's the man who first coined that phrase."

"Oh." She huffed and dropped the card on the desk. "So who sent 'em? You fall in love with someone you put in jail?"

She laughed. "Not exactly." She bent to lift a box onto her desk.

"What are you doing?" Pamela narrowed her gaze. "What the hell's going on?"

"Packing." She put more personal belongings into the box on her desk.

"I see that. The question is, what for?"

She took a handful of books off a shelf. "I've

resigned."

"What the hell for?" Pamela's voice rose with her surprise.

"I'm going into private practice."

"All right, where's my friend? What have you done with her? You know, the Ice Queen?"

Rachel laughed. "I'm right here. I just want to try defending clients instead of prosecuting them."

Private practice offered her a higher level of anonymity. It allowed her personal life to remain private if she chose, and she did. The risk of having some reporter delve into her life became less likely when she was no longer a public servant on the government's payroll and answerable to the taxpayers. Despite how it looked to Pamela, the decision to resign hadn't come lightly.

She'd tried for days to get over the Sinclair brothers, to push her experience with them into the past and get on with her life. Unable to stand the confines of her lonely home, she'd quit her vacation early on the off chance that would work. But when she caught herself lifting her skirt before taking a seat, the memories of Master's touch and Sire's kisses flooded her mind.

Then the flowers arrived.

She gave up any attempt to fight a losing battle and tracked down the number for Olivia Montgomery. They'd had a long talk which helped Rachel decide her next move.

"Rachel, are you sure you know what you're doing?"

She picked up the card. Read it again. "For once in my life, I do."

* * * * *

Jon closed the door on his last patient of the evening and sank into his chair.

He had spent the better part of a week working himself to the bone, trying to get *her* out of his mind. He'd even slept on his office couch one night because he couldn't stand the thought of going home to find no sign of Rachel, and Jack pacing the floor like a snarling tiger.

His cell phone vibrated, but when he saw who it was, he ignored it.

He and Jack had never risked so much on a sub before. Many used the bondage scene to go from one sexual partner to another. They were more interested in the lure of the fetish world than in living it as a lifestyle with a full commitment to their masters. Kat's club, and others like it, enabled them to do that.

Although he and Jack had used the club to troll for subs, they always went there with the hope of finding one woman who'd willingly take that final step. Before Rachel, a couple seemed to fit the bill, but only for a little while. Both had wanted to explore their sexuality until it got hard, more demanding. Then the *game* was over. They both bailed. He hadn't lied to Rachel when he'd said BDSM could be dangerous. He just hadn't explained that the dangers were more than physical.

There were a few exceptions, like Dylan and Ryan. They'd been fortunate to find Olivia, but they'd discovered her far from the red velvet and steel cages of the bondage clubs.

So when he found Rachel outside the club scene, his and Jack's hopes soared. She'd responded so well to their training that she slipped past the guards they'd erected to protect their hearts. Now, as each day passed with no word from her, their hope plummeted and their hearts bled.

He pulled a black velvet box from his desk drawer and stared at the contents.

It became harder to not contact her as they'd promised. He secretly wished Jack had not told her she'd never hear from them again should she use her safe word. Judging by Jack's waspish attitude lately, his brother regretted that promise, too.

His intercom buzzed. "Jackson's here to see you, sir."

"Thank you, Sharon. Send him in."

His office door opened a second later, and Jack walked in ahead of Sharon. Jack raised his dark sunglasses, perching them atop his head—a move that revealed the forlorn hollowness of his gaze.

"Hold my calls," Jon said, gaining a smile from his secretary before she closed the door.

Jack plopped into a chair, saw the jewelry box, and asked, "Anything?" He didn't have to say more. They expected her to contact them through his office, if she contacted them at all.

Jon shook his head, and Jack cursed under his breath. He closed the velvet case with a snap.

The waiting drove them crazy. This morning it became unbearable, so Jon broke their promise and sent a bouquet of flowers with a cryptic message. It may have doomed them, but he prayed that wasn't the case.

"I sent her flowers."

Jack's gaze shot to him.

"I know. We aren't supposed to try to persuade her. I

know we made a promise to let her make the next move, but damn it. Those tears of hers were real. The night we dropped her off...she felt something. She said she didn't want the night to end. Now she's just being stubborn."

"I know." Jack's voice was flat. He raised a hand to wearily rub the five o'clock shadow that marred his normally clean-shaven face.

"Then we have to do something. We should go after what's ours."

Jack pushed to his feet and started pacing. "Don't you think I want to go to her and drag her back home? Hell, Jon, I love her as much as you do, but if we chase her now, we'll be chasing her for the rest of our lives. She has to want this lifestyle. We can't force it on her. She must meet us half way."

Jon raked fingers through his hair. "Fuck. What are we going to do?"

"We're going to trust our pet to come to us. We don't have any other choice." His words preached patience, but his tone simmered as if he were ready to explode. After another lap across the imported Oriental rug, Jack stopped. "I hope like hell you at least sent her roses."

Jon smiled, and then laughed.

The phone rang. He snatched the receiver. "Sharon, I said hold my calls."

"If she had, you'd regret it," Katriona said.

He rested his forehead in his palm. "Kat, I'm kind of busy right now. Can this wait?"

"No. Where's Jack?"

He punched the button for the speaker. "He's here."

"Hi, Kat."

"Finally! I need you both to get over to the club. ASAP."

Their friends had tried repeatedly to get them out of their slump. They just didn't get that this time, things had changed.

"Look, Kat, I appreciate the—"

"Jon, listen to me carefully. There's a sub here requesting the Masters of Sin."

"Find someone else. We're on hiatus indefinitely."

"She's not my slave to pass around. She needs you two."

"We don't need another sub, Kat."

"Damn it. She storms into my club like some dominatrix on a mission. She's not a member, has no collar, and won't leave. I've got things under control for the moment, but I don't know what else to do with her."

No collar?

"Kat, are you telling me Ra—"

"I gave my word. No names. But if you don't get here soon, you and Jack are going to have one pissed-off pet on your hands. She's been here over twenty minutes already, while I've called all over creation looking for you. Don't you ever answer your damn cell phones?"

They hung up and made it to Incognito in record time. Kat met them at the door.

"No one's touched her. Apparently she called Olivia before showing up and arranged to have Dylan and Ryan here. Smart girl. They're holding off the pack."

When they reached the main room, the rumble of conversations snapped to an abrupt silence. The crowd in black leather straps, latex, and chains parted like the Red

Sea.

Jon didn't know about Jack, but if his reaction was anything like his own, they'd both suffocate. And they'd damn sure die happy men.

Rachel knelt on a raised platform in the center of the room. Rose petals covered the floor. Her head was back with lips parted as she took steady breaths and held the pose. A soft spotlight fell on her face and creamy shoulders. Her ivory breasts were uncovered, except for the nipples. A single red rose petal covered each tip. Her hands braced her as she leaned back, no doubt to keep those petals in place, but with her hips and bare pussy lifted toward them, the effect was the most erotic vision imaginable.

"Rachel..." Her name came out on a sigh.

Her mouth curved. Red silk covered her eyes, making her position even more vulnerable. On either side of her, Dylan and Ryan stood like sentinels in leather pants and expressions of total Dom intimidation.

Jon wanted to yank her into his arms and haul her gorgeous ass out of there for some more intimate play, but she'd chosen the club to make a statement. She could've submitted to him in the privacy of his office, or called Jack's cell phone and arranged a meeting, but instead she displayed trust in their friends by making her public declaration in the club. For now, he'd honor that decision.

After an exchange of nods, her temporary guardians moved over to Olivia, whose grin sparkled as bright as the platinum collar around her neck.

Jon walked toward Rachel, praying the vision didn't vanish like a mirage on a desert highway. Club-goers shuffled around them to watch.

He glanced at Jack. By silent agreement they circled their pet. Her breath hitched as she sensed their presence.

"Hello, pet," Jack said huskily.

"Hello, Master." Her voice was breathless.

They'd not yet touched her, but her arousal was already evident. Hell, so was his. He expected the zipper in his slacks to give way any second.

"I see you received the flowers," Jon said, making her grin.

"Yes, I did. Does Sire approve of my use of his gift?"

"I do." He lifted a handful of soft petals, smelled their fragrance. "But something's missing."

Her lips dipped into a moue.

He looked at his brother and pulled out the velvet case.

"Sit back on your heels," Jack said. Only God knew how badly her legs hurt from holding that position as long as she had.

She sat back as told and put her hands palms up on her spread thighs. The petals fell off her nipples to flutter between her legs.

Jack untied the scarf around her eyes. She blinked repeatedly until her sight adjusted to the change in light.

"You came to Incognito without a collar, pet. We can't have that."

CHAPTER ELEVEN

Jon opened the box. The choker was similar to the one Olivia wore all the time, which was to be expected since the same jeweler had designed the custom piece. The choker was subtle enough that it could be worn in public without drawing undue attention, while the tiny padlock pendant hung as a constant reminder to the sub of ownership.

He studied Rachel's face. "Do you accept our gift, Rachel? Will you wear our collar?" The answer he longed to hear shone brilliantly in her eyes.

"Yes. Willingly."

He removed the jewelry from its case and held it out to his brother. Jack pinned him with a questioning look. They had additional plans to bind her to them, but this time Jack would be the one to take ownership. He gave Jack a smile as he collared their pet.

Jon noticed he was careful not to touch much of her flesh as he did so, and knew what would come next. Looks like Kat would get that demonstration after all.

"Who do you belong to, pet?" Jack asked.

"You, Master. You and Sire."

"Who commands you?"

"You and Sire do, Master."

Jon signaled to Dylan to lower a rope from the pulley overhead.

"Raise your arms," Jack said.

While Jack secured her hands with the rope, Jon obtained a spreader bar for her ankles from Kat.

"Do not try to stand, pet." The rope tightened, stretching her torso, lifting her off her knees. Her breathing became heavy.

While she hung suspended by wrists, Jack secured her ankles to the spreader bar, which held her ankles about four feet apart. Then Jon cranked the pulley to raise her farther off the ground. When his brother nodded, Jon stopped and helped him swing her legs forward until they could tie off the bar to the front of the platform. This left her hanging at about a forty-five degree inclined angle with the front of her body toward the ceiling.

Her head fell back between her arms. Her eyes were open and looking around. Even viewing the room upside down, she couldn't miss the rapt attention she drew from the club-goers, most total strangers to her.

As much as he knew public exposure could increase his sub's erotic response, he wanted Rachel focused solely on him and Jack. So he tucked a corner of the silk scarf previously used to blindfold her into her collar and let the rest fan out over her face.

Her body stretched out before them to view and enjoy. He wanted to touch every inch of her, lick her, kiss her, have her suck him...but not this time.

"You're so beautiful, Rachel," he whispered. He fisted his hands to fight the urge to reach for her. "I love seeing you spread out before me like this, unable to move, open for anything I want to do."

She moaned.

Jack leaned close to her other ear. "Your body longs for our touch, doesn't it, pet?"

"Yessss."

"You're already wet for us," Jon murmured. He didn't touch her. Neither did Jack. Instead they let the softly spoken words stimulate her mind. "We can see the cream glisten on your pussy. Everyone can."

The scarf flittered as she expelled air in quickening pants.

"Your nipples are so hard," Jack said. "They've missed our mouths on them, haven't they? They remember how it feels to have our tongues and teeth nip and play."

A whimper was her only answer. Jack smiled at him. Still, they didn't touch her, but both blew cool streams of air across the heated peaks. Her tummy sucked in as her chest expanded, a vain attempt to draw closer to the gentle caresses.

"Master...Sire...Please."

"What is it you want?"

"I want you, Sire. I want Master. Please, I need you in me now." Her words were urgent, strained, and pleading.

Jack shook his head. "That's not what you need, pet. Tell us what you really need."

Again Jack blew across her breasts, while Jon moved to where he could blow across the damp petals of her shaved pussy. Rachel's hips bucked.

"Come! Please, I need to come."

"Not until we give permission, pet. You can't come

until then, can you?" Jack asked.

"Noooo." The word came out on a sorrowful groan.

Jon leaned closer to her ear again without actually touching her. "You know why, Rachel," he murmured. "Your mind thinks you can't come, because your body knows we haven't given you permission. We own you. We control your body. It answers only to us. Would you like us to prove it?"

"Yes... Take me... Please."

Jack didn't touch her anywhere. "We don't have to, pet. You don't need our touch."

"Yes," she hissed. "Yes, I do, Master. I do. Please, Sire. Please help me. I need to come."

"You'll come soon, pet, but only at our command," Jack said.

"You feel that tension inside?" Jon asked, letting his breath warm her ear. "We haven't touched you, yet your body winds up and ticks according to our will. The tingle in your pussy grows because I say it can."

Her reaction was half-mewl, half-whine.

Still, he let his words paint the carnal pictures to which her body responded. "That tingle sizzles around your clit and teases those sensitive nipples of yours. I know. I can see them bead for me. So hard and tight. Feel it, Rachel. Feel your pussy throb with each heartbeat. The tension builds at the memory of each touch we've given you, every stroke and caress. Remember..."

Her chest rose rapidly, evidence of the stimulating effect their words had on her arousal.

"Yes, Rachel. I know you feel it," Jon continued. "Your body recalls every lick...every thrust...deep inside you...until you're ready to explode. You're on the edge, aren't you? Hanging over that precipice, because that's where we want you to be."

Jack whispered into her other ear. "You'll come when we say, pet. I want to see this luscious body dance at my command." Then raising his voice for those around the room, he said, "Come now."

Her body reacted with a vengeance. Her hips jerked. The tension seized her as the climax swept over her in waves. Her pussy drenched with moisture.

As much as Jon wanted to power his cock deep inside and take her even higher, he held back, fully clothed, and watched the pleasure they evoked wash over their pet. As the trembling began to settle down, he said, "Show everyone who commands this delectable body, Rachel. Come again. Come for us."

She screamed as her body obeyed, overwhelming her senses with an intense explosion. Her thighs quivered. Her arms shook. She sucked in huge gulps of air.

He and Jack gathered rose petals in their hands as the orgasm subsided.

When her body hung motionless once more, Jon said, "Now you're truly our pet. Ours to play with when we wish. Ours to command in every way. Obedient to us alone. I want to see you dance again."

"Come, my pet bitch," Jack said as they let the rose petals rain down over her body.

Whether her mind wanted to or not didn't matter. They controlled her body, so it erupted on command and continued as each petal traveled lightly over her skin. By the time the last one fell, her exhausted body shuddered uncontrollably, and she sobbed beneath the scarf.

Jon cradled her while Jack worked with Dylan and Ryan's help to remove the bindings. Once released, she curled into him as if she sought succor. Olivia stepped forward with a blanket, which he let her drape over his precious bundle. Kat offered them one of the more private rooms, but they declined. He carried her out of the club and into the back of Jack's Suburban. Ignoring the seatbelt law, he kept her sleeping form in his lap all the way home.

* * * * *

Rachel came awake in the familiar surroundings of Jon and Jack's master bedroom suite. After registering where she was, she recognized the warmth of the two men who lay on either side of her.

Slowly, she sat up to survey her surroundings. The covers had been shoved down sometime during the night so that Jack's chest and Jon's back were visible. With a wicked grin, she toed the covers lower to reveal her master's flaccid cock and Sire's fine ass.

Jack stirred a bit, turning his face away from her.

Her hand crept to her throat. She fingered the silver choker and tiny padlock pendant.

She belonged to them. Instead of being offended by their domineering ways, she reveled in the knowledge that they wanted her, cared for her...loved her?

"If you love someone, set them free..." she whispered, paraphrasing the words on the card. Although they hadn't said it to her yet, she believed it was true, which was why she came back. "...If they come back, they're yours."

She'd come back, and they'd come to the club for her. So now she was theirs, but by the same agreement, they were hers. She grinned at that thought. They could command her body. They'd captured her heart. But she'd made them hers for all time. And it was time to show them that sometimes a pet can have ideas of her own.

Slowly she rolled to her knees so she could scoot to the end of the bed. From there, she eyed her men. Jon lay facedown, preventing her from reaching his cock, so with one hand she stroked his thighs and ass instead, letting her fingertip slip between the cheeks on occasion.

Jack's cock had hardened a bit while she moved, which made her look up to see if he was awake. His eyes were shut, his face softened in repose. Carefully, she bent over him and licked the inside of one thigh. He didn't budge. She licked again, just brushing the tip of his sex. The length flexed, but he didn't stir.

Jon moved, though, lifting one knee so his leg bent. This enabled her to reach his testicles, so she fondled them and returned her attention to Jack.

She ran her tongue from the root to tip before sucking him into her mouth. His cock became rock-solid in an instant. She timed her circular strokes on Jon's balls with the movement of her lips on Jack's cock, until a big hand settled on the back of her head.

"Mmmorning, pet." Jack lifted his hips to meet her downward stroke.

"A very good morning at that," Jon said, rolling over onto his back. He brought her hand to his cock, which grew several inches.

Similar Cheshire-cat grins spread across their faces.

Looking sinfully sexy with their whiskered faces and sleep-ruffled hair, they propped themselves up on elbows to watch her serve them. She redoubled her efforts, sucking on one a while and then switching to the other as her hands continued to pump both.

They were so hard she expected them to blow any second when Jack grabbed her wrist and Jon said, "Stop."

With an unhidden pout, she reluctantly obeyed.

"There's something we want to do," Jon said. "Something we haven't done with you before." Much to her satisfaction, he sounded a bit breathless.

"I'm all yours," she said with a wide smile.

"Yes, but we want you to be more," he said. "Rachel, would you marry us?"

She blinked. Stunned. "How...?" Her eyes felt like ping pong balls as her gaze bounced from Jack to Jon and back again.

"Legally, you can only marry one of us—" Jack started.

"I can't choose between you two. I won't!"

"You don't have to," Jack said. "We've already decided that for you, pet."

She frowned.

"As far as the courts and the public are concerned, you'll be the wife of Dr. Jonathon Sinclair, but in our home you'll belong to both of us. You already do." Jack fingered the padlock pendant at her neck. "We'll have a wedding as big or as small as you want so you can exchange vows with Jon. Afterwards, we can have another private ceremony for me. Maybe on a ship during our honeymoon?"

She wouldn't have to give either of them up. They'd

figured out a way. She trusted them completely, so why should this matter be any different? "Make it a small wedding," she said then grinned. "Does this mean I'll never see either of you drop to a knee?"

"Minx," Jack said and pounced.

Giggles erupted as he and Jon tickled her senseless. Their roughhousing evolved into ardent touches and passionate kisses that made her heart race and pussy wet with anticipation.

Jon lay on his back and pulled her over him. "Straddle me."

Somewhat surprised, she paused a second before obeying him. They'd never let her be on top before.

"I told you there was something we hadn't done with you yet," Jon said as he ran his hands up her arms and over each breast. "That's because we reserved it until now."

Jack, who'd gotten off the bed moments earlier, now moved around behind her to kneel between his brother's legs. His fingers curved around her hips as he lifted her onto Jon's cock. Working her way down on him, she watched Jon's blue eyes go black with passion. He rose up on his hands, while Jack cupped her breasts. He kneaded and held them for his brother as Jon kissed and laved each peak.

Her hips moved in an urgent plea when he sucked hard on one tip. Jon released her to kiss a trail up her neck and capture her mouth. One of Jack's hands centered on her back and pushed gently forward. Jon pulled her down with him, never relinquishing his hold on her mouth.

Caught up in his thorough kiss, she was slow to react to Jack's persistent fingers, which readied her for his penetration. She tried to pull away from Jon's kiss as his brother's cock pressed through the tight ring of her sphincter muscles. Jon held her still and kept the kiss going. Jack's entry was slow and deep. She moaned into Jon's mouth as they filled her more than she thought possible.

Finally, with one last nudge, he embedded himself in her ass as far as his brother was in her pussy. Jack leaned over her back, and Jon released her lips. They surrounded her, filled her, overwhelmed her, and they weren't even moving inside her.

"We're one," Jack said, his sultry baritone showing the strain of holding himself in check. He pressed a kiss to that sensitive spot on the side of her neck. Then he lifted her left hand in his.

Jon gave her a mischievous grin that she'd come to treasure. His hand neared hers, and that's when she noticed the jeweled band he held poised near her left ring finger. It was platinum, with three Princess-cut diamonds, the center one slightly larger. She looked to Jon, whose gaze pinned her in place even more than their bodies held her immobile. The sincerity and love was all there for her to witness. Tears threatened her eyes.

"We love you, Rachel," they said in unison as Jack held her hand, and Jon slid the engagement ring onto her finger.

The End

Author Bios

Anna Leigh has been reading and penning romances for as long as she can remember. After she met and married her very own real-life hero, romance took on a whole new meaning. She now knows married life can sizzle and romance can be erotic—even in her own home.

Madison Layle avoided her childhood chores on the family farm by curling up with books, and disappearing into other worlds of fantasy, adventure, and romance. With maturity came the love of her own real-life hero (a.k.a. "my darling hubby"), and a real understanding of why her parents locked their bedroom door.

Madison and Anna Leigh first met online through a critique group, a meeting which sparked a strong friendship and a fun partnership. Together, their writing has taken on a spicier flavor, so while their hubbies are off at work, they let their imaginations soar....

Visit them anytime at any of their online haunts:

www.incognitoseries.com
www.madisonlayle.com
www.annaleighkeaton.com

Or "Unleash Your Darkest Desires" by joining:
http://groups.yahoo.com/groups/desires_unleashed

EXCERPT

Incognito: Winning Angela

By Madison Layle & Anna Leigh Keaton

Angela picked up the matchbook to light the candles. Her hand shook as she held the flame to the wick.

She'd spent hours trying to make sure everything was perfect. Trying to figure out the exact words to say and still, she drew a blank. Looking around her tidy, economy apartment, she wondered whether she was insane to attempt to live with two men who were such polar opposites. They all lived alone, had their own little quirks.

Will we all be ready to kill each other in a month?

She sank into a chair. "This is crazy. I'm nuts."

Fidgeting, she straightened one of the butter knives by a plate, silently congratulating herself for being wise enough not to cook anything that required sharper instruments.

The oven timer dinged at the same time she heard a knock.

Jumping up, she nearly toppled the chair in her dash to the door. A peek told her Blaine was as punctual as always. With a big, held breath, she put on a casual smile and opened the door.

"Hey, Angel."

With a bouquet of flowers in one hand and a bottle of their favorite wine in the other, he leaned in for a kiss. Their lips touched as the beeping timer registered in her brain.

"The lasagna! Come in. The flowers are gorgeous...and the wine, thank you. Make yourself comfortable. I'll be right back." She darted for the kitchen.

Blaine chuckled. The door clicked shut.

She snatched her hand back with a muttered curse, having forgotten to grab the oven mitt in her haste. "I'll be out in just a sec. Make yourself at home."

She set the pan of pasta on a hot plate and turned on the tap, then dug under the kitchen sink for a vase.

"Angel?"

She reared up, bumping her head on the cabinet.

"What?" She rubbed the sore spot and filled the vase with water.

Sarcasm laced his words as he asked, "Are we expecting a guest for dinner?"

She carried the crystal vase out of the kitchen to see him standing by the table set for three. "Well..."

A key turned the lock. The front door swung wide.

Garrett strolled in. "Hi, honey, I'm... Fuck me."

"I'd rather not," Blaine said through gritted teeth. "But apparently my angel has."

Her gaze jumped back and forth between the two men she loved more than life itself and knew she'd made a huge mistake. Blaine in his tailored, charcoal Armani looked as if he'd just been slugged in the gut, while Garrett, endearingly rumpled in jeans and black T-shirt, looked like a thundercloud ready to strike.

How could she have ever thought this would work?

As the door clicked shut again, she thought it sounded more like a death knell.

"You've gotta be shitting me, Ange. Not Jack's pup-in-training."

Her heart sank, but before she could respond, Blaine spoke.

"At least I'm housebroken. You don't even have the decency to knock."

Garrett rattled his keys, and she winced. "Don't need to when I have a key, asshole."

Angela stepped between them. "I see introductions aren't necessary." She set the vase down, grabbed the wine bottle from Blaine before he thought to use it as a weapon, and tried to ignore the killer glares the men exchanged like two dogs ready for a junkyard brawl. "Garrett, enough. Blaine, have a seat. Dinner's getting cold."

Afraid to leave them alone for long, she ran for the kitchen and back again with the salad bowl. "Here, dig in. I made lasagna, Garrett, your favorite." As she headed back to the kitchen, she called out, "And Blaine, I have one of your favorites. Chocolate fondue for dessert."

Garrett snorted, but as soon as the pan of pasta touched the tabletop, he grabbed the serving spoon and filled his plate. Blaine eyed him and reached tentatively for the salad tongs. Angela headed back into the kitchen to open the wine and steal a quick gulp for courage. Make that two. Then, with three glasses and the bottle in hand, she went back to face her future, for better or worse.

"Thank you for the wine," she said again to Blaine as she set the glasses on the table.

"You're welcome." He got up and held her seat, then took the bottle and began pouring.

She wondered whether he'd pour the third, but she shouldn't have bothered.

"Got a beer?" Garrett asked, taking another bite of the lasagna.

"Sure." She ignored Blaine's scowl as she fetched Garrett a bottle of draft.

She returned to see Blaine still holding her chair, so she gave him a smile and sat, handing the cold bottle to Garrett. He used the table's edge to pop the top that he could've easily twisted off.

She kicked him under the table, making him grunt. He didn't look up, but the toe of his boot rubbed her calf. She hid her frustrated groan behind a sip of wine. The damn man was acting the jerk on purpose. He wasn't usually this big of an ass.

She glanced at Blaine who ate without a word, and she wanted to sigh. Why the hell did she ever think the three of them had a chance?

They didn't speak as they cleaned their plates and Garrett went back for seconds, then thirds. When she brought out the desert, he stabbed a strawberry with his fork.

Blaine removed the cloth napkin from his lap, folded it neatly over his plate, and then brushed a hand down his tie. "Lovely dinner. Now if you'll excuse me," he said, looking at Garrett with more than just a hint of rancor. "I'm through sharing a table with this Neanderthal."

Garrett grinned and poked a slice of banana.

Her hand shot out to clutch Blaine's arm. "Please, don't go."

"Angel, this is pointless. I've sat here for the past forty-five minutes listening to Mr. Caveman chew his food."

She laced her fingers with Blaine's, refusing to let go, then reached for Garrett's hand, needing the support for what she was about to propose.

"Do you love me, Blaine?"

His lips thinned as his gaze slid to Garrett.

"Look at *me*. Do you love me?"

"You know I do."

"And I love you, both of you. I'm keeping you both."

Garrett gave her hand a reassuring squeeze.

Blaine pulled away, and she felt the wound in her heart rip open. "That's not your decision to make. I told you. I won't settle for second best."

She shook her head and clung to his arm with both hands. "That's not what I mean. I want you both, equally. Together." Oh, damn it. She was bumbling this if Blaine's look of confusion was any indication. "I want us all to live together."

"You're crazy." Blaine gulped down the rest of his wine and used the glass to point at Garrett. "No way am I going to live with...with *that*."

"But he's not that bad...usually."

Garrett didn't help matters by reclining in the chair with folded arms and a stupid grin on his whisker-stubbled face.

"He's a chauvinistic pig, and I can't believe you've been..." Blaine stopped, stood and straightened his tie, one of his nervous habits she usually took time to treasure. "He's not good enough for you."

Garrett slammed a hand on the table, making her jump. "You think because you were stupid enough to spend an entire paycheck on one pair of pants that you're good enough? Let me tell you something—"

"No! Stop it. Both of you." She stood and glared at them. "Either you told me the truth, Blaine, and love me enough to try things my way for a month, or you lied and I've been nothing but a piece of ass that's stupid to boot. Because crazy as it is, I fell in love, head over heels in love, with both of you."

Blaine looked skeptical when he asked, "A month?"

Garrett earned Blaine's scowl by saying, "I'm in."

"In where?" Blaine looked at her. "We can't possibly both live here in your one-bedroom apartment."

"No. Garrett has a house—"

"You want me to move into *his* house?" He looked so appalled she could almost picture what he thought Garrett lived in.

"Are you offering to let me bunk at your place, hotshot?" Garrett asked with a challenging smirk as he leaned his chair back on two legs. She swore to herself that if he propped his feet on the table, she'd knock him over.

"No, I—"

Before Blaine could say more, she grabbed his face and made him look at her. "You said you wanted a home with me. I want that, too. I want you with me always."

"Angel..."

"He has a large house on the beach. A month. Please. At least give it a try. For me?"

Winning Angela

His blue eyes softened, yet wariness remained. He raised his hand to cradle her face, his thumb caressing her cheek. "Angel, what you're proposing is impossible. What are we supposed to do, swap nights? Have a written custody agreement? Week on, week off? It's still only half."

"I don't want it to be like that. I want you both in my bed. Every night."

Obviously stunned, he dropped his hand, and his eyes rounded.

"You want me to sleep with him, too?"

Garrett mumbled a curse.

"In the same bed," she said. "Sharing the bed. Sharing me. He's not gay."

Garrett blew him a kiss and grinned.

"Damn it, Garrett. Knock it off." She scowled at him then checked on Blaine. He looked decidedly green around the gills.

"I...God, Angel. I don't know if I can..." He glanced from Garrett to her. "Share. Like that. With him...there."

She gave him a sly smile. "Yes. You can." She slipped four fingers into his waistband and yanked him toward her. Rising on tiptoes, she slipped her other arm around his neck to pull him down for a kiss.

After a shocked moment, his tongue twirled with hers. Without releasing his mouth, she made quick work of his belt and pushed his slacks and boxers down. When they dropped, he tried to grab them, but she pushed him so that he sat hard on the chair.

"Angel?"

"Don't move," she said, watching his knuckles whiten on the chair's wooden arms.

She pulled the bowl of melted chocolate toward the edge of the table and heard Blaine swallow.

As she kneeled between his thighs, Garrett moved his seat around the table to sit a few feet away but directly in front of Blaine. So he could watch. Garrett liked to watch. All the better to prove her point to Blaine.

"Sweetheart? This isn't a good... Ahh..."

She'd gotten a little chocolate on his shirt, but most of it hit the target as she held the base of his cock in a tight fist. She swiped the tip with her tongue, circling the head, and then sucked him deep into her mouth.

He grew rock hard in less than an instant, and he hissed as the chair creaked under the strain of his grip.

The chocolate mixed with his pre-cum and made her forget everything else around her as she focused on tasting all he had to give.

"Angel, don't... Stop. Oh, damn."

She wasn't sure whether that meant, don't. Stop. Or don't stop. But she chose to believe the latter, since she didn't intend to quit now. She cupped his sac, fondling him lightly, as she took his cock repeatedly in and out of her mouth.

A glance up told her he'd closed his eyes. When she increased her pace, he let his head fall back, and his hips lurched forward.

She moaned her encouragement, let the rumble surround him, and increased the pressure.

His hands grabbed her head, his teeth clenched, and she knew he was close. With an inner smile, she slowly drew back, letting her teeth gently graze the silken flesh then pulled him in hard to the back of her throat.

Winning Angela

With a sound of surrender, he came with a low groan, and she drank every drop of his salty seed. She spent extra time licking him clean while his shallow breaths calmed and his hands stroked the top of her head.

"Now I see why that's one of your favorite desserts," Garrett said.

Made in the USA